"There is no b[...]
so well a[...]
the gatherin[...]
and sullen separation."
—ALLEN TATE,
former poet laureate of the United States

"Undoubtedly the best historical novel of
the old-fashioned spectacular genre in
American literature . . . As a spectacle of war,
the book has no equal."
—*The Nation*

"Passion is piled upon passion in Kantor's words,
and war, marked and flaming, stalks
through the pages."
—*Chicago Daily Tribune*

"A stirring, utterly American book of
men and women and war . . . It is a work
of distinction."
—*Saturday Book Review*

LONG REMEMBER

MacKinlay Kantor

Introduction by Jeff M. Shaara

A TOM DOHERTY ASSOCIATES BOOK
NEW YORK

This is a work of fiction. All of the characters, organizations, and events portrayed in this novel are either products of the author's imagination or are used fictitiously.

LONG REMEMBER

Copyright © 1934: renewed © 1961 by MacKinlay Kantor. Reprinted by permission of the Kantor Estate and the Estate's agent, Donald Maass, 121 West 27th Street, Suite 801, New York, NY 10001.

Introduction copyright © 2000 by Jeff M. Shaara

Map © 2000 by Anita Karl and Jim Kemp

All rights reserved.

A Forge Book
Published by Tom Doherty Associates, LLC
175 Fifth Avenue
New York, NY 10010

www.tor-forge.com

Forge® is a registered trademark of Tom Doherty Associates, LLC.

ISBN 978-0-7653-7781-4

Forge books may be purchased for educational, business, or promotional use. For information on bulk purchases, please contact the Macmillan Corporate and Premium Sales Department at 1-800-221-7945, extension 5442, or write to specialmarkets@macmillan.com.

First Forge Editions: July 2000
First Forge Mass Market Edition: November 2014

Printed in the United States of America

0 9 8 7 6 5 4 3 2 1

To Irene

Note

It is worthy of remark that whatever astuteness Abraham Lincoln possessed as a prophet, was not reflected in his address at Gettysburg, on November 19, 1863. With all sincerity he declared, "The world will little note, nor long remember, what we say here, but it can never forget what they did here." Seventy years later, one realizes that Lincoln's speech represents the only common and popular knowledge of Lincoln, Gettysburg, or the war between the states.

The major characters of this novel are fictitious. To the best of the author's knowledge, there was no one named Bale, Fanning, Huddlestone or Duffey living in Gettysburg, Pennsylvania, in June or July of 1863.

M. K.

Contents

Introduction

There are stories enough to fill great libraries—stories of marching armies, the rattle of muskets, the screams of dying men. We know so much of generals and privates, cavaliers on their fine horses, or the man leading the glorious charge up that famous hill. In these pages is quite another story, drawn with the extraordinary skill of a man who brings us into one small town, in no way unique, and into the life of one man who is considered very much unique by the people who know him.

Dan Bale is a confirmed civilian, a man with no allegiances, who has a distinct disdain for the chest-thumping passions the Civil War has produced. He returns to the small town of his youth, a journey home for a sorrowful personal business, is searching for nothing, expects little else. He is a man disconnected from his world, a man who could be from any time. He has grown up mildly angry, journeyed far from home, seeking nothing from a life that has given him only a faint nod of kindness. He seems void of passion, annoyed at himself that somewhere in a place he tries to hide he has an inconvenient and unavoidable strain of decency. It is Dan Bale's astounding misfortune that his return to his family home should in fact be a stumble into a place where madness and fear and the horror of death will engulf a people whose only sin is that they live in a town called Gettysburg.

In our so very modern of times we choose to believe that it is better to become detached, that our world is too annoying, too troublesome to venture into. We read newspapers and watch television, and sit comfortably removed from the horrors of our time, staring dispassionately while images too grotesque to fathom wash over us in a numbing cascade. If we are suddenly uncomfortable, we turn the page, change the channel. To many, involvement means risk. To many more patriotism is an outdated, misguided, and laughable notion. Dan Bale could easily live in our time.

Today, as in 1863, many people spout noisy pronouncements about the depths of their own courage. Whether we believe our own boasts, or whether the noise is simply a mask for our fear, it is often the soldier who will alone discover the truth. No one shouldering a rifle will be able to predict how he will react under fire. No loud bravado will ever accurately portray how carefully you will aim, how much precision you can muster, how you will truly react to that *other* man with the gun who thrusts his bayonet at your heart. The hero and the coward may share everything else, may even be friends, brothers. But when they are pulled into the great hell of war, the true character of a man emerges, and only then does he meet his own soul. This is a theme critical to the telling of this story. To Dan Bale, this is meaningless chatter.

Passion is at once liberating and dangerous. More often it is a misguided passion of one kind or another that creates the war itself. But sometimes, it is the war that creates the passion, swirling men and women together with an unexpected fire, transforming the coolness of reason or even propriety into hot lather. For Dan Bale, passion is an unwanted surprise. But there are surprises beyond his control, beyond his own turmoil. In Gettysburg, Pennsylvania, in July 1863, the mosaic texture of small-town life is swallowed alive by the extraordinary hell of a great war. But through the eyes of one man, the lives of the people unfold in a magnificent blend of passion, horror, and discovery.

"Now he lived in a feverish and blasted world, and suffered the knowledge that he had helped to make it feverish and blasted . . ."

—Jeff M. Shaara
April 2000

Book One

THE WOMAN
AND THE
BUZZARDS

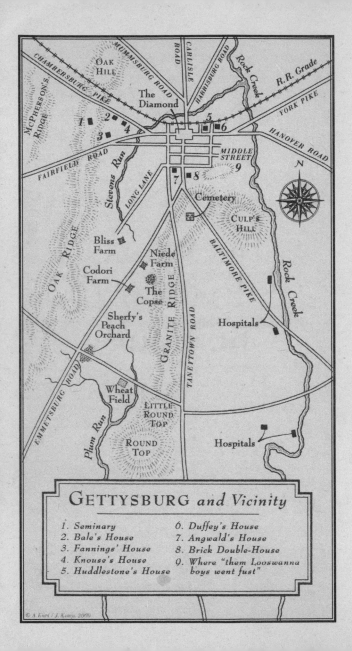

GETTYSBURG *and Vicinity*

1. *Seminary*
2. *Bale's House*
3. *Fannings' House*
4. *Knouse's House*
5. *Huddlestone's House*
6. *Duffey's House*
7. *Angwald's House*
8. *Brick Double-House*
9. *Where "them Looswanna boys went fust"*

© A. Karl / J. Kemp, 2000

1.

At Hanover Junction it was necessary for him to change trains. For a while he sat alone on the edge of a baggage truck, his luggage on the platform at his feet. He smoked and looked up at the sky. There was a moon somewhat past the full, but brown and serrated under the mackerel scales of thin clouds. At the far end of the platform a squad of loafers stood talking. Bale had avoided them purposely. The station itself was deserted except for a night agent who sat in his little den, clicking mysterious jabbers to a mute length of wire.

Presently the agent came out of the station and moved across the hollow wooden platform, a bloody lantern in his hand. A clicking and a thud of metal marked his pause at the switch-post. He came back, carrying the vivid green lantern which he had replaced with the red.

He spoke to Daniel Bale. "Looks like we might catch a little rain, maybe."

"Shouldn't wonder," said Dan.

The agent stood there, weaving the hissing green lantern back and forth. His shape seemed strangely lop-sided in the darkness. Bale bent his head slightly to bring the man's body into full silhouette against

the soft, kerosene yellow of the station windows . . .
The man had only one arm.

"About this time, first part of June," said the agent,
"we generally get a deal of rain around here."

More abruptly than he had intended, Bale observed, "I see you're shy one wing."

The agent's warm young voice gurgled. He spoke
as one who is expecting pity and veneration to be lav-
ished upon him, and who feels that they are wholly
his due. "But," he concluded, "my wife don't mind a
bit. She says she'd rather have me wanting a chunk of
meat than not have me at all. And anyways, when you
figure how it happened, I guess I'm not sorry. When I
signed the roll I figured I might get killed, maybe. I tell
you, friend, there's a good many better men than I be,
lying down there by that crick this minute. Bet your
boots."

Bale watched a crumb of tobacco fall from his pipe
and slide into the forest of his beard; it bounded from
wiry hair to wiry hair, making its own tiny illumina-
tion as it went. He thought, Now it's coming, he's
bound to ask, and I wish—

"You done a turn with the colors?" blurted the
agent.

"No."

The green lantern jerked at the abruptness of the
reply. When the agent spoke again, he was halting and
apologetic. "Well, I always say that a man's first duty
is to his family. Course I wasn't married till I come
back . . . You're married, friend, I take it?"

"No," Bale told him. He tapped the bowl of his
pipe against the edge of the truck, and a host of red
flakes sprayed into the darkness. "I don't hold with
some of your notions. I am not in favor of this war, or
any war. I'm sorry you've lost an arm, and sorry for

most of those who are dead. But I don't intend to go to war, if that's what you wish to know."

He became aware that the rails were checking and crunching under the squeeze of distant wheels. A whistle squawled half-heartedly beyond the black belt of trees.

The agent cleared his throat and spat over his shoulder. "Well," he said, "some holds one way, some another. I don't mind saying there's plenty of Copperheads right in this county."

"I'm no Copperhead."

"No, no. I never said you was. Say, you don't need to be in no hurry to pick up your valise, friend. The train won't go for twenty minutes—the one heading west. This here one goes north."

He went into the station, carrying the green-glass lantern with him. A plume of smoke wavered off from the open doorway. Bale could hear the man whistling, *Now, Moses, what makes you so strange and forgetful* . . . Steel was banging and frying and torturing itself, not far up the track. The engine rounded a curve and spread its buxom shaft of light down the cindered roadway. It came on like a hissing, malodorous animal, tiny freckles of orange showing through cracks and bolt-holes in a hundred places. The two coaches behind it were rickety, and illuminated by futile, brownish lamps.

Dan jumped down from the truck and pushed his extension-case into the shadows where it seemed reasonably safe and out of the way. He walked away from the train as it gasped terrifically up to the station. There would be more people, and he had seen all the people he wanted to see for a long time. Not many years before, he had suffered recurrent nostalgia for the settled complacency, the solid and ever-present population of even a rural community in the East. That was all past. One could not travel for six days, pushing ever farther into a scrambling and more tightly-peopled country, without seeing all faults, existent and nonexistent in mere men and women.

In his brief conversation with the one-armed agent, he realized that he had been wholly absurd. Six days before, he would not have mentioned that empty sleeve to the man who owned it.

On this train, waiting to transfer to the west-bound coaches, undoubtedly there would be some old friends and neighbors, or at least old neighbors whom he had once regarded as friends. They would talk about the war. Where he had been, the war sank into a civilized phenomenon below the southeastern horizon, a capitalistic trap which waited to seize the unwary. Even so, many men had gone to it voluntarily . . .

The light of the railway engine, stationary now, hunted past him; he could see it picking out the trampled weeds which grew close beside the roadbed and turning them into artificial, green paper weeds. A rising ripple of human sounds drifted up through the *whuff, whuff* of tired steam; people were climbing down from the cars and all talking about it . . . Bale turned aside into the tide of gray darkness. He stumbled across a rusty side-track, down into a dry ditch, and walked squarely against the bones of a rail fence. Beyond that, at the top of a slope, tiny nine-paned windows shone in an invisible house. This spot called Hanover Junction had never amounted to much and never would . . . He put his boot on the bottom rail of the barrier, and swung up and over, dangling his legs on the inner side. The edge of the rail was sharp and uncomfortable, but he sat there nevertheless with his back to the station, staring up at that skulking moon.

Something in his pocket was hard and bulky. He dug it out: a small apple. He had bought it from a boy at the train window, early in the afternoon. He took the dead pipe out of his mouth and bit into the apple. His teeth told him that the skin was soft and loose and wrinkled, an apple which had survived in some cellar since the previous autumn. The pulp of it was winy, aged, sour-sweet. He rolled the damp morsels over and under his tongue. Close at hand, the tingling June silence encompassed him; he was in a world apart from the stew of the little railroad junction, and in this world there was no sound but the rack of his own jaws, chewing and chewing.

Another engine was moving closer; it had a cracked bell which swung intermittently, a dull and splintery tolling. The brakes began to tighten and fight with the heavy wheels. Mustn't stay there too long. There would be no other westbound train until the next day.

He thought about his grandfather. Quite possibly the old man was dead, by this time. The letter had been delayed, for Bale was on a trip to the timber with Lucas Mite, hunting for green oak posts, when that letter reached Minnesota. He had come as soon as he could, but perhaps that was not soon enough. There was no reason why he should touch his grandfather's live flesh again. Already they understood each other thoroughly, with an honesty which needed little affection to bolster it. Cancer, the letter had said, but of course he had suspected that all along. It was a dreadful death; he hoped at this moment that all was done with Pentland Bale.

Closing his eyes to the dried-up, metal moon, he could see only the house and the town which he had left seven years before. He was twenty-five years old; he had been in a far place, and was now drawn back to Pennsylvania by this imminent death. It was not at all as he had imagined his return. He had made no fortune, not even a figurative one. He had a few hundred pages of manuscript, blotted and interlined and crossed out. Probably he would never be able to form those notions according to the pattern in his brain. He had firm, stone-knuckled hands and a brown beard; there had been much hunting and much chopping with an axe, and his shoulders were knotted and spread from the weight of the sacked wheat which they had tossed about. Physically he was a different person. There was no measuring stick by which he could check the growth or shrinkage of the creature who lived inside.

A man's voice swam up out of the roiling clatter beyond him. *Boooord.* Dan threw away the apple core, and pressed his feet back over the rail. He ran up the embankment and stumbled across the side-track. Out in front of the station, the one-armed agent was gazing up and down, looking for him. As he ran, Bale could feel a water of pity for this person, pumping in his throat. He thudded up the platform steps and snatched his grip from its hiding place.

"Thought you was lost," the agent cried.

He said, "Thanks. Is this the one?"

"Hurry up. She's moving—"

He caught a gritty iron bar and drew himself up on the stairway of the squeaking car. Burning flakes of soot tore past him; he could feel them settling on his cheeks and kissing his hair. Then he stood at the door of the coach, breathing rapidly, and blinking into the face of the tin lamps.

Perhaps they were the neighbors of his childhood, perhaps they were more than that. At this moment they were only heads above the slatted wooden seats;

they were bonnets and beards and children asleep. Carpet-bags, haversacks, cloth-wrapped bundles stood along the aisle. Bale picked his way carefully past them. A baby, fat pink lump wound up in an old plaid shawl, was saying earnestly *H'la, h'la, h'la,* and its mother fumbled with the front of her dress while the father held up a newspaper to shield her. People filled this coach—too many people. The war had unsettled the world; it bubbled the sediment and the froth together and kept them sloshing about. Forever, these motley Americans were riding up and down their land on the cars.

There was a vacant space beside a black slouch hat with a white trefoil and a number on the front. Bale sat down, squeezing his leather case between his feet. The man who wore the slouch hat stared pettishly ahead and did not acknowledge Dan's nod. He was about twenty-three, beardless, a thick yellow mustache twisting down to cover his long lips. A white silk handkerchief had been stuffed around his neck to keep stray perspiration from soiling the collar of his uniform. Bent across his shoulders were corroded oblongs of gilt braid.

He moved his unbuckled scabbard aside, and flicked a tuft of ashes from his cold cigar. Then, from the corners of pale blue eyes, he seemed suddenly to see Daniel for the first time.

The officer turned, his mouth curving slightly under its tawny brush. "I'm a sucker," he said, "if you're not Dan Bale."

Bale extended his hand. "Hello, Ty."

"Well," said the officer. His voice was shrill, taut, weary. He stared at Dan. "Thought you had left Pennsylvania for good."

"I thought so, too."

"Are you just coming back, now?"

"Just tonight. You haven't been home recently, have you?" he added, with an unhappy eagerness. "My grandfather's near death. That's why I came back from the west."

The soldier shook his head. "First time I've been home in seven months, and I'm only here now because I'm sick. No sense in my coming. My wife managed it; she had Colonel Baxter send me."

"You're married, then?"

"I married a girl from Philadelphia," said Ty briefly. They were silent for a moment, their heads bobbing on their shoulders as the car lurched and quivered.

"I see you're an officer, Ty."

"Captain. The Seventy-second. Philadelphia brigade."

"Well, that's good," Bale muttered. He wondered what else he could have said.

Tyler Fanning shrugged. "It's damn hard work, if you ask me. Hardest work I ever did in my life . . . I got hit with a piece of shell at Antietam Creek. Sick as a dog for weeks. Couldn't keep anything on my stomach."

"Are you all right now?"

"Could be better," Fanning spat upon the floor, and smudged the place with the toe of his glistening boot. "We heard once that you had been scalped by the Indians."

Bale felt awkward. He began to wish that there had been a vacant seat beside someone other than Fanning. "No," he said, "they didn't get me, that time. They came near it. A lot of bad Wahpakootas—those are Sioux—burned everybody out, in our neighborhood."

"Rebels or Indians, they're all the same. We'd be better off if they were all dead."

Bale said nothing. He realized that he was not looking at Ty Fanning, but was frowning intently at a varnished knot-hole in the seat ahead of him. He wrenched his gaze away. Across the aisle a fat, red-faced farmer was snoring with mechanical regularity, a blue handkerchief spread over his bald head. All around, people dozed or snored or whispered or clacked; the air smelled of stables and soot and coal-oil and fried chicken; but sometimes a puff of wind twisted down the aisle, and then you could think of chilly green woods and dark fields where the hay was ripening.

. . . They were neighbors, boys who lived in the same town, and only a field apart. Two years in childhood are a generation. There is apt, Bale remembered, to be a holy clique of twelve-year-olds deeply scornful of the ten-year-olds who worshipfully trail them. In a smaller town, they would have been pushed together by the narrowness of circumstance. As it was, they met on common ground only at the Willows, and in the pasture between their homes, and at fires.

The Willows were three in number, growing from a common stump that lifted on oozy roots at a bend in the meanderings of Willoughby Run. Bale shut his eyes: he saw Tyler Fanning standing on the roots, warm and muddy water sloshing two inches below his toes, pressing his hands together in front of his ribs for an awkward dive that was more of a fall. Tyler Fanning lived in the second largest house in town, and he wore a blue velvet jacket, and his mother went to drive in a carriage driven by a freedman. But nevertheless he was thin and whining and querulous when you got him naked down at the Willows. He had knobs on his knees . . . Captain. The Seventy-second . . . piece of shell at Antietam Creek. Ho! the wars . . .

Dan felt his jaw stiffen. He tugged nervously at his thick beard.

"Where'd you get the growth?" asked Fanning.

"I left my razors at home when I went to Minnesota."

"That's how long?"

"Nearly seven years."

Fanning grinned, not pleasantly. "Look out someone doesn't take you for that son of a bitch Stuart."

"Who?"

"For the moment," Ty whined, lazily, "I forgot that you've been in the backwoods and aren't conversant with present-day affairs."

Bale said, "Only as they concern my soul and body. I might as well tell you that I'm no Copperhead, but I'm not Coming Father Abraham or anything like that. I may be a misanthropist, but not because I'm afraid."

"Don't misunderstand me," replied Fanning. He sat up a trifle straighter. "What I meant about Jeb Stuart was this: he came up here last year and paralyzed Curtin and the whole damn state. Burnt stores, stole money, and took away all the horses."

"I heard about that. Naturally, we get some news out there on the prairie. But he didn't reach home, did he?"

"He went south at Cashtown. And he's got a beard like yours. Look out one of our Dutch neighbors doesn't take a sickle to those beautiful brown—" The grind and groan of metal killed his words; the train stopped, lurched forward, stopped again, started again. At the rear of the coach the baby began to moan once more: *H'la, h'la, h'la.*

Bale asked, "Any children?"

"No. I've been married only two years. And the war and all. I'm man enough." He gave a thin laugh. "You'll have to call on us. Mrs. Fanning would be pleased. You aren't married, I take it?"

Dan shook his head. "You might tell me some news, if you don't mind. Grandfather didn't write often, the last year or two. What about Andrew Leen?"

"He's in New York. A printer. Married and a father. The younger boy—remember Noah?—he ran away and got killed at a place called Front Royal, in Virginia. Elizabeth married one of the Brennemans, over by Cashtown."

"Somehow," said Bale, "I feel very old. I've been on the road six days, and every hour I've had more and more of a creeping palsy."

Fanning chuckled. He squeezed the dead cigar between his fingers. There were gauntleted gloves thrust neatly beneath his sword belt. The scabbard thudded against the floor whenever he shifted his leg. "If you don't mind, Dan," he suggested, "I'm curious to know your views on the war. You're not afraid—of course. But convictions without a quoted sentiment— Damn it, you know what I mean. We've got a few of your Minnesota troops in the east here. They make ornery soldiers and wonderful fighters."

"Quite probably," said Dan, "I would make a wonderful soldier, but I'm not so sure how I'd match up with the rest of Minnesota when it came to fighting. I mean your kind of fighting. Caissons and platoons and sergeants and things like that, of which I know nothing. You'll have to excuse me, tonight. I'm in more or less of a daze."

"You always were a queer duck, Bale," smiled Fanning. His pale eyes were narrow and expressionless . . . yes, he's the soldier, he is it, this is the right thing for him to do, he is suitable clay for them to shape and, Almighty God, how they have shaped him!

This talk, Bale told himself savagely, has brought it on. Why did I have to sit down beside this man?

In the back of his brain, far beneath an aching area of his skull, some brown, niggerish creatures in feathers and loose cotton shirts and ragged blankets, crawled and peeked beyond a woodpile. He heard their squawl go gibbering over the world. Lucas Mite dragged his Sharps rifle across the molasses barrel. Behind him, a dry voice whispered, "I can't git that one." Molasses dripped and burbled from the perforated barrels . . . and remember how we found those Gardener kids—they had taken them by their heels and swung them—

But they were only animals, he insisted. They were not men. They wore trousers, some of them, and months before they had squatted in front of people's doors, whining for Little Tea, Little Sugee, Little Whisk. Some of them wore clothes, but they were not men. That was not a war. It was shooting at wolves, at snakes, at enormous ghosts who gobbled in the cold daylight . . . Must keep insisting . . .

He said to Ty Fanning, "Tell me about Doctor Duffey. He was the one who wrote me about my grandfather, but I've been wondering how he's keeping himself."

"Didn't you see the Missis? She's aboard this carriage. I saw her get on, at the Junction. There she is—right ahead. Mrs. Duffey."

Bale stood up. He moved down the littered aisle toward a leghorn hat with painted wooden strawberries dangling from its crown, a hat which roosted cozily above the seat, with an enormous gray bonnet as its neighbor. "Mrs. Duffey," he said. The gray bon-net came up like an opening trap: it showed the face caught inside—a pock-marked woman's face with sal-low skin and bright hazel eyes. Mrs. Duffey's thin fin-gers had escaped through holes in her black silk mitts, and held a stiff bouquet of wooden knitting needles. She cried, "Great heavens to Betsy. Dan Bale!"

"I've been sitting back there with Tyler Fanning. He just now told me that you were on the train."

She squealed softly; the mass of brown yarn sank deep into the hollow between her thin knees; she snatched at his hands and squeezed them. "You gave me a start. We were looking for you, but not so quick."

"Then Grandfather isn't—?"

Her eyes wiggled intently. "I don't know, Dan. He was still alive yesterday morning when I went over to Collie's. You know, Collie has been down with the fever—you remember Collie; that's my niece who married Joe Kohnkopfer. And her sister-in-law was getting married, and all. Mealy went with me, for the wedding. Heavens to Betsy, you ain't even spoken to Mealy."

He didn't recall Amelia Niede, except as a thin child with white hair who sat outside Pock's grocery store in her father's farm wagon. Now she was pretty in a pale, bony fashion. She had a slender neck and coral lips and listless blue eyes. It was her hat which boasted the painted strawberries. He told her, "I apologize, Amelia. I wouldn't have known you unless Mrs. Duffey had told—"

"You used to call me Aunt Eva."

"Unless Aunt Eva had told me."

Amelia said, "I wouldn't have known you either, Mr. Bale." She kept her hands folded in her lap. It was hot in the coach, and Dan could see little glistening dots of perspiration dwelling amid the fluffy hair at the girl's temples.

"Why'd you grow that beard?" demanded Eva Duffey, sharply.

"It came natural, out west. But Ty tells me that I look like Jeb Stuart."

Mrs. Duffey sucked at her tongue. "The war."

"I've heard nothing else since I started east. Out there, we think about—"

"Yes?" she demanded. "What do you think about, out there?"

"Or at least I do. Other things."

Amelia smiled drearily. Mrs. Duffey kept gazing up at him; he had the odd feeling that her eyes were sterilizing his face. "You were going to write some philosophy, or some such. A lot of books."

"It's always in the future," Dan said.

The train went jolting across a gap in the rails; rows of heads jerked with each uneven shudder of the old coach.

"Tell me about the doctor."

"Oh," said the woman, "Adam's fine. He's got his hands all wrapped up in lint, and for two days he did nothing but curse and blaspheme."

"Wrapped up in lint?"

H'la, h'la, h'la sang the baby in plaid, a deadening sound which had begun with the world and would be present forever. Dan looked back up the car. Tyler Fanning had leaned against the seat, his body rigid, his pearly eyelids closed. His hands played with the brass corrugations on the hilt of his sword.

"Yes. He was making some kind of tonic—he had a spirit lamp going—you know how careless he is.

The lamp exploded and he had to beat out the fire with his hands."

"They—?"

"Oh, they weren't cooked. Just nicely brown. Underdone if anything." She cackled; you felt that this was something which she must regard as a joke, because there were so few jokes in the world. "And swear. Like two troopers. He's been swearing about the war ever since it began; should have been in the calaboose for it, if you want my honest opinion . . . But that happened two weeks ago, and Elijah's had to drive old Salt for him and wait on him generally."

Dan said, "I meant to ask about Elijah. He was in my mind, but I did not ask Ty Fanning because they've never been friends."

"And now, of all times," nodded Mrs. Duffey. "Elijah's eaten up with jealousy of Tyler Fanning."

Amelia Niede said, without much emotion, "He is not."

The gray bonnet bobbed around. "Well, we hear from you at last, Mealy. Don't you mind her, Dan. She's downright glad Elijah Huddlestone can't get into the army. He's her young man, you know."

"He is not," said Amelia.

"I'll go back and sit with Fanning," Bale told them. "I'd be pleased to help you home with your things, when we get there."

Eva blinked. "Elijah'll be at the depot with the carryall, and maybe Doctor, too. If he isn't, I'll feel like scorching his breeches for him. You can ride up with us."

"They'll know, of course, if Grandfather—"

"Don't you worry, honey," said the woman. The

words squirted out as if she had been holding them back for a long time. "Pent Bale is an old man and a good man, and he has nothing to fear from God. I guess he's been pretty lonely, and Adam says he's glad to go."

"I would be," said Bale, "with a cancer." She clawed at his hand . . . He went back to sit beside Fanning.

The young captain opened his eyes—half-opened them and squinted at him—the lids were rimmed with a weary pink. "You had quite a confabulation with Mrs. Duffey. Who's the lady with her?"

"Amelia Niede."

"Oh, yes. She's not bad looking, for a German girl. She goes about with young Huddlestone. Remember young Huddlestone?"

Dan said, "Young? He's a year older than you. Yes, we were good friends."

"He has a rupture or something," Ty told him. "And a bad heart. Can't get into the army. Too bad." He dropped his cigar to the floor and squeezed it into a soggy puddle beneath the sole of his boot. Then he drew the slouch hat over his forehead and closed his eyes. Opened them once more to look at Daniel Bale and say, "I could get there quicker, walking. Plague this train. Demon will be at the depot, if they got my telegram. We'll drop you off at your grandfather's."

"Doctor Duffey may be there, with Huddlestone."

Ty sighed, "You oughtn't to crowd in on them in that dinky little rig of theirs . . . my stomach feels like the devil."

This time he shut his eyes for good. Presently he was snoring.

He slept all through their brief stop at Hanover City. The train champed away, northwest now. There were tiny, square ventilating holes cut in the bulbous bellies of the swaying lamps. Angular patches of yellowness—neither light nor shadow, but seeming to smell of hot oil—jerked and swung across the heads of the passengers. The laboring engine drew its strength from blood-vessels and narrow lungs stretched beneath those coaches; you felt the spongy tissues quiver and hiss and give up their all. The whistle made piping and wolfish sounds, the bell clanked despairingly.

They stopped, and someone was knocking upon a wheel with a little hammer. Through the open window, soft soot wallowed in; Bale gazed out past a signal light which seemed nailed against the silver trunk of a beech tree. There were no beech trees, out west . . . a horse's hoofs went *kock, kock, kock* in the muffled dust of a nearby road.

A thin man in a checkered coat came swiftly through the car. He stood upon the rear platform and waved a lantern and called hoarsely, "Now, Henry. Now comes it!" The engine leaped, trying to break the cars in two. *H'la, h'la, h'la* . . . and give that baby something to eat, so it won't howl any more. And everybody seems to be asleep, with the wheels chewing and chewing and chewing as the yellow squares quiver and dance.

Brakes began to screw tight, bringing a sooty world to life. "Gettysburg," summoned the gaunt Dutchman. "All is out for Gettysburg."

2.

The double doors into the parlor had been closed, and when they were pushed aside with much squeaking and crunching, Bale could see that his grandfather had a damp napkin spread across his face. There were two candles on the mantel-shelf, and guttering group in the candelabra which stood on the Drum table. With liquid affluence, tiny tongues of yellow kept washing over the black panels.

Old Mrs. Wurke whispered, "The coffin from Mr. Sketchley comes. He helped us lay him out."

A wad of short-stemmed red roses had been crammed into a gilt-and-blue jardiniere on the floor beside the coffin. Mrs. Wurke's slipper made a soft, ringing sound against the jardiniere as she scraped past. She peeled back the damp white cloth from the dead face. Pentland Bale looked sick and disgusted and made of paraffin. Already his jaw had sagged, and the hands of the willing undertakers had not been skillful enough to draw the wrinkled lip fully over his yellow incisors. A faint, sick-room putridity mingled with the smell of crushed roses.

"All right," said Dan. "Put the cloth back. You ought to have some windows open in here." He tried to open two of the windows but the cases were jammed and solid, painted shut.

"He never know anything for three days. Just right still in his bed, kind of dazed like."

"All right," said Dan again. He stood at the double doors and motioned Mrs. Wurke into the hall. Then he shoved the doors together. The front door stood open; he went out upon the narrow gallery and took a few deep breaths. The old woman waited in the lamp-glow of the hallway, chafing her wrists.

Clouds must be thicker overhead . . . he could see no suggestion of that shop-worn moon, and the long street was a ringing den of tree-toads. The roadway faded into midnight up a long slope where it veered toward Cashtown. Bale felt the buzzing pulsation of train travel still quickening unnaturally within his skin—a steady, draining katabolism which he could not shake off. He was more aware of that than he was of his grandfather's death, and the fact that he was once more standing on this lead-gray porch, feeling the bushy night of Pennsylvania around him.

He had seen Doctor Duffey and Elijah at the depot—them, and a ragged white horse switching his mane and grunting angrily, rubbing bony flanks against the worn shafts. They had told him. In that moment they were only faces who talked and told him that one portion of his life was ended—the last thong which tied him to his childhood was gnawed and parted . . . ho, the wars . . . a captain of the Seventy-second Pennsylvania Volunteers had slumped down in the Fanning carriage at the farther end of the platform and waited for him, moody and uncaring, solely uninterested, while the limping freedman came to gather up Bale's leather satchel.

Doctor Duffey protested, "No, no! You'll be coming along with us and not squeeze us a particle. When you get home, Elijah can sit up and keep watch with you awhile."

"I'd be glad to," lied Huddlestone.

Bale told them, "I'll ride with Ty. Or I could walk, for that matter. If Grandfather's gone, there's no need for me to hurry any more."

"Dead for twenty-four hours," said Duffey.

"I'll look for you. Get around as soon as you can—"
He went riding off with Fanning while the Duffey
carryall racked unevenly up the hill behind them. He
thought himself a traitor to some ancient cause. It
would have been better to crowd those four people
and their bundles. Ty said, "One long belly-ache for
months . . . that's a fact. Inside and out of me, a belly-
ache. And no hope in sight. You watch, Dan Bale—
one of these times I'll get killed. I'd rather, too, than go
through Antietam again."

They were only faces who talked, and told him
nothing at all.

He went back into the hall. He said to the little old
woman, "Well. I'm going up to bed. What time is the
funeral?"

"For two o'clock tomorrow."

"All right." Those were the only words which he
found it easy to say to this tired, shrunken toiler in
calico. "Thank you for everything, Mrs. Wurke."

She began to cry. "I was pretty fond of Mr. Bale. He
was pretty good to me, these three years."

"I'll want you to stay and keep house for me,
awhile."

She made bubbling, soapy little chirps and swal-
lows. "Yes. Yes . . . I . . . be glad to stay by you."

The second story of the house was bisected by a
straight hall with a window at the rear and a door
leading to the upper gallery in front. At the head of
the stairs. Dan stopped and looked out of the rear
window—southwest, through darkness which hid a
scurf of young oak trees and a sloping pasture. The
Fanning house stood beyond. A lot of lamps were
burning, over there. He wondered what sort of a person Tyler had married . . . remembered the time when
he and Tyler Fanning had a battle out in that field,

flinging dry white weeds at each other, pretending that the weeds were spears. He wounded Ty. In the neck. The broken shaft of a sharp reed scraped the white varnish from his skin. "Oh God," screamed Ty, "oh God oh God oh God oh God."

Dan walked on through the smelly thickness of the hallway. His own room was at the front, on the northwest side. The door never had closed tightly—now it was just as sagging, just as cramped and crooked as it had been seven years before. He brought out a box of sulphur matches; the thick head of his match popped like a torpedo when he scratched it. There was a lamp with a tin reflector, in a bracket on the wall. The room began to grow slowly all about him—that same room, coming to uneven and shadowy life once more. He screwed down the ragged orange flame and replaced the lamp chimney.

Mrs. Wurke had been sewing in there; she had left unhemmed aprons and a mass of yellow tissue patterns on the bed. Dan removed the pile and put it upon a chair. He sat down on the bed, thudding his leather bag at his feet . . . sat down heavily amid high-piled feather mattresses—the cords sagged under him and the big maple frame made squeaks and clickings.

Finally he got up and went over to a three-cornered closet which had been built across a corner of the room, and drew aside the curtain and looked in. The clothes which he had left hanging there must have been put away in a trunk. Now there was nothing inside but a fishing rod, a broken shotgun and an old umbrella. On the shelf were a stack of cigar boxes, a paper-wrapped bundle, two bottles. He opened a cigar box. Marbles. Those came from long ago, when he was a little boy. He remembered that big gray-blue "cloudy" with a red eye on its side, one which he had taken from Elijah Huddleston. Another box: penholders and lead pencils and crumbs of dry tobacco, and a daguerreotype of his mother and father, and a shriveled horse-chestnut. Why had he kept that buckeye? Some significance, forgotten . . . These were tender, stupid ectoplasm of a childhood and youth long gone.

He didn't open any more boxes. "This stuff should be up in the garret," he thought. He shook one of the dusty bottles, and a black syrup roiled oozily about. Liniment. The other was one-third full of bourbon. He lifted the mouth of the bottle to his lips and tasted the liquor; there was dust all over the neck, he could feel it gritting on his tongue . . . Put it away, put it away.

A mahogany table, which he called his desk, stood between the two front windows. There was a copy of the New York *Tribune* spread over it, to protect books and other objects from dust. August 16, 1860. Someone had placed that paper there nearly three years before. There were his books—he'd taken only a few with him. Because, when he went west, it was just to look around. He went out with Ike Herriott, but Ike was intending to settle there. Dan Bale wasn't going to settle; he was just going to look around. He had looked around . . . Ike Herriott was dead, and not a lot older than Dan. Only twenty-five—twenty-seven years old, somewhere around there, when the west got him. Settled down . . .

Rollo At Work. He looked at the brown ink on the flyleaf: Daniel Bale from Pentland Bale, Esq. A presentation for good behavior. 20 of Nov 1848. And he could remember much of Rollo. Most of the time Rollo was picking up chips, and he and his Cousin

James both had wheelbarrows. There was a colt named Elky. They went to the Squire's . . . Dan thought, "Grandfather, in your black coffin and with that wet napkin over your slow-rotting face, do you remember why you made that presentation for good behavior? I don't."

A loose step shuffled in the hall outside. "Water I thought you would have," said Mrs. Wurke.

"Oh," he said, "thank you." He took the huge, white pitcher and set it upon the wash-stand. She offered him a linen towel with a pink border. Then she said good night and went away.

He hunted through the crammed, haunted drawers of his desk until he found a pair of scissors. His razors and whetstone and shaving mug were in the wash-stand drawer. In forty minutes he had sponged himself, and removed his beard. The dark, bony face which glared out of the lamp-lit mirror was no face which he had ever known. He didn't even keep a mustache. Cut it all off. It seemed the thing to do.

The sheets on the bed hadn't been changed for a very long time. They felt damp and unearthly until the warmth of his body dried them out. He lay there in darkness, listening to the treetoads, and a dog which bawled somewhere west along the Pike. Later came a momentary patter of rain, and a wind to bang the loose shutters. Pentland Bale and all his ancestors came up to sit around the bed, but Dan didn't mind them. He kept rubbing his sore, smooth face and wondering nervously, "Why did I do it? Why did I cut it off?" And God, he thought, during the eternity before he slept, I hope Grandfather didn't suffer too much. Not too much. I hope Doc never tells me if he did.

And Tyler Fanning was struck by a piece of shell at

Antietam. Somewhere there is a vast, mistaken dis-
placement called a war.

He slept, and though he didn't know it, there were
still lights burning over at the Fanning place. Ty was
vomiting.

3.

This Doctor Adam Duffey, who came in and sat
down at the foot of Dan's bed before he was actually awake, in the morning, was a surviving genius
of his childhood. Nearly twenty-six years before, he
had driven up to that pink brick house on the Chambersburg Pike, and come inside to wash his hands,
speak bitterly to a cringing midwife, and snip the wet
cord which bound Daniel Bale to his mother's body . . .
One of the boy's earliest memories was of Adam
Duffey, shirt-sleeved, a wad of tobacco deforming
his spongy cheek, pounding up drugs in a mortar.

Now he slid in, cat-footed, his battered silk hat
clasped between two red thumbs which protruded
from the gray, sausage-shaped bandages that were his
hands.

Dan lifted himself on his elbows, and blinked.

"Praise Peter," exclaimed the doctor. "And you've
cut off your saintliness."

"What?"

"The handsome beard, and it's gone." Duffey cocked
his oversized, silver head on one side and pressed his
mossy brows together. "You want to be a young man
of fashion, once you're back among white folks
again."

Dan said, "I'm just waking up. I didn't know where I was, or who you were. Close the door."

The doctor pushed against the door with the toe of his scuffed shoe. He turned around and looked at Dan again. Fresh sunlight dashed in a long slant through the windows and matted over his sagging, pulpy face. "Well, my boy," he said. "Pentland Bale is gone. May he rest easy. A good man, and many a worry you gave him."

"Not the last seven years."

"Don't fizz up so willingly. Where's all your fine philosophies? In books—in books you ain't never written."

"I dreamed about him all night," said Dan.

Duffey nodded solemnly. "It's an unsettled world we're living in. The ghosts are uneasy, and not to be blamed for it. You used to laugh at my banshees."

"I'd still laugh at them, and it gave me satisfaction." Dan pushed hairy legs from beneath the bedclothing, and dropped his feet to the floor. He yawned, and shook his head.

"Very well. Laugh. But I saw Ike Herriott. I saw him die, and I woke up in a faint."

Bale grunted, scratching sleepily at his knees.

"You don't believe me," Duffey accused him. He sat down in a rush-bottom chair, spreading his short legs apart and dumping the bandaged hands into his lap. He wore a frayed coat of heavy black broadcloth and a waistcoat with scarlet and white poppies climbing over it on a gold-threaded vine. The rims of his pockets were frayed into a pasty fuzz; ancient saturations of food and medicine had left their pattern upon his clothing. You felt that he had been placed in those clothes at maturity, and whatever genial chemistry transpired within him had stained its evidence on the loose shell of his garments. The big, square thumbs were nervous, twitching things; his deep-set eyes were dreamy globes of cobalt. He had a vast and ill-conducted practice, concerning which he kept no books or records of any sort. People came from Harrisburg to consult him—from York, from Carlisle. And forever he was very poor, and eternally he owed a butcher's bill.

He pulled the wrinkled brown lids over his eyes and leaned his head back against the chair. "It was like this, my boy. I felt very much a part of young Isaac. He was the smartest neophyte who ever wielded a scalpel under my direction. His folks in New Jersey were big folks—good people, and grand. Well, said I, take my blessing along of theirs, and go into those new lands so far away, and never forget to tell people to raise tomatoes in their gardens."

"Are you still tomato crazy?" asked Dan.

"Your own grandfather said I was. He and other good folks like him. Love-apples, said they. A horrid poison to taint the very blood. I say now that there is life in tomatoes—strange, powerful infections of life that folks will know well enough, some day when I am gone . . . I wasn't intending to talk about tomatoes. It was young Ike, and how I saw him . . . You left here in 'fifty-six, you and Isaac."

Dan said, "Yes, 'fifty-six."

"All right." Duffey opened his eyes, and the damp, gleaming knobs of blue were suddenly mystic, fanatical. "It was the night of the eighth of March, Eighteen Hundred and Fifty-seven, and that day I had delivered a woman of twins. The babes were slow to come, and I was that tired, and old Gus Luckenbill had fractured a femur by falling from his hay-loft. It was a terrible busy day. And Mrs. Culp down with digestive fever . . . Well, I fell into my bed beside Eva, more dead than alive."

He aimed his two thumbs at Dan's face. "And maybe it was two o'clock in the morning, when ghosts walk abroad if any time, and I heard someone a-calling me. 'Doctor,' said that Somebody, 'Doctor.' Up I sat in bed, and ready to go to the door. And then I realized that I had seen *him*, tussling with Indians. They was dressed mainly like civilized people, all but one—and he had feathers—but I knew them for Indians. And I had seen him die, with his cerebrum spilled out like sweetbreads in the snow."

He stood up, breathing heavily. "Well."

Dan growled, "I don't believe you ever saw anything of the kind. Doubtless you made all that up from my letters. We never knew whether the massacre took place on the eighth—it was near the eighth, sometime. I was at Fort Dodge, and went back to the lake with the relief expedition. He did have his brains out, when we saw him—if that's any satisfaction to you. He was frozen stiff, of course; it was cold that year. He was carrying a Sharps rifle, and it was broken in two at the breech. There may have been a hand-to-hand struggle. Probably there was. But you're the same infernal liar as ever. I wouldn't trust you with a wildcat dime."

Duffey went over to the window and stood looking down at the leafy road, grinning softly. "Oh, Dan, I looked forward to your coming back, and now you've not the sense you left with. I doubt not that next thing you'll be in this terrible war, bursting people with bombshells, like the devil you are."

"I'm not going to war." Bale stood up, lifted his boots, and threw them down again. "Doc," he said,

"I've got to put on some other clothes. That suit was my best, but it's suffered sadly in travel. Maybe I can wear some of the things that are put away here. Will you ask Mrs. Wurke to come upstairs?"

"And you naked as a six-weeks foetus? I will not."

Dan cried, "Doc. It's good to see you." He reached up his hand, and Duffey patted it with his bandaged paw.

"How long will those burned hands incapacitate you?"

"I'll have these bandages off in four more days, or take down my sign. Now, I'll go back downstairs and find that poor woman—I've a good tonic I want her to take in no small doses. This was a hard pull of the poor soul, Dan my boy. You should give her a bit of a present."

Bale nodded. "I thought of that last night. Probably Grandfather remembered her in his will—you know how meticulous he was about such things. And she was here for the past three years. But if he didn't, I'll see that she gets a tidy sum."

Duffey stood there, swallowing awkwardly. "Dan," he whispered, "it is defilement to mention such a thing in a house of death. But—I wonder if you—it was a long time, and folks are paying in greenbacks—"

Dan said, "You old—" He bent down, hunting among his things, so that the doctor could not see his face. "What's the bill, Doctor Duffey?"

"To you it would not be one penny. But Pentland Bale was a rich man."

"Middling so."

"I say he was rich. My bill is—is fifty dollars, gold." He gulped like an embarrassed child. "Praise Peter," he whispered. "Money. It's the curse of all. It caused this war, Dan—it caused sorrow and desolation and the mourning of widows."

Bale found his money belt and unbuttoned it. In one of the pockets there was a thick wad of paper money, and from others came the metallic thud of coin. He counted: "Sixty—eighty—ninety—a hundred. There's a hundred in greenbacks, Doc. Count it."

"It's too much entirely. And I'll be taking all your money."

Dan told him hastily, "I read the New York papers yesterday, on the cars. Greenbacks are fifty-eight cents this week. That's fifty-eight dollars, and I've got a lot left. You know that I owned a half-interest in Lucas Mite's flouring mill, as I wrote to you. I sold out before I left."

Duffey regarded him with sagging jaw. "Sold out! Then—you're not going back to the west?"

"I have no idea what I'm going to do. Now, go off and give Mrs. Wurke her tonic. And ask her about my old trunk. Folks are apt to be arriving at any time: they won't like to see me naked."

The doctor stuffed the immense wad of green paper into one of his coat pockets, and took out a snowy handkerchief of pink and white silk. He touched it to his eyes. "You're a man, Daniel," he whispered. "It's an uneasy world. I wish I knew what would become of us all." He opened the door and waddled into the hall. "Elijah," he said over his shoulder, "is down in the buggy. He waited there while I came in to see if you were awake. I think Elijah is afraid of people who have died, poor lad. And him wanting to be a soldier."

"Send him up," ordered Dan. "I may need help with the trunk, anyway. And ask him to bring this pitcher full of water when he comes. If you make a body servant out of Hud, I don't see why I can't do the same."

He heard the rumble of Adam Duffey's descent, the monumental talking of walnut boards beneath their moving burden of meat and bone and broadcloth . . . By standing close behind the muslin curtain, he could look down across a narrow front lawn with its guarding palisade of blue-white fencing, and see Duffey's carryall standing beneath the biggest elm, a wheel cramped against the box and old Salt reaching up with ugly yellow teeth exposed, trying to wrench off some elm leaves.

Elijah Huddlestone sat in the driver's seat, with one foot elevated on the spotty leather dashboard. Last night he had been only one of those talking faces. Now he was an extremely tall young man in white shirtsleeves and checkered waistcoat, who wore a round, fuzzy hat drawn well down on his forehead. He had a slender black mustache curling around the corners of his mouth. There was a sense of petulance, of balked desire, in the Elijah who sat there. From that distance Dan could not see the shape of the man's hands, but he knew that they were just as slender-boned and girlish as ever, and every bit as white.

Duffey called softly from the front porch. Elijah wrapped the reins around the whipstock and came up the brick walk, rubbing his hands on the seat of his trousers.

Presently he was tapping at the bedroom door. Dan wrapped himself in a sheet and turned the knob. Elijah started. "The devil. You look like a corpse, wrapped up that way . . . oh," he added lamely, "I'm sorry." He came in and placed the heavy pitcher on the washstand, and presented Dan with a ring of keys which had been jingling in his hand. "These are the ones you'll want, the old lady said. She said there were two trunks in the spare room; your things are in the big one."

"Thanks, Hud." Dan dropped the sheet and poured water into the wash-bowl. He buried his face in it, rubbing with yellow soap, and lifted blindly to hunt for the towel.

"There. Right beside your hand."

"Thank you."

Huddlestone sat on the edge of the bed. His slim fingers played nervously with the flaps of his waistcoat. He radiated the uncertain discomfort of one who feels that he is expected to return intimacy for intimacy, and cannot bring himself to do it.

"Sorry I'm not dressed," Dan said, "but I had to put on some other clothes. I haven't any that are more presentable than the ones I was wearing. Maybe there'll be some, put away."

"You gave me some pantaloons and a suit-coat when you went west," Elijah reminded awkwardly. "I couldn't wear your clothes now, though. You're too wide."

"Come out west and we'll widen you."

"No, I guess Pennsylvania's more my pattern."

They heard the uneven richness of Doctor Duffey's voice from the floor below. Outside, the white horse wrenched his head about, shaking off flies. The jangle of his harness mingled with the distant, drowsy clacking of chickens. Somewhere near at hand a big farm wagon was rattling on the road.

"It must be good to get home," Hud suggested timidly, "even with your grandfather dead, and all."

"He should have died sooner. He hated to be sick."

Hud nodded. "I used to see him sitting out on the

porch. Or at the window in his library. He looked pretty sick, for a long time before he lay a-bed."

"Well," said Bale, "he's easier, now."

"Yes." He had the stiff, fuzzy hat in his hand, tapping it against his knee. "I see you've cut off your whiskers."

"It seemed necessary."

"I see."

"How do I look?" Dan asked, bluntly.

The younger man sat back less timidly against the disordered mass of bed covers. "Why, somewhat wider. I think I'd say that you look kind of more settled, some way. Like you had married and settled down. Though you haven't married, have you?"

"You seem to be on the road, Hud."

Elijah flushed. "Mealy's a nice girl."

"And very pretty." Dan turned away, buttoning his drawers.

"The old man don't like me, so well."

"What's he got against you?"

"Simply that I'm poor!" Elijah exploded. "Poor as Job's turkey, same as always. I'd been working in Pock's store all last year, but then I got a chance to sell subscription books with a Boston publisher. It's an atlas of the world and a household medical cyclopedia and *A Thousand and One Gems of Poesy*, all in a uniform binding, stamped with genuine gold leaf, one dollar and forty cents the volume, or the three for three dollars and a quarter. I've been riding around with Doc, driving for him, and then canvassing while he was busy with patients. Did pretty well, too, but since Doc burned himself I've had to go in and ladle medicines and help him with pills and things."

Dan said, "No more chance with the books, then?"

"Not much. Doc is paying me. That is—he owes me the whole amount, to date."

"He can pay you now. I settled our account with him just a few minutes ago. Get your money before he spends it all on canary cages or patent rocking-chairs."

"I'll dun him within the hour," Elijah said. They both laughed, then sobered at the quick remembrance of what lay in the parlor downstairs.

Dan said, "It will always be a mystery how my grandfather ever let Doc come within a league of him. Grandfather had a horror of people with spots on their clothing."

"Doc is pretty spotty," nodded Elijah.

There seemed to be a mutual recognition of the fact that whereas once they had been close friends, circumstances precluded an instantaneous revival of the relationship. They would extend alternate tendrils, grasping willingly at them, tugging at the tendrils to discover whether or not they were strong enough, and perhaps at last trusting their full weight to the viny fabric which would be woven between them.

"Come on back to the spare room," Dan said. "I've got to search for some clothes." He thrust his legs into the wrinkled trousers which had served him on the journey and, bare-armed, opened the door into the hall. Tenderly Elijah placed his hat—evidently his only one—on the bed, and followed.

Doctor Duffey downstairs; he and Mrs. Wurke were in the dining room . . . "but just because they're advertised in the newspapers, with poetry and what-not, doesn't make it a fact that Hostetter's bitters are . . ." Someone rapped at the side door; abruptly Duffey ceased speaking; they heard the limping tread of Mrs. Wurke. Dan stopped and listened. "It's old

Mrs. Knouse," he said, and went on to a blue-painted door. "This is it. Or used to be."

It was a narrow room under the eaves in the ell. One cobwebby window looked southwest across the corner of Fanning's pasture and over the wheat fields along the Emmetsburg road. The room smelled of preservatives and dry feathers and mice; it was a bed-chamber being transformed slowly into a lumber-room, a repository of household ghosts. Calf-bound books, scabby and worn, were stacked upon the spinet in the corner, and several oil paintings lay face down on the faded patchwork which covered the bed. A thin permeation of gathering dust whispered over everything. "Those trunks in the corner," said Dan. "It's the bottom one. Help me lift off this critter on top."

They grasped the huge hair-trunk by its dry leather handles. Huddlestone's face was suddenly pale, but he cemented his thin hands around the ring. Bale stared at him across the rounded top. "By God," he said, "I forgot."

Elijah's lip curled. "Forgot what?"

"Look out!" ordered Dan. Rudely he shouldered Hud out of the way and threw his own weight against the trunk. It leaped, teetered, began to slide. "Look out," gasped Dan again. With his shoulders against the bulk, he let it thud to the floor without too mighty a crash. The window casing jiggled lightly.

"I'm sorry, Hud."

The thin man said, "Oh, don't mind me." He walked over to the window and stood looking out, and prob-ably seeing nothing. "I think it's better, anyway," he mumbled. "I got something new a couple of months ago." He turned and drew the loose cloth of his trou-sers tightly across his groin, so that Dan could see the shape of the truss which bunched underneath. "Old man Niede's got more than one thing against me. Maybe I oughtn't to blame him."

"Tell him to go to the devil," Dan said. He kept his face pushed down toward the trunk, and fumbled noisily with keys. Presently he threw back the lid, and a wave of camphor struck him in the eyes. He folded back the cold, limp garments, hunting and hunting.

Elijah scraped around for a few minutes, drumming on the window. Then Dan heard a metallic thud. Elijah had found a gun in the corner. "What's this, Dan? Was it yours?"

"No. I don't know—it's just a musket."

The rusty lock clicked. "Tell you," said Elijah, "this is a Sixty-nine."

"A what?"

"Buck-and-ball. A lot of the troops are using them now. She loads with three buckshot and a ball, or more if you want'em. She'll shoot the daylights out of anybody at point-blank range."

"She's better off up here, then," Bale said. He found a pair of heavy linen pantaloons; those would do, he decided, if he could discover a coat to go with them. They'd always been much too large. There was a black alpaca vest which might be all right . . . He straightened his back and found Elijah standing very erect, on the farther side of the bed, the dusty musket clamped against his side. "Ready," said Hud. He snapped the heavy gun into a quick diagonal. "Take aim. Fire." The lock went *pik*.

Dan shrugged. "You go at it as if you knew how."

"We've been drilling all spring. Bart McKosh is the new drill-master. He lost a leg at Fredericksburg, you know."

"Who's we?"

"Oh, Charley Deffenbaugh and old man Gubbe and Ernie Dryer."

"I thought Ernie Dryer lost his hand in an accident at the carriage works."

"Yes, but he gets along well at drill. And a lot of folks from the college, and some of the Sem boys. Why don't you join with us?"

"I'd be of no use to you. Not the way I feel."

Hud shouldered the musket, thudded it down again. "Say, did anybody tell you about Wesley Culp? They say he's in the rebel army."

"He ought to have known better."

"I suppose," Elijah nodded, "that it was because he was down south before the war, and all."

"You ought to know better, too," Dan told him. "Everyone ought to know better. But of course they don't. Human beings belie their designation every day, and have been doing so constantly for two years. The only hope is to keep on until all the fools are killed off. Then we might have—not peace, but at least a diversion of energy towards something else."

There were welts of color on Huddlestone's cheeks. "Perhaps"—he tried to make his voice smooth—"you don't believe that the Union is sacred. Is anything sacred to you?"

"Nothing," said Dan. "I reckon human life comes as close as anything else, though. Did you ever kill anything?"

"What do you mean?"

"Did you ever kill anything?" repeated Dan.

Elijah's face froze into a furious, pearly white. "Why, you damn fool, we went hunting together all the time when we were boys!"

"Yes," Bale told him, "and we killed squirrels and partridges and two deer and I don't know what all. And out west I killed two Indians that I know of, and maybe more. They were animals, too. That's what I try to tell myself, always. But I've felt funny ever since."

Huddlestone put the musket back in its corner, making a great to-do over placing the butt in its original position. When he turned he was smiling quietly. "We're drilling on the lawn east of Deffenbaugh's place Thursday night. If you should be walking out, stop by to watch. We drill very well."

"I have no hope for you," said Bale.

They stood there and looked at each other; laughed a bit, nervously.

"Sometime we'll have to argue this out," Elijah said. "Doc ought to be through with his prescribing by now. I'll have to go down and see."

"Remember me to your mother."

"Thank you," nodded Elijah. Dan closed the trunk, locked it, and led the way up the hall to his own room, with the bundle of smelly clothing on his arm. Hud picked up his hat and wiped imaginary dust from it. "I'll be at the funeral, if Doc doesn't need me to drive."

"Funerals are heathenish spectacles," Bale said. "Grandfather would never attend one. Now he is compelled to." He went to the railing of the stairpit and looked over it as Hud went down. Adam Duffey came out of the parlor into the lower hall, his face very red from some restrained emotion. He had been viewing the corpse. He lifted his bandaged hand as he saw Dan's head above him. "Take courage for the future, Dan, on this sad day," he whispered, in husky ritual. "And we're glad that you arrived in time to lay him away." Then they went out at the front door, he and Elijah. Dan went back into his room and spread out the retrieved clothing upon his bed.

4.

Mrs. Wurke gave him a late breakfast and not a very good one. There were interruptions. Old Mrs. Knouse came from next door, to peek and spy. She said she wanted to know whether there wasn't something she could do. Julius Orcutt, the lawyer, came. He and Dan found Pentland Bale's papers in a little leather portfolio, locked in the top drawer of the library cupboard. Orcutt carried them away, walking on tip-toes until he had reached the street, looking as if he possessed some grave secret which he should never tell anyone but Dan.

He had whispered about the weather, and about Vicksburg. Dan could remember Benjy Orcutt, vaguely, as a fat child with buck teeth and a drooling lower lip. Now Benjy was before Vicksburg. Mr. Orcutt displayed the ambrotype which he carried in his breast pocket in a folder stamped with the American flag. Benjy had his hair cut very short, and he was still fat, and he looked younger than eighteen.

At last Dan left the table, abandoning the fried eggs which were now cold and leathery. Mrs. Wurke stood in the kitchen door, wooden in the starchiness of a blue apron.

"You didn't get no good cooking yet, Mr. Bale."

"It's all right. I had plenty . . . Something seems to be the matter with my appetite today."

"For your dinner I would make *gut* pie-plant pie, like Mr. Bale always ask."

"Now, don't you worry about me," he mumbled, and walked through the living room into the front hall. Those double doors, closed and morguish, were more than he could endure. There was no reason for keeping a corpse in the house. Some decent mechanics should take care of such tragedy, he thought: deft hands should lift a person from his bed as soon as he died, and bear him out into the world of wet earth and drenched leaves, and let him become a lush part of it all.

Another rig stopped at the gate. A single buggy drawn by a sorrel mare. A wiry, stooped creature in a flapping linen duster jumped over the wheel and limped up the walk, taking off his hat as he came. This was Finis Sketchley, a wizened kernel of a man, who was cabinet builder and coffin maker and layer-out of the dead. Seen through the weathered mosquito-bar which covered the outer door, he was something repulsive and even pitiful, though his knobby shoulders were sifted with sunlight.

He rapped upon the leaden-glass panel beside the door.

"Mr. Sketchley," Dan said.

The old man was winking rapidly with one eye, a nervous impulse which had flickered all his life. "Howdy, Dan. I heard you was back from out west, sonny." Bale opened the door and the little man scurried inside. His voice dropped into a stage whisper as he nodded toward the double doors. "I just wanted to see if he's all right." The S sounds sputtered like steam in the dim hall.

"Go ahead." Dan went out on the lower gallery. He filled his pipe from a handful of damp tobacco which he had dumped into a coat pocket. There was a great crying and protesting of ungreased wheels, far up the Chambersburg road. He knew even before he looked that nothing ever changed in Gettysburg. Grandpa Germels was coming to town with his ancient red ox-cart, the inevitable white-haired grandchild beside him.

Dan leaned against a pillar of the porch, studying the lavender cat-faces of pansies lifting from mossy bricks of the front flower bed. The red cart wailed closer and closer; when he looked up, Grandpa Germels was pointing with his goad toward the Bale house; the child was staring. The pink-bearded man jerked his square head down, lifted a clumsy hand in salutation, and moved on, east. The little boy kept looking back.

Presently the double doors crunched together once more, and Mr. Sketchley emerged, moistening his lips with a pointed tongue, rubbing his spread fingers with a large handkerchief. "It's all right," he said. "In summer I don't like to wait so long for the burying." Still in that rusty whisper . . . there was a streamer of smoky black crape tied to the handle of the doorbell, and a breeze flung it across Sketchley's face as he came out. He pushed the clinging stuff aside.

"We got everything fixed, up at Ever Green. The grave and all."

"Well," Dan said, "that's your job."

"And I got that Bearman boy coming back on the train tonight. We'll bury him tomorrow morning."

Bale said, "Adolph Bearman? Coming back . . . ?"

"He died after he got hurt in that Chancellor battle. Ain't nobody told you? His pa is bringing him home from Virginia." He trotted away down the walk, scooted up over the wheel, and the mare started off before he was fairly in the seat.

Dan stepped from the porch and walked slowly through the side yard near its encompassing fence. The wooden cistern cover was new—bright yellow boards, probably built within the past month or two. The old one had been lichened and rotten-looking and strangely beautiful, even when he last saw it seven years before. He glanced across the fence toward the Knouse home, and a yellow curtain twitched at one of the windows. Old lady Knouse was watching, peering and wondering. "Poor relic," he thought. "Why does she watch me?"

In the back yard, he sat down on the round bowlders which formed the curb of the nasturtium bed. His house was beautiful in that kind morning sunlight— its green-gray shingles, its walls of powdery brick, its back porch with the morning-glories creeping up taut cotton strings. A great deal, he thought, has happened since I sat here last. There has been a war, and Ike Herriott was killed by the Sioux, and my grandfather must submit to Finis Sketchley's hands. There are still morning-glories. A new cover for the cistern . . .

South past privy and deserted stable and woodshed, the lot sloped away, south and west, its tangled rose bushes giving way to a narrow vegetable garden and a longer field of bluegrass. A big sweet-gum tree marked the extremity, where chocolate-colored rails ruled off the Fanning pasture. Then the ground slid rapidly up toward the seminary grounds, and the Fannings' house in its distant grove, surrounded by sprawling outbuildings. As Dan looked he saw a carriage creep out of the driveway, down the lane, and east in the road from Fairfield.

He thought that Ty was going out for a morning drive. Perhaps he would stop by. Dan hoped that he wouldn't.

The cupola of the seminary was an egg-shell against the solid, warm blue of the sky. Southeast, under mealy haze, the Round Top hills nosed up. Dan squinted. Yes, they had cut off timber on Round Top. It looked naked and marred ... Chickens clucked drowsily, over at Fanning's. A Sunday clucking, though this was Tuesday ... Somewhere a cow bawled. There was a placid opulence about this morning; you wished that you might be a vegetating part of the earth; you could smell the honey, the hot bodies of drying grain.

For seven years he had tasted the windy breath of a new country. But this land from which he had sprung was mellowed, trodden; the fields had been turned over many times. He could not conceive of its ever having been a cup of unripened green wine. Low hills locked it in; tight, complete; we have you, you have always been ours, you are drenched and seasoned with the sweat of quiet people, and their decaying bones have made you sweet.

He thought, "Virginia must be somewhat like this. And men are tearing it to shreds ... Blundering about with brass guns—"

Beside the nasturtium bed, clover had come matting up in indefinite fairy rings, and in one of these rings he put his shoe and watched the delicate leaves yield beneath oppressing weight ... He began to feel the emptiness of yard and house, the hollowness of a town which no longer belonged to his blood. He saw himself as a child, and his grandfather was leading him home up Chambersburg street, from the scene of some boyish crime. His long, yellow fingers clamped on Dan's ear. Dan saw their shadows flickering over a vanished wooden sidewalk: child and grandfather, one struggling and impish, the other as tall and conscientious as a Puritan eternity.

Later he realized that some creature was jingling in the yard behind him. He turned quickly, then stood up. A fat white dog with clipped ears and a long rat tail, was nosing soberly along the picket fence; a tiny bell hung from the dog's brassy collar and tinkled eerily.

"Cybo!" Bale cried. He had supposed, of course, that the dog was dead. Though he was barely full grown when Dan went west. "Yu, Cy," he called softly. "Yu-yu-yu-yu-yu." Cybo rolled toward him at an awkward gallop, his tail erect, his pink nostrils expanding. He snuffed at Bale's knees, looked at him vacantly, and ran over to nose against the corner of the back porch.

Dan walked toward the front. He expected to find Tyler Fanning there—just why Ty should come, he did not know—but instead he met a woman at the corner of the house. They very nearly bumped together. "Excuse me," Dan said. He thought in that first moment that she was the most desirable woman he had ever seen. She wore a dress of light-weight black silk, ruffled and spread into a sweeping richness around her, supported by the stiff carpentry of hoops. From a lowcut froth of drooping lace her neck rose like the stalk of an exotic flower. She wore a small straw hat with cloth violets foaming down against a mass of carelessly-bundled hair.

Hair the color of rye whiskey.

"Excuse me," he said again.

And this was Tyler Fanning's wife, because Demon was behind her with a gigantic market-basket in his hands. The basket sagged under a shock of fresh pink roses, a bushel at least. *Excuse me* . . . She had green eyes, large and somber; her upper lip was long, her mouth pulpy and wide and very soft.

"You are Daniel Bale?" she asked.

Demon ducked and nodded behind her.

"Yes, ma'am," Dan said, "and you must be—"

"I'm Mrs. Tyler Fanning."

He knew that he was bowing.

"Mother Fanning wanted me to bring a few flowers. She is indisposed, and cannot attend the funeral. Demon, you have the basket."

The old man gabbled, "Yes, Miss Irene. Yes, Mist Dan. I got it heh."

"Thank you, Demon," said Bale. "Take it in to Mrs. Wurke, won't you?"

The servant edged past them with his damp, fragrant load, then turned and rolled his eye at Dan. One eye was blind, dead and blue. His face was a scrolly mass of pockmarked brown tin. "Mist Ty, he captain, Mist Dan! Yessu. He captain! He make 'em damn rebel scoot." He cackled happily, and limped away toward the back porch.

Dan said, "It was kind of you, and kind of Mrs. Fanning, to remember my grandfather. I can see that the roses in our garden are very poorly. Neglect, no doubt." Oh, you—I cannot remove my eyes from you—they have congealed warmly against your skin—

"We are rich in roses," she told him primly. She had a white glove drawn tight over one hand and forearm; in the other little square-nailed hand she held its mate, a twisted scrap. "Tyler said that you rode from the Junction together in the cars."

"Yes. He looks ill."

Her eyelashes were long, thin, ginger-colored. She had high cheek bones, full nostrils. That mouth again . . . you woman, I . . . "He is not well at all. He had a bad wound, and has not yet recovered. I wrote to the Colonel, who was a friend of my father, and made him send Ty home. If only for a few days."

"Yes," he said. Yes. No doubt the best thing. Too bad he can't stay a long time. Look at that comical dog; I would have thought he was dead by now. Your face is saying a great many strange things. What do you think of me, anyway? . . . What do I think? Why, I think you—and I'm not sure—I should know better than to have such a thought in my mind—perhaps after I have seen you many times . . . You should always wear black. Why should I? I don't know: you should. You are in mourning for some madness which came about when you were born. Some mighty madness, a bestial and hungry kind—

"But he was ill again last night, and did not sleep until late. He's sleeping soundly this morning."

"It's very good for him to be home. I suppose the Fannings are very proud of him—"

If it's hungry and bestial, it's the kind of madness I want. Sometimes I have dreamed of things like that. When I awoke, I was tremendously ashamed. Yes, yes, that's the sort of a world we're living in: it makes you ashamed of the sun, the spices in the soil, the consistency of living flesh . . . I know, because I've been ashamed of it all, just as you have.

Demon came scraping back from his errand, the empty basket on his arm.

"It was kind. Thank you, a great deal."

"Not at all, Mr. Bale. A very tiny tribute to a respected neighbor."

He walked out to the old carriage, and clutched her hand as she lifted her foot to the step. He was numb; he could not feel the pulsation of her fingers, the weight she leaned upon him as she took her seat. She raised a flimsy parasol; Demon climbed upon his perch and took up the reins. Mrs. Fanning inclined her head. The fat mares went lunging away through the ruts, the tight harness glistening across the sweat of their backs. Cybo trotted between the rear wheels, tail drooping now, a stubborn little white caboose.

Before the carriage was out of sight, a middle-aged man in a long coat had appeared from somewhere and was standing beside Dan, combing a thin beard and dusting off his shiny lapels. "Daniel. Indeed. So you're Daniel! I am the Reverend Solt. I was your dear grandfather's pastor. I respected him, sir, and loved him as a true servant of the Lord . . . vineyard . . . arms of our Saviour . . . funeral at two o'clock . . . do not know how many Masons . . . and music; the chaplain will . . . and God our Heavenly Father, so we must not grieve for the departed."

"Yes," Dan said. Yes. Yes. For God's sake, what do you want of me? Oh, I'm sorry. You mean it. You cannot help yourself; there are so many people like you in the world. You cannot help—

"Daniel, I came to you feeling that you might find comfort in a moment of prayer."

"Very well," Bale told him wearily. They left the fragrance of the outside shade and went into the house. Reverend Solt hesitated at the closed parlor doors. "Not in there," Dan said, sharply. They moved into the library across the hall. Reverend Solt put his flat hat on Pentland Bale's desk, and slid down on his knees, facing a narrow Windsor chair. He looked questioningly at Dan, knotting his creased, farm-worn hands together. He had not been a minister all his life.

Dan said, "I'm sorry, Reverend Solt. I do not wish to offend you or my grandfather's memory, nor do I wish to be a hypocrite. During these years, my ideas— If you will feel satisfied, praying for me instead of with me, please go ahead."

The minister's eyes filled with tears. He bent his forehead against the hard edge of the chair; with one hand he motioned rapidly for Dan to kneel beside him. He began a hasty, full-hearted chant which was wholly honest and passionate, and yet which he must have uttered many times before: "Oh, Lord, our Father, our Heavenly Guardian and Redeemer of all, we come to Thee in a midnight of sorrow and loneliness. We beseech Thee to shew us that our way is not Thy way, that we have not Thy all-seeing wisdom to understand when the pangs of desolation strike at our hearts. Oh, Lord our Heavenly Father, in Thee is our only refuge, in Thee we trust when we come thrice cast down. Oh, Lord—"

After a few minutes Dan felt rather absurd, standing there behind this man with his struggling, hot, clasped hands and his wet bald head. He went down on his knees as quietly as possible; no doubt the Reverend Solt would be happy at last when he turned and knew that Dan, too, had been kneeling.

Bale squinted at the pink-and-tan pattern of the faded carpet. Of course he was thinking of her. It seemed unreal, even to have knowledge of such a woman. For the first time in his life he was aware of the desire, the plan and hope to do willful evil, something without remorse and never to be eradicated.

5.

They wore white cotton gloves; they were lodge brothers, all much younger than Pentland Bale had been, and two of them were men to whom he had loaned money. They held the tight ropes. The coffin

lurched as one of the men near the head let the cord
catch in his hands. Then it went down, even and
enormous amid the crunch of ropes. A light breeze
caught the little Masonic apron tied across the box,
and rolled it back, flopping. Dan heard the chaplain,
whispering through his asthma once more: "And now,
Brother, you dwell in the City Foursquare . . ."

Reverend Solt put his gaunt arm around Dan's
waist. Somewhere in the breathing crowd Mrs. Wurke
could be heard going *ah-hloo, ah-h-hloo* . . . there was
a gush of sympathetic whispering. The Masons began
to file past, middle-aged, lumbering. Each of them
dropped a twig of evergreen into the open grave.
Meadow larks soared and dipped, whistling across the
hill. A horse neighed; the buggy-wheel scraped against
a tree.

Ever Green Cemetery was a good place to lie; it
seemed that Pentland Bale's stiff body would feel a
flicker of relief, now that all this incantation was done.

Straw bonnets, bonnets of ribbon: Mrs. Knouse,
hawk-nosed and ludicrous in her llama lace shawl. The
curved clods making that mound of excavated earth
had the slick grease of spade marks on them. Again the
horse whinnied.

People turned away. The crowd was lifting and
moving with one impulse, like a bird which had rested
there and now wrenched itself into reluctant flight.
Finis Sketchley muttered to an elderly workman who
had been skulking behind a row of cedar trees. He
came over and began to move the bundles of limp
flowers aside, preparatory to filling the grave.

A few women voyaged past Daniel, moving islands
in the widespread machinery of their skirts, clutching
quickly at his hand, then ducking their heads and
sailing on with handkerchiefs at their noses. The

crowd thinned, thinned. Eva Duffey came past. She whispered, "Adam couldn't be here. Elijah left him at Shultz's. The baby's got running-off-of-the-bowels."

"Come, Daniel," said the Reverend Solt, earnestly.

The carriages began to creak and clatter. A child squealed, and someone put a hand over its mouth.

"Thank you, Reverend Solt," Dan said. "I do not believe I'll go back to the house just now." He saw an aggrieved glare in the man's eyes; Reverend Solt had been preparing a lecture for his benefit, he knew. "If there's nothing else you need to do, you might go back and sit with Mrs. Wurke for a time. She's upset."

The minister nodded sourly. He pressed Dan's hand, and went striding off toward the diminishing row of rigs. Elijah Huddlestone stepped across the corner of the open grave; he glanced into the hole; there were little spots of color in his cheeks. His mother was with him—a dumpy woman in mended poplin, with no bridge to her nose, and false teeth that clicked when she talked. Elijah did not resemble her, but he did look very much like the father who had died when he was three. Mrs. Huddlestone was what Pentland Bale had always called "a widow woman." Mrs. Syrena Huddlestone. Plain Sewing & Dressmaking Reasonable. There was a faded black-and-gray sign in front of the chunky house near the Diamond.

"I see you did get here, Hud."

"Yes."

Mrs. Huddlestone patted his sleeve with her calloused little fingers. "You poor boy. Come all this way and never get to see him."

"I'm glad he's gone," said Dan.

"Yes. Yes. Poor soul. Poor old man. It was a nice funeral, Dan—I never see better . . . You got to come over and take supper with Lijy and me this week."

"That's kind. I'd like to."

Elijah hesitated, hung back. "Are you going to stay around—here?" There was a faint contempt in his question.

"No. I thought I'd take a walk. Get the smell of funeral flowers out of my nose. This—it—"

"I know," Hud nodded. "They're bad business— funerals. There've been a lot of funerals around here since you went west." He saluted with his forefinger and walked away to the Duffey carryall. Eva Duffey was already in the back seat and Mrs. Huddlestone was climbing in beside her.

Finis Sketchley had put a long smock of blue-checked denim over his black suit, and was helping the workman to fill in the grave. He shook his head at Dan. "This is a good lot," he said, winking spasmodically. "High and dry. There ain't any trees for the birds to drop stuff all over the tombstones."

Dan looked down at the rounded slabs, all of them washed and bleached by years of exposure. Telitha F., devoted wife of Pentland Bale. Daniel S. Bale. Mary N., wife of Daniel S. Bale. Baby. Rest, Darling . . . Grandma, father, mother and the baby sister who had died four days after she was born. And he couldn't remember any of them. This was now a world in which he stood with no living flesh of his own. "It would be different," he thought, "if I were married. Maybe it would be."

The last of the carriages was rolling back to town down the hill; only the hearse and a light wagon remained. Fifty yards away, two men were shoveling out another grave, working leisurely, pipes in their mouths, their knees already out of sight behind the brown embankment of earth. That must be the one for Adolph Bearman. Yes, it was on the Bearman lot . . .

Died after Chancellorsville. Bale thought, "There was no earthly need of that." Adolph Bearman had been grinning and mild-eyed, selling apples and grapes from door to door. Wounds received at Chancellorsville.

He said to himself, "Somebody's to blame, and I hope they suffer for it." At least these dead, tragic and prosaic, cancer-eaten and bullet-pierced and consumptive alike—at least they could rest quietly on the rim of that green cup. No harm should ever come to them.

Meadow larks flung their watery seven-notes high and low. Dan walked out through the ugly brick gateway. There was a sign.

ALL PERSONS FOUND USING FIREARMS IN THESE
GROUNDS WILL BE PROSECUTED WITH THE
UTMOST VIGOR OF THE LAW.

A good thing. Keep youngsters from hunting pigeons and quail up there . . .

His hat had been left in the carriage and now he combed eagerly at his thick hair with clawing fingers, ruffling it, cutting loose furrows until his finger nails scraped on the scalp underneath. His heavy coat was stifling him. He took it off, and the vest underneath, and put watch and purse and tobacco into his pants pockets. When he came to a convenient covert of berry bushes he stuffed the discarded clothing there. Then he walked on down the Taneytown road, opening his shirt collar as he went.

In the west, there was South Mountain. As a little boy he had pondered on that. South Mountain . . . how could it be in the west? But there it lay, a low bulwark of purple, two-dimensioned, a painted barricade against all eternity which fell beyond. From the parceled valley where Plum Run had its birth, farms went curling toward the highland in genial rolls. And the sun over them all, to hatch drowsy sawings from a million insects hidden within the barley.

The town had tumbled into a round chancel northwest of the cemetery hill. It tried to draw a coverlet of trees over its face; it was rooted to this soil by the threads of country lanes which twitched off among the swales of green. This path led to Taneytown, that lower road led to Emmetsburg. So many cart wheels had crushed these patches of dazzlement and shade; the memories of peaches and corn and butter were solid from wall to wall; their riches had stained the fence rails to a mellow brown.

He saw cattle lying in the woods beneath him, comfortable little bulbs of russet and white. That was the Niede farm. A blue apron wavered on the porch of the toy house beyond. Perhaps that apron was Amelia . . . He remembered how he and Elijah and Andrew Leen used to go into that pasture after berries; remembered the berries, warty and cool and bitter sweet. It seemed as if he could hear the tinny sound of a little pail, thudded softly by the hands of children who were vanished forever.

This was a trance, he knew—an absurd dreaminess which the sun had soaked into him . . . He climbed over a fence and went down the slope toward the Emmetsburg road. Little field and little field again, and many warm stones, and most of this ridge land was pasture, or hayfields where the cows might do their gleaning after the grass had been cut. When he reached Niede's rye at the foot of the ridge he walked carefully along its edge with the bearded weeds, already tough, swishing against his legs.

In the road beyond a farm wagon lumbered toward the town, and a row of little girls—white dot and pink dot and yellow dot—were ambling south near the Codori place. He passed the drowsing cattle; they watched him, broad-faced, inevitably docile. Their droppings lay in pasty pools among the rocks. Over toward Little Round Top, crows were flapping above the trees. "Out west," Dan thought, "there are the hawks and eagles." Pennsylvania summer . . . he was here in a valley where he had walked as a child, and all this earth had been shaped and herded over a long time.

He came up to the Niede house through an orchard. A row of beehives, warped gray cubes, ranged on trestles beside the wall; the bees were a cozy wind all around. A thick cherry tree was turning a slow lime-yellow under the ripening sun. Dan climbed the wall. Robins flipped up from the garden as he came.

Uncle Otto was sitting in an old green rocker close against the shaded well-curb. A shaggy dog, lying beside him, lifted its head. Uncle Otto seemed asleep; his fat belly rose like a pudding with each slow pressure of his breathing. He opened his eyes and gazed calmly at Dan. His hand went up to caress a white beard. "Ach," he said, "it is young Bale. No hat mit, and it is struck dead by de sun."

"Good-day, Mr. Spohn."

The old man motioned clumsily toward the well-curb. "Down sitzen. De little Amelia on der locomotive mit, and says it is not killed by de scalpers, west."

"No," he said, "I didn't get killed."

"Old man," nodded Uncle Otto, solemnly, "he is die."

"Yes. We've just buried him up at Ever Green."

Otto Spohn shuddered up out of his chair. His feet were wide and bare and very soiled. "I have it buttermilk, now," he offered.

"Thanks. If you don't mind, I'll take a drink of water instead."

"Is bad," declared Otto, "and in der blood it makes so—so—" He struggled awhile, hunting for a word, then shook his head and padded over to the gaping slant of the root cellar. He went down the mossy steps very painfully, holding to the crooked casing above him.

Dan let the chain down into the well. Far below he could see a round dollar of blue in which his head and shoulders were framed. The bucket sucked into the water with a hollow splash, and made a shimmering puzzle of the deep illusion . . . He hauled it up, and drank. The old dog at his feet sighed, turned over, and went to sleep again.

Uncle Otto came up out of the cellar with a brown pitcher in his hand. "Everybody is die sometime," he said. He shook his head and drank mournfully. "Maybe too *der alt* Otto Spohn, once." He gurgled into the pitcher again, and set the empty vessel down on the curb. Thin buttermilk dripped from drenched tufts of his beard. "And comes maybe to see de little Amelia, young man." He tried to look very wise.

"I was just walking," said Dan. He looked toward the barn and saw Henry Niede, Otto's nephew and the father of Amelia, standing there with a bucket in his hand, gazing suspiciously at him. "Oh, the devil!" he thought. "That ignorant Dutch savage is afraid somebody's going to seduce his little pullet." He stood up. "Thanks for the water, Uncle Otto. *Danke schön.*"

The old man sighed, a little puzzled, and groaned down into his chair again. Dan walked past the smoke-house and wagon shed; Henry Niede stood in the deep shadow of the upper barn door, watching him come. Bale nodded at him. "Good-day, Mr. Niede. I stopped by for a drink."

Niede's face wrinkled in a crafty, narrow-eyed smile. "Why, howdy-do, Dan Bale! I didn't know was you, now. I thought was some other feller. Well." He came forward, dusty-armed, his boots shuffling in loose strands of hay that were spilled about the sill. "Well, and your grandfather was buried today. Ach, that is too bad for the old man."

"He was sick a long time."

"I guess you're just about the only heir, ain't it?" The man seemed fighting to keep a honeyed eagerness out of his voice.

"Yes," Bale said. "It's likely there won't be any more, either. I seem to be cut out for a bachelor. Good-day, sir." He lifted his hand and went on, past the barn. He could feel Niede's eyes squinting, burning after him with an unholy avarice. He thought, "They're all alike. Money. Money. Doc was right. It's money which has caused war and the major unhappinesses. He'd sell that girl for a body slave if he could get his price— Niede would. Not that I want her . . ."

The farmer had driven his vision from him; he was insensitive now to the droning tranquillity. You could put people down in any violet meadow, in any hillock of clover, and see their petty defilement before an hour had passed. Defilement: himself, along with the others. Without hesitancy he had hoped to plant sensual germs within the head of his neighbor's wife, and had imagined that they grew out to enfold him and draw him into the mutual festering of their desires . . . He vaulted over the fence and went back toward Granite Ridge, swinging across a field east of the Codori farm. The froth of daisies rippled and tossed as he crumpled it.

At Codori's, someone was sharpening a scythe. The juicy *weet, weet* of a cold whetstone keened against the solid blade: there were weeds to cut, grass to mow, the forests of the grasshoppers must be shaved down.

Ahead of him, beyond the low stone wall, a round grove of rock-oak saplings pushed themselves together. For all their slenderness, you knew that they had been there a long time, wrapping their roots around the bony hill and straining for the sap of their tough nourishment. Arbutus grew there; once the boys and girls of Dan's school had gone Maying, suckled in that legend by an elderly teacher who was an Englishman. They had whooped and tumbled among the bowlders, those boys, while the girls had fallen to their flower-plucking like honest little peasants. The arbutus trailed pink skeins over the stones; the tiny corollas were lined with rose. And all this had happened in some other century, when butterflies had richer cream on their wings, and schoolmasters in shabby beaver hats were very kind . . .

He spread his hands on the rim of stones and stepped over the wall. The bunching copse had hidden something which he could see now: the Fanning rig with Demon asleep in his seat and the mares idly swishing their tails at hungry flies. The bars by the Taneytown road were let down, and creasing wheel tracks curved from gate to grove.

The horses twisted their necks and sniffed in his direction, and where was the woman in black, and where was Tyler Fanning? Bale circled the northern edge of the copse; a mound of bright color lay in his path; Ty was flat and senseless upon a folded tartan blanket, the military hat covering his face. He had a cigar in his outflung hand, but the chewed butt of it was sliding through his limp fingers. No sword or belt or gloves or military blouse: just the wrinkled white shirt and blue breeches and the long, glistening boots dumped out across the blanket.

Dan heard a little sound; he turned. Mrs. Fanning was sitting some distance away, leaning her shoulders against the wall which bounded the north side of that pasture . . . He heard his feet, sounding enormous and clumsy in their march toward her. As he approached, he saw her mouth bend in a smile—not the polite smirk of one who brought roses to a dead old man, but a flutter which moved with her eyes and made something tender and secret of her whole face.

She explained, "We've been for a drive through the countryside. This seemed like a place where it would be nice to stop; I've never been here before."

"I thought you must be having a picnic."

"No, we've nothing to eat . . . Tyler didn't wish to stop, but I insisted. Maybe he'll feel better, now that he's slept some more."

He asked, "May I sit down?"

"Do." She moved her legs an inch; her square little hands drew at the hem of her skirt and folded it more tightly beneath her. You could see the sleek varnish of her right thigh and the upper calf of her right leg, swelling tightly under the smooth black silk. She was not wearing the hoops which had supported her gown that morning. "You must excuse my appearance," she said. "I was—being comfortable."

He said, "I don't know the trivial politenesses any more. There's little ceremony on the prairies. People have to work too hard." He sat down, not too near to her. "I wasn't expecting to see anyone, either. My coat is under some bushes near the cemetery."

"Is—everything over?"

"Yes. He's been put away." He could feel the afternoon sun squatting in yellow brittleness around him. "You should be in the shade, Mrs. Fanning."

"No." Her eyes closed and she tossed her head with a quick, nervous thrill. Her hands went up to pat the iridescent mound of loose hair. He thought, "You are a lady, but now you look like a girl in Mother Merry's house at Dubuque." Then her eyes were open again, hard and green, and again she smiled. "There's something medicinal in this sun, perhaps. A habit-forming drug. I like it. It's hot, but I like to feel it soaking through me. I've had strange dreams all this day, being under it. And—other times. When Mrs. Fanning is asleep in the afternoon—or doesn't want to talk, and no one else is there—I go out into the meadow and lie flat in the long grass and let the sun pound me. The meadow behind your house . . . It's not genteel. You must tell no one."

He felt that an intense coarseness was creeping into his voice, and desperately he tried to keep it out—make his words limp and casual and reassuring. "I like that field. Ty and I played there, sometimes, when we were boys. After I was older, I used to sit out there at night. Near the thorn-bushes, where there's a marshy place below. Sometimes I'd fall asleep and not wake up until morning."

"How odd." That little brandy voice of hers—so smooth, and holding a spiny breathlessness beneath its surface. This was the first time that Bale had ever been aware of a woman's voice, as a thing tangible and quite apart from her. "Didn't your parents come to search for you?"

"There wasn't anyone but Grandfather, and he'd be asleep."

"You were an orphan. Mr. Bale? Your parents—"

"They died before I could remember them. It was an epidemic. A baby sister came; she died, and then my mother, and my father followed within a week. But I can't remember."

The woman said, very gently, "Your home does not look as if it had concealed so much tragedy. It's pink. I can see pink blotches of it through the little oaks, when I look from my window . . . I like the wooden pump."

"Yes," he nodded uneasily, "it's a very fair picture, that house. I don't know whether to keep it or not." A shadow switched over the grass at his feet; it was gone; there had never been any shadow in the world. And then it came back, and hung there. Dan looked up at the sky. "Look there!" he cried. "Buzzards! Two of them."

She placed her hands calmly together, but her shoulders moved with a shuddering squeeze. "They eat carrion, do they not?"

"Yes. I thought all of them were gone, around here: I haven't seen any for years. We don't get them in Iowa or Minnesota—too far north. Maybe these came over from the Blue Ridge."

Now the buzzards were swinging in a high and solemn circle, above Codori's farm to the west. The angle of the sun made their blotting shadows rub across the copse, blur and vanish in the sloping field, become a reality close at hand and then only a suggestion, the thinnest taint which ever sat above the meadows and the grain. "Something's dead, over by Codori's," Bale said, "probably a calf." The motionless birds were fastened by invisible threads twisting in the white-blue sky so far above them. They did not twitch their wings. The threads turned them lazily about.

"This is too perfect an afternoon," Mrs. Fanning whispered. "I don't like them. I wish they'd go away."

A revolver shot banged; Dan lifted nervously on his haunches. The woman did not cry out, but her body jerked as if something had struck her. She exclaimed, "I didn't know he was awake—" Tyler Fanning was standing erect at the edge of the copse; he lowered a revolver in his hand, then raised it again. The buzzards had broken their invisible tether and were planing down above the field.

With his left hand, Ty drew the black hat more firmly over his forehead; he squared his shoulders. The navy revolver banged again. Behind him the sedate mares were quivering, ears erect, hind-legs braced. Demon wailed, "Eeyo, Becky! Eeyo, Bright! *Hol' on . . .*" He tumbled down to grasp at their bridles. The buzzards kissed a grove across the Emmetsburg road, then cut sharply higher and drifted off into the west.

Dan stood up. Ty came toward them slowly, blowing the smoke out of his gun and plucking caps off the cylinder.

"Ty," the woman said. Her voice was sagging, the voice of a much older woman. "We didn't know you were awake."

"Didn't you see me get up and haul my side-arm out of the rig?" He nodded at Bale. "Hello, Dan. Where did you drop from?"

"I was walking . . . Mrs. Fanning has been kind enough to let me sit down and chat with her for a while."

Ty blinked his pale eyes. "Did the shots startle you?" he asked, a shade too kindly.

There was a vise of silence, for a moment. "No,"

Dan said. "We've had considerable shooting, you know, out where I've been."

"You cut off your whiskers, didn't you?"

"Yes. Last night."

The young officer shrugged. "Damn it all, Irene. Why'd you let me sleep so long?"

"It wasn't long. Just a little time."

"You knew mother was expecting us back. For a reason."

Slowly, the girl began to climb to her feet. Tyler did not move. Dan offered his hand to her, but she waved him aside. The loose gown hung from her tight waist, badly wrinkled by her sitting upon it. She shook out her skirts: you could hear the watery sound of her petticoats underneath. She looked steadily at her husband. "I don't care if we miss those Harrisburg people altogether," she said to him. This was something Dan was not expected or intended to hear; he turned away. "It's much more pleasant sitting here in the sun. And much better for you to be resting out in the fresh air."

"The devil it is," Tyler snapped. He swung on his heel and walked toward the carriage. Then he spun around to say something more, but he began to cough; the words curdled in his throat; he coughed with violence and some pain until his face was a sallow red. "Come *on!*" he cried at last, catching his breath. "We're too late for any use!"

His wife moved slowly after him. She took a few steps, then turned to bow to Dan. "I enjoyed our talk," she said. A rag body, a china face all expressionless in its enameled grin.

"Maybe," said Dan, "we'll meet again. In—another field."

He did not intend to utter those words. For so many days he had been kept by stifling exigencies from saying the things that were in his mind, and this relaxation, this melting down under a warm sun, had made him speak to her—load the trivial words with all the meaning they would bear . . . He felt her eyes leave her body and come over to him and glue against his own and search the hidden darkness within, and wonder what truth he was speaking and how much of that truth she should accept . . . She turned swiftly. She went away through the short green blades.

Ty called, "Bale. Give you a lift to town."

"Kind of you . . . I must go back through the cemetery."

He walked out of the field, past the lowered bars, and crossed the road. Behind him came the squeak and jumble of the carriage moving along uneven ground. When it wheeled north into the road, Dan was already past the elderbushes which hedged a wheat field near the summit of the ridge. The horses' feet were muffled and wooden on the hard-packed dirt; a tail of thin dust floated lazily up from the rear wheels, and Dan wondered why Cybo hadn't been along.

He looked back at the little rock-oak copse, the tumbled stone fences, and the limpid haze of the western ridge and South Mountain beyond. Those buzzards had come back. They were flying higher and more cautiously, as if at any moment they expected Ty Fanning's revolver to spurt at them again.

6.

Mr. Orcutt showed him the will, read paragraphs, re-read them in a dry and mildly approving voice. He opened document after document. Two houses in Trenton, New Jersey. The farm near Paoli. The half-interest in the Philadelphia book-bindery. The fourteen hundred and twenty-seven dollars in the bank. All the tiny, overlapping little claims and indebtednesses which hinged locally around the name of Pentland Bale.

"He was a good business man—your grandfather. A shrewd man, and he prospered accordingly." Orcutt took off his glasses and wiped them with a loose end of the rusty scarf he tied around his collar.

Dan shook his head. "Not shrewd. He was entirely too kind for shrewdness. You have listed several thousand dollars of bad debts on which you feel that little can ever be realized. Those weren't the doings of a shrewd man, and I deplore the adjective."

The lawyer curled his lower lip back between his even, yellow teeth and pressed it lovingly. "However that may be, Dan, your grandfather has left you very well off." He swallowed. "I will be glad to offer any assistance which I may in—the carrying out of your stewardship."

"Thank you, sir." Dan stood up and reached for his hat.

Orcutt looked surprised in a plain, stony way. His hand closed on the sheaf of papers. "You wish me to execute your affairs for the present? Naturally, I expected to attend to the will, the admitting to probate, and ordinary forms. But these other matters: collections, the receipt of these various monies—"

"If you assume them all for the present, I shall appreciate it. Perhaps you may care to shoulder the care of them indefinitely."

Orcutt nodded gravely. He lifted his head with the felicitous pride of a man who takes abnormal comfort in his own honesty. "I will endeavor to serve you, Dan, as I served your grandfather." There was a tiny prickle of pink light in each of his dull brown eyes. "Dan, there is a rumor going about the town. I heard it first yesterday, after the funeral. Two rumors—"

Dan said, "This is a village. Rumors—"

The lawyer clamped the bent gold bows over his gaunt ears. "Two camps of rumors, I might say. One group has it that you are a Secessionist—a Copperhead." He gulped over the word as if he had stepped across a puddle of dung. "The other group, in which I am happy to join with hope, declares that you are going into the army; that already you have been offered a commission with the Minnesota volunteers."

"They're both wrong. I'm not a Copperhead, and most certainly I am not going into the army."

Orcutt's assistant, a youth who had been reading law books in the office for the past year, came limping up the rutted stairway with the mail. He looked like a sallow, clubfooted monk in his baggy gray waterproof. He placed letters upon the lawyer's desk, nodded at Bale, and went rustling and dripping into his cubby-hole opposite the cold stove.

"I'll be going," said Dan. Orcutt made no reply. Only when his blundering fingers had lit a candle to push back the growing darkness of the office, only then could Dan see that the man's eyes were narrow and watery behind his round spectacles.

One of the letters was shaking in his hand. "Benjy," he said, with difficulty. The damp, thumb-smeared envelope had a crude red-and-blue cartoon in its upper left-hand corner, one of those myriad cartoons which blotched on half the envelopes clogging the mails. It depicted a scrawny rooster in a liberty cap trampling on a scrawnier rooster with a Jeff Davis beard . . . Dan moved his feet.

Orcutt's damp glance slanted up at him. "Wait," he said. "Benjy was expecting to be a corporal soon." He spread the coarse wad of paper closer to the candle, and began to read aloud with no further apology or explanation.

My Dear Father:
Here we are still outside the works and I am
writing this on a cracker box. I thought sure by the
time I penned another line we would be inside and
the stronghold would be ours. But old Ulys, which
is what the boys call him, hasn't sent us in yet.
However they cannot withstand us very long now
as a fellow came within our lines yesterday and said
the food over there was a minus quantity and he
hoped we wouldn't give him any mule-beef. Tell Ma
I never rec'd. the last three bundles she sent. No
doubt they have been eaten by somebody afore this.
Ralph Tolis got sick a Friday and was sent back to
the hospital. It is a kind of stomach fever. We pray
that he may fully recover his health and spirits at
once. The weather has been very hot and there is
considerable grumbling and not a little sickness, but
you know dear Parents that I will always look out
for Number One. Tell Grace we have yet no word
from Clark and it is feared he fell in the last assault
or was taken prisoner. That is something which I

would not want to happen to me I can tell you. The
boys are playing a good deal of Bluff, but no one
has much money and most of the betting is done in
paper currency (fractions at that) or secesh shin-
plasters which are dear at any price. You can buy a
bushel for only a mite of change. There is artillery
fire on our right daily, but thus . . .

Orcutt stopped short and put the letter down.
"No," he said, "I presume that he has not yet been
made a corporal. My apologies for having kept you
waiting." He removed his glasses again and looked at
them critically, holding the jointed lens before the
flame. "I," he began, "ahh—" and then stopped and
said nothing more.

"I hope he comes through safely," Dan said.

Orcutt scraped his throat. He stood up and offered
a loose hand. "I trust that I may serve you with satisfaction," he declared. "Will you call again, within a
few days?"

"Yes," said Bale . . . He went down the knotted,
slanting cavern of the stairway. Outside, clouds were
solid and dark gray and very low, rubbing close
above the square red chimneys of the town. Even this
rainy world was a hundred degrees lighter than the
den where Julius Orcutt sat ready to serve him with
satisfaction . . . He thought of Benjy Orcutt, waddling
after a tribe of scabby-legged boys through the soft
fields along Pitzer's Run. Fat buttocks, crooked teeth,
stiff yellow fuzz. He thought, "And whatever humanity lives within his father—whatever kindled the flicker
in his eyes—that spark will be puffed out when *it* happens to Benjy . . . Vicksburg is so far away."

He turned up his collar, and thudded along the wet
walks which bordered Chambersburg street. He

hoped that the rain would stop before supper time; since no one observed mourning any more, he was going to the Huddlestones' for supper. He fancied Mrs. Huddlestone babbling to Elijah that Dan Bale oughtn't to be left to brood alone, now that his poor grandfather was dead, and most young folks gone away to the war, the war, the war.

"I'd rather get killed," said Tyler Fanning, "than go through Antietam again." And no one had made the idiot go. There hadn't been any draft when he went. The draft was at hand, now, and maybe it would take Dan Bale along with the rest. It was one of the immutable gnashings of a nation's jaws: if it pulverized him, he must watch with open eyes, watch it squeezing his chest in two, but never fall back on the hypocrisy with which some others had bolstered themselves. Let them get out a band of martial music, he decided, and the most ordinary oafs became knights until they are spoiled by it. Isn't that so, my dear? Yes, she'd say, but Tyler isn't an ordinary oaf. He's embittered and childish and wholly wrong, but you see how well he let himself be shaped for the slaughter. There must be a knightly fancy underneath, and maybe it was that knightly fancy which I married. I don't know. It all seems sullen and stupid, now . . . Yes, my dear, yes, yes, whiskey-hair, slim neck, yes, hard green eyes—yes, most bitter mouth in the world, and you will forget it if ever we meet, alone at night, when the insects are fuming around us and the grass is smooth and dry, yes, you will forget it if ever we meet in another field. *Another field.*

His hands had little gulleys of perspiration: the bent folds of their flesh. He walked on, going home through the rain to try for satisfaction in Plotinus. But any satisfaction ran away from him.

7.

Some of the churches held prayer meeting on Wednesday night, some on Thursday. By this time, Dan knew that there were prayers all the time—little imprecations which old men shaped as they weeded their peas, blundering entreaties that baked in women's heads as they shook the ashes out of their kitchen stoves. He heard the whole town, the hot green countryside, praying all around him. It was hard to sleep at night.

He sat on the edge of the front porch, his feet close beside the drowsing pansies. Slow-gathering night began to show itself in blue dust that hung along the turnpike and made a witchery of every paling. This was Thursday evening, and two bells turned heavily on their beams, far across the town. A B-flat bell and another which he couldn't name.

Old Mrs. Knouse trotted out, the fringe dripping from her shawl. Her bonnet jerked briefly at him. She clacked, "Goin' to the drill?"

"The drill?" he echoed stupidly.

"I was pretty sure you wouldn't be goin' once to meetin', Daniel." She chuckled. The prim little gate banged behind her; she scooted away, east, along the path which led to the first board sidewalk, tucking up her skirts unnecessarily as she circled the shallow puddles left from yesterday's rain. The pink sunset was kind to her knobby shoulders.

Dan waited indecisively, rapping his pipe against his palm. That was what it all meant, of course. It seemed as if he had heard military music in some hidden distance, for the past half hour. And an hour before some boys from the seminary had sauntered past, poking and threatening one another with guns. He had supposed that they were merely larking around.

"Elijah's army," he said, with ashamed malice. Hud had not mentioned the drill, since the discussion on Tuesday. *Sometime we'll have to argue this out—*

He cried to himself, very suddenly, "Of course I'll have to go! He's expecting me to see him. The poor devil—truss and all—he's proud, he wants to march—"

He got his coat and hat. A coolness came down from western mountains as the sun oozed lower behind them. Mrs. Wurke had gone to church; the empty house breathed behind Dan as he went away toward the village, a house still smelling of elderly death, pained by it, and refusing all tranquillity.

The Knouse woman was a little goblin, far ahead. He walked slowly, not wishing to overtake her. Few people sat on the stoops and galleries along the way—none whom he recognized except Mr. and Mrs. Clinkhofer, sitting in fat, doughy silence as they had sat for all the evenings of his life. The martial music shrilled up again, far ahead. A fife, maybe two, playing *O, My Love She's But a Lassie Yet.* The boards were hollow and thudding under his feet; you could still smell a misty penetration of the rain which had come on Wednesday.

It was a long walk. This town strung itself along ten roads, dusty or muddy spokes which ran out from the hub, the Diamond. It was a little town but the long avenues blended into gray distance before the houses had ceased. The homes were red and pink, yellow and white; they squatted, with thick walls and no eaves at all, like the placid cattle which chewed their cuds in Niede's beech wood-lot. You thought: a dairy town, a place where there is thick grass in every rear yard and cool butter in the pantries . . . Overhead, a tree-toad broke the nearer silence; it stopped its sawing, frightened at its own wheeze, then began once more. The bells for prayer meeting had ceased ringing. Distant clumps of bushes stood out with the momentary distinctness of early evening, then sank lower into blue dusk. A drum lived somewhere under the earth, a huge and empty resonance which supported the faraway fifing.

There were a few rigs in the Diamond, and early lights burned in several stores, but the people had all moved farther on, along York street. Huddlestone's house was dark. There were more rigs ahead, and people walking. Dan could hear the mottled fever of their conversation while he was yet two squares away. That was Deffenbaugh's place; Japanese lanterns shone along the low porch, though colors could still be distinguished in the tardy gloaming. Horses whinnied up and down the side street; this was all like a fair, and Dan smiled half-ashamed as he found himself walking faster. The martial music began again. He thought, "That was a game we played when we were children, and now they're using it with their drill." *Peddler, have you boots for children* . . . the drums rattled and banged.

They had a big sign, painted with black letters on an old sheet hung behind those four paper lanterns. Ladies Aid Ice Cream & Cake Benefit U.S. San Comm. There didn't seem to be many customers; a couple of little girls were standing beside a kitchen table eating their portions, and at the end of the porch Grandpa Deffenbaugh was doing something with a big wooden tub. Women fluttered up and down the path with plates and baskets. But the main horde of people froze in a thick crust around three sides of the field

which bordered the home on its eastern width, held
back by a white fence.

Inside the pasture Elijah's army was going up and
down. Dan counted: thirty-four of them. Four squads
of eight, with two shorter boys closing file in the rear.
At one side, braced against his crutch, stood a sickly-
looking man with one leg. That was Bart McKosh; he
used to drive the butcher's cart for Mr. Rosenvelt.
He said, "Left oblique. March!" Dan nudged closer; a
woman spoke to him. Her face—half hidden and it
was growing dark . . . the Wade girl from Breckenridge street, the younger one. Her father had been an
invalid for years, and her mother used to do all the
mending for Pentland Bale and his grandson. She
made Dan's shirts, and Ginny helped with the seams.
"Why, Gin," he called, "I didn't know you. You're quite
grown up!" She nodded amiably, and moved away
through the crowd. Bart McKosh said: "By fours . . .
huh." His voice sounded thin and peevish, much as Tyler Fanning had sounded. He crutched slowly toward
the middle of the field.

Dan could pick out Elijah. His height made that
easy. He was in the front rank, looking straight ahead,
and supremely conscious of the staring faces so close to
him. The dusk came, thicker and thicker. None of the
men wore a uniform. They were in their shirt sleeves; it
must be hot work, drilling. Someone began to applaud:
there was a loose patter of hands all along the fence.
Bart's voice squealed up again—dropped with a snarl.
You couldn't understand his words. He seemed to be
saying *quahaw! hoord—har!* Clumsy feet came down,
true and even on the turf.

The fifes and drums started a new tune. There
were five musicians in a little knot in the center of
the lawn, around whom the squads swung in their

futile wheelings. Old man Holder was beating the bass, and one of the other drummers seemed to be a colored man; he had white hair. Dan squinted. It was Demon, Fanning's Demon. The fifes larked higher; they sounded like birds. Dan felt his toe thudding mechanically against the damp earth.

He said to a man who leaned upon the fence beside him, "What's that piece?"

"'Garry Owen.'" The man kept chewing calmly on a burnt match; he did not turn his head. There was a flash of silver from his open coat. Presently his eyes shot side-ways. "Oh," he said. "It's young Bale, ain't it? Don't you remember me? John Burns."

They shook hands. Bale asked, "What's the badge?"

"Constable. I'm constable, now. I teamed awhile with the army. But they made me come home. Said I was too old." His face was calm, dissipated and leathery. His sad eyes rested coolly on Dan's. "And I know more about soldiering than that whole caboodle out there." He kept chewing and chewing at his match; presently he spat it away, a flattened cud. Out in the field, Bart McKosh jerked his harsh syllables. The feet went *nud, nud, nud* in Deffenbaugh's trampled pasturage. John Burns kept grunting *left . . . left . . . left*. He chuckled stonily: "Hay-foot, straw-foot, hay-foot, straw-foot." He said to Dan, out of the corner of his wrinkled mouth, "I know all that truck. Knowed it for a long time. Teamed awhile down in Maryland, but they sent me home." Somewhere in the crowd there was a growing murmur. Dark. It's getting too dark. Can't see anything.

Those varied, ill-assorted shapes went swinging past, very close. "Hey, Charley," yelled somebody, "look out. Here come the rebels!" A lot of small boys tittered and echoed the words. "Look out, Charley. I'm a rebel. Boowoowoorr! Boo, I'm a rebel—"

John Burns told Dan soberly, "At that, I've seen worse drilled milishy afore this." The hand-clapping began again, louder and more sustained. Bart McKosh wailed *quah-haw . . . ult!* Boys slid over the fence to approach the shadowy squads. The army broke ranks, and melted across three sides of the field.

Over on Deffenbaugh's porch, the paper lanterns were gay and heathenish; a woman began to ring a dinner bell. The crowd spilled slowly up over the lawn.

A thin totem with a musket in its hand came toward Daniel. "Hi," said Elijah.

Bale told him, "I was just going to give you a hail."

Huddlestone put his long leg over the pickets and slid across the fence. People pushed away from them; John Burns was gone; the wheels of light vehicles began to rattle in the road. "Well," Elijah challenged, "what do you think of it?"

"It was a good drill. Though I don't know much about drill."

There was a mighty hauteur in Elijah's voice. He tossed the gun over his shoulder. "I don't think we're so bad . . . You'd better think it over, Dan."

"I've thought," said Dan, "for over two years."

"You going up for ice cream? The Ladies Aid is treating us soldiers."

Dan said, "No. Too many folks in the way."

"Mealy and Ma are over on Doc's porch. Why don't you come over for a spell?"

"All right." Bale felt in his pocket, and brought out a fold of paper currency. "While you're up there, buy some ice cream and cake. Deffenbaughs will lend you a basket or something. For the ladies, you know."

"No, I'll buy it. I—" Hud hesitated, then reached for the money. "That's thoughtful of you. I'll meet you at Doc's." He went away toward the orange and green lanterns, still holding his shoulders painfully straight.

Near the corner, and with people ambling along in little groups ahead of him, Dan felt a hand on his sleeve. He turned. A fat man had stepped out of the shadow of a big sycamore tree beside the road. "Bale," he said, "I've been wanting to get a word with you."

Dan asked, "Who is it?" Just a meaty body and a stubborn, round head in the gloom.

"Elmer Quagger. You remember me. I used to work for Bedford Fanning. Foreman of his shoe factory."

"Yes," said Bale. "I remember. How are you?"

The tension on his sleeve increased. "Come over here by these bushes a minute." They moved into the deeper shadow.

Dan asked, "Well?"

"I've heard stuff about you, Bale. Wondered if it was—right."

"I don't know what you mean."

Quagger cleared his throat, and his damp voice had a little more character to it. "There's folks around here that might like to talk to you. If what I hear tell is—right—" He chewed soundlessly on nothing. "You ain't in the army. We sort of wondered how you feel about the war, and all. You ain't the only one, maybe, who is a friend of true liberty."

Dan said, "I—you mean—" The truth began to convulse itself in his brain. He's taking me for one of those—those— He asked, "You are talking about Copperheads?"

"That isn't a word folks like to say, Bale. But if

you're a friend of true liberty—if you believe in freedom and fair play, and the downfall of imperialistic tyranny—"

Bale clenched his fist. "You—God—damn—" His arm kept trembling; he forced it down against his side. "Can't a man have an idea of his own without being claimed by your gang? If I wanted to fight, I'd fight. North or South. It wouldn't matter. If I wanted—" The round hulk in front of him was so mute and puddinged, so sickening and quiet. His hand shot forward; he seized the man's coat collar.

Quagger said, with no fear: "Go easy, mister! If I'm wrong, I'm wrong. But go easy on me. I got a knife here—"

"Don't you flash it in front of me," Bale snarled. He hurled Quagger back into the yielding bridal-wreath bushes, then turned and walked away. Behind him he could hear the man thrashing about in the shrubbery. Two small boys advanced, peering, wondering at this commotion. "Go along with you," Dan ordered. The boys fled down the path out of sight. They sent back derisive hoots from some hidden refuge. Flowers inside Grandma Leen's fence surrounded the dark world with their poignant spice . . .

Bale crossed the road, meaning to turn down a side lane toward the Duffey house. But somewhere, back near the Diamond, there was a growing hubbub. He looked back. People beneath the gaudy lanterns at Deffenbaugh's were all looking west; some of them were walking rapidly away from the porch. Younger men were running. Dan stood there. This was an unnatural realm of nervous crescendo, a perverted village where he had never lived before. The war had done this. It was the fault of—

Somebody roared, "News! Big news, folks!" and a

light bobbed out into the middle of the highway. There was no help for it; he had to go back, of course. *News. News.* He walked as fast as he could. He did not begin to run until he was past Deffenbaugh's and with every stride he hated himself for running.

A middle-aged man in a plaid shirt sat in a gig. Barney Endsor: for twenty years a justice of the peace, a clerk, an assessor. His horse shivered in a plaster of foam and dirt, and a bunch of leaves had been caught inside the gig shaft. A younger man stood with one foot on the hub and held a lamp high in the air, a yellow torch with furious insects battering against it.

Endsor was spreading a paper in his hands. "Louder," people demanded. "Louder, Barney!" Barney's voice lifted tautly: "And undoubtedly the greatest cavalry engagement of the Rebellion, when Federal cavalry under General Pleasonton's orders crossed the river near—"

"What's it all about?" Dan asked of a boy beside him. The crowd nudged tight, filling in on all sides. The tired horse shied back. *Whoa,* blame you . . .

The boy said, "Battle. A big battle. Barney's just drove in with a Philadelphia paper."

"'Our Troops Victorious. Stuart routed and driven back on Culpeper. There was sharp firing at Beverly Ford and Brandy Station Tuesday, but the scope of the battle was not known for some hours. Now it appears that the timely advent of the Nationals has prevented the rebels from embarking on a raid which may have been aimed at Washington, or possibly a reconnaisance in force north of the Potomac into Maryland. It was held more probable, however, that the rebel general Lee was concentrating his cavalry for the purpose of—'"

Barney kept pausing to spit against the dashboard.

He was pleased at the reception, the riotous interest which Gettysburg had accorded him. His red hands trembled as they held the wadded edges of newspaper. It wasn't often that a man driving into town with news like this could find a ready-made audience in Deffenbaugh's yard or anywhere else.

Already the listeners were seeking professional opinion. Men choked close behind the gig where a thin, brown-faced boy in a tight blue jacket was standing at ease, pancake cap over one ear and thumbs hooked inside his belt. A woman giggled: "They're asking Milo Vandercook about it. He just got back on furlough yesterday."

The boy was not yet sixteen. His voice was husky and unhardened. "Well," he was saying, "tell you. It's like this. That was all cavalry. See? Course I'm"—he strangled with his own importance—"I'm in the infantry But old Joe Hooker ain't going to let Lee out-smart him. Bet your buttons he ain't. Old Joe, he—"

"What'll happen if Lee comes up acrost the Potomac, Milo?" somebody called.

The boy wrinkled his forehead, and grandly he sucked a wad of tobacco into his cheek before he replied: "By gravy, if he does, we'll just lick the poop out of him!" The men grunted, laughing, poking one another. The few girls moved away hastily, sniffling as they fled from this delightful vileness.

Dan found Elijah on the edge of the crowd, craning his neck. "What is it?" Hud asked. He had a willow basket on one arm, but he still carried his musket.

Bale explained, "Endsor just drove into town with a paper. There was a big cavalry fight somewhere down south—Beverly Ford, I guess it was. Beverly Ford and Brandy Station." He took the basket from Elijah. "Come on, Hud. We'd better get this over to

Doc's before it melts away. The ladies won't relish it, melted too soft." Elijah kept looking back, and Dan growled, "Oh, come on. That was away down in Virginia and it happened last Tuesday."

"Well," Elijah said, "I'm coming as fast as I can." But several times he turned and gazed again at the black, jostling mob beside the gig. Then a few long strides brought him abreast of Dan Bale. "You can't believe much of that nonsense in the papers," he declared. "Probably that was just another skirmish. Every time they have a little skirmish, the newspapers talk like it was a battle that amounted to something."

Book Two

ELIJAH'S ARMY

1.

Ty was downstairs, packing his things. He had carried not an ounce of baggage when he came—nothing but sidearms and gloves. Now he was filling a knapsack which he had brought while on his previous furlough. His mother prepared a housewife kit for him; he would never use it, but if the sullen acquiescence with which he received the gift was of any satisfaction to her, she might feel that her solicitousness had been worth while.

Doctor Duffey had called, the afternoon before, and had delivered himself of sundry philippics on the subject of army surgeons before he arranged for medicines. There were two vials of sedative pills, a bottle of tonic and one of a magnesia compound. Ty was to take the tonic daily, the magnesia before each meal, and the pills as needed.

He worked briskly, silently, packing these articles with clean handkerchiefs and socks, and adding two boxes of cigars and some wine. The knapsack was one presented to him by a German officer during the first months of his service; it was of lightweight russet leather, and bore a tooled eagle crest on the flap.

From the top of the hall stairway, his wife looked down at him. She stood without speaking, rubbing her hands back and forth on the polished mahogany of the railing. It was impossible for her to admit any kinship, even flimsy and merely marital, with the slim man who bent above that knapsack in the lower corridor. Sunlight crept through diamonds of pink and gold glass beside the front door, and made smoky dabs of color on the deep, brownish purple of his blouse and the faded blue of his breeches.

There had been no sexual relation between them for more than a year . . . Irene Fanning wondered, in this dry moment, if ever the taint of raw sex had existed in their physical union. In the first year of their marriage her mind was pulsing with a fever of expectancy. (This was the epoch of braided jackets and red-striped bloomers; the Seventy-second were still Fire Zouaves, and they dreamed of a heraldic war ornate as the flash of their white gaiters.) A five-day honeymoon, two furloughs: *this is it,* she had thought each time, *maybe this will be the hour.* Now the notion of any fulfillment was a tired wraith to be chased out of mind and forgotten whenever possible.

She did not despise her husband for his impotency. Rather an emotional pity had come to possess her: wounded . . . a piece of metal driven squarely through the lining of his body . . . think of it, inside, inside, where all is soft and warm and wet and a part of honest nature. That awful intrusion had saved a sympathy for him which otherwise would never have been born.

She called, "Did you get those socks off the bureau?"

He lifted his face; wooden cheek-bones, thick mustache. "I didn't want them all. Just the wool. Three pairs."

"Didn't you want any writing paper?"

"I've got all I need at camp. No use lugging any more of the damn stuff with me."

He wrote every fortnight, as regularly as possible. *My Dear Parents & Wife, Thank you for your missives which were rec'd. in due time. Pleased to learn that all continues favorably at home. With the army, matters are much as before. We moved to this point on the 16th inst., the 72nd being detached from the Brigade for special guard duty at the bridgehead here. Have not been engaged with the enemy since I last wrote, though according to Dame Rumor we may expect action soon. Regret to say there was a double execution at this camp yesterday; two deserters; it being a matter of comment that the guilty parties were not reprieved by executive clemency. Without the strictest sort of discipline no army can—*

"Did you find the silk handkerchiefs?"

"Yes." He added a muffled, "Much obliged, I'm sure."

His mother came lumbering from the kitchen—an unwieldy, round-nosed woman with eight silver ringlets, like flat coils of wire, pasted across her forehead. The polished parquet thundered as she moved; her bosom was a shaking bulwark of fichu and lace and old-gold chains.

She cried, "Honey boy, you never got those medicines!"

"Yes, I did. They're already in here."

She blocked the living-room doorway, a living pavilion of distended brown silk. "Did Gretel bring the grape conserve?" She screamed, "Gretel! Gret-*ell*. I told you to get a jar of grape—"

"For God's sake," said Tyler.

Irene said, "He didn't care for it, mother. And the doctor said that he shouldn't eat anything with nuts."

Mrs. Fanning made a damp, grunting sound. "My baby boy," she gasped. She kept striking at her mouth with a little wad of folded lace. "I've got a great notion to write to Colonel Baxter myself! I don't know what he's thinking of! You aren't fit to stir foot out of this house—"

"I got my orders last night," Tyler said. "Probably I'm as well off down there as here. Maybe I'll get killed and it'll be a good riddance of bad rubbish." He chuckled ghoulishly, and now there seemed to be a mounting color in his cheeks. He snapped the buckles close against leather straps, sawing with all his strength at the bulging russet.

His wife came slowly down the stairs. "Demon's ready. I hear the wheels."

"Call father," quavered Mrs. Fanning. "Oh, call f-f-father—"

Irene went into the library. Mr. Fanning was behind his desk, his carpet-slippered feet neatly paired on a green footstool, and a Philadelphia *Press* open in his hands. He wore a yellow linen coat and a white waistcoat, dusty with cigar ashes. His head was quite bald, but the gray mutton-chop whiskers along his cheeks were curly and luxuriant. He put down the paper and removed his spectacles.

"They are ready?"

She nodded. "Demon's out in the carnage."

He caught up the paper again, and lifted the glasses before his eyes. "It says here—in the *Press,* June the twelfth—'Thus have a little energy, promptitude and bravery in the beginning thwarted a movement which, had it been suffered to mature, might have been fraught with shame and disaster to our arms.' And perfectly correct, perfectly, perfectly." He folded the straight bows of his spectacles and slid them into his upper waistcoat pocket. "I don't for the life of me see why Tyler was summoned back. There is absolutely no threat of invasion, now."

He squeezed Irene's arm as he went past her, and through the doorway into the hall: a tall, stooped man slightly lame in one foot, and walking always with his toes turned in. "It says here in the *Press,* Tyler—" The closing door deadened his words.

"Ty's going back," said the woman. She leaned against the library table; the carved edge of it squeezed the limber hoops against her body . . . "He's going back. Maybe he'll be killed. Poor Ty. And vomiting at night, that way—so often. Oh, ghastly, ghastly. What would he have been like, if the war had never happened? Would we have loved each other? . . . It doesn't matter, now, because the war has happened . . . He's cruel, but he cannot help being cruel. The cruelty is a congenital part of his selfishness, and can't be cut away or ameliorated.

"I made my bed . . ." She flailed the words out of her brain . . . "I made it. Now I've got to lie in it, whether with a coughing, cursing man who hates himself as much as he does the rest of us, or whether I lie there alone after he is dead."

"Irene," her father-in-law called.

She opened the door. Mrs. Fanning was rubbing her cheek against Tyler's shoulder and making the same grunting noise which she had made before. She turned her tiny, bleary eyes toward the girl. "Your poor little wife, Tyler. Your poor little wife. She just can't bear to see you go—"

"I can't stand a lot of slop," Tyler said. He pushed his mother aside and picked up the knapsack. "You going to the depot with us, Irene?"

"Yes. I'll get my hat and parasol."

She joined the two men in the carriage. Mrs. Fanning leaned beside the porch railing, crying, tearing down the trumpet-vine as she clutched at it for support. "Mother!" Mr. Fanning shook his head at her. "It's our boy's duty, my dear. His place is at the front with his regiment, suffering the fortunes of war for good or ill. We shall pray that it be for good."

Demon groaned from his high seat. "Aaamen." He nodded his white poll, the tiny kinks of it glistening like spun glass.

"Shut up, Demon," Ty snarled. "You don't need to start in, too. It's enough to make—" His harsh cough went shoveling to the bottom of his lungs.

"There'll be no invasion, mother, no invasion. The *Press* says—"

"Get up!" shrieked Ty. The mares bounced forward; Demon straightened the reins, muttering and blinking. The carriage wheeled out into the lane. "See over there, Tyler," his father directed. "They are cutting down the woods on the hills. On Round Top. See?" They heard the light tap of the closing door, and the fresh torrent of Mrs. Fanning's wails in the hallway. *Oh, Gretel, Gretel—*

"My dear boy." The older man plucked at the curly chop-whiskers of his left cheek. "Your mother's lot is not an easy one. We watchers at the hearthside must keep our hearts buoyed up with hope and prayer. It is a far cry from our little village to the tented—"

Tyler muttered. "She doesn't have to act like an old fool." His father stiffened, swallowed, and tightened his jaw. Irene watched the tiny froth of dust which lifted with each upturning of the right-hand front wheel. She heard Cybo sneeze underneath the rear of the carriage. His bell tinkled, tinkled.

They turned east toward the village. "It seems difficult to realize that Pentland Bale is gone," said Mr. Fanning mildly. "I wonder if Daniel will keep the old house, and live there."

Irene lifted the little green parasol above her head. She felt a sudden, guilty dampness in the hollows of her palms. She kept looking at the carriage wheel.

"No doubt he will," Ty was saying. "Especially since he doesn't appear willing to risk his precious neck down south."

The woman raised her eyes. "You said that he didn't believe in war—that it was against his whole philosophy."

"A lot of people developed that same idea as soon as hostilities commenced." Tyler chuckled; his eyes seemed to be brighter, unfilmed. There was a hint of color in the skin of his face. "After all, it isn't such a bad life—the army . . . Dan Bale is a queer piece, but he's got an awful determination. Like to have him in my company for a while. Show him a thing or two. He might make a good soldier if he was willing to buckle down to it."

Irene looked across the fields toward the Bale house. Mrs. Wurke was out at the pump, but Dan wasn't anywhere in sight.

This was Sunday morning. When Tyler received the telegram summoning him back to his regiment, the evening before, he had learned that an engine and a tool car would leave Gettysburg for Hanover Junction some time after eight o'clock the next morning. His mother groaned and gabbled when she found that Ty was to begin his journey in a "work train." It was not in accord with her notions of Captain Fanning's military career, which were worked out and labeled long before. In her mind she had it all plotted:

He lived in a tent, as did all other soldiers. The

tents were snow-white, they stood in even rows, mile after mile. Pennons flapped from their ridge-poles. Tyler sat at a rude desk writing letters home, writing orders, writing despatches. Sometimes a bugle blew. He went out, then, to oversee a drill. The army filed past, rank on rank, glistening steel, garish buttons, pristine gloves. The army saluted Tyler. He sat his horse, rigid, stern, young . . . Still her boy, her boy. "Captain, the rebels are advancing." "Convey my respects to General Hooker, sir, and inform him that the rebels are advancing." Cannon began to boom in measured, spaced billows of sound; there was the "roll of musketry." Smoke became thick and white. Far away sounded the rebel yell. "Advance, friends, and give the countersign. Forward, march! Present arms! Fire! . . ." Tyler rode up to the rifle pits of the enemy; he unsheathed his sword and waved it gallantly. "Forward, men, onward and forward and onward and take them in the flank, take them in the rear, for the sake of Old Glory . . ." "Wait. Stop. Halt! The captain's hit." "Are you struck, sir?" "Yes, General, I'm afraid I'm severely wounded." "My boy, you've done noble work today. Take him to the hospital at once . . . Your wound is not fatal, I trust, sir. The nation needs men like you. Pennsylvania is proud of you, Captain Fanning . . ." Then, inexplicably, he had come home on furlough, very sour-faced and thin and yellow, and had thrown up a whole stomach full of veal broth and barley. War, she understood, was a ghastly and hateful business. People were wounded, and they ruined the best hooked rugs in their mothers' houses. And had to ride back to Hanover Junction with a lot of pick-axes and Irishmen.

At the foot of the short hill sloping north from the Diamond stood the railroad station. The main track ended at the depot, but a temporary spur curved on toward the new cut in the rocky hill northwest of town. A row of freight cars, transformed into laborers' shanties, lay along the side track; scrofulous children peeked out at the carriage as it jolted in a circle and halted close to the platform. Someone was singing in a flat tenor: *swate Lily, she's the pride of my life, if she'll only be my wife* . . . you could smell potatoes frying. A giant in a soiled orange undershirt was sitting on a pile of ties, smoking a pipe.

Tyler climbed out of the carriage. His wife watched with slow amazement: the set of his shoulders, the stiffening of his neck. He was not the same man who had come home, who had lain for six nights in her bed, who had coughed and sworn indiscreetly and answered all her questions in sullen monosyllables. He was an officer, very proud and peremptory, no matter what curling smudge there might be in the soft place above his bowels.

He called to the big Irishman, "When's that burden train due to start for Hanover Junction?"

The man pointed up the rickety track, where knots of smoke puffed out around the curve. "She's after taking rails aboard." He looked at Fanning with clumsy admiration. "Will you ride to the Junction with her, mister? . . . Maybe you'll be in General Vincent's army. It's me own brother that's with General Vincent. Patrick Callan is the name, mister—"

Tyler swung on his heel and walked back to the carriage. His boots went *wunch, wunch, wunch* in the rough bed of cinders. "It'll be along in a minute. Get that knapsack out, Demon."

"The new connection west of Gettysburg will be of considerable advantage to our city," said his father.

"It's taking them an almighty long time to build it."

"Labor is at a premium, and materials come high."

Tyler squinted at the smoke, cottony against the pocked green of Oak Ridge. He sucked his cigar. "At least if the rebels come up here, they'll be spared the trouble of destroying this road."

"Nonsense," declared Mr. Fanning. "They could never penetrate this far."

"Jeb Stuart did."

The older man creaked down from the step; the carriage swayed back at the release of his weight. "A hundred thousand armed men would rise in their might if Lee ever showed himself north of the line."

Tyler laughed unkindly. "I can damn well tell you what Lee did to a hundred thousand of us last month."

His father's face was tired and grave. "Your wife, my son! Save that for the camp and barracks, if you please."

"Oh, Irene doesn't mind. She's accustomed to my little blasphemies."

"Yes," the girl said, "I don't know why I should object to that. Things are different nowadays, father."

Demon said, "She comin', Mist Ty. She make great big smoke."

Tyler threw away his cigar and came over to the carriage wheel. "At least you don't slop all over me, lady," he said. "I declare, I've a better soldier's wife than a lot of chaps."

"Ty." She put her arms around his neck.

He whispered quickly, "Maybe we ought to have a child. Give you something to think about . . . I've been too damn miserable, that's all. Probably I'm a poor excuse for a husband. The war takes it all out of me . . . just the same, I'm glad I'm going back. Mother would put me in the madhouse, in another week. Give us a kiss."

She kissed him; his lips were dry and his breath hot and unpleasant. Then he caught up the straps of the russet knapsack and hurried out across the tracks; his father followed, limping, the sharp pebbles punching up through his carpet slippers. Tyler had drawn out a clean silk handkerchief and was stuffing it inside the collar of his blouse. His sword swayed evenly beside the gathered folds of purple cloth in his rear; sunshine glittered on the polished flap of his revolver holster. He walked with an alert, nervous importance, as if he had stepped out of a stuffy room which was never to his liking, and now breathed the keener air of swishing winds.

Irene nodded in her mind: "He's glad he's got that over with. I wonder if he has anything to do with those women—camp followers, they call them. Maybe he'd be glad to, because they are a part of his adventure. He'll be a general if he lives, and if it all lasts long enough. Even getting killed in a battle would give him much satisfaction . . . Goodbye, my lover, goodbye, goodbye, once I thought I loved you, once I thought we might be happy. I made my bed, and now I'll lie in it all alone." She closed her eyes and listened to the gigantic respiration of the locomotive as it limped closer and closer.

When she looked again, Tyler was waiting near the roadway in front of the pile of ties, his haversack on the ground beside him. Mr. Fanning stood there; he bent down to remove a cinder from his slipper; he was talking to Ty, but she could not hear what he said. Scampering ahead of the deliberate engine came a group of boys, bright-faced, their hair slicked down in Sabbath baptism. Among them trotted a taller youth in army blue, his jacket open, his cap far back on his head. Vaguely, Irene remembered him as the

Vandercook boy who had brought spring fries to Mrs. Fanning, the year before. Now he was a returned hero, his shoulders square and his lips wise with fledging assurance . . . He's the greatest person they ever saw, she thought. Greater than God or officers or Tom Thumb or anybody. He's a soldier, home from the wars, home from the wars.

Tyler shrieked, "Halt!" The boy stopped, a stiffening quiver of blue, his hands slapping against his thighs. The children fell away from him, scattering as Ty came toward them.

"Don't they teach you to salute, Private?"

The Vandercook boy muttered something. His hand cracked up, down again.

"What is your regiment?"

"Eighty-seventh Pennsylvania—" Then their voices vanished under the whistle's screech; the engineer leaned out of the cab, switching his hand back and forth. Tyler grasped the boy's arm and jerked him from the track. Brown steel came sliding across in front of them, wet with oil, wreathed in drifting smoke.

She could see Tyler lifting himself up on the tool car as it rolled past. A knot of workmen rode there, swaying with the train's motion, or squatting on the pile of rusty rails. Ty's hat coming up, then the knapsack lifted high, then his sword glitter. He was on the car, going to Virginia, going off to Owen's brigade. He saluted his father, then he took off his hat and bowed toward the carriage. Demon waved the whip, and hooted.

Mr. Fanning stood beside the track, flapping his gaunt hand, staring after the cars. The wheels clicked faster, there were yellow flakes in the smoke. The boy soldier stood sheepishly; his friends whinnied and giggled on the depot platform. They began to call: you could hear their voices as the engine went grouching off into hazy distances. "Haw-haw, Milo." "Hey, Milo, you just about got put in the guardhouse." "I bet once if I was a soldier by the army, I would salute a colonel." "He is not a colonel; he's a captain." "He's a—" "Ask Mr. Fanning. Mr. Fanning, he's a captain, ain't he? Ain't he a captain, sir?"

Tyler's father said, "Yes, lads, he is a captain. Maybe Milo will be a captain some day, if he conducts himself properly." They began to titter at the Vandercook boy. "I bet you never get to be a captain, Milo. I bet you never seen a rebel, Captain Vandercook."

Milo threw a handful of gravel at them. His face was very red. They galloped off, howling. Mr. Fanning put his handkerchief back into his coat pocket— the handkerchief which he had been waving at the receding train. He came over to the carriage. "He is gone, my child," he said. "We will pray today that no ill may overtake him. And Reverend Solt is going to eat dinner with us." He climbed wearily into his seat. "They should have let Tyler remain for the duration of his furlough, as promised. This is all a tempest in a teapot. The very thought of an invasion is ridiculous, newspaper twaddle, all of it."

Irene kept wondering if she had not looked at Ty for the last time. She felt a growing unsteadiness in her throat. He would be killed. She knew it. She was certain. He would be killed. She wondered whether she would marry a second time . . . Oh, Heavenly Father, she thought suddenly, I am a wicked woman. I am wicked, wicked and evil and heartless. Her hands lay in her lap, weak and cold.

2.

The wistaria vine hung close to her window. She had loved to think that it was tropical, a female cat-creature more animal than vegetable, holding some watery mystery in its pointed little leaves. All the pendulous orchid tufts were long gone, and now it was a clambering jungle of solid green. The gray snakes of its trunk were hidden below the porch roof; the vine came up without reason or support, the only daring thing which could put its soft paws near Irene Fanning's window.

It was not like the rest of Pennsylvania, she knew. Not like a small, tight town with good people doing good things, and a very few bad people doing bad things. Nothing was compact or regular or disciplined in its nature . . . All about her was an oppressive, interlocking existence, and so she loved the vine more than she could say.

The dusk came toward the window, dry water, growing thicker and more heated with every slow moment. A thunderstorm twitched in the hills beyond Greenwood; vapid lightning shocked with a formless quiver. It would rain in Gettysburg before the night was done. Tyler was far down in Maryland; Irene had counted him out of her life, inch by inch, hour by hour, car-length by car-length . . . She wondered what the Potomac looked like. Like the Delaware or Schuylkill, no doubt, but somehow sleepier and more southern. There would be many negroes, and pontoon bridges, and cavalrymen who rode along rocky trails beside the water, silent hulks against the sky. Washington threw a silver dollar across the Potomac, she had read. And maybe President Lincoln would go to walk on the banks, a cadaverous lawyer from Illinois with the weight of the whole war bending across his back. Banjos playing in night winds across the dark blue mountains, up from the south . . .

She shuddered. Tyler had told her about the south. In a nagging, profane whine he had said the necessary words about Antietam Creek: It was a town called Sharpsburg, and they had to attack across open ground. He said he was coming from Second Brigade headquarters on horseback, when he got hit. He thought the horse had run into an iron pipe stretched across the road—that was the way it felt—an iron pipe striking him heavily in the middle. Then he didn't know anything until he was lying flat on the ground, clutching a bunch of sharp weeds in his hand. The horse was dead, a few feet away. He could feel something immense and wet inside him, as if he had swallowed a hot, steaming sponge. A big corporal named Hatchworth picked him up over his shoulder and carried him back to a hospital; on the way, he could hear the rebels coming. The rebels went back, still yelling, after the artillery opened on them. It was cannister at point-blank range, Ty said. Whatever that was. It sounded ugly . . . And while he was in the hospital, somebody stole his watch. He lost twenty-seven pounds in something like three weeks.

That was Maryland, that was far over the line, that was as far as the south had come. Now he had gone back to it all, and his wife knew that he would be killed, and she hated her soul and body because of the nausea which she did not feel. Killed. He'll be dead and buried. You'll be a widow, widow, widow.

Lying there on the bed in the density of summer dusk, she pressed her hands over her eyes. The green

saturation of wistaria lay across her life—there was
no calm darkness behind her closed eyelids but only
tropical vines, crawling and climbing, and they were
coming slowly alive, and they had snakes for the vine
part of them.

The stairs creaked and sagged, then the boards of
the upper hall. "Daughter," said Mrs. Fanning. Her
voice blasted the mousy echoes of the room. She said,
Dotter. Candlelight showed yellow in a long crack beneath the door; Irene arose, and turned the knob . . .
Mrs. Fanning was standing there with a white, flaring
candle in an earthenware stick. Her great breasts
heaved from the exertion of ascending the stairs.

"Father and I are out on the porch with Mrs. Knouse,
daughter. She missed meeting, just to come over and
see how we were. You oughtn't to be up here alone."

"I'm going to sleep, soon."

Mrs. Fanning began to cry. When she cried, her face
curled up in a dozen thick, fleshy folds; you thought
that she was laughing, until the tears started to come . . .
"Mother!" said Irene, feebly enough.

"Oh, he's gone, my child, he is—gone! I'm trying
to take refuge in prayer. Mrs. Knouse just said that
the only true consolation is in the Rock, the eternal
Rock. And poor honey boy, he wasn't like himself.
He wouldn't take any grape conserve. You wouldn't
let him," she sobbed, in bleary accusation.

Her husband called from the lower hall. "Mother.
Now, mother—" He stood at the foot of the steps; far
out on the porch was the faint crunching of old Mrs.
Knouse's rocker. "Must not give way to grief, mother.
Must not give way. Bring our little lady down with
you."

"She's going to retire, Pa," groaned Mrs. Fanning.
Massively, she started down the flight.

Irene said to them both, "Goodnight. Now—" the words were slabs in her throat, they were things of matter and with dimensions and size and thickness, pieces of words—"don't worry. Please. Ty will be all right. Goodnight, my—dear parents." She had said that at last, it was over and done, she had claimed them. She closed her door and quietly turned the wooden button. Voices below stairs became muted little whispers which hissed up through the floors, and now she could disregard them and pretend that they no longer existed. Down in the back yard, Demon was mumbling to Cybo as he came from the barn. "You fat old dog. You pretty worthless old dog, Cybo. Gretel she say you took fresh eggs lass week, you old no-good old dog."

A church bell was ringing. The Lutheran bell. Up at the seminary, a boy whistled shrilly, and another answered him with the eternal night-cry of youth: "ee-ow-ee-ow-ee-ow-ee-ow," faster than you could follow the sound.

Irene lit the candles on her bureau, and closed the window shutters. Little insects came frittering through the slanting wooden leaves; they were mad whorls about the cottony candle flames until the heat kissed them to death. The girl took off the dressing sacque which she had worn as she lay upon the bed. Her clothes filled the camphor-scented darkness of a huge wardrobe closet: silk, muslin, lace, silk, poplin, merino, silk, silk, layer and fold and rustling promise. The Fannings thought it inconsiderate of her to have so many clothes . . . Her father's estate yielded her nearly five thousand dollars a year . . . And she sent to Paris for thin stockings, and she wore them each day of her life, and Mrs. Fanning found a smutty horror in her doing it.

She removed the heavy petticoat, the stays, the thin little drawers, the shirt which drooped close against her hot, pear-shaped breasts. When she was wound in a long cotton nightgown and when her hair was let down, she felt weary and housewifely and no longer very sinful. She was a soldier's wife, and that day she had sent him back, and she had been brave about his going. Last night his boots had stood in the corner; he slid under the sheets beside her, the golden male hair of him brushing her tender skin. At least there had been that much to their marriage: the awful physical intimacy had been a common piece of their existence for six days; they had been close, had slept side by side.

No curlers, no cap for her mass of coarse hair. It drenched all around her neck and shoulders, loose, tingling. Standing there on the rug beside the bed, she clenched her fingers and drew a long, shuddering breath . . . "I'll read," she declared, "I'm not sleepy and I can't go to sleep, but I refuse to dress and go downstairs. I'll read the *Press* and the New York *Tribune.*"

She lay with her shoulders deep in feather pillows, a Blazing Star quilt drawn up to her knees, and the pewter candelabra moved to a little walnut table beside her bed. The rustle of long newspaper sheets kept frightening tiny gray and pink moths which hissed over her. She wanted to get away from the war, but it was hard to do so. It kept poking out at her in thick, uneven columns: Incident on the Rappahannock. Letter from Mother of Five Soldiers, Two Have Been Wounded. The Rev. Mr. H. R. Gillbroughten will address the Christian Commission on Tuesday next. President Abraham Lincoln has been invited to attend services by the Union League in Philadelphia, July 4.

Women experiencing pain, annoyance and illness from female troubles should not neglect Dr. John L. Lyon's French Periodical Drops.

Fernando Wood. It was a very foolish name— Fernando. She didn't want to read about him, she was weary of seeing his name in the papers. Among army surgeons, there were one hundred vacancies which should be filled at once. Foes of the legal tender notes prepare denunciatory campaign. Fernando Wood. A *Life of Chopin,* by F. Liszt, had just been published . . . She read about it, a column and a half. Brandy Station, Beverly Ford, Brandy Station, and latest advices from vicinity of Vicksburg. Religious serve for contrabands in Camp at Alexandria, Va. The Chief Executive replies to critics in case of Mr. Fernando Wood.

A girl she had known in Philadelphia—Miss Alice Springer—had been married to Mr. Barnabas Veatch of Northampton, Mass. Mr. Veatch served for some months with the Massachusetts volunteers until compelled to resign his commission due to ill health & wounds, and was now engaged in commercial pursuits. Two lives lost in the burning of storehouse, Bleecker street, in New York City. Pathetic Tale Recounted by Ohioan. Finds dying son among wounded in a railway station. His Last Words. Provisions bring high prices in Rocky Mountain town: an account of his journey by titled English visitor. General Halleck declares ambulance system as suggested is an unnecessary novelty. And inexpedient to introduce into our army administration at this time. Fernando Wood, Fernando Wood.

Governor Andrew Curtin has urged a Careful Watch on Our Southern Frontier. Would arm citizens at first threat of invasion. But Held Unlikely. And if you'd be relieved or spared from ills that crush the unprepared, Hostetter's Bitters use—for note: They are the surest antidote.

Then she knew that she had been asleep, long asleep, with the papers matting over her and the candles shrunken to dribbling stubs of tallow. How long she had slept, she did not know. The house was quiet. The same dog which barked each night, was wow-wowing up near McPherson's woods, and Cybo gave supercilious sniffs in reply from the back porch.

Irene folded the papers, puffed out the candles and swung both shutters back against the wall. It was hotter and the window sill was dry; it had not rained yet. Two windows of the Bale house shown, minia-ture oblongs of saffron, and there was one light up at the seminary . . . She thought of the field which stretched down toward Bale's: a sloping rug of grass and clustered shrubs and thickets where tiny enam-eled insects shuttled back and forth in the blackness. Another field, another field.

She could lie in her bed, but she could not go back to sleep. It started in her feet and in her finger tips—a hardy stiffening of desire, a sun warmth which blushed through bones and muscles. Now it's in the ankles, the wrists, coming ferociously up the arms and into the soft hips, and leaves them hard as leather. Cautiously, and all in unholy terror, she slid her hands down across her abdomen. A thousand little veins went throb, throb under the thin layer of cotton cloth. Her breasts tight-ened, slowly, terribly . . . Made my own bed now I'm lying in it. Alone. Alone. Oh, good God in heaven.

And then it seemed as if she were dying, her breath battled with her pulse, the air came out of her lungs and in again, and did her no good, as if she had never breathed. She stared up into the frail gloom above. Wistaria, wistaria, a cat creature climbing—humid, alive, outside that room. A widow and never a wife, never, never.

Enormous lushness crawled over her body and weighted her down, crushed against her rigid mouth and bosom and loins, fed itself on the surge in her ears and the quiver of every striving cord. With a weak sob, she turned on her side. She could look through the open window . . . Far down in the dark pasture, a match flame twinkled, crimsoned in one isolated twist against the midnight, went out and there was nothingness. Only a lonely field, and a man walking there.

Another field, another field. She said rapidly to herself: "Oh, that fiend! I hate him, I hate him more than anything else in the world. Why did he have to say it? Maybe he knew I'd understand. I wonder if I showed it—the understanding. Is he there, walking back and forth, expecting me? He thinks I am a strumpet; it was an unpardonable insult for him to look at me as he did . . . I told him about my going out and lying in the sun. Now he's living nearby, and walking in the field, and he told me—he told me—"

When she slid from the bed to the floor, it was with a solid purpose, a frantic capitulation. Mad. I'm mad. I cannot help it. I'll go out, there is no hell like this, I'd rather be wounded in my innermost entrails as Tyler was.

Working with insensate hands, she found her slippers. There was a silk cloak in the wardrobe. She drew the folds loosely around her . . . Dark in the hall, oh, so dark. Mr. Fanning's sleep whistled from his room: droning human sound, pathetic if she had stood there listening to it. She did not stay. She could smell her own body, talcum and flowers and burning flesh. Slowly, with deliberate caution, she went down through the black house.

Out behind the kitchen Cybo jingled up, panting like a fool. "Go away," she whispered, "lie down, lie down." A night wind made its eerie trickling in the big ash tree. And ridges and hills all around, good people sleeping, young boys up at the school dreaming of war; out in this field one man is walking about. "No," she said, "I'm utterly damned, but I will be happy, I will be eager and receptive for once in my stupid life."

She crept between the hard rails of the fence. If she had not looked through the window and seen the flame of that match . . . a powder train leading to all passion and all wish to be possessed. He knew that she was watching from her high purgatory.

Twice in her life, she had seen him. She wanted to shriek and tell the whole audience of nature that she was not responsible, this was none of her doing . . . The grass reached up, feathery and without any dew, and stroked her legs.

Her feet found a path which twisted among the bowlders and hummocks; she went like a cloud. There was no past or future. Her tongue crept out and laced over her lips, and then they seemed glued together tighter than ever before. In this quarter-light close to the ground, lived shadows and bushes and half-buried rocks which were blue with lichens in the daytime, and Irene Fanning was a moving part of them all; they owned her, they held a shroud around the way she went.

Near those thorn bushes . . . low, marshy place. That was where he lay, where he stayed all night, the tryst he had named for her. This is my whole life, she thought: I've got it here in my hand like a bird, and slowly and deliberately I am crushing it—driving the thin little bones into the frail skin, the downy feathers. Juice of my life, it drips between my fingers.

A thorn frond dragged its needles over her bare forearm. Cruel and eager, it sprang upon her. Voices. Two men were talking—he isn't alone—two of them—

She sank down on her knees. She lifted the scratched arm to her mouth and moistened it. The sundered nerve ached against her wet lips with steady vibration.

"No," a man said, "it's correct. McKosh is positive. That's the reason I came over to tell you. He had word from Harrisburg."

Dan Bale. "I think they're getting all het up over nothing."

There was the sound of a heavy shoe kicking the turf.

The other man laughed. His voice was exultant. "They're going to organize a full-sized army—maybe two. This region will be in the Army of the Susquehanna. Major-General D. N. Couch will command it."

And he was Elijah Huddlestone; he had sold her things at Mr. Pock's general store, he had sold three books to Mrs. Fanning, he was tall and thin and had a black mustache, his mother made dresses for Mrs. Bedford Fanning—all this, and she had not known his voice when she heard it first.

"What good will it do anyone?" asked Bale.

"Good? Good?" His voice went away, fumbling, for awhile. It came back, strong and assured. "Listen to me: if the Butternuts ever get up here, they'll burn us out of house and home, sure as you're a foot high. That's war: burning things, capturing things, taking things from the enemy. We're enemies—"

Dan said, "I'm not. I don't wish to be a professional enemy. I'd rather let my emotions decide—I'd rather hate a man because I knew certain elements in him needed hating."

"Christ Almighty," gasped Elijah.

"Well," said Dan, "that's the way with me, Hud."

"It don't need to be. It's your country."

"The whole business is our country. The whole shooting-match. Why can't people realize that? Why do they have to kill part of their country because they love it?"

Huddlestone grunted. "Nobody can talk to you. I doubt if it's worth it, anyway."

"Possibly it isn't."

The other man said, "Christ" again, and then he was silent.

A match crackled. The flame picked out half of Bale's profile. He was sitting on the ground beyond the thorn-thicket. Long legs shadowed beside him; Huddlestone was standing. The match went out. Irene could smell charred tobacco, coarse and sweet.

"You want to be a soldier," Bale said. His tone was very low; barely it reached her ears.

"Why, yes. I—"

"That's all of it. You were born past your time. Perhaps there used to be some sense in war, but there isn't any more."

Huddlestone laughed. "I guess you were born way ahead of your time, Dan. Nobody else seems to see it your way."

"Maybe I was . . . It looks as if it were something neither of us could help." He said, "I know. You dream about it at night. It's a kind of longing which dwells all around you and slips in and takes possession, once you let your mind be unoccupied. I've had it, about other things. I imagined myself a great philosopher. Plato, Plotinus, Jesus Christ, John Locke,

Ralph Waldo Emerson, Daniel Bale. You drew something from the Greeks and bolstered it up with an Asiatic notion, and proved it by Dan Bale! I'd put it all in books, this distilled philosophy. They'd study me in universities."

Huddlestone muttered an obscene word.

"It's all of that," Bale said. "It was a boy's dream. I've got over it, more rapidly than you ever got over yours."

Elijah began, "Now, listen to me. I never was crazy about being a soldier until the war broke out. I never—"

"Oh, bother. We played soldier by the hour, and you were always captain."

The other man cried, "Yes, and I'll be a captain if I can get enough recruits! They have to be from eighteen to sixty years old: of course many of the younger ones lie. If I brought in forty men, I'd get to be a captain right away. Twenty-five—I get a lieutenancy. Fifteen, second lieutenant. I call that a handsome opportunity."

"Handsome opportunity to get shot by some poor farmer from Tennessee, if that nets the world anything. No militia commission is worth—"

"Listen," declared Elijah savagely, "we're not going to be state troops. We're going to be a United States organization from the start. The government'll pay us."

"How long do you have to sign up?"

"For the existing emergency."

Bale emptied his pipe. A torrent of fireflies. "Who said this was an emergency? What do they want in Pennsylvania, anyway? I suppose they want Pock's store and your house, and mine; I suppose they'd throw away their lives to capture the seminary or Codori's farm or Little Round Top. Don't be a fool,

Hud. If they go after anything it will be Philadelphia or Baltimore or Washington."

"You must know all about it."

"Well," said Dan.

They were silent. You could hear them breathing through the gloom. Over in the mountains the ground rumbled.

"Thunder," Elijah decided. "I'm going home before I get wet." He started away, crushing through the weeds. In the hollow beyond him, frogs went *glahh . . . glahh*. "You're not going to sit out in this field all night, are you?"

"Just awhile."

They said, "Goodnight." The rail fence creaked as Huddlestone crawled over it.

In Irene's mouth was the taste of blood. She slid out her tongue and let its tip trace along the pattern of her mouth; she wondered if her lips were red, wet and dripping with the sap which had come out of her arm . . . Juice of my life, she thought again. They want to spill it. Huddlestone wants to open the bodies of men he's never seen and doesn't know, and rob them of a strange tonic which keeps them alive.

The mountains lunged together once more; the ground trembled softly. There was a blank, lavender spasm along the horizon.

Ty had ridden away on a train—its wheels were still clicking with every whisper of her pulse. And now she could imagine that over beyond South Mountain a mighty car of war came bundling its way through the barley hills, pressing down the nap of wheat and clover. It was not a chariot of the past, no juggernaut, nothing oriental or fantastic; its only fantasy was in the horrific size of wheels and the bald fact of its being in Pennsylvania. North it came, north and east,

squeezing the hills aside . . . full train of war, loaded
with a screaming freight of wounded men, a jumbled
cargo dead or alive. Ty rode on the prow of it, and
now he was joined by Elijah Huddlestone. The rocky
earth sighed and quivered, and dreaded the pressure
which crackled toward it. That's war, she told herself,
now I know what war is, and may it never come to
this town. Buzzards, may the fields never be able to
understand you.

Muscle by muscle, she rose in her place. She must
go back to the house. She was no longer shaking with
the delirium of physical desire. The two men had
taken her madness from her, in their talk, and with a
last flicker of passion she hated them for it. Now she
would go back to the silent bed, the snoring house,
the existence which she had cast aside. She would
wrap that existence around her, let its stiff folds cover
her body and her soul . . . Silent woman, proper, mod-
est, aloof, and respected by any man who looked at
her. A soldier's wife, a soldier's widow. Mrs. Captain
Fanning expressed the following articles, gratefully
received by the U.S. Sanitary Commission: 2 doz. hospital shirts, 2 doz. pairs felt slippers, 4 doz. sheets, 2
doz. pillow cases, 25 yds. san. sheeting, 2 cases surg.
dressings, jellies, wines, farina, also tinned milk, des-
sicated vegetables and Other Articles Too Numerous
To Mention. Soldier's Wife, soldier's—

The thorns took her in their teeth; it was a vine, a
sinew of pain which had curved out of the midnight
and torn her again. She sobbed, and tried to strangle
the sound as it came.

A match flared, close before her eyes.

Bale said, "Why, you—you—"

Then she blinked into twisting darkness: the wraith
of the little flame sputtered and curved in front of her

glazing eyes—now it's purple, now getting green, now it's pink again.

He asked, "Mrs. Fanning, what is it?"

"I'm—caught in some vines."

Again, a match. "I'm sorry. All tangled. Do stand still, please. That's right . . ." His hand went mauling, caressing around her left arm. "Blackberry vine," he said. Then the tiny blunt swords had been lifted away, but her whole body felt as if it were wrapped in them still. "Well," he began, and then said nothing more. The match went out.

She said, "I am here—I've been here—I mean, it was difficult to sleep. I wandered out for a walk."

"Huddlestone and I were talking. Elijah Huddlestone. Perhaps you heard us."

"Voices," she said. "I heard—voices."

The man was looming closer and taller, all the gigantic night-prowlers of eternity muddled into his lone shape. He said, sharply, "You came—"

"I came because . . . Mr. Bale, I must go. I must—"

"I've thought we would meet out here," he said. "But not like this. I didn't think it would be this way." His touch branded her body; her skin was cold, clammy as the film of ghost-flowers.

He said, "Wet." His fingers slid away. In the circle of a new match-light he lifted her limp arm. "Blood. You are cut by those briars. I must fix it for you."

"At home—I'll wash it there. It isn't serious. Mr. Bale, I ask—" She heard her words go fluttering off like wet moths, clogged with chilly darkness.

"Come over into the kitchen; I'll dress it. I am quite a surgeon."

"That woman." Irene felt her mouth making the words. Now I'm saying that woman, the old lady who works for you, your housekeeper.

"She went to Mummasburg after dinner, with her nephew, for a few days." His hand was between her arm and her side. She looked up at him. Grim shape, dark shape—

No. No, Mr. Bale. I'll worry. I came out to—walk. The—the Fannings. They do not know I'm gone. There'll be a storm . . . she was walking, the two of them walking in stony blackness. It was no longer possible for her to know whether she shaped the words and pushed them from her lips, or whether her brain merely staggered silently beneath their weight and her lips were set and unyielding . . . Forever, vines. Wistaria sent her out there, the cat creature, the tropical passion, and the other vine caught and held her.

Bale's arm slid tightly around her legs, outside the long cape, his other arm grew around her shoulders, he lifted her over the fence. "Mr. Bale," and this time she heard her voice, grave and distinct, "I would rather not. I feel that it would—"

Then he brought her into the kitchen. There was the soapy smell of old wood, washed to its core, smooth as powder. A kerosene lamp burned with steady wick near the northwest window, and a big brown insect was trying to get inside and roast himself. He plunged at the pane with ticking resignation.

Irene leaned close against the rosy cloth of the long table. Curdling streamers of blood ran slowly down her wrist, drying and thickening as they oozed.

Dan brought cold water in a basin, and a bundle of shabby table napkins, soft and white. With her right hand the girl wrapped the drapery of heavy silk more tightly around her body; through a mist of oil light she looked down at rumpled brown hair as Dan bent beside her. "Hold it up," he directed. "That would be better. Here's salve and everything. Your skin is—"

"The scratch is—deeper than I thought."

"Yes." Their voices died and left them, dumb and sodden creatures, marooned with no power of speech. Icy water began to drip from the girl's fingers.

Suddenly, Bale lifted his head and leaped past her. He stood in front of the northwest window, gazing intently through the pane. She saw his fist clenching, squeezing the damp and pinkish cloth. The frenzied insect had ceased battering with all suddenness. On the clock shelf, a brass pendulum grated stubbornly back and forth behind painted glass.

"What is it?" the woman whispered. She stiffened with horrid, outlandish fear. "The window. Was— was there someone—?"

He closed the inner shutters. He came back, and took her hand again. "That bug, or whatever it was. A sound, you know." He laughed, a harsh whinny. "But it occurred to me that I had better close the shutters."

"Oh." And then, "Yes. Someone might—"

He continued with his bandaging.

"There's no need to wind it so thickly, Mr. Bale."

"Most certainly. It must be kept clean and— protected."

Thunder boomed and tumbled overhead. They listened. The volley pounded away into the north.

"Artillery must sound like that," She drew a long breath.

Bale fastened the bandage with windings of white cotton thread.

She felt her lips twitch in a rubbery smile. "It was very kind of you to—do this."

"It's nothing." He lifted ragged scraps of cloth from the table, put them down again. She could see the muscles of his throat stirring, relaxing, tightening once more.

The door swung open; the aperture framed a world grown suddenly violet, quaking violet light, very thin. A hoarse wind raced through shrubbery beyond the picket fence and enormous raindrops thudded like bursting eggs upon the porch roof.

"You can't go, yet."

"I must."

Rain crashed down, a blinding sea. Purple light ruled the world again, then utter darkness. Dan pushed the door shut and turned the knob.

"Mr. Bale," Irene cried. She could not face him; she looked down. Slowly she could feel her breasts toughening, paining her under the high-necked nightgown. She pressed her hands to her temples.

He stood close in front of her. "You were out there in the field," he said rapidly. "I was there, too. I know why I've been there every night. Not for Elijah's sake; he just happened to come over; he went calling around the yard for me, and I heard him . . . Not because of him. I've been there, hoping that you might—" His fingers curled around her hand.

"Don't kiss me," she heard a far-away voice, lone woman's voice, trying desperately to take refuge in counterfeit dignity. "Don't kiss me—Mr. Bale. I shall go mad if you do."

His lips burned hers. She had the feeling that some mysterious starchiness had gone out of the fabric of her, in that long moment. I'm married, she wanted to tell him, I'm married to Tyler Fanning. Almighty God, I'm married . . . Mrs. Captain Fanning. The thunder burst against her ears . . . She began to forget everything, she did not want to remember wistaria or the thorny field or anything else.

I suppose, she tried to say to herself, this is something I've been waiting for, all my life. If only it weren't

for that light—and the window. I know he saw something or someone outside. *If that awful, gasping
kerosene lamp* . . . the lamp went out, blown out, left
them together, locked against one another. He lifted
her, her feet lost the floor; rain slapped against little
windows. Oh, she cried inside herself, how wicked I
am, how completely fallen from some stupid estate.
Don't take your arms away. Closer, harder, never take
them away, wind yourself around me, in and out of
me. I felt this lunacy an hour ago, but I never thought
it would come again.

3.

Monday evening, Elijah Huddlestone went to
bed on a hard sofa in Doctor Duffey's parlor.
The old doctor had ceased wearing bandages on his
hands two days before, but the new skin was still
thin and sensitive. It was difficult for him to hold old
Salt's reins, or harness him, or manage a dozen other
necessary chores. The procreative impulse of Adams
county was not willing to let him take even an essential vacation; Mrs. Carl Bearman gave birth to a fat,
pink daughter about supper time. Elijah Huddlestone
was important to the Bearmans and to the doctor, in
those hours.

He drove back to Gettysburg at ten o'clock, with
Duffey a dozing cargo in the rear seat. The doctor
awoke only when they rocked across the railroad
crossing. He yawned. "Seems as if we had been to
Carlisle and back, Elijah my boy. And there's Emmy
Funk's tumor, and old Kaufman ready to stop breathing at any moment. Indeed, he may be gone now."

At his own gate, Duffey creaked to the ground and went up to the porch. A light, inside: Elijah heard the crackle of Eva Duffey's newspaper . . . She had sewn a dozen pairs of mittens for the doctor, out of clean white flannel, to permit the use of his hands. He had four pairs, now, in a damp and bloody bundle under his arm . . . Elijah leaned out from beneath the carryall top and looked at the stars. It was a perfect night, not too warm or humid. The Milky Way was a sugary mass.

Adam Duffey called from the front door, "He's no worse, praise Peter. Eva hasn't heard a speck of news, but no doubt we'll hear before dawn. Will you sleep on the sofa?"

"I'll drive home first and tell Ma," said Elijah.

Mrs. Duffey called, "That sofa's hard as the Rock of Ages. You go to bed in Aunt Alice's room, Elijah." Aunt Alice was the doctor's relative, who had lived and died with the Duffeys long before.

"Oh, the sofa's all right," he told them. "I'll put old Salt up, and then come in."

"Did he have plenty of feed at Bearman's?"

"Too much," Huddlestone said.

He drove around the square, slapping Salt into an unhappy trot for part of the distance. In front of his own home he dropped a halter hitch around the painted wooden post, studded all over with rusty nail-heads, and went up a path between worm-eaten rose bushes. The whole yard smelled too precious and too sweet; he thought of Pentland Bale's funeral.

His mother slept in the one room on the second story, a wide, low-ceilinged place with a boxed stairway leading to it. Elijah lit a candle after he had closed the front door, and moved to the stair door. "Ma," he called to the little woman above.

There was a muffled sigh as she roused herself. "Lijy?" she asked.

"Doc wants me to sleep over there."

"Is somebody dangerous?"

"I guess old Peter Kaufman is pretty sick . . . They've got a new girl at the Bearmans'. We just drove in from there."

"Which Bearmans? She-that-was-a-Bittner?"

"No, the ones out on the Newville road. Carl, it is." He swallowed, wet his lips, and then asked, "You haven't heard any news? War news, I mean."

She echoed, "War news," mouthing the words because she had removed her false teeth. "No, Lijy. Why?"

"Oh," he said.

"Get you a clean night-shirt. There's two fresh-ironed in the kitchen. And be careful you don't drive too fast. I don't like that old Salt," she added sleepily to herself.

He said, "All right. No, I won't. He won't go fast anyway." He closed the stair door and tramped into the kitchen. The candle-light revealed a flat dish of oil pickles and two slices of bread, on the kitchen table. His mother always left something for him when he was out in the evening. "Lijy likes a snack," she told people. He spooned up a generous portion of the limp, syrupy flakes and spread them upon one slice of the dark bread, then plastered the other slice over it. The sandwich tasted very good . . . if he were in the army, he could have no late evening snacks. Though his mother might, and probably would, send him jars of pickles whenever possible.

He held the sandwich clamped in his mouth while he thumbed through the heap of clean, ironed cloth-ing. He folded the night-shirt and jammed it into his coat pocket. Then, food in hand, he went back to the front room.

The single flame of his little white torch made the familiar place waver with a calm mystery. Over in the corner was the tall "dress form" which his mother used in her work. It had a quilted bosom and quilted hips, with wire mesh in the back and below. Saucers of pins and the flat snake of a measuring tape lay before it like votive offerings. The figured bombazine for Mrs. Bedford Fanning's new Sunday dress weighted down the sewing table. He thought, "I'll wager it takes a lot of yards to cover her up."

In the opposite corner of the room stood Elijah's Vincennes musket, with a saber bayonet fixed. He set his candle on the window sill and picked up the heavy gun. "Right shoulder shift—arms!" he whispered, and juggled the musket about. He felt his knees stiffening, the small of his back harsh and tight. He about-faced, the gun across his shoulder. The dress form loomed before him, a headless creature which yet managed to seem monstrous and smug. He grunted: ". . . Shoot the guts out of you, you rebel son of a bitch!" The dress form waited, humbly, for him to shoot. Then he felt silly, and slammed the bayoneted gun back into its corner. What if someone had been walking home, late, and happened to look through the window—

A thick book on the mantel-shelf: he took that, and blew out the candle. He went out to the carryall, book in his grasp, munching the last of his cucumber-pickle feast. Twin tulip trees beside the fence rustled sleepily.

He made the circuit of the black square, put old Salt away in the smutty barn, walked around to the Duffeys' front porch and entered the house. The doctor and his wife were in bed, but Eva had moved her lamp into the parlor adjoining the office, and had spread a sheet and comforter on the sofa. Elijah undressed. His hands smelled of horse. After he had removed his truss and donned the cotton nightshirt, he went out to the kitchen sink to wash . . . Pendulous flesh, heavy ache, a useless fold of his abdomen bulking down. He pressed his body against the low side of the sink as he washed.

Back in the parlor, he lay on the couch with a mound of rocky little pillows at his back. He screwed the lamp flame higher.

Elements of Military Art and History, by Edward De La Barre DuHarcq. He had paid a fortune for it: four dollars. His mother had said nothing when she saw the book; probably she thought enough. But he had intended to buy a new hat and some shoes, out of the money he made from book selling, and he had bought neither. No one should object to this acquisition of his, if he sacrificed in order to get it. He'd never let Daniel Bale know that he had the book. He knew all too well what Dan would say.

He tried to read about Waterloo. *Blücher.* He wondered how that was pronounced: Bloosher or Blutcher or how. In spite of his interest, he began to feel very sleepy. The cucumber taste oozed stealthily into his throat . . . Stubbornly, he read on. Paragraph after paragraph of tight little print. The boys of Gettysburg began to form between his eyes and the type. He saw them all, McKosh and Deffenbaugh and the seminary lads. He saw himself. Miraculously, he was hard and fierce and strong, and his loins were firm as driving-harness. *Captain Gubbe,* he ordered, *take your men and deploy as skirmishers. Fall back slowly if they strike our front; I want time to re-form my line.* Miraculously, too, in spite of the braided eagles of his rank, he had the Vincennes musket with him. He felt its massive butt prancing against his shoulder; they came toward him in ghastly phalanx—line after line of headless, quilted enemies.

He slept uncomfortably, his neck crooked across a green hair-pillow. The lamp flame grew forked and burned in varnished soot within the squat lamp chimney. He slept; the book slid deep between his legs.

In a pearl-blue dawn he awakened, chilly and cramped and sore, to find the dry lamp wick stinking as it smouldered, and to hear Doctor Duffey out in the hallway saying kindly, "Did you come all this way by yourself, Marta? You wait and go back with me." A child's voice murmured something. Elijah stood up and blinked. His ruptured abdomen puffed with sudden pain; he put on the truss before he went to the hall door. The doctor was there, solemn and sleepy, looking like a dressed-up herald or innkeeper from some medieval pageant. He wore a short night-shirt which hung straight from his round middle, and showed the firm calves of his hairy legs through splits at the bottom.

"It was Marta Kaufman," said Duffey. "There she goes."

In the soft dampness of early morning, the little yellow-haired girl stood on the block at the roadside, struggling to reach the broad back of a farm horse.

"Old Kaufman's grandchild—she says he's slipping fast. You get dressed, Elijah, and put old Salt into the carryall. I'll be ready by then."

Huddlestone watched Marta go riding away on the clumsy chestnut stallion. He shook his head. "I wonder if there's any war news?"

"War news? No doubt, no doubt whatever. There's hell and damnation every day, and especially on the finest of mornings." The doctor sighed his way up the stairs.

Elijah pinched the glowing wick in the parlor, and drew on his clothes. He tried to imagine that this was a call to arms: while he slept in his tent, the sentries had come racing in with news of a morning assault. That was what happened to the Union army at Shiloh, people said—only the sentries didn't get there soon enough to warn . . . He stopped in the kitchen and drank deeply from the blue dipper which hung over the water pail. The water tasted of moss, of frog pools and staleness. He hurried to the barn, and prodded the white horse out of its dreams. The eastern sky was frothy with apple colors.

He jangled along the pasty driveway in the carry-all, but Doc hadn't come out of the house yet. Huddlestone snapped the leash of the hitching-block in the ring of old Salt's bit, and went into the house. He found the unshaven doctor, silk hat on the back of his head, hunting through a cabinet for some hidden potion.

"It's the strychnine I'm hunting," the old man said, over his shoulder. "Maybe it's just as well I don't find it, poor old feller."

The office was a cluttered, smelly hall along the north side of the house; a partition between two rooms had been taken out in order to fashion it. The walls reeked with red-and-blue charts of the human body, and steel engravings of famous surgeons. In the exact center of the apartment stood a long, high table covered with black oilcloth, and with a padded cushion for a head-rest. Against the south wall rested a row of unmatched cabinets, some with glass doors, some without.

In this room was the supreme attainment of medical

arts, as practised in Gettysburg. On that big, black table, Duffey had more than once proposed to relieve Huddlestone's rupture by an operation. He believed it possible to do so, but could promise nothing . . . Elijah shuddered when he thought of ether, of the drugged helplessness from which he might not return.

He said, "Doc, there's strychnine in your little satchel . . . no, I mean the old one on your desk. This one." He caught up the bag, and Duffey followed him to the door, flexing his stiff fingers inside the white flannel mittens. Outside there was a peculiar tonic quality to the air—a vast and flowery emptiness within all atmosphere, and into this vacuum you might plunge your face, and drink deeply, and be refreshed.

Doc climbed into the carryall beside his driver. Sitting thus, he seemed nearly as tall as Huddlestone, for the aged cushion on the driver's side was pressed to a deep hollow by years of the doctor's weight; Elijah sat in the round hole, inches lower than the surrounding surface. The carriage had a decided right-hand slant . . . They turned left toward York street, and west once more through the Diamond. Cautious smoke crept up from a few kitchen chimneys; an early workman thudded his way south under the arching trees of Baltimore street. "It's a great morning to die, Elijah," said Adam Duffey.

At the extreme edge of town, when they had passed the Knouse and Bale houses and moved up a long slope toward Cashtown, they saw a strange caravan poised for a moment on the rim of Oak Ridge, then spilling rapidly downhill toward them. Elijah pulled over with one wheel in the weeds.

The wagon which rocked unsteadily in their direction was an ancient vehicle, with blistered blue paint scabbing on its wooden sides. Two deep-chested horses, muddy-hocked and panting, tossed their heads and began to shy away from the carryall. The wagon was crammed with children, upended chairs, lamps, women, cloth bundles. Behind it rode a pale boy on another horse. A lame shepherd dog, staggering on three legs, began a challenging bark which ended in a howl.

"It's Antiques and Horribles," grunted Duffey, "sure as you're born!"

The wagon crashed to a halt opposite the rig. A fat-eyed man in sweaty denim waved a broken willow switch. "They come to Jambersburg!" he roared.

Elijah flung the reins around the whip-stock, and climbed out. He stared up at the crazily laden wagon; wild eyes blinked down. "What's the matter?" Doc called past him.

"Rebels!" bellowed the farmer. Saliva dripped from the corners of his straw-colored beard.

Elijah saw the blue-green world skating past him in a tilted whirl. "Where? The rebels . . . where?"

"To Jambersburg they come at night. I guess is maybe millions: they take my colt, they kill the *kelver!*"

A woman wailed: "And jickens they kill. Maybe they burn our house down once—"

Duffey had joined Elijah in the road . . . They stood there marvelling, listening, letting old man Kaufman die unaided . . . The straw-bearded man— his name was Christian Zeigenfuss, and he said he had a son in the One Hundred Forty-eighth P.V.— was quite mad with horror. His farm was four miles from Chambersburg; in the first blackness of the previous evening, the family had looked out and seen a host of dark horsemen rush into their yard. More came, and more; the lane was choked with them. They wanted water and food, and they paid with great wads of ragged paper which could never be money. They talked in a strange way; they wore torn brown shirts; they were rebels. Yes, they had taken his colt—it was a fine sorrel colt, worth a fortune. And after the whole posse moved on, a party of three men had come back and killed two calves. They killed them and bled them and cut them up by the light of a burning brush-pile, before the eyes of Mr. Zeigenfuss. Yes, and chickens—how many, he did not know.

Perhaps within a few hours the rebels would return; they might have learned in Chambersburg that young Dias Zeigenfuss was a Union soldier, and then they might kill the whole family . . . The farmer's tribe packed as many valuables as they could muster, into this wagon. They fled. The world was ending, outrageously, all around them. Ach, yes, Chambersburg had been burned. They looked back and saw vast red flares against the sky. Other people with faster horses had passed them, but must have turned off somewhere along the way. Mrs. Zeigenfuss had a brother who lived near Hanover; perhaps the rebels would not find them there. Millions of rebels. They laughed while they killed the poor *kelver*. They had guns, and most of them wore two pistols. One man, cried the pale thirteen-year-old, had no less than four pistols. And Chambersburg must have been burned; probably every soul there had been killed. There were enormous pink spots in the sky—

Elijah kept telling himself, "This is true. I'm standing here, talking to these people; they've seen the rebels. The rebs are here, in Pennsylvania. We're invaded . . . That little dirty-mouthed girl: she's looked upon the enemy." He thought of turning old Salt and whipping him up, racing home for the Vincennes musket. He had powder, but no bullets as yet. The bayonet . . . "God," he said to the doctor, hoarsely, "they might even come here. What in time is the army doing?"

Duffey shook his head. His round eyes were very bright. He assured the hysterical travelers that Gettysburg people would at least give them breakfast and let them rest for awhile. He and Huddlestone stood beside the carryall and watched the Zeigenfuss family scrambling down the hill, horses and wagon and featherbeds and all.

"We must hurry, Elijah—poor Kaufman, he was slipping fast, Marta told me! Hurry!" he squawked with a burst of amazing wrath.

Huddlestone flailed old Salt across his gray rump. The horse snorted, and lurched into a stiff gallop. From the top of McPherson's hill the two men gazed west along the misty strand of the Pike. The sun crept clear of the horizon and gilded distant ribbons of forest, caught a jeweled flash from some farmhouse window.

"Praise Peter," Duffey sighed, "no enemies in sight." He meditated for a moment, clinging to the seat as the carryall bounded and wailed across the clods. "I don't know what they'd want with us, to be sure. I've got no calves for them to butcher, poor hungry creatures that they are."

Elijah sobbed, "Bastards." His lips felt shapeless and woolly. "The boys'll all be out as soon as they hear the news, Doc. I ought to be back there." *Elements of Military Art and History* began to unleaf itself in his brain; page after page, an incredible volume. "Somebody ought to send a message to Harrisburg," he heard himself yapping at the doctor.

Old Peter Kaufman had been dead for ten minutes when they reached the farm. He was ninety-one years old, and had long been ill of heart trouble.

4.

Three church bells and the fire bell were splintering in a wicked medley; it seemed as if some leafy lining of the village had been shredded to reveal a brass pulsation which had always existed there, but only in this hour was being heard.

In his night clothes, Bale went out on the upper balcony and looked for smoke. North, east, southeast, the rim of trees was unsmudged. He thought, "They're ringing as if there was more than an ordinary fire. I wonder if—" But no, no, it was too absurd. He went back to his room and dressed. He splashed his face over the washbasin and ran down the stairs; he was alone in the house; Mrs. Wurke was not to return until Wednesday ... It was impossible to consider food while that mysterious palpitation of iron and brass kept echoing, and less than a mile away. He shut the outer door, and ran through the gate.

Blue, golden, breathless, the morning arched overhead. Mrs. Knouse was poking her head out of the front door, weird wrappings of faded yellow caught around her neck and shoulders. "Daniel?" she cried. "Daniel?"

"What?" he asked.

"Is it a fire?"

"I don't know, Mrs. Knouse, I'm sure." Past her lot, he began to run. His feet came down in a hollow trample on the first length of wooden sidewalk.

Far behind there was the growing mutter of a rapidly approaching vehicle, the mingled wheel-whirring and rattle of loose hoofs which might have been a runaway. A man's whistle pierced up as Bale turned. The Duffey carryall was bounding over the ruts; Doc leaned out, waving his hat . . . Dan swung into the highway. Old Salt bore toward him, neck stiff and eyes puffy as oysters. Elijah sawed at the reins: whoa . . . *whoa!* Dan caught a side-rod and swung himself sprawling into the rear seat. He cried, "Are you killing old Salt, or what?"

Elijah brought the lines down in a murderous slap on the animal's back. Doc was leaning over the seat.

"The rebel army's invaded Chambersburg, Dan," he said. "Hang on. Elijah thinks he's a Jehu—"

"How do you know?"

"We met a party of folks running like all hell was after them. Likely they've spread the news in town. Hear the bells?"

"You can't hear anything else; I thought it was a fire." He had a feeling of bafflement, a deep and disappointing perplexity. "Well, Hud," he cried, "if that is true, you're one ahead of me."

Elijah laughed, a high-pitched carol. He said nothing. The back of his long neck was red . . . The carryall swayed around the half-turn to the left and straightened out again. Here the homes were built close to the sidewalk; people hung out of windows, and children gaped from every porch rail. A straggling group of youths with schoolbooks under their arms . . . running in the road, they howled wolfishly as the rig shot past them. Duffey groaned, "And that's part of Gettysburg's army. They want to have the war right on the seminary campus, I doubt not."

"Look here," Bale cried, "are you sure the story's true?"

The doctor's forehead pushed up in fleshy rolls. "Dan, you should have seen that Dutchman . . ."

"There he is," said Elijah. They rocked out into the Diamond, and Hud was pointing with his whip: across the way stood a loaded farm wagon with a fringe of men around it. Elijah turned for a scant second, and his eyes met Dan's. "Talk to that old scare-cat, Dan, and you'll believe there's an invasion. It's not a lot of talk any more." He swung the heaving, gassing horse toward the hitch rack by the grocery . . . Those bells were still clanging, pound-pong-pong, as if they were the metal heart which kept life pumping through the whole town.

A buckeye tree grew up through the rusty brick sidewalk beyond the rack, and against the trunk of the tree a wide board had been nailed. A tall man, hammer in hand and mouth made speechless by its load of tacks, was fastening a white paper oblong to the board. In a semicircle around him more men were grouped, trying to read over his shoulder.

"Look there," Doc said, "they're nailing up the news."

Mr. Pock called, "It's a proclamation from Andy Curtin."

The man with the hammer turned. He nodded vacantly at them; he was Julius Orcutt. Dan saw those same reddish lights in the dull eyes as they rested on him. Painstakingly, Orcutt expelled another tack from his mouth; his hammer drove it home.

There was a continual scattering of weak guffaws. "Wants a lot of soldiers already."

"You better go, Henry. You'd make a good soldier, uh?" The men moved closer in the semicircle.

Elijah finished tethering old Salt, then turned and started rapidly across the Diamond. Only the fire bell was ringing, now; the church bells seemed worn out, but a nervous *throm, throm* of bludgeoned iron still made the air stagger. Before Huddlestone reached the wagonload of refugees, Bart McKosh stepped out to meet him. The veteran wore a pair of blue pantaloons pulled hastily over his soiled flannel night-shirt; one empty trouser-leg hung loose against the crutch, swaying as he moved . . .

At Dan's elbow, Mr. Pock was murmuring, "Welcome to anything I got. I tell you, gentlemen, I won't fight with 'em. If they come to town they can take my whole stock, and never hear a peep out of me. I got a growing family, and—" A patriarch with a stringy beard grunted: "*Gesetz ist mächtig, mächtiger ist die Not.*" There was a dry, apprehensive chuckle from the little group around the tree.

People came in a thin scurrying from every street which fed into the public square. Children . . . the young men, thought Bale, where were they? How many regiments had gone from southern Pennsylvania; how many companies out of this county? Here were white-beards, silver-hair, the paunches and knobs of middle age. And young men: there were himself and Elijah, and the one-legged Bart McKosh, and a mutilated gawk named Ernie Dryer. Boys from school—pink noses, cow licks, unformed chins—they carried Ovid and Cicero and Scott under their scrawny arms . . . Young men of Gettysburg, he cried to himself: where have you gone, and how are you finding it there? You rebels raiding Chambersburg, are you young too?

Close at hand sounded the rapid pat-pat of hoofs; children scooted to safety as a gray horse whirled out of York street. Astride it joggled a man whose dark coat and hat seemed hung in a light veil of dust; the slanting sun caught a dozen glitters from the buckles and buttons and sword which were a part of him. The crowd beside the farm wagon turned to stare with new suspicion as he loped past them. This was no idling soldier, home on furlough: he was too purposeful, too hot and dusty.

He halted in front of the men under the buckeye tree; his big mare sniffed suspiciously toward old Salt. "Major Haller, acting under orders of General Couch." Stirrup leather crunched as he swung down. "Who's in charge here?" The major dusted his hat against his baggy knee.

"Kendlehart's president of the council," someone muttered.

"You've seen Governor Curtin's proclamation, people. You're apt to be invaded, any moment. I want to talk to your borough officials, immediately."

Julius Orcutt stepped down into the road, hammer still clenched in his hand. "Dr. Kendlehart is not present at this moment. Can I be of any assistance? My name is—"

The major shrugged. "I'm informed that you've got some sort of militia in this town. Correct?" He twisted his head impatiently. "What's that infernal noise?"

"Fire bell," came a chorus. "John Burns is ringing it."

"I wish to heaven John Burns would stop it," grunted the officer.

"It's to call people out. The whole rebel army is in Chambersburg!"

Major Haller said, "The whole rebel fiddlesticks. We've heard all about that—it was Jenkins' cavalry, on a raid. It's rumored that they kited straight back to Maryland last night. However, that is neither here nor there. I want to talk to your townspeople about this militia company. It is imperative that we Pennsylvanians organize for defense at the earliest possible moment."

The fire-alarm had stopped suddenly, shorn off; its cessation pained the empty air . . . Bart McKosh and Elijah were hurrying across the Diamond; even at a distance you could see the fever in Elijah's cheeks. McKosh looked more dark and sallow and browbeaten than ever. He hurled himself along with prodigious leaps of his single leg . . . The army officer walked forward to meet him.

Doctor Duffey's mittened paw closed on Dan's arm. "You've still got a grip," Bale said . . . The old doctor was staring past him with glazed and squinting eyes. "Watch," he kept saying, "over there by the corner. Watch! It's Constable John Burns, and he's a fire-eater if ever I see one. Look—the poor old relic is lugging his musket along—"

Burns began to chant before he had reached Major Haller: "I got military experience—fought in two wars, I have. Teamed with the army down in Maryland . . . ain't so old as I might be—" The men could barely hear his words. He glared at the officer with bitter, Indian eyes; his loose jaw kept wiggling from side to side.

"My hands are coming back to me," Duffey chuckled harshly. He pulled Dan toward the carryall. "Look how I can take hold . . . And do you know, this puts me in mind of when I was in Philadelphia and we had the plague. Cholera."

"This is worse than cholera," Bale said.

"It takes hold in the same way . . . Would you mind riding home with me? I want to see if I can drive old Salt without too much pain and trouble. Likely I'll have to do my own driving from now on, if Elijah goes off to shoot at folks."

Dan said, "According to that officer, it was only a raid. They've gone back south again."

Doc climbed into the carryall and unwound the reins from the whipstock, working with slow and flabby gestures. "Devil a bit of satisfaction I can find in that. They'll be back for a full meal . . . this is a terrible war, Dan. *Tutchk,*" he ordered old Salt. Sullenly, the white horse hobbled in a half circle; the wheels scraped against the body of the rig.

"He was treated shameful, poor horse. We'll be taking it easy now, no matter who has pups. *Tutchk.*"

As they squeaked toward York street, they passed a bulky man who was walking rapidly away from the crowd beside the Zeigenfuss family. He lifted his head for a glance at Bale, then turned away again.

"Elmer Quagger," nodded Adam Duffey. "Said to be a Copperhead."

"Yes. He is one. That's what people are whispering of me, no doubt." He looked back over the seat; Quagger was staring malignantly after him.

Duffey cocked his head on one side. "What is it?"

"Nothing. Quagger—he reminded me of something . . ."

"Reminded you?"

"Yes. I don't know what. It doesn't matter." For a few minutes he tormented his mind, trying to decide why Quagger's vicious glare had confused him. Then he gave it up. Quagger was no one to fear. Still—his face—

Duffey sighed. "Yes, I'll be wholly capable of driving. Eva can help me with the harness and so on, if Elijah goes off to fight . . . You come with me, Dan, and we'll have a bite of breakfast. I doubt Elijah realizes there's such a necessity as breakfast in the world."

"That rupture of his," Bale asked. "Do you think he—?"

"Jesus," said the doctor. "It will kill him completely if he tries to be a soldier. But the war's killed plenty before him."

5.

It was early the next afternoon before Dan saw Irene Fanning. She had not been out of his mind since the hour when he surged over her body, but the great riddle of their attraction, their immediate and mutual sin, was buried deep when the bells began to ring.

He thought that his brain must be boxed into four compartments—shelves or drawers or cubicles. In one of these lay his past life, and in another his fumbled knots of philosophy. The two remaining boxes were stewing with treacherous thoughts of the war and of Tyler Fanning's wife. He tried to keep them penned, each consciousness in its proper place, but paper by paper, word by word they would curl up and occupy him, plaster his soul, blow forever behind his eyes.

In the rain of Sunday night he had felt only the proud possessiveness of a male, the glut of pure satisfaction. She was willing; she was no child; he had bent her scruples aside if any actually existed. He had seen aright when he diagnosed the bitter desire in her eyes. This must be one form of love—he was not certain—he had never lain with an intelligent woman before ... All her emotion, whatever sensitiveness and tender pride she possessed, was undiscovered and nonexistent ... Only when he walked back with her through the wet pasture and left her to creep alone into the house of her betrayed marriage, only then had he felt the self-abomination of the skulker, and not for long.

Most desperately he had wanted to see her on Monday, but she did not appear, though he watched the Fanning place for hours ... Certainly she would be in the crowded Diamond on Tuesday morning. He ate a light breakfast with the Duffeys, and went back up York street. Drums and fifes were playing, at the college grounds, where Major Haller was examining the Gettysburg volunteers. A coterie of men still gathered near the grocery, trying to digest Governor Curtin's proclamation. Dan stopped and read the message. He could recognize the dogged, futile blast for what it was; the pathos of a perplexed nation seemed wailing in every massive phrase.

An army of rebels is approaching our border ... I now appeal to all the citizens of Pennsylvania, who love liberty and are mindful of the history and traditions of their revolutionary fathers, and who feel that it is a sacred duty to guard and maintain the free institutions of our country, who hate treason and its abettors, and who are willing to defend their homes and their firesides, and do invoke them to rise in their might and rush to the

rescue in this hour of imminent peril. The issue is
one of preservation or destruction.

"That officer, he says Abe Lincoln's called for a
hundred thousand men."

"What I want to know is, what's the army doing?
Whynt they chase them rebels and give 'em a trim-
ming? Whynt—"

"But Ezra says they got to go for six months already. They won't take 'em by the army less nor that;
six months is all."

"—Got harvest ahead, and the hay ain't in. And
maybe he gets killed yet."

The old sage with the yellow whiskers nodded his
head. He was a creaking, rheumy-eyed man with a
bad breath; his name was Truckenmiller, and neighbors
were fond of telling how he had worn out three wives.
All of his sons had run away as soon as they were
grown, but now he was too old to harm anyone . . .
He said, *"Blinder Eifer schadet nur."* But no one was
paying much attention to him. He sagged on the
broken bench in front of the store, making little dents
in the dust with the tip of his cane.

Then he looked up again and poked his cane at
Dan. "Maybe you go," he said. "A strong young man
to make war, *ja? Das Alter wägt, die Jugend wagt.*"

The scattering conversations stopped, dead. People
behind Dan turned to stare at him, and those in front
of him were studious in their close scrutiny of the
proclamation . . . Bale thought of telling the moth-
eaten tyrant that youth had more reason for careful
consideration than age. But it would do no good.
These people had made up their minds concerning
him; perhaps there were those who envied him his
solitary courage, but he rather doubted it. He moved

silently through the group and walked around the corner into Chambersburg street . . . Far to the north, on the campus, there was a burst of cheering. The drum corps skirled up: *Zu Lauterbach hab ich mein Strumpf ver-lor'n* in a grandiose and gaudy spasm. Dan wondered if Demon was there, playing. And then the woman came into his mind and stayed until he went home and fell upon his bed.

He dozed awhile. Disordered dreams trooped across his sweaty slumber, and all the time he was aware that more wagons went past the house than had gone past in many days, and off in the green distance the drums rattled and throbbed . . . He got up at noon, and bathed, and went down into the kitchen. The bread remaining in the house had dried out since Sunday; he should have brought more from the baker's. But there were cheese and fresh milk and soda crackers, and he opened a jar of peaches. He ate, and washed two days' accumulation of dirty dishes; all the time, the clock whispered gutturally at him. He thought: "That's the clock. Same one. It was ticking Sunday night . . . beside this table I wrapped the bandage, here I put my arms around her. We went into the living room to the couch. So remarkably unreal and remote—an experience in the life of someone else." He walked to the window and peered across at the Fannings'. House, barn and out-buildings baked in a mid-day glare; chickens wandered drearily about in the scratched blue shade. And Demon nowhere in sight; his mistress must have permitted him to go to the village with his drum. But surely he couldn't go to war, if anything so idiotic occurred—

Dan took a bucket out to the well. Beyond the fringe of hollyhocks, past the faded palings of the yard fence, he could hear the jingle of Cybo's bell. There was a growl, a scuffle; someone cried *shoosh!* Cybo sprang through a gap in the barrier and scuttled across the Bale yard.

Mrs. Knouse rose up out of larkspurs, her mouldy face shadowed by a sunbonnet. "That dumb critter," she scolded, "he makes dirt in my lilies!"

Her chin was brown and dripping; she held a trowel in one gloved hand and a peach-basket in the other. "I will not leave my plants for them bad men to take," she explained, fiercely. There was fresh earth pressed across the front of her gray calico apron. "Not these bulbs, you bet. I'll put 'em down in the cellar where they can't be stole."

Dan heard himself asking, "You mean—the rebels? Why, that was just a raid. They went right back south. And Chambersburg wasn't burned, they've learned: only a building or two. Just cavalry, according to word received downtown. It's said that they headed back toward Hagerstown and—"

She shrieked, "If they come here, they'll never find my *tulpen!* These are exquisite plants, Daniel, and if they come to Gettysburg they'll never find 'em down in the cellar under my washtubs—"

He said, weakly, "I don't think it's that serious," and went back into the house with his water pail.

He sat at Pentland Bale's desk and tried to write a letter to Lucas Mite in Minnesota. But the letter was flimsy, a puny recounting, not at all the sort of a letter Mite would expect . . . Doctor Duffey, he thought. No, he's busy enough; I shan't bother him. Hud will be drilling with those youngsters, or God knows what. And no one moves, over at the Fanning house. The place is bewitched. Only Cybo goes jangling across the pasture with his idiotic bell; he trots under bushes and prowls in the brown timothy, and lies in the hot sun and lets flies bite him . . .

Room after room, all empty, all grotesque and stolid and inhabited by unfriendly presences. The day was stifling. He took off his shirt and tramped up and down the stairs, trying to make vague errands for himself. At four o'clock he had what he thought was a very good idea. He lifted the trap door in the kitchen floor and crawled down into the pit beneath, hunting for whiskey. He found it: a keg. Pentland Bale had declared that it was an improvement on the old-time Monongahela . . . Dan filled a decanter and carried it up to his room. He read Meister Eckhart and Coleridge. He read two copies of *Arthur's Home Magazine* . . . Later he drank more whiskey and was moderately sick. Over behind the seminary someone kept shooting with a musket. Practising marksmanship, learning how to kill a man. The wide reports rolled in, round and precise and portentous, until dusk put an end to them, and boys began to halloo up and down the Springs road.

Then he had been asleep and he slid up out of hot darkness because a voice was calling him. "Hey—" a man wailing at him, over and over, "Hey . . . hey, Dan!" Dan shook himself; his lead body became bristling to life. He got up and crept to the window. There was a black smudge against the dimness below, and that smudge was Elijah. "Hello," he croaked to the smudge.

"I didn't expect you'd be asleep," Huddlestone said.

"No, I wasn't . . . I guess I was, too."

"I'm very sorry. But I wanted—"

Dan told him, "Come upstairs. The door is unlatched." While he lit the lamp, he could hear Elijah poking cautiously up the long stairway. Dan opened the door . . . Hud was in his shirt-sleeves, and bare-headed. He looked at Dan. "Why, you didn't take off your clothes when you went to bed."

"No," Bale said. He slouched back loosely on the bed. "Liquor's over there on the table. Help yourself."

Elijah grinned. "Drinking all by yourself? That is odd. I didn't know you drank much at all."

"I don't."

Huddlestone took the glass stopper out of the decanter, hesitated, and dropped it in again. "I want to tell you: it looks like we're going."

"Going—where?"

"Harrisburg. We'll likely be mustered tomorrow afternoon by Major Haller. We'll be part of Couch's Army of the Susquehanna."

"Army of the Susquehanna." Dan heard a hard, tight voice which might have been his own. "We look at reality, and we do not see it. It is colorless, without any form or surface or consistency. We listen for reality: it has no sound . . . no shape. Nothing that we can grasp or smell. It remains unnamable." The voice stopped speaking; only it breathed heavily.

Hud asked, "What ails you? God."

"That was a Chinaman," the compact voice went on again. "Lucas Mite introduced me to him. A very strange man, Mite. He came from Connecticut: I think he killed someone there before he came west. And he has a conscience. He tries to assuage it with Shake-speare and all sorts of things. Well, he had a little book—a paper one. The person who wrote it claimed that it was translated from the Chinese language. There was a man named Lao Tze, who lived a long time be-fore Jesus Christ. He wrote a book called the *Tao Teh King* . . . No reality."

Long silence. Elijah looked somber, and swished the whiskey about in its carved red bulb.

"He was only a Chinaman with a queue, probably," Bale said. "No one to be concerned about. Even if there isn't any reality which returns always to the realm of nonexistence."

"You must be real drunk," Elijah said.

"Yes. I must be."

Insects muzzled about in the elm branches near the window . . . a dog which always barked, up near McPherson's.

"Well, I wouldn't have routed you out if I had known you were this way. I mean," Elijah added peevishly, "talking about men from Connecticut and Chinese people and reality, and all. This is pretty serious business, being invaded, whether you believe it or not."

Dan said, "The devil." He moved over to the washstand and bumped against it heavily. He took up the pitcher.

"That water is foul if it's been here long," Elijah muttered. "Give me the pitcher." He wrenched it out of Dan's grasp and went away downstairs. Bale sat at the big table with his head on his arms. He heard the pump squawling . . . Hud came back with fresh water for him, and he drank deeply and splashed his face in the bowl. "Thank you," he said. "I hope I haven't offended you."

Elijah sat on the sill of the open window. "No, I'm too excited for anyone to offend, I guess. Being mustered in—"

"I want to understand it correctly. You mean that you're all going into United States' service?"

"Not all. Bart McKosh can't go, naturally, and Haller said no one would think of accepting Ernie Dryer—not now, anyway. And those musicians are just a kind of pick-up to help with the drill. But most of the rest—"

"They'll take—you?"

The insects buzzed for an uninterrupted moment.

"Of course they will. What did you think?" He spoke sharply. "They say there's all kinds of ruptures in the army nowadays. And—well, I know a lot about this business. I've studied and— Likely they'll make me a corporal or sergeant, right off. I'm only sorry I couldn't seek out a lot of recruits and get a commission, but that may come later."

"I see."

Elijah was folding tiny creases in the loose cloth of his pantaloons. "There's considerable stew and fuss. The war department refused to take volunteers for less than six months, so Governor Curtin's trying to get them to accept us just for the emergency—until we've helped repel the invasion. Haller says he expects permission from Mr. Stanton by tomorrow afternoon. Then we'll go ahead. There's all our crew who've been drilling—that includes four boys from the Sem—and I understand we'll get at least fifty out of the college. Maybe we'll have nearly a hundred."

Dan asked, "And then?"

"Why, we'll be sent to Harrisburg. They seem to think the rebels will head for there, if they come north again."

"Do you actually believe that you will see fighting, Hud?"

He stood up, restlessly. "Of course I do." His dark eyes seemed very large in his thin face. "Dan—the reason I came over here tonight—it isn't so late, only about ten o'clock—Listen, Dan. I want you to drop everything. Come along with us. Be a good fellow, why don't you?"

Bale cried savagely, "Not for you or anybody."

"Do you realize what this invasion means?"

"Well, what does it mean?"

Elijah clenched his fists. The knuckles were squeezed and bloodless. "This is our country. They're coming up here. I mean, they're going to try to. A man who won't fight for his home is—" He stopped short, swallowing.

"Yes," Dan whispered, after a moment. "You can't understand how I feel. But I'm not going to kill anybody, ever again. Think of this, Hud: suppose you'd been brought up in South Carolina. You and I met, enemies. We killed each other. Why? We'd have been friends if we were neighbors here in Gettysburg. And because I killed you, your mother must be robbed of you for the rest of her life."

"Hell," said Elijah.

"Well, that's it."

"Then you won't consider it?"

"No. You ought to know that."

Huddlestone smacked his palms together. "All right." He walked toward the door.

"How about Amelia Niede? Does she know you're going?"

Huddlestone stood stock-still. "I saw her this morning for a moment. She was with Uncle Otto and her Ma, down at Pock's. She—Mealy's a nice girl . . . I'd like to talk to her some more before I go. If I had any money to spare, I'd hire a turn-out and take her for a drive in the morning. But I had to square a grocery account with the money I got from Doc."

Dan fumbled in his pocket. "No," Elijah snarled. "Do you think that was why I was telling you?"

Bale stood up clumsily. He had a wad of paper money in his hand. He went over to Elijah. Huddlestone backed away, his face rigid and his eyes bright. Dan caught his right arm and held it; Hud struck, blindly and quickly, at Dan's face . . . Bale caught both the man's wrists in the trap of his big hand and held him, in spite of his writhings. He pushed the fold of money into his pocket. He said, "Are we friends, or are we not?" He dropped Elijah's wrists.

Hud breathed rapidly and stared at the floor.

"Oh, now—" said Dan.

"How much was that?"

"I don't know. I haven't the faintest idea. You know what Doc always says: money, it's the curse of us all. It's caused wars and sadness and devilment, or something like that."

"I can't take your money, Dan."

Bale said a short word. He sat down on the bed.

"I cannot. You should be able to understand."

Dan sneered, "Because I'm a Copperhead? Because I'm a coward who won't go out and kill for the sake of the Star-Spangled Banner and Father Abraham and General D. N. Couch and the Army of the Susquehanna?"

"That's not it. But—you're drunk and—"

"Not that drunk. I know what I'm about . . . Go away, and quit driving me to distraction." He lay back on the bed, closing his eyes and putting his hand over them to keep out the tawny glare of the lamp.

Elijah shuffled around on the matting at the door. "All right," he said, finally. "A loan, then. Until I come back. Will I see you tomorrow, Dan?"

"Doubtless," Dan said. He heard reluctant feet going away down the stairs. He lay there on the bed and wondered whether he should take more whiskey . . . *ho, the wars!* "Doubtless," he said aloud to the echoing room. Then he blew out the lamp and lay down once more. Wondering, murmuring darkness. Before morning he dreamed of Doctor Duffey and Elijah going to war in the carryall. Their old white horse was shot; he stood still in the shafts, trembling and dying by inches. "Isn't there something you can do for him?" Elijah kept appealing. "Poor old Salt! Poor old Reverend Solt . . ."

He came back into the world when everything was grayish-pink and a thousand birds haunted across the fields. Their immutable warbling rippled through the room. He went to the window and looked out at a layer of mist which lifted from meadows across the road . . . This life must be shed. Mrs. Wurke would be home all too soon; then he could not wander, lone and crazy, through his own house.

Dan sponged his head and shoulders, put on a clean shirt, and went out to the well. A mirror of orange was lifting in the east; the belated and sleepy roosters in Fanning's barnyard were wailing about it. Dan went into the cool kitchen and hunted until he found a willow basket. In it he packed the remainder of the cheese, half a loaf of dry wheat-bread, butter, a knife, and a jar of quince preserves. One of the Germels boys had left a pail of milk in the little buttery off the back porch; the milk appeared mysteriously each night; you left an empty bucket and a bit of fractional currency on the wide green shelf, and miraculously the milk would be there in the morning, as if elves had brought it . . . Dan washed an empty wine bottle brought from the pantry, filled it with a pint of milk, and plugged the top with a roll of newspaper. He put Coleridge into the basket, and a late book of Emerson's which he had never read; it had been bought by Pentland Bale during his last illness. He put in a slab of writing paper and a lead pencil, then took them out again; no, he could never be one with the dainty souls who sat themselves down in clovery dales and poured out their souls amid the murmur of thrushes. If he had anything to give the world, it would bear itself through a less beautiful travail . . . The doors stood open behind him. He walked south across the pasture, carrying the basket.

He looked at the Fanning house. It was a cube, lifeless, a desolate rock laden with old vines. The chickens gabbled shrilly, telling him.

From the Fairfield road he went south opposite Long Lane. The sun pushed above Granite Ridge and shone on a dwarf in Henry Niede's barnyard, and animal dwarfs over west at the McMillen farm . . . He stepped among the spongy hummocks which give birth to Stevens Run. Thick woods, south past the Bliss place; the birds were busy and trilling there, and all the ridge was a smother of plumed trees. Blue haze made a million dimples between the puffy foliage. Green lilac tufts, he thought . . . the trees bring peace, but somehow it hurts you to look at them too long.

6.

At one o'clock he finished his bottle of milk and ate the last of the toast he had browned over a wood fire. He picked his way down the west slope of Little Round Top, sliding among the great bowlders with the basket on his arm. He washed at Plum Run and wandered east through the gulley to the Taneytown road . . . Green silence: he came out into the narrow lane, and a woman on a bay horse was bobbing toward him from the north.

She was Mrs. Tyler Fanning; she rode a colt which had been trained as the elder Fanning's saddle-horse. It trotted gingerly, wondering about this side-saddle, its ears stiff and pointed . . . The woman held her face high; she came forward in metal dignity, and her lips were colorless. She wore a habit of dark blue, and her hat was in her hand; the dust lay like flour on every fold of her garments. Before this, she must have been galloping hard. The colt breathed too fast, and his bridle was gray with suds.

Bale stepped into the grass beside the road and put his basket down. "It's a good day to ride," he said.

The colt skated away through the dust, but the girl brought him back. She did not look at Dan Bale, but far beyond him. "I don't know what to say to you." She spoke harshly. "If you were me, would you know what to say? Please do not tell me that it's a good day to ride—"

Their eyes met and clung coldly together.

"If you'll get down," he suggested, "we might walk a bit. You can tie the colt or lead him, just as you choose . . . He's a good one. What do you call him? I've seen him out in the—"

She said, "Dazzle. His name is Dazzle."

They muttered together: "whoa, hold on, Dazzle, good boy, Daz"—Bale grasped the bridle; the girl rested her hand upon his shoulder as she lifted her knee, shook out the wide skirt, and slipped to the ground. She seemed very small beside the tall young horse . . . There were tiny lines drawn in soft spokes around her eyes. "He'll behave, tied," she said to Dan, "if the flies don't annoy him too much. Do you put him over there in the shade."

Dan unsnapped the reins and knotted them together for an extended halter. "There," he said, "he

can get his head down if he wants any grass." He tied
the leather around a peak at the fence angle ... He
could feel blood in his wrists and temples pounding
with the jarring spasm of pebbles—clots of pebbles
moving through his veins. I wonder if my lips are gray,
he thought. They feel gray. Her face is like it was when
Tyler yelped at her, that other afternoon. There is still
a bandage on her arm, to remind me.

He offered his arm. She took it in a stiff clutch.
They walked down the road; she was holding the
long riding skirt by its braided loop, and the shadows
of their bodies dissolved in a grotesque pool beside
them.

"You despise me," Dan said. "Probably it's natural
that you should."

"Natural?" she repeated, as if she were very tired.

He tried to speak without emotion. "I was the ag-
gressor. Whatever wrong has been managed, you can
charge against me."

"I have tried to charge you with a great many
things," the girl said, "but—I've been so hideously
mixed up, body and soul."

He halted, and seized her hands. "If you knew how
I felt, would it be any easier?"

Her laugh was a brief, hopeless pleading. "Mr.
Bale, are you going to tell me of your great love for
me?"

"It may be that. I don't know. You've been with
me—my mind, ever since. And before."

She went on, dully: "You tried to fling me out of
your mind, and failed. That is a greater compliment
than I could have expected."

They were walking again. "And because you are a
gentleman—a sensitive one—your conscience has

been active. If you are a Christian, you may consider both of us utterly damned, and hate me for it."

"That's not true. Not a word of it." He swore softly.

"I wonder," Irene Fanning said. Her eyes lifted, holding a steady question.

Beneath the shade of the big beech tree, Dazzle nickered inquisitively. A slow rumble of wheels came in a rising echo, not far up the road . . . The girl pressed her hands nervously. "We must not be seen here, Mr. Bale. Not this way. At least no one knows about—about— No one else."

"They'll see the horse."

"I could have left him tied—and gone for a stroll—"

"In here," he whispered quickly. He pushed the branches of elderberry aside, opening a tunnel into the thick shrubbery. The woman crowded through; Bale followed, drawing the green leaves together. There was a low ditch behind the matted bulwark; clover hay grew tall and unclipped, spilling past the broken bars of a fence. The approaching wagon joggled closer. "Down," the man whispered. He drew her into the cushioned jungle of hay; her throat was hot against his wrist.

The wheels and hoofs stopped for a moment as the driver paused to gaze at the bay colt. Then the vehicle creaked again; it rolled past the elderberry ambush, a rusty team, a faded old Stanhope with the bearded driver mumbling to himself. Dan thought: that old man Truckenmiller again—I would have thought him too shaky to drive alone . . . The wheels muttered out of hearing.

Dan whispered, *"Das Alter wägt, die Jugend wagt."*

"What?" she asked.

"Youth ventures—starts ahead—while old age considers. That villain of a Truckenmiller—he quoted it in town yesterday."

She said, "We must—" and made as if to rise.

He fastened his arms around her body, and drew her down. He kissed her roughly, again and again . . . Her lips trembled against his neck. "Oh, I'm mad," she sobbed.

"I love you, Irene. I—"

"Not—not—"

"I know it is. I can't forget."

The colt neighed and stamped, annoyed with waiting.

Irene said, "I must—go. Dazzle . . . he's fractious; he'll break loose! And here we— Like this—"

He crushed her into the yielding grass.

"Madness," she cried weakly. "Darling, darling! Oh, God, I feel like a strumpet. It never was like this before!"

He said, "Not another flicker of time . . . nothing but you—"

"The world will—kill us, for this . . . Outraged—"

He lifted her body close beside his; on their knees they faced each other in the reeling shade. "You'll divorce Fanning," Dan cried. "You've got to do it. You don't love him. We'll go west at once. Cut loose from Gettysburg, from—Oh, my beloved—" the words poured from him, inexhaustible fund, he could go on saying these things to her, day after day without end— "think what it will be! Casting everything else—"

"You don't know me. Only this sin we've done—"

"Call it sin. God knows it's beautiful."

She groaned, "Oh, I'm shameless. But I desire you, desire you, *desire you*—" She shuddered, and closed her eyes. She struck fiercely against his chest. "We must go, at once."

"Tonight," he said. "My dear, tonight—"

They stood up. She brushed blindly at the netted branches. "It's too terrible—that way. Because I leave the house, with both of them there—I feel like a thief, or a murderer, or— Since Sunday I've lain in my room, pretending to read, trying to think. It's as if the world had been cracked, far and wide, and I was afraid to step outside for fear I'd sink through."

"Listen," he said. "Dear, can you listen? I'll buy a good team today. We'll go away—tonight. I can draw a thousand dollars out of the bank at once, if need be. We need not come back; everything can be settled, later."

She shook her head. "If you stop to think, that is childish. And I would never do such a thing to Tyler and his parents, no matter how little love I bear them. No—we must consider, for a long time."

"You doubt me. You don't believe—"

"I doubt myself—Dan." Her face flushed lightly as she said the word. It was as if in speaking his name, sanely and in no great stress of passion, she had committed herself to a greater intimacy than ever before.

They went back to the colt. He had trampled about and got one leg over the line by which he was hitched. He squealed and arched his neck when they came near him. "He's good," Bale heard himself saying. "Got a lot of daylight under him, and a rather steep rump, but he's a rare breedy stamp."

"Mr. Fanning bought him in Emmetsburg," Irene said. "Please hold Dazzle close to the fence. I'll mount there."

After he had aided her into the saddle, Bale still

held the colt's bit. He curried at the shining neck with stiff fingers.

"Tonight . . ." It strangled him—choking word—

Her face grew whiter and whiter. "I don't know. I must think."

"If Mrs. Wurke comes back, I will send her to Mummasburg. It's farther from the line, and her relatives are terrified at the thought of invasion. She'll be glad to go."

"Don't do that," Irene commanded, sharply . . . She cried, "Oh, my hat—I did have one."

Dan went back to the thicket and found the little felt hat with its white feather, a crushed morsel in the clover. The woman took it in her hand, and bowed.

"Irene," he said.

"Goodbye—Dan." She whirled the bay; he danced high on his hindlegs, shook his head, and blew a relieved snort from his nostrils. Then he rocked up the road at a frantic lope . . . Mrs. Fanning did not look back, but gave her full attention to holding Dazzle.

Bale went down the shady row to pick up his basket. He thought, Now that any peace is irretrievably gone, I could never wish it back. So hardy and alive; sensitive to this leaf and that pool of sunlight, hearing all sounds . . . who would believe that adultery was like this, like this? He thought, Tyler Fanning— I'll pity him from now until Doomsday, but I can never hate him. Likely enough he'll be past hating me. I'd fight for her, yes, I would even kill for her if I had to. This is not the same ravine through which I walked an hour ago; I have never seen it before . . . And get rid of Mrs. Wurke, poor creature. Give her money; send her away; get rid of her; there must be no interference, no intrusion upon my woman and me. I must lay plans, I must buy a team—if I could persuade Irene to leave with me tonight—walk out of this trivial existence, shed all memories, and never dwell in the past again.

He left it all behind him: the rock-skulled hills, the timbered dens, the thickets of Plum Run gorge where catbirds meowed and peeked at him. A thousand steps: pace, pace, pace again: and he was not conscious of having driven his body up the fields. When he came to the Emmetsburg road by Sherfy's peach orchard, a dust cloud was moving from the southwest. It resolved itself into flashing spokes, lacquered staves, a black gelding—all the panoply of a gay cutunder buggy driven by Elijah Huddlestone. Dan stepped aside as the rig sped toward him, but Elijah whistled, and drew on the reins.

Amelia Niede sat on the seat with him, and her white muslin dress was well sprinkled with dust. Again she wore the hat with painted strawberries, and patches of rose were smothered in her flat cheeks; Elijah had kissed her this day—the first kiss he had ever given her . . . If he went to the war, he might come back an officer. Officers were men of importance; in some magnificent way they acquired manners and property and short beards, and people spoke to them with deference; not even Henry Niede could look with contempt at an officer . . . There was something the matter with Elijah, with Elijah's private parts. People whispered, "He has a rupture," but like enough that would never interfere with him, in war . . . If Elijah became an officer with lapels of blue-black plush, they would be married at the Lutheran church, and live in the village, and never again would Amelia have to milk six cows. They would have their pictures made, she and Elijah; he would sit in a chair, knees crossed, and she would stand beside him, and the photographer would tint their faces pink. She squeezed her bony fingers closer together.

Elijah yelled. "I'm hustling right back to town. Maybe Major Haller's got word by now. You climb in with us, Dan."

"No," Bale said, "I'll walk home across the fields . . . I've been picnicking in solitary contentment."

"You look like it agreed with you, I must say. See here: remember I told you last night that we'd get at least fifty fellows from Penn college? Well, there's fifty-seven already signed the roll!"

He waved the tasseled whip; his eyes were open wide, and he wore an immense stock which seemed ready to garrote him. "The major says we're apt to leave for Harrisburg any minute, once he gets permission for the 'existing emergency' enlistments. I tell you, Dan, the country's full of rebels! They're pouring into Maryland like flies; the *Star and Banner*'s been posting bulletins all day. Some folks say it's only rumors; I don't believe it. They're holding mass-meetings in Philadelphia, and Governor Curtin's ordering cannon from—"

"Go on to your blamed war," Dan ordered.

"I'm acting as temporary sergeant. We'll drill tonight, if nothing happens before then . . . see you!" he called, and then they went flashing off, wound in the hot smoke of the road. Dan stood in the grass, waiting until the dust had settled. Yes, he said—yes, they say there is a war off there behind South Mountain, behind the rolls of forest . . . quickly, quickly I will bind myself against you, will feel you beating upon me like a hot heart, hear the breath shiver out of your mouth, and it is all surfeited with a power which we never knew existed before . . . war, behind blue hills over there. Slaty rivers of men pouring up the roads where we've never walked. Elijah says so.

When he reached his house, there was a folded sheet of paper tacked against the mosquito-frame door. On one side was printed in soiled black type: *will guarantee colt to stand and suck at the above-stated price, or service with no such guarantee at Terms To Be Arranged.* On the other side was written in blunt lead pencil, "The mother stille not so well, and Aunt Emma to stay until knows what the army do. Respy, H. Wurke." As Dan read the note, he felt a blind fever of passion climbing in his brain. Mrs. Wurke would not return from Mummasburg this day; God knew when she would come. Until knows what the army do . . .

He went inside, to exist, to drag out the monotonous ages until night. He lay down; he could not sleep; he could only crave the ultimate hour. A bugle ta-ta-taed far away, every few minutes, and the hazy Pike was thunderous with wagons. Mrs. Knouse had locked herself in her little brick house, tulip bulbs and all; she peered from narrow cracks behind her shutters, watching for screaming hordes of rebels who would come to uproot her flower garden.

Elijah Huddlestone was sworn to the service of his Republic, that afternoon, and Dan did not know it; he did not see Elijah before the volunteers went clamoring off to Harrisburg, waving their shabbiest hats and howling:

Sam built the wagon,
The old Union wagon—
The star-crested wagon—
To give the boys a ride . . .

The younger boys sang in quartets, their arms locked around one another: *No more ciphers, no more books, no more master's cranky looks* . . . Bart McKosh and Ernie Dryer and old John Burns were left behind . . . The recruits reached Harrisburg in a steady rain, and had to wait in the downpour for hours, and they wondered if this was war.

7.

Monday evening a troop of independent cavalry from Two Taverns came clattering into Gettysburg to report to Major Haller. They were farm boys, mostly—mounted on shaggy farm horses which squealed at all the clanking and hullabaloo around them . . . All day, piled-up wagons of refugees had been grinding in from Fairfield, from Greenwood and the hills beyond. The drivers crouched in voluble terror, staring wildly over their shoulders at the rainy horizon behind.

Ja, men declared, the rebels had come through Hagerstown. Johannes Merckenburg saw them; Frederick Sturtz had a sister living there, who had sent him word. Mrs. Henry Kreck had fled from their wrath, with her five children packed in a New Rochelle wagon; she had driven all night, and one of the children sick with scarlet fever . . . *Ja,* there was a terrible old general with one leg, who had stolen a fine brougham somewhere; he drove with his good leg propped on the seat before him, and only the idiots of the countryside would stay to be eaten alive. Soldiers spread out on every road, they spotted the pastures with their fires, they burned Adolph Schilling's fences, they took every horse from the Hamms. Ach, they would pay, but their great rolls of dingy paper were not money. The wild men with long hair, the men who talked as no human beings had ever talked, were dark and patched and very, very hungry. Chickens disappeared; you heard them squawking horridly; then they squawked not again. The cherries were eaten. Who was it said that those men with long hair had eaten a baby or two? *Ja,* it was all too true; they had eaten children; it was known ... They seized upon Otto Roush's new wagon, and took it away with them. They sang satanic songs; the pigs squealed for mercy, and were butchered in every farmyard. Many children they had eaten; only the fools would stay. Army after army came clanking in from the south, and cowardly folks ran out to give them coffee and gingerbread, and to cheer at the dirty pink flags they carried.

They cut the ears from pretty girls; they strung the ears like beads and hung them around their necks. Ach, it is a terrible thing which happens to a young woman who is caught by them, all alone ... *Nein,* I have not seen it myself, but it is true. A hundred of those men will carry her away into the forest; she will not be found again. And afterward, they will cut off her ears.

Tuesday the wagons still came. You saw the dried, snuffy faces of old women peering down; white-haired children bawled, their noses ran and were not wiped clean. Kittens spilled out of peach baskets, and were left to yowl in the mud behind. There were runaways ... Wagons, wagons through the turnpike gates, wallowing in from the west. Chambersburg had been seized again by hosts, by gaunt thousands ...

And Wednesday, the procession still came. The heavy-hoofed cavalry from Two Taverns had splashed away up the Harrisburg road: men cried at them, *Verrickt!* and go once the other way, for that is where the rebels come.

8.

It was after dusk on Thursday evening, and Dan Bale was walking out of Pock's store with a sack of groceries under his arm when he heard the faint squeal of a fife. Loafers who had clustered under the buckeye trees were moving across the Diamond and peering down the black tunnel of York street . . . The fife trickled closer; drums were making an uneven roll, and behind this tuneless murmur was a weary drone of cheering. Lanterns began to drift out of dark houses. The word passed from square to square: our boys, people said. It's the milishy.

There were more than a hundred of them. They straggled into the Diamond in a shambling file with the lanterns of townspeople leading them on. An officer whom no one had ever seen before, was marching ahead; he kept swinging around, limping backward, staring down the indefinite line. "Close up, men," he entreated. "This isn't any picnic, just because some of you have sweethearts watching." People were calling from windows, from doorways; the drums and the fife cut their medley short. "Close up, close up! *Raaat ob-leek* . . ." The dim figures stumbled, closed a few ragged gaps. *"Ult! . . . To the left—uss!"* Yellow lanterns got in the way. So many of the soldiers seemed thin and stooped, frail shapes oppressed by unfamiliar and monumental burdens. "*Kommm-pah-neee* . . ." His command of dismissal rose high above the sudden hum of conversation.

The officer added, "Men. Remain within call. Don't leave this town square without permission." He walked wearily toward the lights of the hotel, holding up his sword scabbard as if the weight were too much for him.

Dan watched one figure, much taller than the rest, detach itself from the crowd. He went forward hesitantly, with the groceries still under his arm. He asked, "Elijah?"

"Yes," a cracked voice said. Hud loomed in front of him; he seemed like an amazingly thin, long-legged monkey, trained for bizarre pranks, with the little cap cocked tightly over one ear.

They shook hands.

"What's all this? We didn't expect you back this soon."

Huddlestone explained, "We were ordered here from Harrisburg. The rest of the regiment's out at Swift Run, but we fellows moved on tonight. A lot of the local boys are here."

"Regiment?"

"They've put our set in with about seven hundred more. We're the Twenty-sixth, now. The Gettysburg boys make up Company A . . . The train got off the track at Swift Run; I shouldn't wonder if it was the doings of Copperheads."

"Was anyone hurt?"

"Not to notice. The balance of the Twenty-sixth will be here in the morning."

Dan asked, "What's the matter with your voice?"

"Matter with it? I don't know—drilling, like as not. We've been having the devil's own time: muster wasn't completed until Monday, and we left Harrisburg yesterday, to feel out the rebels over west."

"You mean—" It was impossible; a patently childish design which had somehow found its way into the affairs of war. "You mean that your regiment had only two days of training, and now you're going against the—enemy?"

Elijah thudded his musket upon the ground. "Well, you know our own bunch—most of Company A— has been drilling for months. Of course, some of the rest—"

They stood there, mute blots of darkness, staring through the gloom. "Can you stop out at the house with me and have a bite to eat?" Bale asked. "We'll get up a bottle of sherry—"

"No, I'm sorry. If I can get leave, I'll go over home to see Ma. I don't suppose Mealy is in town."

"You could drive out there," Dan said, "but they'd all be a-bed."

"Probably. Well, she'll probably hear about us and come in, in the morning. I don't know how soon we'll move out of town—not till the rest of the regiment gets here."

Again they shook hands. Dan left Huddlestone in front of the grocery store; in the wan light of the windows he could see that Elijah's uniform was new and stiff, though already muddy, and he wore a broad splash of chevrons on his sleeve.

"You're a sergeant?"

"Well, the men think so." Hud's drooping mustache twitched; he seemed leering as he grinned. "Goodnight, Dan. Get down early in the morning; we may march before very late."

Under the direction of a bearded officer, squads of the tired men were trying to stack arms in front of the shop platforms. The muskets kept sliding down with a bristling clatter. "No. *No!*" the lieutenant was growling. "Hook each over each. Like this. You, there, private—hold yours. Now you lean yours on. Now—you." Bale could hear the clinking and thud of their guns, hear the hollowness of spoken words, all the way to the little bridge over Stevens Run.

The night-barking dog on McPherson's ridge was making no sound; perhaps he had been housed and muzzled against the fear of a raiding enemy. Now Dan could realize the pervasive menace back of the leafy hills. The few stars looked flat and swaddled by wet clouds, and the moon was only a vague sickle beneath them. Somewhere at the end of this road were other men with muskets; no one would have to direct their armament . . . Silently, he went into his brooding house. He felt oppressed by monstrous desolation.

The Fanning place showed no gleam of light; it might have been swallowed in a thousand miles of steppes. And nineteen hours before, Bale and the woman had agreed that they would not be together this night . . . He sat on the couch in the black living room. In that space, their wrapped bodies had lain. He felt the inevitable, prickling surge of remembrance . . . her hair in his mouth, the smell of her clothes. His throat made a rough sound.

After he had gone to bed, his nervous brain kept leaping about, centering on Elijah in broad chevrons, Elijah with a pancake cap, frightened school-boys trying to stack arms, a captain who limped with the pain of raw leg muscles. He dreamed: Lucas Mite walked through the dry prairie grass of autumn, through deep blue-stem, with a gun in his hands. Dan could see Mite's face as clearly as he had ever seen it: rusty beard, the big-pored nostrils, the sad gray eyes so level and cool. Mite was hunting for prairie chickens, the birds cheeped about in dry tangles underfoot, you could never find them . . . Lower, he bent, lower—pointing his shotgun this way and that. Then, without one shiver of warning, a wall of spectral cripples in new uniforms had risen up all around him. They opened their mouths; they said nothing; they blinked blind, white eyes . . . And from this dream, half roused by the wailing cry he made and coasting into deep forgetfulness again, Dan did not awake until the next day.

The sky was bulging with gray clouds. Children's voices soared with the common shrilling of startled poultry, but beyond their murmur was the dull, earthy march of men who walked together. Startled, Bale leaped out of bed and to the window. Through the motionless elms he could see a broad, purplish tide coming up the road; splotches of faces above the deep color, mingling, bobbing, row after row.

He had not intended to sleep like that. Sleepless nights, hours of passion, the eternities of brooding had worn him down. Now there were a hundred things which he must do, distressing tasks he must complete; he had a sickening notion that there was something concerning Elijah Huddlestone and all the rest, which only he could arrange . . . He snapped his suspenders over his shoulders, cursed monotonously as he forced his naked feet into his boots. He ran down the stairs. The head of the column was passing as he reached the front fence; bare-calved boys scampered alongside, wheeling their arms in circles, screeching. "You blame kids skeedaddle back to town, now," a youth's voice shouted. "Want that the rebels should get you?" The heavy shoes, squad and trample and squad again, trying to keep step . . . why do they have to carry so much with them? Tall knapsacks, stuffed and enormous; the sausages of blankets; canteens, pouches, belts, bayonet scabbards rattling, a multitude of seminarians and lame men and old men, all trying to keep step, like burdened peddlers in their chafing uniforms.

"Hud!" he called. This must be Company A; there was old man Gubbe, but a few years younger than John Burns, trying to measure his pace with the college students. They carried their muskets like hoes and brooms and buggy whips, every which way: shouldered, sloped, hung by the slings. Pink face, wax face, the gnome face of a lawyer's clerk—Almighty God, it was that lad who'd read law with Julius Orcutt, and he had a club foot—they were letting him go. This was all nightmare, a nightmare worm which marched in the morning on fifteen hundred feet.

Elijah, so tall. "Dan . . ." He waved his musket.

"Good luck," Bale heard himself rasping.

So new, right off the shelves—their dark clothes. The hard leather belts squeaked and whined, stiffness reluctant to go out of them. Pink face, stubble face, gnome head all turning, twitching around. The boys began to call under their breath, the snub-nosed, the crazy young . . . that fellow Bale. Yep, where's his gun? Oh, he left it out west; fightin' Indians. Somebody hooted, clapping his hand against his mouth: "owwwow-wowwow." "Silence in the ranks!" howled Elijah. The laughter sighed down; only a titter now, a mumble of shoes over the damp macadam.

Company B, Company C . . . he didn't know them. He turned and walked back into the house. The little boys were returning down the slope, pointing their sticks at every tree and bush. Bang! Bang! A throng of women stood far back by the Pike gate, bulbous pyramids of pink and brown against the hazy foliage. A bell at the seminary began to ring.

Long after they were gone, Dan imagined that he could hear the mumble of their march past the door, hear the gray-haired officers chanting at them . . . He washed, dressed himself for the day, and went to build a fire in the kitchen stove. It was far into the forenoon; he had slept like a sot.

He ate, listlessly. The hours trembled by. He picked up his hat. Go to town for tobacco . . . yes, bacon. He'd forgotten so many things, the evening before. This day was darker and darker, a lead casket shaped around the world, and when he stopped to turn up his coat collar against the gray drizzle, it seemed as if he could hear the sound of firing. He leaned beside the gate, listening. Five minutes. Ten . . . Maybe it was thunder, a reluctant spasm of the rain-clouds. Still, it had come to his ears as no thunder ever came before.

He walked to the Diamond. The roads were empty of refugees; no high-piled wagons in sight. Clink-hofer's grandchildren played quietly, cradling dolls in a Boston rocker on the deep porch. "Bye oh bye oh bye," the white-braided-eldest girl sang, a tuneless rhythm thrown out by the plastered wall. And Mrs. McBride was calling across the road to some other neighbor, "Yes. Then you just beat it up with two eggs, but be sure you take out the yelks first." The red bricks and board canopies of the business section sent back the mighty echoes of his footsteps, an accusing slap, slap like spanking hands. There were only six rigs in the entire Diamond. Everyone seemed to be hidden away.

Julius Orcutt met him as he mounted the step in

front of the grocery. "It's coming close, Daniel," he said.

Bale nodded.

The lawyer had a brown paper envelope in his hands. He was mutilating a loose corner of it between his thumb and first finger. "They are the last we have to send. If the Southrons attack them—"

"It's murder!" Dan cried. "God damn it, what are people thinking of?"

Orcutt drew in his chin. "They're thinking of our great country, Dan—that's what they are thinking of! Would that you'd think of it, too."

"You go to hell," Dan said. He stopped, knotted his fists, and then went into the store. Five men were looking at him; they had heard what passed outside. Mr. Pock sidled nervously from behind the counter. "Something?" he trilled.

"Yes, tobacco. I want a pound of bacon . . . no, two pounds. Your medium-best coffee: the small size sack. Sulphur matches" . . . the group of customers pushed close together. One of the men whispered a word or two. "Correct!" someone said explosively.

Bale went outside, carrying his purchases in a broken wooden box. Orcutt was standing beside one of the canopy posts, waiting for him. "Mr. Orcutt, I'm sorry," Dan said.

The lawyer put his loose hand on Dan's sleeve. "We have always been friends. Pentland Bale and I— These are parlous times. A man speaks in wrath, and does not know why."

"Don't think the worst of me."

"I shan't, Daniel, I shan't. I know that you are not one with those—those—" He gulped, touched his hat, and went away up the hollowed stairs to his office.

People were in the road by the turnpike gate again, heedless of the rain, crowding expectantly around a ten-year-old boy who sat on a folded scrap of blanket, astride an old white mare. Face after face turned toward Bale as he came forward, then all twisted back once more.

"Your Pa send you, Roger?" rose out of the buzzing.

The child on the horse, nodded. His face was frightening—his lips were so utterly bloodless.

Dan asked of young Mrs. McBride, "He's brought news?"

She bobbed an affirmative. "Yes, they struck against the enemy out by Marsh Crick. This is Ed Striger's boy, he brung the word, just now."

"What happened?"

"Our boys give way. Up toward Mummasburg. They went north with most of the rebels after 'em, Roger says."

The boy repeated, "There was a lot of shooting. A lot. Ma and Aunt Kate got down in our cellar. Pa's laid up with ague, but he said I should ride to town and tell folks."

The town council, people said. Yes. He ought to go right down to Mr. Kendlehart and Mr. Orcutt and the rest. The white mare stood sadly, head bent and tail all knotty with burrs. As Dan went on toward his house, he could look back and see the crowd scattering, as if moved by a horrific impulse, and never intending to gather again . . . No more sound of firing. So he had heard muskets, and not the echo of thunder. Perhaps Elijah was killed.

"No," he said aloud.

He walked into the dim kitchen and thumped his grocery box upon the table. *Dan . . . oh, Dan.* It was a ghastly whisper. He thought for a moment that some wraith had cried aloud inside his ears, a baleful ghost which would torment him forever. *Dan . . . Dan!* It was in the buttery. He stumbled across and flung open the door. Two faces stared out of the dimness, the smells of sour milk and cold eggs. Elijah, and some face he did not know. Huddlestone was lying on the floor: the other man squatted against the wall with a gun in his hands. "Christ," Bale said.

Elijah smiled feebly. His chin was dirty with powder; it looked as if his mustache had melted and run. "We just scooted in here a minute ago. You were gone. We've been running like all hell, through the woods . . . Are the rebs here yet?"

"No." Dan dropped to his knees. "You're wounded? Hurt?"

"I've just got an awful gut-ache, from hurrying so . . . This is Fisher. He's from here; Penn college. We got cut off." He took a deep, shivering breath. "Ran into them, three or four miles out. God," he sobbed suddenly, anguished and bitter, "you ought to see them! We haven't got any soldiers like those."

"Is anyone killed?"

The Fisher boy nodded. "Guess so. It all happened so quick. The regiment retreated up toward Whitmer's farm, with most of the rebs chasing them. Those gray sons a' bitches gobbled up most of Company B. The boys were yelling, 'I surrender, I surrender, I won't shoot, you got us.' It was terrible. Huddlestone and I got chased off, over past some bushes."

"We laid low," Elijah gasped. "Then we watched our chance and cut for it. Nobody saw us, I guess. But the regiment'll be dead or cut to pieces by night."

Dan cried, "Take off those uniforms, right away!

I'll get you some other clothes. The rebels won't know, if they come—"

Huddlestone shook his head. He grasped the two lower shelves on either side, and pulled himself up. He scraped around in the corner for his musket; through all their flight he and Fisher had kept their guns and ammunition, though their other accoutrements were gone. "No. We thought they'd be pushing us, but if they're not in sight yet we've still got a chance."

"A chance—?"

"We'll get along south, towards Maryland. Our army's down southeast of here somewhere; they can't be sitting in Virginia all this time. Maybe we can find them, instead of getting caught. No use in our going towards Harrisburg; the Butternuts will be all over north of here, in a couple of hours . . . Fisher and I said we'd rather die than go to a prison pen."

Dan said, "Now, be sensible. You'll die if you keep running around the country this way—"

Elijah's teeth showed in a snarl. "Come on, Tom Fisher!" He leaned heavily against the door casing.

"Wait a minute," Dan ordered. "Stay here." He ran through the house and out to the front gate. The rim of the western hill was smooth, unpeopled. He went back to the fugitives. "Come on," he said. "Let's get over to Fanning's. You'll never reach Maryland on foot, not if the Confederates are close behind you."

The drizzle had ceased, but clouds still blocked close above the trees, humid and oppressive. The three men climbed over the pasture fence. Huddlestone's face was green and drawn; he moved as if his joints were grating together, and the younger soldier gazed at him with some concern. Bale put his arm under Elijah's arm-pits, and half lifted him along the twisting path. "I'm all right," Hud kept sighing. "Let me alone. Damn it! I can get along—" Fisher trotted ahead, carrying the two muskets.

Cybo lunged at them, pink-eyed, barking. They kicked him out of the way. "In here," Bale directed. "This is the cob-shed. Lie low for a minute." He raced up to the rear stoop and pounded upon the door jamb. "Mrs. Fanning!" he called.

"She's resting," came Irene's voice, tight and disbelieving. Then she appeared in the kitchen doorway, and slowly her hand crept against her mouth . . . She whispered, "Oh, come in—quickly! Gretel's gone to Spangler's . . . everyone's gone except mother—"

Inside, the startled shadows bending beside them, he fed on her mouth. "It's a world gone to rack," he whispered.

"Lover." Her arms binding him for a moment. "But—here? You must not—oh, Dan, you—" She whined in fright, falling away from him, and knowing suddenly that this was Tyler Fanning's house . . . Tyler Fanning's people all around—specters of her betrayal swooping close—

Bale pointed toward the barns. "The militia's been scattered by the rebels. They're close—coming in along the Pike. Elijah and another fellow are hiding out there in the barn. There's a chance for them to avoid capture by hustling south at once; the main Federal army is on the way north, they think . . . Will Mrs. Fanning let them take a horse and any sort of a rig, and try it? I'll pay for it, if they are unsuccessful."

Irene said, "Of course. I'll tell her. Of course they mustn't be—" She caught up her gown and sped in to the front hall. Her voice rapped out, fiercely, "Mother!" and there was an answering groan upstairs. The stairway echoed crazily as the woman's pointed heels stabbed against it. Dan waited, trying not to look at the room around him . . . A despoiler, he thought. I can't forget. In my house it is not the same. Here—

"The Jenny Lind." The girl's voice echoed down from the top of the stair-pit. "Mr. Bale, mother says for them to take the Jenny Lind. The top was broken when Demon had the runaway, but it rolls nicely still. It's at the far end of the shed . . . Take the colt. He's broke to harness, and the rebels will carry him off if they come to Gettysburg . . . Father's gone in the carriage, with Demon." The ceiling quaked as Mrs. Fanning climbed out of her bed.

Dan called, "Very well. I'm buying the colt, if anything goes wrong. Please tell her." He ran to the cob-shed: Fisher was peering out through a crack. Elijah sat on a saw-horse while Dan and Fisher rolled the broken Jenny Lind buggy from its deep ruts in the straw. They hunted savagely for single harness. Dan went into the stable run and led out the bay colt. Mrs. Fanning was standing at an upstairs window, wailing damply, a pink wrapper caught around her. "Father loves that colt . . . he's gentle. Even my daughter-in-law rides him . . . poor, poor boys! And your dear mothers, they must feel—"

Bale shoved Elijah into the splintered seat beside young Fisher, and handed their muskets to him. Elijah clasped the guns in his trembling hands. "Dan, I'll get myself some of those devils yet. Chase us around the country this way—" They waved at the pink hulk in the upper window. The colt danced out of the driveway; ungreased axles screeched without mercy . . . They went pitching south, and east again; the wheels were throwing out a thin soup of mud. They went out of sight behind the nearest grove.

Mrs. Fanning staggered back from the window. "They make me think of honey boy. What if he'd be captured and court-martialed and— I can't stand it! Dan, Dan!" she cried. "Will you go down to the factory after father? The Confederates—coming—"

"They've heard the news downtown by this time, Mrs. Fanning. He'll be here before long, I'm sure—if not, I'll look out for you until he comes." He considered for a moment. "Perhaps it would be a good idea for you to hide your valuables. They say invading armies seize them: I don't know."

Irene stood on the back stoop, twisting a handkerchief in her hands. "They've been hidden since Monday, Mr. Bale." Her face called, oh lover, it has been so long since the last realization—so many hours—yes, you know—you feel the separation of our starved and pitiful selves—

"I'll keep an eye out for you, until dark," Dan said. "If Mr. Fanning doesn't arrive soon, I will be back." He strode through the wet weeds of the pasture. By the time he reached his own yard, he could hear a marvelous, sodden murmur beyond Oak Ridge—the sound of a hundred and fifty wagons rumbling on a damp and rocky Pike.

He went out through his gate and looked up the hill. In the low mist, a troop of cavalrymen loomed tremendously on the summit. Seen through the haze of wetness, they were spectral and Tartaric. More crowded there . . . More. He heard a yapping word of command; a horse squealed; then the herd began to pour down the long slope toward him. Resounding hoofs . . . He heard Mrs. Knouse cry out; her door slammed, and she was moving things against it.

Book Three

THE
CHAMBERSBURG
PIKE

1.

Irene bundled Cybo into the cellar, shut the door, and came up to the hall. She could hear the clinking of bottles in Mrs. Fanning's room, hear her windy groans, and the dull clanging of heavy chinaware as she leaned against the wash-stand. She was taking turpentine, a few drops in a spoonful of alcohol; the treatment had been prescribed once long before when Mrs. Fanning suffered an internal hemorrhage, but still she persisted in inflaming her kidneys with it . . . Spirits of turpentine came out into the hall, sweetish smell of invalidism, and now the whole upstairs was an apothecary's shop.

The girl turned away from the stairs. She had neither the courage nor the desire to go up and embrace Mrs. Fanning, moan sympathetically, touch her stuffed body with its hot, wet skin. She thought, "And she did let them have the colt and the Jenny Lind. Other people might not have let them. Maybe she would never have done it, if it hadn't been for the thought of Tyler." Irene went out on the porch and looked southeast across the sloping meadows. A wagon was moving south in Long Lane, two horses whipped into a straining gallop, the wagon loaded with tiny gray and black dolls. At that distance, and in the gray haze, the heads of the dolls seemed disconnected from their bodies. She wondered idly why a human body seemed to come apart when viewed from a long way off. That was an uninterpreted analogy which she could not pursue—too remote and incapable, she thought—suspended here on this high porch behind the budding trumpet vines . . . The wagon was moving slower, slower; it stopped, and a doll went chasing back to pick up something which had fallen into the road. Then image and wagon blurred together once more; the toy horses twinkled out of sight past a row of peach trees.

Wheels hummed closer at hand. Mr. Fanning and Demon rioted up from the Fairfield road; the mares rocked wildly and they were frightened, their coarse manes slapped in the wind. Demon was holding his arms stiffly extended as he grasped the reins. He had lost his hat. Irene ran to the edge of the steps and pressed her palms beside her mouth.

"Look out!" she heard a woman's thin voice screeching. "Becky's tug strap—look out—"

The team swayed aside and the front carnage wheel ripped through a lilac bush, broken branches whistling against the box. Becky and Bright stopped in their tracks, snorting and blowing; the loose tug was trailing around Becky's legs and she kept trampling it nervously.

Mr. Fanning climbed down and labored across the damp lawn with a faded carpet-bag in his hand. The bag was heavy and he carried it clumsily. He did not look back at Demon and the tormented mares.

"The rebels are—"

She said, "Yes, yes! Any moment. We know . . . I thought the team was running away."

"Where is mother?"

"Upstairs." She tried to say, "Turpentine. She's tak-ing—" It was the first time she had ever seen Mr. Fan-ning when he looked untidy, with his waistcoat hanging open and soiled cuffs far down over his hands.

"This bag," he muttered. "It's from the factory. Pa-pers and letters—my contracts—I have currency from the safe, more than seven hundred dollars, part gold. We must—"

She nodded. "Give it to me. I will hide it."

He took a deep breath, then pressed the handle deci-sively within her grasp. He limped on into the hall, and she could see his white, delicate hand trembling as he rested it on the newel-post. "Mother," he called, "I'm coming—" and went up the stairs as rapidly as he could go.

A sound was driving itself against the girl's ears. As she looked across the mound of shrubbery beside the porch, she was positive that the poplar trees shim-mered, the fences were blurry and titillating, all up-rooted and quivered by the pulsation of the long ridge. Wagons and men, whip-snappings, some kind of struggling outcry and chatter, all minced by the stupendous turning of wheels . . . wagons with sick men, wagons full of sacked grain and gunpowder and corned-beef, an awful migration pushing its sound ahead.

This could not be the invading army so soon, so soon. "Why," she thought daintily, "they haven't given us time!" The bag of papers and money weighed against her leg; she imagined that she had Mr. Fanning's whole factory, his past and present life and a good share of his future, all his assured comfort, there it was in her hand ready to be hidden. The barn. No, invading armies burned barns and haystacks. The house . . . Tyler had told her what happened to house after house in Virginia. Down in the ground, deep under a blanket of beetles and white roots, that was the place for burying.

There was an abandoned well beneath a Baldwin tree, just across the driveway. Once, said Mrs. Fanning, it had been covered by a wooden platform, and Tyler had barely missed going to his death when the rotten planks gave way. Now the hollow menace was covered by two limestone slabs; quack-grass wove a skein around them.

The woman ran across the driveway and knelt beside the stones. The damp stain of grass was pushed through dimity and muslin and silk, printed on her knee as she rested there. She clawed a sodden corner of ancient wood from beneath the left-hand slab and forced the flat bag through the opening. A little chorus of gravel and the dust of rotten wood went trickling down into mysterious water far below. With numb hands she wrenched off the wide sash around her waist and tied it to the handle of the carpet-bag. Half-hitch, half-hitch, half-hitch; it was the only knot she knew. She fastened an end of the sash to the wormy corner of hewn plank, and forced it back into place . . . Wet grass rubbed and gritted between her fingers as she tore up handfuls of it and strewed them around the corner of the well. Before this, she had removed the bandage from her arm—that long wound which the Fannings knew was caused by a jagged splinter in her closet—but it seemed that she was courting suppuration, rubbing pollution after pollution into the encrusted scar.

At last she stood up, her gown all stained, and she looked at the well. "It's safe," she said, half aloud, "if they don't become suspicious and begin to pry around. And if the planks don't give way—" Past the barnyard, down the sloping road in front of Bale's and Knouse's, moved a thickening tide of men. "Some have horses," Irene said to herself, "and some have none." Long poles thrust up, muffled and wound with dun rags. "I suppose those are their banners—covered because it's rainy. Tyler calls them 'colors cased.' Some have horses, some have none."

She mumbled it over, again, again, as she moved up the driveway. It was like a counting-out game which she had played long before. How long? Fifteen years? Oh, the war had been a war for all of fifteen years . . . *William-Trimmity-is-a-good-water-man-catches-hens-puts-them-in-pens-some-lay-eggs-and-some-lay-none-White-Foot-Speckle-Foot-oh-be-gone-and-O-U-T-spells-out-some-have-horses-some-have-none* . . . She heard Mr. Fanning cough, up in the open window; he stood there staring at her and jerking his whiskers. "It's hid," she called. He murmured inanely. "What? What's hid . . . oh, yes—"

"It's hid in the old well. I tied it to my sash and let it down."

"They will see the sash, I fear."

"No, I covered it with grass and—and things . . . Look!" she cried. "Past the barn—they—"

He turned away. "Mother," he said, and his voice seemed humble and fumbling, "mother, here are the rebels. You can see them . . . I was assured that there would be no invasion. I told Tyler, in all confidence—" Then Mrs. Fanning was at the window beside him.

His words, falling limply. "What did—Demon do with the team?"

"He took them into the barn."

Demon, Demon, let the team be. Come in the house and hide. Oh, Bedford, and Gretel's still at Spangler's or I don't know where! They took the colt, father . . . no, the Huddlestone boy and— Demon, come inside—

The old man shuffled out of the dim amphitheatre of the barn and stood in the wide doorway, blinking up at the window with his one eye. "Cayn't send me back to Mayland," he said. "Mist Fanning, 'em rebel cayn't fotch me back to Mayland. I got Freedom Papeh in my bosom. Old Mist Capple he give me Freedom Papeh long time ago, so 'em damn rebel cayn't make me slabery no mo'."

Mrs. Fanning squealed. A small man on a wiry black horse leaped the pasture fence and came cantering up toward the yard. He swung carefully past the garden patch, his horse's feet making clean, dark U's along the slaty cabbage rows. Behind him, three more men on foot were scrambling over the fence. The mounted soldier wore a citizen's coat of loose brown weave; he had a revolver buckled around his waist, and a huge grain-sack tied behind his saddle.

He took off his felt hat, and smiled. His teeth were small and even and yellow. There was a wispy fuzz of tawny beard on his chin; perhaps he was eighteen years old. "Quattahmastah's odduz!" he announced. "Have yawl got any speh hosses, ma'am?" The three men came hurrying across the garden, stumbling heedlessly through beans and beets. One of them reached down and jerked up a carrot; he wiped it against his gray shirt and bit out a large, orange bite, and all as he ran . . . They carried rifles slung over their shoulders, the butts chafing against their thighs.

Mr. Fanning grasped the window ledge with both hands. He said, shrilly, "I have no horses to spare, sir." Down in the cellar, Cybo was barking without a pause for breath.

The youth bowed politely; he looked toward Irene, and suddenly there was a silver spice in his narrow blue eyes. "Lacy," he ordered, without turning his head, "look in the bahn."

Demon was waving something wadded and dirty in his hand. "Freedom Papeh! Cayn't fotch me back to Mayland, Mist Rebel—"

"Shut yo' mouth, nig," said one of the infantrymen. They pushed the old man out of the way and vanished into the stamping, scented blackness . . . Bright whickered with annoyance. The men came out, leading both horses. "Two mo' old nags out in the field, Capting," said one soldier. He ran a hand approvingly over Becky's muzzle. The mare blew and jerked up her head. "Sho," murmured the soldier.

The young officer still held his shapeless hat on the pommel of his saddle. "Reckon theh five-yeh-olds; yawl take 'em along. Leave any mo' old nags behind; we got too many now." He fumbled in his coat pocket and drew out a fold of damp paper. He looked up at the window and saluted gravely. "Do you want I should write you an odduh, seh?"

Cybo's yelping: *row, row, row, row.* Mrs. Fanning had disappeared. Irene could hear the reluctant sagging of the bed . . . and now the fat woman was lying down, trying to huddle deep in her sanctuary. She would want more turpentine—

"Will that order be honored in Confederate money?" Mr. Fanning asked, slowly.

"All sech items will be paid at a time subsequent to the establishment of the complete and undisputed independence of the Confederate States of America, seh," the boy rattled.

Mr. Fanning patted the window-sill hysterically. "No. No. I will never see that day, nor will you! Take my horses, but please do not harm my household or my—"

The rebel blushed angrily, and saluted again. He swung his horse in a swift dance. "We hahm no one," he said, but he was looking at Irene as he said it. Once more he bowed; he leaned forward in the saddle. The black gelding thudded across the yard. "Fetch 'em along, Lacy," the captain called, waving his hat. The black skimmed the fence, up and over and down; he loped away, twisting along the path which angled east below Knouse's. The carrot-nibbling soldier ran ahead of his companions and opened the wide gate into the pasture, and closed it meticulously after they were through. Bright and Becky filed through the bushes, each ridden bareback by a soldier, with the third man bringing up the rear; the mares were wrenching their necks and neighing at Demon.

The old negro crouched beside the manure pile. He began to keen shrilly to himself. "Take Bright and Becky to slabery . . . em damn rebel cayn't take Demon, but take my fine team . . ." He was humming, swaying his head, building a foolish song out of it. A tear coasted slowly alongside his flat nose.

Mr. Fanning groaned from the window: "Daughter! There's no help for it. We should be thankful if they spare our home. Come into the house at once; these are soldiers, my girl—enemies! A woman—"

"I know all that," she said, drearily. "There are more troops over there in the road. Past the Bale house. I'm—" she began to mumble, and she did not care whether he heard the words or not—"I am going over there and—ask Mr. Bale what to do, about the horses. Maybe we can get them back. Maybe he—"

She reached the fence, bent her steel-skirt around her knees, and began to slide between the rails. *My child* he kept calling, *come back at once!* She began to run, the rough green weeds slashing at her clothes. At that moment she did not care how much her father-in-law was outraged by her brazen going-away. This car of war had come pushing through the hills, as in her nightmare thoughts: it was here, trundling down the Chambersburg Pike, and she had best see it as it came. She could not slump in a hot room which smelled of turpentine, and pray and sigh with aliens. Dan, she thought: I must be with him. I would rather be at his side.

She looked back when she was nearly across the field, and she could see Mr. Fanning standing out on the kitchen stoop, waving his arms at her. "Gone crazy," she said. "He is sure that I've become mad. And I have become mad, but not on this day . . . in this same field, and long ago, days and days and days."

Two shabby, dark-eyed men were drinking water at the Bale well. Muddy haversacks and rolls of ragged blankets lay on the step behind them: they wore their muskets slung, and the damp barrels gleamed softly . . . They moved back from the well, forcing a somber, steady gaze at Irene as she hurried past. "Brothers," she said to herself. "They look so very much alike. They look like pictures of Israelites in the wilderness. John the Baptist . . . some queer, unhappy prophets who carry guns as they go out to spread a peculiar gospel. But like enough they are cutthroats." Then Dan Bale was beside her, and he had caught her hands.

He said, "I'm glad you came," and she nodded politely, as if this were a party, a lawn social where her presence was expected and desired. He released her hands: the rebels might see. Twenty feet away, beyond the ivory fence, the army moved in front of them. "Here's more cavalry," the man said in a matter-of-fact tone. "White's cavalry, those men told me. Some more passed a few minutes ago."

They were boys, but no boys like those who had gone up the road that same day. They cantered carelessly, wild hunters released from a dun frieze which hung all along the rainy Pike. They owned flapping hats of shapeless felt, drawn low over their eyes; their yellow faces were pinched and flat as the profiles on greasy coins.

Boy and boy again—one with drenched fuzz on his cheeks, one with the hairless face of an Indian girl, long snarls of hair brushing their collars. They had been foaled to the saddles, they would ride in them until they died. And every cavalryman had the dull butt of a carbine thrusting up beside his leg; they were weighted with revolvers, but few of them carried sabers. You could see embossed letters on holster flaps and saddle skirts as the troop jangled past. *US* . . . again, *US,* and the men for whom those leathers had been stamped were trellising Virginia thickets with their bones.

Behind these riders, the soaked macadam was forested with gray men and sloping muskets: they crunched up out of the hollow horizon and streamed down the hill past this gate. They were infantry; they came by fours with a peculiar, swinging stride which was half a run. The western valleys were shaking with wagons. Lone officers drifted beside the column, mounted shepherds: they wore waterproofs, they wore wet yellow jackets or blue Union capes. Their eyes rested momentarily on Bale and the woman with him—flat, pin-pupiled, the eyes of men who had seen altogether too many things, and were concerned with secret contemplations which no one else could ever define. Sorrels, blacks, roans, chestnuts, a very few grays, the horses were painted with clay, and in some strange manner they had all become of the same shape and gait: they held their heads alike.

A rout-step army, the noisy stretch of leather straining from buckle to buckle, loose shoes which rubbed and blistered and made the wearers walk like lame men. Voices above the mutter of their marching. "And Extra Billy's brigade, they got no Pike up that way . . . town is this?" "It's Gettessbug. Says they got them a shoe factory; place wheh they make shoes . . . stole them eggs at all. The lady made us a giff."

A young boy's chant, the key-bugle voice of one who had been a sophomoric orator at some drowsy academy: *Backward, turn backward, O Time in yo' flight, make me a child again just fo' tonight*. There was a rattle of laughter. "Yeh," someone called, "and a gal child at that—"

"They took Becky and Bright," Irene whispered.

He said, "They rode out of the gate below Mrs. Knouse's, a minute ago . . . I went out in the back yard when they first came by, but I could see Demon opening the stable door, and I knew that Mr. Fanning was home. Why did you come over here?"

She looked down at her knotted fingers. "Everything—went to pieces suddenly. I hid—" she lowered her tone—"I hid a bag for Mr. Fanning, and the next minute those men were in the yard. It seemed the natural thing for me to do, in some way—come over here, and stand beside you, and watch—"

She looked up, and his face was pale under its

brownness. "I did not do that," he said. "You'll have reason to doubt me. I should have remained with you, no matter how it made me feel . . . I think of you," and the trudging men tried to destroy his words with their canteen-clatter and multiple footsteps, "I think of you all the time. I have no peace, and no wish for any." He drew her back from the gate. Two men were beside them, the two sad Ishmaels who'd been drinking at the well. "We're obleeged," one of them murmured. They began to pull their hats over their ragged manes as they went out to the road.

A man called, "Major, what men are those?" A group of officers was working past the advancing infantry, legs of horses sliding and scrambling in the shallow ditch. One animal sprang ahead of the others, and its rider nosed it in between the two soldiers and the marching, head-turning files. "What is your command?" the officer snapped. He had the cragged forehead, the ascetic mouth of a religious warrior; a Masonic ring glittered on one of his thin hands as they clenched the reins.

"Taunton's foot-scouts, seh—".

The word went back to the other officers. "Taunton's men, General. But they've fallen behind."

"They should be beyond the head of the column, up with White." You thought: here is one accustomed to speaking in courtrooms and political rallies. The voice seemed absurdly civil, rising out of this seasoned, tigerish horde. The general pushed close, past his jingling staff; his thin horse had two white stockings under the plastered clay. "I am General Gordon." He bowed to the woman and to Dan. "General John B. Gordon, of Early's Division. Have my men been committing any misdemeanor on your premises, sir?"

"No," Bale said. "Not these men—they merely

asked for a drink of water. But some of your foragers took my neighbor's carriage horses." His glance went from Irene, back to the Roman-faced general.

Gordon had the eyes of a young judge who dreams of senates, who stands forever through his dreams decrying in measured sentences the rascality of a thousand Catilines. He took off his little cap with its splintered bill, and he bowed again. "Madam, I regret that the necessities of military strife call for the temporary acquisition of your property. Rest assured that not one man of the Army of Northern Virginia would appropriate a stick you own, were it not for the cruel exigencies of—"

"Oh, go away!" she cried.

Gordon stopped short; his sparse beard appeared to bristle. He turned his horse down the ditch. The staff officer with the Methodist face spurred quickly after him. Over his shoulder, the major called to the two wondering foot-scouts, "You men fall in with the Thirteenth until we bivouac!" and then went on, jolt and squeak and rattle, with the hoofs of the general's horse tossing wads of mud at him. The other officers saluted, bowed toward the gate, and racked behind.

The girl said, rapidly, "I don't know why I interrupted him. They were not my horses—they were the Fannings' . . . I was very rude, wasn't I? Wasn't I rude, Dan?" she kept demanding. A thin laugh was shaking in her throat, and her lips were blue.

He muttered, "Come. Come into the house, for pity's sake. I'll get you some wine. Oh, my dear," he cried, "if I were able to stop this whole thing! And we've seen no horrors; only the pageant, only—"

Mr. Fanning came hurrying through the yard; they could hear his gasping approach before he rounded the corner of the house. His shapeless pantaloons were drenched to the knees by the wet field-grass. "Thank heaven you are safe, girl! I came for you as soon as I could leave mother. Gretel is back from Spangler's." He demanded: "Daniel, why didn't you bring Mrs. Fanning home?"

"It's safe enough . . . Mrs. Fanning was upset about your horses, and she—"

The older man nodded. "Daniel, our administration has shown once and for all time, what it thinks of Pennsylvania. Permitting this—these—" Limply, he motioned toward the last company which shuffled along the road . . . The long approaching thunder was all around, now. "Wagons!" Bedford Fanning cried. He kept kneading his blue-veined hands together. "Wagons by the score! Look there—daughter, Daniel!—coming down the hill. They must have looted Chambersburg and Hagerstown of every last thing. And I have six thousand dollars' worth of boots and leather in the factory, this very moment!" His Adam's apple was jerking above his disordered stock and loosened collar. "If Tyler knew—"

Feverishly, he began to work his hands from pocket to pocket. "Tyler . . . ah, yes. The mail came. Somewhere I have letters. Two, from Tyler. They are marked on the same day, at Baltimore. Ah." He brought them out, dog-eared oblongs. "One is addressed to you, daughter, and one to his mother and me."

"Thank you," the girl said. She took the envelope; she did not look at it; the gray-topped wagons rumbled, and Mr. Fanning's voice had crept up until it was a screech.

Bale took his arm. "Did—Mrs.—Fanning—tell—you—colt—buggy?"

The man's bald head bobbed crazily. "Yes, yes! I don't blame—" he cried. In the whole of creation, there was nothing but this crunching grind of wheels. "Perhaps even now," he shouted in Dan's ear, "I will have Dazzle back. If those thieves had taken him, I'd never—"

"Hud and Fisher must be safe. Did you see them turn off the Fairfield road as you came home?"

"No. I saw nothing. I—"

"If they reached the Baltimore Pike before the rebels, they are safe. The Confederates are moving on Harrisburg; I heard them talking about it. They're not moving south from here."

Irene's shoulders began to sag. She kept staring intently at Dan and at her father-in-law, even though her face was white. "I feel so strange," Dan heard her say, "as if something inescapable had come to us—a car of war—some—"

He brushed Mr. Fanning aside, and picked the woman up in his arms, and carried her quickly into the house. She did not faint; she still kept looking at him, wide-eyed, and trying to master the jellying of her lips. "Feel so strange," she said.

"There's sherry on the top shelf of the cupboard," Bale told Mr. Fanning. He pushed open the library door and brought the girl inside; he could hear the older man limping out to the kitchen, opening a door, pawing among sacks and bottles.

Dan whispered fiercely: "Dear. Dear. You've got to get hold of yourself. You cannot do this. You—"

She nodded. He held her on the smooth cherrywood settee, with Pentland Bale's portrait glaring up above. "It was—Tyler's letter. I feel as if—as—" She sobbed with hot breath, "I don't love him. Oh, believe me, darling. I never loved him! But I'm sorry, sorry, sorry—" She took a deep breath, and closed her eyes. Mr. Fanning came in with sherry in a Willow cup.

The wagons made all the window glass dance in its tight frames. There were still a few mounted men riding alongside the jumbled train, but the main army had gone around the half-turn, across Stevens Run, far into the quiet nave of Gettysburg. The gate in front of Mrs. Knouse's home was still fastened by its little wooden block. No rebels had walked in her paths, or dug up her flowers . . . The mist was thickening into a definite rain; the lines of shambling, stolen horses bowed their heads and quaked on, invading, invading.

2.

There were three Confederate soldiers standing at the door of the town hall as Julius Orcutt came up the steps. Two of them were privates; they stood on either side of the door, bayonets fixed to their muskets; both men were chewing tobacco. "Just a moment," their officer said, and two guns lifted as one, narrow bayonets pointing at Orcutt's middle.

He said, "I am a member of the council." His face felt very hot, and he wondered whether the rebels would understand that flush, and know what he was thinking.

The lieutenant wore an untrimmed, black mustache which drooped heavily, hiding his mouth. He stood with his feet apart, his gauntleted hands clasped behind his back, and in each of his boot toes there was a broad crack through which the skin showed wet and pink. "What's your name?" he demanded.

"Julius Orcutt."

The officer said a word; butts of the guns dropped to the limestone, *k-kah*. Orcutt's sleeve brushed one of the rigid bodies as he went past. He wondered whether Benjy had ever pointed his bayonet at a man's stomach . . . the long room was damp, shadowy. It smelled of cigars and rusty stoves and wet woollen clothing. A kerosene lamp flickered at the end of the table, and Doctor Kendlehart sat in its blurred circle, writing, with men standing behind him and peering over his shoulder.

Manasseh Pock, the grocer, came sidling around the corner of the table . . . cheese, Orcutt thought, that's it—cheese: his face is sculptured from the rich yellow cheese he sells, and somehow I never realized it before . . . he offered a limp paper which had been many times folded and re-opened. "This is the enemies' requisition, Mr. Orcutt," came his hollow whisper.

I will not whisper, the lawyer vowed to himself. I am a good Union man, my only son is before Vicksburg, my wife's brother wore white cross-belts and was killed at Buena Vista, and we have his picture at home on the mantel-shelf.

"I regret that I was delayed. My wife has been indisposed—"

Outside, one of the rebel sentries moved his feet. Orcutt lifted the dirty foolscap sheet before his eyes, then lowered it and shook his head. "My specs are at the office."

Mr. Pock took the requisition from him.

"Headquarters Early's Division, Second Corps—"

corpse, he read it—"C.S.A. In the field near Gettysburg, Pennsylvania, June the twenty-sixth, eighteen sixty-three—"

"Louder, please," Orcutt snarled at him.

Pock whispered closer, shaking his head sadly. So much of this, he seemed to be thinking between the reading of the items, will come out of my store. Sixty barrels flour, seven thousand pounds pork (but they would take bacon, they say), twelve hundredweight sugar, six hundredweight coffee, one thousand pounds salt, ten bushels of onions, one thousand pairs shoes, five hundred hats.

"Is that all?" asked Julius Orcutt.

"Or—ten thousand dollars in money! They place this levy on the whole of the borough and county."

The lawyer took the paper from his hand, and looked at it. The script was a twisting fuzz . . . so many years, he thought. I should never have tried to memorize English Common Law by one candle . . . He let the requisition fall from his hand to the table. "The consensus of opinion, gentlemen?"

"We have been discussing the matter, and have reached a decision," Kendlehart said. "One moment—until I affix my signature." The pen-point grated sharply. Doctor Kendlehart lifted his letter and slanted it close to the lamp, although the room was not wholly dark. He read, deliberately and gravely. *Gettysburg, Pennsylvania, June twenty-six, eighteen hundred and sixty-three. General Early. Sir. The authorities of the borough of Gettysburg, in answer to the demand made by you upon the said borough and county, say that their authority extends but to the borough. That the requisition cannot be given, as it is utterly impossible to comply.*

"Well enough," Orcutt declared. He imagined that

he could feel a warm strength of muscles, flooding suddenly across his chest and into his shoulders and hips—why, he was thinking, even I could shoulder a gun if— "But I decry the abject humility of your tone, sir."

Kendlehart motioned for silence, and went on reading.

The quantities required are far beyond that in our possession. In compliance, however, to the demands, we will request the stores to be opened and the citizens to furnish whatever they can of such provisions, et cetera, as may be asked. Further we cannot promise. By authority of the Council of the borough of Gettysburg, I hereunto, as President of said Council, attach my name.

Orcutt was aware of their defensive glare, the whole tribe . . . oh you burgesses with fat buttocks, he snarled in his heart: you goat-beards! "Is that unanimous, sir?" he heard a counselor-at-law demanding, coolly and very far away.

"Practically, Mr. Orcutt. We feel that—"

"Orally, I hereby tender my resignation as a member of the council. My written resignation shall be in your hands at the next meeting." He could not see; his eyes were coated with tears. He turned away, trying to find the door.

There was a ghostly whispering, whispering behind him. "You have nothing to lose," Pock whined. "Look at my position! They'll strip my shelves and cellar, and a pretty time I'll have trying to collect from the government."

Orcutt turned. "I would not give them one onion." He was throwing a death's-head grin squarely at them. "Not one onion—do you hear me? Not a pinch of salt or a boot-strap or a rotten potato. Let them kill us, if they dare, and take them. That is my opinion, my friends . . . Feeding the men who have killed, the men who are trying to kill—our sons. The union—" he groped in the well of his chest, tried to find words, they were not easily marshaled now. He wanted to say something about the flag, about forefathers who had died at Bunker Hill and Valley Forge, but all he could think of was Benjy: Benjy had the croup, and he was heating turpentine and lard in a pan over the wood-range, making it tingling and aromatic to drive the croup out of Benjy's chest.

He saw a tall rectangle of light all around him; it was the door and sentries still stood there, one on each side, bayonets and buckles. He heard a low chant in the street—the rustling, husky whisper of many men singing, and singing different songs . . . *come on, come on, come on, old man, and don't be a fool.* Gray shapes, scores of them, along the sidewalks, bunched under canopies, huddled against trees. Docile, and resting in the rain. Horses whinnied and stamped, along the street under the buckeye trees, all around the Diamond. The songs kept on, and the rain dripped, talking to itself and to this incursion. *O Mollie, O Mollie it's fo' you Ah must roam, Ah'm Jubal Eahly's soldier, Dixie is my—*

The film of momentary rage and bafflement was washing from Orcutt's eyes; he could see more clearly at every step, even with this night fog, rainy dusk squeezing down over the village. The Dryers' little girl stood alone on the step in front of her grandfather's harness shop, staring at a row of ragged men who squatted on the sidewalk before her. "Sho, I et two little gals lass night, dint I, Muley?" "You sho did. I et one myself." The child glared with fearless incredulity. "You—didn't—either," she kept murmuring. "You—didn't—either—I bet." Orcutt went on, picking his way past the huddles of resting soldiers. A line of freight wagons, farm carts, Conestogas, ambulances, was plowing directly across the Diamond, east toward the York Pike. Then perhaps they would not be staying here, perhaps they would go within the hour.

He heard a familiar voice, but distorted by sheer rage, rising close at hand: "Mind, mind! Leggo o' me, you damn Secesh—" A big circle of men had formed by Pock's store. A tall man, Orcutt could look over the packed shoulders and twisting heads and see old John Burns being dragged across the sidewalk by young soldiers who held his arms pinioned against his sides. The constable was holding back with all his might, rigid as a poker, his stubborn feet scraping as the captors hauled him forward. There was all the venom of rattlesnakes in the old man's eyes.

Someone rode rapidly against the edge of the crowd, on the opposite side; a big horse surged into the group, head drawn high. "Look out," shrilled a voice, "it's ol' Jube . . ." Elbows, knees, gouging metal—men stepped upon Orcutt's feet, stumbling, giving way as the rider pushed into the circle. He was saturnine, round-shouldered; his beard was a mass of stained strings. "What the God damn hell's the matter?" he screamed.

"Gen'ral Eahly, seh . . . this fellow was abusin' us—"

"Hell," squealed Early. "He's old enough to be yo' grand-daddy, boys."

Burns lifted his hot eyes. "I ain't so old, you damn rebel. I'm constable of this borough, and I'll enforce the law, and I don't need no Secesh thieves to put me about my business. I been in the army, too—teamed down in—"

The general forced his big bay around, and headed back through the scattering infantry. "Call the provost and place him under arrest," he ordered. Other officers rode forward to join him. "Lieutenant Dilse has jest repo'ted . . . town council, seh." Early's wiry voice skewered up again: "To the devil with the Yankee council!" and then Orcutt could hear him saying something about York. Two soldiers emerged from the crowd, with John Burns clutched between them; they trotted him off across the Diamond. I wonder if they will shoot him at sunrise, Orcutt thought. No, no, that is outlandish.

He went up the dusky stairway into his office, lit a lamp, and stood for a long time looking at a steel engraving of John Marshall, as if he had never seen John Marshall before . . . Bugles began to blat, all through the heart of the town, and out into the rainy country beyond; you heard their tight, brassy squawl relayed beyond the reach of any ears. Orcutt sat in his old chair with a handkerchief dampened and folded over his eyes, and tried to sleep. Sleep! when every nerve was pricking and alive, when the cells of his body crept out like mice, fleeing around the office . . . then he could feel them stealing back into his fingertips again. A brief oration resounded outside: the commanding voice of one trumpeting his verbiage to the patient troops who were his bench and his jury. *Soldiers! Your march through the enemy's country has been marked by Victory and Plenty*— Orcutt thought, "Another lawyer. A rebel one." He could hear the jingle of scabbards, the droning orders, the incredible sigh of two thousand men picking themselves up and moving obediently once more. But he was afraid to look out of the window, for fear they would not be marching away after all.

By the time darkness was thick and certain, they were gone. The rain held an intense glow of burning freight cars, east of town, and distantly men could recognize the sound of axes and crow-bars ripping at the rain-soaked railroad bridge. Julius Orcutt went home, holding himself with stiff dignity, the roof of his mouth dry as flannel. "At least," he thought, "I can tell Benjy that I did not treat with them. I have no reason to be ashamed." His wife was sitting in a merino wrapper, waiting for him. She was drinking an herb tea which was said to be good for the heart, and she cried to Orcutt that she had had another chill as soon as neighbors told her that the rebels were gone.

3.

Mrs. Huddlestone had a lamp in her front room, and she came to the window and peeked out when she heard Dan Bale walk up on the porch. Seen through the cheap, rippled glass of a nine-paned window, her face did not seem desiccated by worry but merely drooping in sad folds as if the bony re-inforcement behind it were somehow evaporated. She recognized him; he could hear her murmur, "Way a minnuh, Annyull." She went over to the table where her false teeth lay on a folded napkin, and she fixed them in her mouth before she opened the door.

"I've news of Elijah. Good news," he added quickly. Her mouth opened and shut; the teeth clicked; her dab of a nose began to show pink in the middle of her china face.

"Lijy isn't—hurt?"

"No. I've seen him." He came into the room, but she still stood beside the door, holding it open; she might have been expecting Elijah to follow him in, musket and all.

Wine-colored cloth with tiny fleurs-de-lis in its pattern, lay spread across the sewing table, tenting down two sides and spilling over the carpet like a twilled path for some noble to walk upon. The dress-form was a senseless statue beside Mrs. Huddlestone's chair: its meshed body had been expanded to the fullest— bust, waist and hips—and rich armor of the purplish bombazine had been pinned over its breast.

Elijah's mother had a silver thimble on her finger, and she kept tapping the thimble with her thumb as she gazed at Dan.

"He got away safely, Mrs. Huddlestone. He and a boy named Fisher—a student. I saw them go."

"He didn't get caught by—"

"No. No." He kept repeating it, sing-song doggerel. "No. Not hurt at all. When the regiment retreated, he and this Fisher were separated from the rest. They got as far as my place. Mrs. Fanning let them take a horse and rig. They drove south before the rebels reached town."

Water was dulling her eyes behind their spectacles; her eyelids blurred rapidly. She made a little crowing sound as she nodded toward the image beside the table. "That's for her."

"That—"

"It's going to be Mrs. Fanning's new gown. She wanted me to give her a fit some time before Sunday.

I was sewing on it just now. Ever since The Enemies come to town. Yes, ever since—The Enemies. I kept thinking about Lijy. I was—kind of worried. It was real thoughtful of you to come and tell me, Daniel." The water began to slide over her round cheeks . . . not tears, he thought. Just thin water, a nervous quantity of it which has been in her eyes all this time, and only overflows because it's no longer needed there.

He did not tell her of how Elijah was lying on the floor of the buttery, how he leaned against the door casing, how Fisher carried their muskets across the pasture. The buggy: they rolled it out. They, he said, harnessed the colt. They drove away. Yes, Elijah felt fine . . . The words were crowding in Dan's mouth; it seemed difficult to sort them and select the right ones to give to Mrs. Huddlestone, while she stood there spanking her thimble and blinking at him.

"First I heard about it," she said, "was when the Leen boys come running in the yard—they was trying to find their cat and put her in the woodshed, because The Enemies was coming." She sat down suddenly in her low, padded rocker. The little yarn balls on its arms danced and trembled. "I just kept sewing—kept cutting out the goods. Seemed as if I had to . . . I'm real glad about Lijy. Mrs. Endsor come and rapped on the window awhile ago, and she said the rebels was gone."

He nodded. "I inquired around to make sure. It was possible that the Confederates might have overtaken Elijah, somewhere down the Baltimore Pike. But they didn't go that way. Likely Hud will turn up in a day or two, unless he and Fisher decide to go south and join with the regular army."

The woman let her rocker creak for several minutes.

"Then I'll keep right on with the bombazine, so's I can give her a fit. The Enemies didn't capture any Gettysburg folks, did they, Daniel?"

"Only John Burns. They locked him up, but someone let him out as soon as the troops left. They're all over up north, folks say, on the Hunterstown road."

Again she said, "My." And then, babbling rapidly, "War is such an awful thing. An awful, awful thing, Daniel. I wish Lijy didn't think he had to go to it . . . Let me give you a snack. I feel as if I could eat hearty and give thanks to The Lord, with Lijy safe, and all."

He tried to excuse himself but she made him take two hermit cookies, from a big blue plate which she brought out of the kitchen. Crumbs surfeited his mouth as he went away through the murk . . . he and Elijah sat in their secret den behind the rhubarb bed, eating warm hermits, and Elijah running up to the door again and again to ask for more. A dozen years. He could not imagine such armies then, such a cancer of impending battles . . . He threw the remaining cookie into a forest of bushes; it seemed heartless and wasteful to do so; he walked toward the Diamond. The rain was a steady rustle all around, and the baggy macintosh which had belonged to Pentland Bale, swished and crackled as Dan moved in it.

With the morning, he thought, little boys would come splashing down York street. They'd appear not as they did ordinarily, after a rain—to squash the puddles of mud about, to work up mud puddings at every little bog—but to search for the dismantled droppings of the soldiers. Things would lie scattered among the ruts which marred the tenderest portions of the Pike: wads of chewed tobacco, torn straps, ears of corn, a ragged pair of drawers, and a scrap of money printed in Richmond. And always and always would be the apples of manure, high-piled, low-piled, sown freely—soft, hard, tan, greenish, yellow—long windrows of hasty excretion, the last record of an army which hurried as its beasts emptied themselves.

Men stood in groups on the porch of the Emblem Hotel, though only a few lights shone in the stores. There was a gobble of voices mingled with the hollow dripping of wooden eaves . . . "and put all the women-folks and children in the Presbyterian church or somewheres, and get what guns we can together" . . . "saw more soldiers already on the road from Mummasburg, and cannons by them" . . . they jabbered boldly, now that the gray men were gone to York. Dan passed the porch railing, a yard from the nearest group. Someone grunted, "Who is that?" and the chatter dulled down for a moment. A low voice muttered, "Any Copperhead could let 'em come in his yard and get a drink." Bale turned, and came up the steps. Sides of faces, whiskered profiles showing brown in the glow of hotel lamps. "Who said that?" he asked.

Nobody answered, but they were all looking at him. A one-legged shape clicked across from the doorway, balancing on a crutch. "Don't you mind that, Bale," Bart McKosh said. "Fanning's nigger just told me how you got Huddlestone and Tom Fisher away. If I had two good legs I'd kick the poop out of anybody says you're a Copperhead."

"I'd rather do it myself," Dan replied. "Thank you, anyway." He went down the steps and on around the edge of the Diamond.

A few doors west of the square, and on the south side of Chambersburg street, was a black vacancy between two buildings. Dan remembered it as a torment of his childhood, when first he was old enough to

come home alone at night. Daytimes the cavity was
innocent enough: a narrow waste where grass grew
tall, where rubble coasted slowly into a weedy exca-
vation which once had been a cellar. At night, and to
a frightened boy, the ten-yard gap was charged with
evil; no goblins but gibbered there, spitting their de-
cayed breath in your face no matter how fast you
ran . . . And now the phantasmagoria had come once
more. They twitched forward through the rain, and
one of them was an old man who carried a lantern in
his hand.

The goblin was saying, repeatedly: "Come out. Go
ahead. Walk careful, or I'll shoot." Feet sliding closer.
The voice cried, "And don't try to scrootch down in
that hole . . ." There were three figures, fumbling and
sodden, scourged by the rusty shaft of lantern light.
Once more the old man lifted his voice: he was John
Burns. "Who's that there? Stop, so's I can look at these
fellows."

Bale waited. Three hunched shapes stepped up on
the wet bricks. The lantern swung close to Dan's face.
"Oh," Burns said, and Bale could not analyze his tone
or sense what disapproval was there. "Hold this light
for me, Mister Bale. I got two prisoners."

One of them said, "Wawl never teched nothin'—"

"Jest a-restin', seh. A-restin' from the rain."

"I was pretty sure I heard somebody in that old
smokehouse behind Peiffer's." This was an honest duty
which Burns was doing; he did not gloat, but there
was a metal of reclaimed pride about him. "Hold
still, you." He jerked at the slide of the lantern.

Bilious skin, boys who had been very weary for
days at a time; they looked as if their thin faces had
been twisted from cheek to chin by some vicious

sculptor. Both were hatless; one wore a homespun shirt with no collar, and the other had a Zouave's jacket from which the buttons were gone. "Stragglers, I'll be bound," John Burns announced. He held a revolver in his left hand.

"They're not over fifteen," Bale said to him.

The old man growled, "I wasn't much more'n that when I fit the British. Come along, the two of you. I'm going to lock you up." He took the lantern from Bale and herded his prisoners away toward the Diamond. Someone yelled from the hotel porch, "What's goin' on over there?" The constable grunted, "Got two stragglers," but they could not have heard him over at the hotel. Then he seemed to ask the two Confederate boys a question; Dan caught the word, "Hungry," and there was a quick mutter of soft voices. Lantern beams bobbing, they splashed away through the mud . . . He will feed them at once, Bale thought. He will go to great inconvenience to find food for them; he will tramp back and forth in the rain, carrying things; all the time, he will threaten them with his revolver. The roof of the jail will lie between them and the rain. Let them thank whatever fortune they know, for this imprisonment.

And long before he reached his dark house, he was aware that his fear of the vacant lot between two buildings, the memory he held of fleeing past, the recaptured sense of whispering demons who herded in their stealth—all were forever muted and brushed over by this later hour. He would see Burns' rusty lantern swaying in dreams for years to come, no matter what else came to happen.

As he crossed the bridge over Stevens Run, he heard a splashing at the brookside, then once more only the slow tinkle of water from soaked timbers: he knew that another dun shadow had stumbled into the darkness at his approach ... someone crawled over the gate into the pasture east of Mrs. Knouse's property before he went past. Like an old comb, the piece of an army had drawn itself down this highway, and its broken teeth lay scattered behind.

Dan's front door was standing open. He remembered that he had locked no doors when he went away; out west, there was not a cabin on his prairies which could be locked when the owner was absent, and the acquisitive, defending fear of this town had not yet marked him. Stragglers: they might take silver ... somewhere in the house was silver. Pentland Bale's gold studs; his watches and books and the hidden, filigree jewelry which Dan's mother had once worn ... He pushed aside the light frame of the mosquito-bar and stood peering into the black hall.

"Dan," Irene Fanning whispered.

She had been waiting for him, alone in that house with all its haunts. *Mrs. Fanning.* It struggled toward his lips: he thought of saying that before it seemed natural and right to call her name.

"I'm sitting on the stairs. Here. I've been waiting."

His hands hunted for her. "One minute. I'll make a light."

"No." And then he realized that her voice was swollen with some peculiar emotion; it was scarcely the voice he was learning to know so well. "Close the shutters first."

He went into the library, feeling for the dusty shutters which had not been closed for a long time. One after another he drew the slatted pairs together. Four windows. Two at the front, two on the side facing the

Knouse place. The corner of the big desk drove itself against his hip. "There's a candle here, somewhere," he called, and he could hear her rustling into the room, feeling her way, arms fending out before her. The match crackled, its dripping sparks scorched the carpet. There was the oily flicker of dead candle-wick yielding itself to flame.

The woman said, "It was raining the first time I was here, too. Wasn't it?" Across shining chair-backs, she stared at him. She had a dark cloak caught around her shoulders, the goods still speckled with raindrops, and the puckered hood hanging loosely down her back. Beneath the cloak he could see the same black silk which she had worn when first he met her.

"Raining," Dan echoed. "Yes. Not like this—it was a storm." He demanded, shrilly, "Is anything wrong?"

"I had to see you. There is something—"

That, he thought. Oh—*that.* The notion was full-born, robust in his mind even as he glimpsed it. She would be compelled to divorce Tyler Fanning, at once. There could be no tenderness in the consideration of such vital need. She'd have to . . . *that.* He went to-ward her, reaching out his hand; the unnecessary chairs got in his way. "You mean that you're going to—that you've found out—"

"No," she said, sharply. "Not that. Not yet."

He stopped. He looked at her eyes, bitter and in-tent. Her hands, clenching the Windsor chair in front of her.

"Not that," she said again. "I'm sorry if you thought—No. For that matter"—her eyes went down, and her mouth twitched precisely over the indelicacy— "perhaps I can never have any—children."

There was something white in the hand she lifted

from the chair-back: a crumpled wad. "I have a letter from Tyler."

"I remember. Mr. Fanning gave it to you, out there." He took the paper from her and began to smooth it, pressing out the wrinkles.

She told him, "I had to bring it to you. It was the only thing to do. Tyler's father and mother ate in their room—what they did eat—and I had my supper alone. I've found a key for my room; it is locked; they'll think I am asleep. Just as before." He could hear the deep sighing of her breath. "I go out like a jailbird or a—woman criminal. A sneak . . . I heard Mr. Fanning reading their letter aloud. It—was not like my letter." Dan was still rubbing the sheet, still looking at her. "Oh, read it!" she cried.

Tyler's narrow, tilted hand-writing covered one side of the double sheet and half of the second page. The letter was dated at Thoroughfare Gap, on the twenty-first of June. "Dear Wife," Tyler said, "I am sending this in care of Chaplain Kraal, who is going to Baltimore and will post it for me. No doubt you will be surprised to hear from me in this vein, but there is a certain matter concerning which I feel impelled to address you. Word has been sent me by a certain party, making a strong accusation of infidelity against you. My first impulse was of anger toward the informant, but on closer study of the matter regret to say I would not be surprised if it"—the lines were more tilted than ever, wider apart, and he had omitted an essential verb—"true. That might explain (if true, and not idle gossip) the increasing coldness evident in your manner to me. I refer to Dan Bale. I am here"—the word was blotted beyond recognition—"my duty, and expect to continue so unless killed, which might relieve the situation for you. This sudden blow and the disgrace of it is overwhelming."

He said: "To my certain knowledge, the informant has never told an untruth, at least not in the years I have known Said Informant, which is a long time. Write to me at once if you can clear yourself. Bale has shown himself utterly reprehensible, and I will attend to him in due time if I survive. Of course I am writing nothing of this to my parents. Your reply awaited with the utmost eagerness. Deeply wronged, but still Your Husband. Capt. Tyler Fanning. 72 P.V."

Dan realized that he was saying, rapidly, driving himself to say it . . . his throat grown raw: "Look here. I cannot understand this. The letter is dated June twenty-first, and he left here on Sunday the fourteenth. We—it was that night, and— This letter of which he speaks—why," he cried, "it must have reached his camp as soon as he did!"

"They've moved. A long way. The regiment was near Fredericksburg, before, and Thoroughfare Gap is a long way from there. I searched it out on the map." Her mouth blurred, the lips bleached and quavering. "I felt I should bring the letter to you."

He said, "That's right and just." He wanted to say more, to tell her how totally unjust the whole situation was . . . rage began to sparkle across his brain. "Now, listen," he was saying, roughly, "this has come as we might have supposed it would come. You must divorce him. There's no use in haggling merely because Tyler is in the army. You have suffered enough at his hands before this. Is there any reason for you to be defamed by some—"

Her face was more brittle and white than he had ever seen it. "You know that it is all very true."

"This is no common infidelity! How could you be unfaithful to a faith which never existed?"

"Maybe," she said, "it existed for Tyler. Maybe I didn't recognize its existence for him."

The candle trickled its pennant from side to side; their thin shadows grew and blurred, dissolved, grew once more on the faded wall paper . . . The girl still stood behind the tall chair, facing him. He had the grotesque thought that she was a prisoner in a dock made of Windsor spindles. "Do you love him? I ask that for the first time. When you were—hysterical— you told me that you didn't love him. Now you must tell me again."

She shook her head. "I don't feel toward Tyler as I do toward you." The blue shadows hunted up from the hollow of her bosom, washed across her set, stubborn face. "I don't—wish him, as I have wished you. I don't—" She whispered, "Please don't make me go on."

He felt an impulse to snarl, *Go on!* But the first rage and annoyance were chilling into solid hatred. Fanning: he was responsible for this. He, and whoever had been the informant. Dan took a deep breath. "The window," he said aloud.

The woman's glance raced to the tall shutters which caged around two sides of the room. "Oh." Her shoulders sagged again. "You mean—that night in the kitchen. Then you did see someone."

"It was a face. I didn't know whose. Just a blur, and then gone away. I thought it was only a tramp— they go past here, sometimes. Army deserters and . . . it wasn't a tramp."

"Do you know who it was?"

"It's all come back; I puzzled, and I couldn't understand why he—There is a man in town named Quagger. Perhaps you don't know who he is."

She said, wretchedly, "He worked for Mr. Fanning. Years! I know—I've heard them speak of him, often. Mr. Fanning said that he was a good man, a church man, but a sympathizer with the south, and so he discharged him. I thought—oh, it was absurd—I thought it might be Mrs. Knouse."

"No. That fellow Quagger . . . He was staring at me."

"Why would he be at the window?"

"Like most of the dolts in this village, he could not understand how I refused to enter the army unless I felt as he did. He approached me, to discuss the matter. I was angry. I—laid hands on him. Perhaps he came to try to do some harm." Bale paused for a moment, thinking rapidly. "No, I think I've got it. Elijah was here to tell me about the militia and the new citizens' army. He must have followed Elijah here; later he saw you and me come into the kitchen—"

The girl's hand strayed across her forehead, rubbing back the damp surf of her hair. "I used to pity women who were talked about. I'm glad I did pity them. Now I can be more charitable with myself."

"He had the courage of his convictions, at least. Quagger had. He signed his name to the letter." Dan's shadow blocked hugely ahead of him as he came toward her. He lifted her limp hands from the chair-back, and put his arm around her. Irene's body seemed to surrender inside its damp wrappings, but her face turned away. "Oh, don't," she cried. "I'm too stained, too maligned and— The Fannings! I have to go on—living there, feeling this—"

He swore in a raw whisper . . . his arms tighter and

tighter, drawing her loins against his: "You have to do nothing of the sort. We'll go. I swear that you must never enter that house again. We'll go, at once. I've money here, in a belt. Write to Tyler—we can post the letter once we're gone."

"You've forgotten. The country is swarming with rebels. West, north. They have gone on east, too. There is no way for us to go. Probably the armies are strewn all through Maryland."

"They'd let us through. They—"

"No, you know they wouldn't. There are no trains here: they're destroying the railroads as they go. If we—did go, and had horses, they would take the horses. We must stay." She cried, "You can go, Dan. You— Go away and leave me. Much the best that you can—"

"You wish me to go? Actually?"

"Yes, yes! Dan—"

He said, "God. Oh, God. I wouldn't go if—" His face came down; he pressed her hands aside; she struggled weakly, and the damp cloak slid down in a soggy pile. In this gown I saw you first, he wanted to say. I could never go away from you now. We are going through something: it is a—phase . . . Damp, abusive, their lips came together.

Just as before, he cried to her without words, just as the other nights. In these few weeks we have met and tasted and taken; you must take, I must give to you, you must take and absorb. "Dan . . ." she groaned, an aching murmur, curling out from the hot crowding of their mouths. "I have to go back, to that house—to *them*—"

"No," he said, "if you must go back, you can go later, but we shall forget the disaster. Tomorrow we may talk about it; the invaders are gone, the roads are safe, you can drive out with an old horse, I will meet you; in a few days you can decide coldly and justly, what you shall say to him. Or I will say it. I will go, and tell him. Whatever you wish . . . not now, not now. Again this is our night."

With the girl sobbing, shivering in his arms, he went over and blew out the candle. The darkness wrapped so tightly around them that they became utterly insensitive to it; it was difficult to think about the next day, or even what home-going might be necessary before morning. He began to tell her, rapidly and many times, that he loved her. It was the most sincere belief he had ever held in all his life, and came tonight with acid intensity. Body, thoughts, taste of your mouth, the feel of breasts and thighs, the astral voicelessness which is your spirit, all of these I worship and want to possess as I possess my own. He told her again and again by word, by touch, by the whole use of his body. The woman left off sobbing; her flesh grew warm . . . "Give, give to me forever," she told him. "Darling, give to me, most beloved—I desire you forever, whether my mind wishes it or not. At this moment all wickedness is pure."

4.

In the blistering sunshine of Tuesday, Henry Niede brought his horses and cattle back from the valley where he had hidden them. Together with neighbors living along the Emmetsburg road, he had herded his stock some two miles down Plum Run on Friday, when the growl of the Confederate advance was heard from the northwest. Although no foraging parties penetrated south of Gettysburg that day, the farmers felt shrewd and not a little thankful that they had led their property out of harm's way. Those were pitiable people out along the Chambersburg Pike—and on the York Pike, east—who had not sense enough to find a secret, grassy den for their teams and milch cows.

The rebels were not smart men, Henry had heard. They would butcher a young, fresh cow without a second's thought, or else chase her along with their roaring, stolen herds to be beef on the second or third day after. If he were a rebel, Henry knew, he would use some sense about the cattle he butchered. And valuable heifers with good points—especially Alderneys—he would not butcher, but save them and bring them home when he came from the war. He could not blame the Confederates for their thievishness, but he felt a cold horror at their waste.

There were complications in hiding the stock. A boy or a man had to remain on guard all the time and keep the animals away from an unfenced wheat field nearby, or from being lost. It was a long way to go to milk nights and mornings, and seemed even farther when you had to drive with the eighteen-year-old blind mare which you had kept on the place. The woman said it was bad for milk to be joggled in a wagon and carried across fences and hills in pails. The cows did not give as they should have given . . . His sorrel colt was a wild one, always galloping and squealing about, and he would be lucky if the colt didn't fall into a gorge and break a leg and have to be shot. And maybe somebody else—not rebels—would steal the *kelver* and carry them off in a covered cart. It was bad, having all your stock in the woods. You would wake up at night and hear them mooing down there, and wonder if maybe a bear might not come out of the mountains over west, and prowl down to Plum Run and do some damage.

Nevertheless, Niede could not bring himself to drive the animals home when the rest of the neighbors did, on Monday. They appeared so confident that all danger was past. The rebels had gone clear to Harrisburg, men declared, and likely would capture Philadelphia too, and go back south by way of Washington. Some man came in from Taneytown on Sunday night, with a Baltimore newspaper. The Baltimore paper was certain that the enemy was cutting railroads for the sole purpose of leaving Baltimore and the capital defenseless when attacked from the north. *Nein,* men said, they will not come back here. They have taken everything along the main turnpikes, and when they go back to the south they will go by other roads. It is safe to bring the horses and cattle out of the woods.

Henry told them that he would wait. He gratified himself by imagining how silly his neighbors would look if the raiders returned on Monday night and found every stall and cow-shed crammed with occupants, ready for the taking. He was too smart for that, and anyway people said that gray riders had been seen on the Newville road again and again, and there were still people fleeing north from Frederick, and crying that more rebels came . . .

The sun had a confident, beaming promise on Tuesday morning. Looking at it as it crept above the pale yellow of the wheat, Niede was forced to admit that the war must be far away by now. His wheat was ready to cut, or would be in another day, and he would need his horses. You couldn't go about harvest when you were spending half your time running back and forth to the woods. And he'd have to see about getting a man. He did have a cheap one—a boy, seventeen years old—who had been bound out by his grandfather. But the ungrateful lout ran away to the war, and hadn't been heard from for six months. Men wanted a lot of wages . . . yes, and some of them even figured it in gold, and they ate as if food could be had for the asking. Times were bad, but he couldn't get in his harvest alone. Amelia and the woman were no good in the field: Amelia acted sullen because her arms turned red, and her mother stood up for her . . . Uncle Otto couldn't even milk. He was a no-good. But he would leave the woman some property when he died. It looked like he was going to live forever.

Niede got up at daylight and drove down to the Devil's Den and walked for ten minutes in the dark, wet woods before he heard the bell-cow. There had been company at this early milking on three other mornings, but now he was all alone. No guard was at hand any more, so if the cattle had ruined anyone's field Henry might have to pay for it. His forehead dampened with chilly sweat as that thought came to him . . . He experienced great difficulty in finding the horses; when they were found, he cursed them and tied them firmly, each to a separate tree. After consideration, he risked bringing the colt home with him, fastened behind the milk-cart and like to upset it a dozen times. It was late, and he had little more than half the milk he should have had. Those calves had been at the One-Horn and the White-face again, the little *esel!* He should have bound branches around their necks, with sharp points to gouge the mothers and make them kick the calves away, but then the branches were liable to pin them in the bushes so that they might break their foolish necks. It was bad, having your cows away off in the forest. He kept telling himself, Damn dirty armies. They ought to be put in jail . . . what I would like to do to them.

After breakfast the sun was smooth and honest above Granite Ridge, and the air was warming rapidly. It would be a hot day, and the little kernels of wheat would dry and grow fat and warm in their splintery husks. The wheat should be cut by tomorrow; tomorrow was July first; you couldn't wait all summer, rebels or no rebels.

He told his wife, as he pushed away the coffee-pot: "I got those horses tied, down there. I should go and bring them home now, and the cattle too."

"Better you had brought them yesterday like other folks," she told him. She did not look forward to wheat-harvest. She was a dull, funny woman. He couldn't make her out, sometimes.

"And if those damn armies had got them, you would think I was a smart man, *ja?*"

"The armies never got Codori's stock. They never got Sherfy's nor Trostle's nor Pitzer's, nor—"

"Ach," he said, coldly, "you are a fool woman!"

She made no response, but went on washing dishes, the strong soft soap foaming between her red fingers.

"Where is Amelia?" Henry demanded.

"By the chickens."

He said, "It's a wonder she is doing any good around here. It's a great wonder she ain't set down to weep over that no-good of hers."

Mrs. Niede turned, slowly, to face him. She had the hard, somber boniness of feature which she had transmitted to her daughter, and twenty years before she had been almost as pretty.

"I don't want you should talk that way," she muttered. "He is now a soldier. Remember you that. He is gone to fight those same rebels you hid your cows from. Maybe you should be glad that there were men like him to make the rebels go away, and not steal things."

"He ran away from them." Henry laughed. "I guess I know what they told me in town. He ran away, and they say Mr. Fanning is like to lose a buggy and colt because he took! Oh, he is a fine soldier." He clumped out to the back porch. Uncle Otto was coming up out of the root cellar . . . buttermilk, always buttermilk he was drinking. Quarts and quarts, which was just as good for the pigs. It would make the pigs fat, but Uncle Otto was already fat and that didn't net a dime for anybody. Amelia was down at the chicken coops; she looked bleached and shrunken in her loose calico gown and blue sunbonnet, like a child dressed up in her mother's clothes. Ach, that girl, he thought. She has got the looks; she ought to find a rich husband. But now she will be an old maid. I would like to beat some brains into her, if I could.

He ordered her, "I want you should come once with me. To get the cattle."

"Henry," cried his wife, behind him, "you should get you a man. Two men."

"And costs maybe half a dollar?" he snarled.

Amelia said, "I'm coming." She left her basket in the corn-crib, and walked toward the porch . . . He had never struck her since she was grown, but always she acted as if she expected a blow from him. Her mother spoiled her. She took money out of the tea-pot, and gave it to her to buy ribbons and truck, and like enough when Henry came in from the field of an evening, he would find that Amelia's mother had let her go off to town with the Duffeys or somebody.

He grinned without humor. "So. You wear the good shoes to feed chickens."

"These are old ones, Pa."

"Your Aunt Gerta, she would never waste shoes while she was doing work. Nor Grandma wouldn't—"

"Aunt Gerta's got feet so bad now," Amelia said sharply, "she can hardly walk on them at all." Her face began to show the mottled pinkness it always showed when she was frightened and angry at the same time.

Henry told her, "Just the same, girl, Aunt Gerta got her a good husband. Was not an old maid when she was twenty—"

"Mealy," came his wife's shrill voice, "your Pa is going to bring back the stock. You come and get you a sunbonnet, because he wants you should help him drive them up."

Niede said, "Come on," and started toward the barn for halters. Then he remembered that he had placed their halters on the horses already—they were tied, down there in woods, kicking at flies and waiting for him. He heard Amelia say, "I've got a bonnet," but she went into the house anyway, wasting time.

Uncle Otto settled himself heavily in his old chair. He called to Henry, talking in *der Alt*, saying something about a fine week for harvest, but Henry didn't turn his head. When his wife wanted to bring Uncle Otto there, twelve years before, he had agreed because he thought the old man would live only a year or two. And he had lived all this time, eating his share—to say nothing of buttermilk and peaches and tobacco—and even if his wife got the larger share of Uncle Otto's property, Henry would not be much ahead.

Finally Amelia came out, and they started across the hayfield toward the ridge. It was a short cut this way, if you had to walk; shorter than going southwest by the Emmetsburg road. Henry carried a rusty, perforated pail in which he had put some lumps of salt wrapped in a newspaper. The pail was no good any more; he could throw it away, down there in the woods, and wouldn't have to lug it home after he had lured the cattle with salt. He would ride Belle and the other horses would follow along, or he could lead them if he didn't have to herd the cows too much. He would give the girl a long switch and she could come on foot, keeping the cattle moving. He began to wish, now, that he had brought his stock home the day before; then the neighbors had helped each other; he wondered why people didn't ever seem anxious to trade work with him . . . he had had to work very hard. And now Amelia was a lazy-bones. He would never have a son. The woman suffered trouble with her insides, after Amelia was born; she lay in bed six weeks, though Henry was certain that she might have got up sooner.

He looked back at his daughter, climbing over the stone fence from Codori's pasture. Ach, and with all her looks she has not got a rich man. There was old man Truckenmiller; he would not live long, and he owned three farms that people knew of, and maybe more . . . Amelia was singing, a thin chant which barely reached his ears. Somehow, it made him intensely angry to have her lagging behind that way, and singing silly songs . . . *some mischief brewing—so that's what you're after, a whole cherry pie—*

He yelled over his shoulder: "Better you hurry, and not sing light songs and nonsense. The *kelver* maybe is lost in the woods." She stopped singing, and trudged behind without saying anything, though once she sobbed when she twisted her ankle. Shoes—wearing shoes at work! A young girl had good strong feet; shoes were for church and weddings.

As soon as they reached the woods, they began to have trouble. The calves had indeed hidden themselves, in a little patch of bushes high among the rocks; how they ever got there was a mystery; they peeked out like big-eyed deer. It took half an hour to climb around and catch them and drag them, bawling, back to the herd. And the sun was high, and the cattle seemed restless. Henry had no sooner mounted Belle than she stumbled over some stones and nearly threw him. He gave her a good stick where it would do the most good . . . ach, she acted like a wild horse, and they would never get home this way!

It was certainly ten o'clock before they got the straggling beasts up to the Emmetsburg road. Ten men would have had a time; Henry knew that the delay was not Amelia's fault, though he blamed her loudly for it. She had torn her dress in two places, her face was a dull red, she had a scratch on her cheek, and there were dirty tear-marks around her eyes. The cattle were wild ones and the horses almost as bad, except old Heine, and he moved as if each hoof were buried in mud above the shaggy hock. Half the day speeding by, and the cattle not home yet. "You bet God is giving it to me," Henry told Amelia coldly. "God is mad because I got a girl that has her head full of crazy songs instead of work like she should." He howled at the animals: "You damn *verrickt,* and get to the road! Throw them a stone once, you no-good—"

At every lane opening, at Sherfy's dooryard, at Codori's, the herd made a lumbering dash for shade and freedom. You had only to leave your stock in the woods for four days to make them as savage as Indians. The sunshine pushed down; they stewed in its pale glare, and Henry began to forget about harvest. He could feel yellow dust settling in his throat, coating his eyeballs, dry and scorching all over his body sweat ... Well, at last they were getting the dumb-heads home. He would like to let them go without their feed this night, and see how they liked it. Only you could not do that to cows; they had to eat, or you got no milk. Precious little milk he would get until they were tamed again ... The animal shadows blotted under trampling feet—

"Pa!" Amelia had been wailing, again and again. "Pa!" He was hot and tired—he had been astir and slaving for many hours, and he hated Amelia and the stock. It will serve her right, he thought, if she hollers and hollers until she has lost her voice and can only croak like a frog. Only when he heard the rapid stutter of many hoofs behind him, was he prompted to turn his head, and then his red rage began to shrivel.

Five men were looming close at hand, and they looked like a whole army. After all, after his scheming and caution and hard work, he was going to lose his herd. These men would take them—five men, and they had guns. Their horses were coated with dust; the long, curved scabbards rattled and clanked ... Henry pushed old Belle toward the fence ... *ja, ja,* he was afraid.

They drew up in a fierce circle around him and Amelia. Ach, they were going to shoot without another moment's delay. "Hey," a dry voice said, "any Butternuts around here, farmer?"

Henry took a deep breath. These men were blue—a bleached and unwholesome blue, but it was not the color of the enemy. High boots on their legs and—

"Cat's got his tongue," a soldier grunted. They turned toward the girl. An older man asked, not unkindly: "How about it, sissy? Seen any rebels?"

Amelia whispered, "No, sir." The cows were all

bunching along the fence-side, ahead, and beginning to eat.

Niede cried, with huge relief, "I thought was rebels sure, mister! No, they're gone."

"When?"

"A-Friday." He wondered why he should be so humble and fawning before these rigid figures, when three of them were young enough to be his sons.

"No more left in the neighborhood, eh?"

Henry said, expansively, "There was an army of them here on Friday. I guess some is left on the roads up north. Folks say they seen 'em. But I guess most is gone to Harrisburg."

The oldest soldier had a scrubby beard; his eyes looked like black nail-heads driven deep in saddle leather. There were wide yellow V's, whole slabs of them, on his arms. "Same story, Andy. Reckon we better report." He spurted a long string of brown spittle into the road: it rolled like a ball. The horses turned, with much creaking and jingling. The older man swung back, and jerked his square head at Henry. "That town Gettysburg, ahead?"

Niede nodded. He kept wondering whether these men might not be fancying his cattle, after all. He had heard that even the Northern soldiers were apt to steal from farmers unless they were watched closely . . .

"They're all Dutch, around here," he heard the man with the yellow V's say to the others. "Well, boys, let's git back to Buford." The dust foamed in choking clouds; long after they had vanished in it, you could hear the *rumpety-rump* of hoofs flogging back.

No rebels . . . Henry Niede felt like a very young man once more, free from the elderly worries and sins which had been crushing him down. "See," he crowed at his daughter, "there is real soldiers, and not like your Huddlestone who runs away in a buggy and don't come back yet!" He kicked at Belle's ribs, and headed toward the One-horn who was straying through a fence-gap into clover. *"Donnerwedder holt!"* he roared. *"Odder ich farschlock dir der Kup!"*

He was pleased enough to reach home safely with his stock, and he did not stop to berate Amelia any more. He drank some coffee, ate a few crullers, and walked in to the village to bargain for harvest help. God began to be good to him at last; in Middle street he met the Brenneman brothers in their wagon. They were trusting, good-natured souls, and they would work for small pay. Henry hurried back home with the pleasant idea growing in his mind that Uncle Otto might have died suddenly during this excessive heat—dead and no bother to anyone, out there beside the well. But a dust cloud, vast and ominous, was pressing north past the Sherfy farm, and Uncle Otto was quite alive, standing out in the road with Amelia and the woman. "Look!" they all cried at Henry as he approached, "and comes thousands of soldiers with horses . . . They're ours," Amelia kept saying bravely to her mother. "Ma, they are *blue*. They're our side." Likely enough, she was imagining that Elijah might be with them.

5.

It was shortly before this that Doctor Duffey stopped at the Bale house, hoping to snatch a few moments' rest in what had been a disheartening day. He was losing a tumor case which he had thought to save, and over in Boundary street lay a child with a shattered thigh-bone, for whom he felt that he could not do enough. In such hours the Irish morbidity of his ancestors acted as his curse, even though their mysticism might be a belated blessing.

He found Daniel Bale in his undershirt, covered with sweat, and swinging a scythe through the rank weed patch beside the old stable. The sun was white-hot overhead, and through all its course the temperature had swelled. Only in shadier tangles near the gum tree was there any buzzing of grass insects; yellow dust lay thick and cooked along the Pike, and old Salt waited at the gate with his head hanging low, suffering agonies of flies with scarcely a quiver.

Duffey sat down on the well-curb, groaning softly. "Come over and pump me a drink," he begged. "It'll be easier than cutting weeds. This is scarce a day for needless ambition."

Dan hung the scythe on a peg under the stable eaves and came across the lawn, rubbing a soaked forearm over his face. His undershirt was drenched and soggy. "I thought I'd take down all the grass in the back lot. There'll be goldenrod later if I don't, and Mrs. Knouse suffers from hay fever."

"Sure," the doctor nodded, "and not a bit of it the fault of your weed patch." His bright eyes rolled up for a scant second, then vanished again under crusty lids. "I've observed that a man can find excuse enough for driving his body to torment when his soul's in the same place."

Dan stopped, with his fingers clutching the pump handle. He asked, "What are you hinting, Doc?"

"You've been bothered to death. Anybody could see that."

"I'll thank them not to see it."

"Go on, and draw me a bit of a drink."

`Bale's lips squeezed together. The pump groaned and gurgled. Water came up through its suction with tardy reluctance, rising nearly to the spout, grunting spasmodically down again, and lifting at last with surrendering spurts. Duffey put his cupped hands out and dashed the water over his face. "That's good," he gasped. "I can't be saying as much for the rest of the day. This is the first good I've found in it."

Dan kept the pump handle moving; he bent down and sucked a mouthful of water from the spout, then spurted it out into the grass.

"Katie Huffmaster," the old man said, as if in continuation, "she was run away with, you'll remember."

Bale sat upon the well-curb. "Yes. The horse was frightened by the locomotive."

"A young horse, a bad one, and they should never have let her take him out alone. Poor child." He droned it softly, over and over. "Poor child, and she's got a right femur shattered. I'm fearing she will be a cripple for life, even if I save her the leg. I started with Smith's anterior splint, and changed to Hodgen's apparatus, without extension. Now I've got her in a fracture box filled with bran, poor child . . . It's hot this day, Dan. Too hot. I sometimes wish—"

Abruptly, he ceased speaking and began to pat his damp temples with a wad of handkerchief. Bale clenched his fist loosely and stared at the tiny pearls of sweat which hung between his knuckles. "What do you sometimes wish?"

"In the future, there'll be things to do. Things better than Hodgen's or Smith's way, or stinking boxes of bran. Praise Peter, and I'd like to see the day. And no more wars," he added. "Dan, the wars will be done."

Bale laughed scornfully.

The doctor lifted his head. "Folks felt like you, maybe, before the days of William Harvey. Yes, years before Ambrose Paré. Dan, I'm thinking you never heard of Ambrose Paré. Yes, before Jenner came along with his small-pox vaccine, they were saying the same thing. I'd like to see this far future, if I could."

"It won't be better. Anyway, I wasn't thinking of potions and cure-alls."

Duffey sighed. He began to polish the stained nap of his silk hat. "I'm thinking of them. Oh, they'll have ways for Emmy Funk's tumor and for Quagger's gizzard, if that's what ails him."

Bale swung around and stared defiantly at Duffey. "Where did you see Elmer Quagger?"

"In my office. He came."

"This morning?"

"Why not? It's a burning sensation, he says, and much gas to bother him. I wondered about his pylorus . . . more likely it's bowels. I came near trying a purgative enemata, but gave him oil instead." He returned Dan's gaze, mildly but shrewdly. "You leaped like a goat when I said his name. Don't tell me you've fallen out with your brother Copperhead."

Dan made a smile of sorts. "Your humor is more than quaint, Doctor Duffey. Sometimes it smells to high heaven."

"I wish I knew what was worrying you."

"Possibly my status as a Copperhead."

"That's not it, indeed. I've been accused as a Disunionist myself . . . Quagger has changed his lodgings," Duffey added.

Dan said nothing.

The doctor gazed kindly at an orange thicket of tiger lilies beyond the fence. "He used to live with the Frielings. But they asked him to move, Saturday, and I don't know where he's living now. And did you hear what they're telling about Quagger and the rebels?"

Bale stood up. He exhaled deeply, and jammed his hands into the pockets of his pantaloons. "No. And what's more, you will not hear me ask."

"He talked about the misfortunes of Governor Vallandigham, and the rebel officers said that Vallandigham was a traitor and the Yankees ought to have shot him. And all black Republicans. Poor Quagger—north and south hates him alike, but if you'd prefer me not to talk of it, I won't. There's no need for you to fizz up the way you do, Daniel, boy."

The silence lay between them, stupid and unwieldy . . . Old Salt was not tied. He took an explorative step or two; the buggy squeaked. "Whoa," Duffey called, and the horse stopped. The doctor set his hat on the back of his head and stood up. He looked squarely into Dan's eyes. "He asked me a question," he said, "about you."

"Who did?"

"Quagger—who else? He asked if I knew you well, and I said I did. He asked if you was a man who'd kill him because he had wronged you, and I tried to get him to tell the wrong, but he would never do it. He said it had been on his conscience, because he had wronged you when he was angry. I'm thinking that his ailments were true ones, but there was a disorder of the brain behind them all."

Dan rubbed his thumbs up and down his suspenders. "Why did he move from the Frielings'?"

"The rebels—or maybe a straggler or two—stole their chickens. Before that, they hadn't minded about Quagger's sympathies, political and all. Maybe they suggested he had given the chickens to the rebels . . . I admit it sounds like a joke to be laughed at. And he looked shabby and unshaven, as if he had been sleeping in the woods."

The old man slid out a pink tongue to moisten his lips. "I'm your friend, Dan Bale. It was me who helped you into this world, and I feel responsible. I'd like to have you tell me how Quagger could ever be wronging you."

Dan exclaimed suddenly. A long dust cloud was pushing up the valley from the south . . . he spun the doctor in his tracks, and pointed. Together they stared through the writhing lines of heat. "Sakes," Duffey whispered, "it's the rebels come back again."

"But they didn't go south. They marched to York."

"This is them, you can wager on it." The old man said: "This war, Dan. This—armies crowding in the roads, overrunning all creation. It'll be the death—"

Dan cried, "Look there!" Far beyond the Fairfield road, beyond Long Lane and against the searing fog of Granite Ridge, a little wad of horsemen was emerging from the welter of the parent cloud. They headed rapidly across the fields. Now they could be seen swinging from their horses, lifting rails out of a fence, breaking a path into the sprawling pastures . . . The two men rested their elbows on the picket railing. From an upper window, Mrs. Knouse was yapping, "Daniel—what is it, Daniel? Is it more soldiers come?" and Duffey wondered whether the woman had been hiding behind limp curtains, straining her ears to listen to the conversation in the yard.

"They're Union, Doc. Nationals."

Duffey said, "There's none about. They'll be more rebels, more and more." He asked himself, and was Elijah Huddlestone caught by them? They came out of the south, the south and—

"I can make them out. They've got blue uniforms."

"You're right, by God," breathed the doctor. "And I'm happy it's so. I was thinking about Elijah."

Dan nodded, without turning. "Yes. If there were Nationals south of here, perhaps he hasn't been gobbled up."

Adam Duffey put his hand on the younger man's bare arm, pressing his broad fingers deep into the firm, hot flesh. "Before it's too late to speak, I ask as a friend that you'll be telling me what the to-do was with Quagger. If I can help—"

"Oh, Doc. Let it be."

A dozen soldiers swung out along the Fairfield road, their horses at the trot. The remainder of the advancing troop stopped for a moment beyond the roadside fence; horses huddled in a close, milling group as if they whispered horse secrets; then two men sprang down and began to tug at the rails. Now you could see the shimmer of their faded blue breeches, hear the muffled hoofs and all the sound of their deliberate approach. Two harp-shaped elms beyond the field were tranquil, motionless: the sun made feathers of their highest leaves . . . an officer said something, metal and unavoidable word, a word said for the millionth time. Behind this clustered outpost, the shallow wheat fields seethed with the smoke of travel, travel— more horses than had ever trotted those roads before. The sound this army made was not the dull, portentous murmur of a Confederate brigade coming over McPherson's ridge on a dark afternoon. The valley throbbed with echoes; men squawked to one another, the horses were glinting with sturdy harness, and no caravans of plunder came gypsying behind.

Duffey said, with conviction, "They look like they was expecting war any moment. Indeed, they want to see it come."

Bale turned, and looked searchingly toward the Fanning house: Demon was out in the garden, a squat brown shape, rooted there forever. The upper windows shone hot and glassy . . . no one moved.

"I wonder if these would be Tyler Fanning's men, Dan?" It was a brutal truth, but his simple question made Daniel suddenly angry and hateful. "What nonsense, Doc," he heard himself snapping. "Tyler's in the infantry!" The dust wound close above the southeast world, a long stair-carpet over the road from Emmetsburg. Inside her house, Mrs. Knouse was scampering about like a beetle in a box. They heard her limping steps, the quick gaspings and exclamations she made to herself as she hastened to perform some suddenly important chore. She popped her brown face through the rear doorway. "It's Union ones, Daniel—I heard you say so. Maybe I can put my bulb-roots back out in the garden where they ought to be. The Lord sends us now a quick answer to prayer." Then she clapped the door shut; the nearest soldiers were hunting speedily across her weedy pasture. Their horses were all chestnuts except for one gray. Eight men—tight and squat in their saddles—the survivors of the herd which had cut across from the smoky farms behind.

Duffey swallowed. He loosened his clutch on a spear of the white fence. "I'd best be driving old Salt out of this before he gets scared," he said. "Who'd ever expected to see these soldiers, an hour ago? Good

day, Dan." And when he had climbed into the carryall and had lifted the reins in his scarred, pink hands,
he cried: "According to Elijah, this is what they're
calling a vidette. They shoo them out along the roads
to watch for enemies. It's a French word—vidette." Old
Salt started warily down the Pike, forgetting the
nagging flies, his ears stiff and pointed and cocked
forward as the squad of cavalry came at him.

The carryall had passed before the soldiers emerged
from the field, and Duffey was pleased that they did
not challenge him. To him their advent was an annoying complication, but minor to the riddle of personal relationship.

Whenever he tried to clear his brain of the jogging,
dusty shapes which his eyes were putting there, he
could only realize that he had told the whole truth
about Elmer Quagger, and had stated his questions
to Dan as openly and simply as was possible. Here
existed an inexplainable rift and barrier that did not
come from the years of disassociation. It was no out-
growth of Minnesota prairies or the life which Dan
had lived there. Strangely enough, Duffey kept thinking of a love affair. If his friend were experiencing
one, there was no understanding how Quagger could
in any way be aware of it, or be involved.

And certainly Bale was not implicated in petty
schemings nurtured by the Copperheads, the Sons
of Liberty, the Knights of the Golden Circle—call
them what you would. Such was not his way, could
not be admitted among his beliefs . . . The old doctor
was as dully depressed by Quagger's unhappy insinu-
ations as by any relapse or lack of progress noted
among his patients. The world gaped at him, stained
and unappetizing. He disliked the war partly because

of the obtrusive patriotism which it had fostered, and
partly for reasons of vague but earnest humanity.
The war had occupied him, nettled him, overcome
him for more than two years, and thus he welcomed
the home-coming of Daniel Bale with supreme enthusiasm . . . That enthusiasm had never been justi-
fied; he had seen little of Dan during these weeks; he
found him complex and stupidly preoccupied, a man
whose very sternness and adult rigidity made him
unapproachable, and thus unsatisfying as a friend.
He thought, you cannot see all that's going to occur,
when you sew a young mother's torn body together
again.

6.

The Federal squad trotted quickly up the slope,
and when Dan went to the front gate he could
see them sitting their horses against the polished western sky, just as he had seen the Secessionists bulking
there a few days earlier.

Old lady Knouse, the eternal Knouse on her front
porch, asking questions, wanting to know things
she knew already. "What went with those soldiers,
Daniel?"

"They're up on the hill."

"Maybe more will come," she nodded.

"Doubtless we'll get our share," he told her, and
she scuttled back into her house. He thought it odd
that she should have a bread-knife in her hand.

He could hear a faint but persistent cheering in the
village. The Union troops were being welcomed as

saviors, as protectors who came from the President himself to right whatever wrongs the rebels had visited upon these innocent people. Bale wondered what would happen to the stragglers whom the old cobbler-constable had seized on Friday night . . . they would be taken to a prison camp, probably. This was a strange occupation for men with minds: tag and tag again; you are tapped by a hand, you are dead; another person is tapped, and he is wounded; the prisoners are tapped and tagged and led away.

He walked out into the road. Most of the cavalry squad had vanished over the hill, but two men still waited at the summit, dismounted, with horses standing beside them.

From behind, down past Stevens Run, rose the rapping of hoofs . . . Stevens Run . . . Thaddeus Stevens was far away from his town, now, and Dan thought how surprised he would be if he knew that soldiers were trampling past his home. Some day Thaddeus Stevens might be even more famous, and people would hear the name of Gettysburg because he had lived there . . . A single rider swung around the curve; the earth exploded in loose puffs as each hoof touched the ground. Still at that easy gallop, the man passed. He was an officer; he had a dusty mask for a face, and his tight jacket was drenched with sweat. He glared hawk-like at Bale as he churned by. More hoofs, back in the town, an increasing rumble and hullabaloo, and more troops coming. The head of a long column bulged around the turn.

The oncoming troops did not lope with the free menace of the rebels; they were uniformed more consistently, they held together in a firm double-file and bright guidons snapped, tiny triangles above their heads. White haze boiled high. You knew that they

had ridden endless roads, had drawn their dark blue
lines up and down map after map, with inexhaustible
gallons of the same blue ink behind them . . . Closer.
They began to be men, even in the heat: individual
bodies had been the raw material of which this military mechanism was constructed. They possessed
mustaches and legs and stomachs, and one had come
from a cow barn and one from a glass factory, but
now they were of a tested standard.

Choking clouds whipped and billowed around
them, the dust fell in adhesive thicknesses over cloth
and skin and metal and horseflesh; still it could not
hide the pride of their shroudings. Blue, government
blue, hot and heavy goods, wool which was too thick
for any need, they steamed inside its firm, buttoned
folds. Closer, closer, two and two and two forever,
with the gaudy notches of their guidons flicking on
ahead. They had no faces . . . this was Tuesday . . . no
one could ever tell how so much dust had been born
since that wet Friday, the Friday which seemed so long
ago. The clay was dried by days of sunshine. Now its
smoke rose up, pestled and pounded, to wash every
human line from the faces of men.

Their mouths were wet scars in the plastered blank-
ness, for eyes they had twin holes. Every soldier with
a beard had become a patriarch, a hoary Methuselah.
In the town, a brass band exhorted with full confidence.

> *. . . mandates*
> *Make heroes assemble*
> *When Liberty's form stands in view . . .*

Far and near you could hear dogs yipping; again
Bale looked toward the Fannings', but still there was

no one in sight except Demon and a hysterical Cybo who danced and pirouetted in the yard . . . Nothing settled yet, he thought. We've laid it all on the table, after some foolish parliamentary law. But here is part of the army, and what if the Seventy-second Pennsylvania should come, ho, to the wars?

All the bordering fields were drinking up a saturation of disturbed dust. You could not breathe without drawing heated particles against your nostril linings. The cavalry moved more slowly in the Pike. An order came relayed down the steaming river of men; distantly, a bugle uttered its piercing stammer. There was sudden, oppressive silence which ticked in the ears, and the column stood there halted on the road. Men twisted their stiff shoulders, began to cough and murmur. Almost directly in front of the gate, lifted a cry: *there he goes!* With a jingling crash, a horse pitched forward and lay shuddering, its fore-legs doubled, its hind-legs stretching and plowing in the dust. The blue rider had leaped clear as the animal went down; he stood with his great, curved saber trailing, wiping his face and gazing down at the mound of ruddy flesh beside him.

"What's the matter, Bryce?"

The man answered, "Too damn hot, sir." Other cavalrymen pressed aside, giving room as an officer rattled along the ditch. He swung down; with the private, he bent over the horse.

Dan called across the fence. "Do you want some water?"

"Yuh." They didn't turn for a moment, and when they did it was to face him with those same inhuman false-faces of grime and sweat. "If you've got an old cloth handy—" added the officer.

When Bale came back with the bucket of water and a piece of torn quilt, the column was moving up the hill and filing left through a fresh gap in the fence, across the seminary campus. High on the ridge among the trees, a United Sates flag wavered, a gay, candied flake that could have no reality, no concern with worn-out horses which slobbered in the road. Still the troops came riding out of Gettysburg, and swung trampling to one side as they passed the stricken animal and the solitary man beside it.

Dan said, "Here's the water. If you soak this old quilt and lay it over his head—" Thick bubbles were swelling from the horse's nose; within the shiny body its intestines rumbled and growled. The trooper looked up at Bale, and shrugged. Eyes like little gray pebbles . . . he was much younger than Dan, younger than Elijah. "No use, mister. He's done for. I'll have to ketch a remount." He drew the carbine out of its holster by the saddle, swung it against his shoulder, and held the muzzle close to the gelding's ear. The report boomed out, slapping upon all nearby hills; a scatter of dust mingled with powder smoke as the bullet drove through. Legs, neck, tail, the dead beast seemed to press itself deeper and deeper into the warm gray bed where it lay . . . gas inside its body still burbled. Thud and clatter, the soldiers skirted past. A deep voice called, "Get that critter outa the road."

The dismounted man was bending down to unfasten the saddle-girth, the holster, haversack and roll of blanket; he did not look up or reply to this order. Dan set down his pail of water and went out to help. "Don't you use a martingale?" he heard himself asking. The soldier said, "Not us. They're all right for new recruits," he added scornfully. He dragged the girth from under the prostrate carcass and piled equipment in front of the gate. "Wait'll I git the bridle, mister." And when he had done so, "Now if you'll ketch holt with me." Each took hold of an out-flung leg; two other men swung down to help them; the four of them dragged the dead animal into the ditch . . . there were little foamy pools where the horse had lain, and scarcely any blood. "Thanky," the soldiers said to Dan. "Mind if we have some water?" They grouped around the pail, drinking very little, coughing, gargling the water and spitting it out upon the ground.

Bale told them, calling through the white haze which drifted between: "There's a pump around in back. Tell them they're all welcome." He went up the path and into the house. It was cooler the instant he had stepped inside the silent, brick-walled rooms. Somewhere a clock was ticking . . . This house, my house in Gettysburg. Grandfather lived here, he lay in that room in his coffin . . . And now the memory was a legend, and nothing else.

He was drinking, in the kitchen, when he heard somebody tramping up on the front porch; the mosquito-bar door rattled as a fist knocked against it. Still in his damp undershirt, he went through the house. Framed against the glare outside was a gaunt, bearded man in uniform, his sword scabbard caught up in his gloved hand. "Hello," his nasal voice was calling, "hello, inside—"

"Yes?" Dan asked.

The man reached for the door handle. "Sorry to disturb you, my friend," and then he was inside. An officer, with dull gilt leaves in his shoulder-straps, and the meal of dust lying over him. He bent forward, whispering as he nodded toward the staircase. "I make bold to ask your momentary kindness, sir. If I shall not disturb your family."

"There is no one else here."

He nodded rapidly; his hazel eyes peered sadly out of caves in his yellow skull; there was something of a schoolmaster about him, and something of a grim wood-chopper as well. "Glenn's the name. Major Titus Glenn, Gamble's brigade." One hand fumbled with a plump leather pouch attached to the side of his sword belt, behind the revolver holster. "I've got an old wound that's bothering me; it's the very nuisance in this heat. If you will be so kind—" You will not deny me, his eyes declared. You dare not. For all the mildness of my voice—

Dan said, "My name's Bale. You're quite welcome to anything I can offer."

"I shan't trouble you for long." Already he was unbuckling his belt; the saber banged against the floor. "Just give me a basin of water and show me the way to your privy."

"Privy?" Dan heard himself repeat the word stupidly.

"I want to do a dressing."

"You're welcome to the kitchen." Dan felt all the embarrassment of a country gawk; the officer walked behind him, and he was unfastening his blouse. "I have bandages with me," he explained, "but try to find a surgeon when you want him!"

In the kitchen, Bale dipped a basin of water from the big wooden bucket on its corner shelf. The last time, he thought—the last time a wound was dressed in this room . . . oh, thin red wound, and never made by a war . . . When he turned, Major Titus Glenn had removed his blouse. He unloosed his suspenders and pushed the wad of trousers and drawers down from his hip joint, though he kept a tail of ragged shirt shielding his nakedness. He said, calmly, as if he had said the same thing in many other kitchens: " 'Scuse me." He rolled his shirt high.

There was a deep-drawn, brownish hole at the left side of his lower abdomen, and another opposite it in the back. Through the wounds a single linen thread had been pulled from front to rear, and was tied in a limp bow-knot at the side of his body. Dan made a sound. The officer nodded quickly. "First," he explained, "they used what is called a tent. Then a seton of oakum, then a seton of candlewick, and finally this linen string. I was lucky and escaped peritonitis." The flesh around each wound was rubbed raw in an irregular and scabby circle. He had opened the leather pouch, it was filled with clean rags; he moistened a scrap of cloth in the water basin, and dabbed it lightly over the sores.

"God," Bale said.

The deep eyes peered at him. "It was a musket-ball, fired in the dark. I had no business where I was, wandering outside our lines." He bent once more to his task.

"Do you think there'll be a battle here?"

Major Glenn tossed the soiled wad of cloth into the wood basket beside the stove, and took up a second piece. "That is hard to say, Mr.—what is your name, once more?"

"Bale."

"Mr. Bale. No, there's no telling. I heard that some rebel cavalry was in the vicinity. We've got men out to the north and west, now; if they raise any of the enemy's pickets we might have some fighting. It's hard to—" The last word blurred on his lips; he had trouble holding the saliva in his mouth, bending down as he was.

"What troops are these?"

"This is the First Division of the Cavalry Corps, commanded by John Buford. Keep an eye out on the road; you're apt to see the General. He's a smart figure of a soldier: still a young man. Watch for a trim man with a yellowish mustache. A clever soldier—"

He fumbled for the leather sabretasche, and brought out of it a folded square of soft cotton which he packed into the hole in his front side; he pushed another cloth against the posterior wound, and tied a long strand of white rag tightly around his abdomen, holding the makeshift bandages in place. The room began to smell of human sweat and the thin, branny odor of serous secretion. "It is Christian fore-bearance on your part, Mr. Bale, to permit my intrusion." He rearranged his clothing, and seemed to don a new gravity as he buttoned the heavy blouse. "You're a Union man, I presume?" he asked with too-conscious ease.

"A Pennsylvanian by birth."

"Married—and the father of numerous children?" There was a sly falsehood in his chuckle.

Dan said, "No, I'm not married." He breathed audibly for a moment; you could hear his breathing and the officer's, mingled together, striving one against the other. "I am unalterably opposed to any kind of war. That is why I'm not in the army."

"Ah," Glenn exclaimed sharply. The front door slammed, and a man thudded into the hall, his spurs dragging. "Major!" The voice was taut, starting echoes through the high rooms.

Glenn pivoted. "Yes, Billy," he called.

A scrawny youth came rattling into the kitchen, heedless of the dust which splashed from him like snow with every movement. His bony hand was playing nervously with his holster flap. He looked cautiously at Dan, then stiffened and saluted the major. His arms snapped down. "Colonel Clendenin was wondering about you, Pa. He sent me back. The whole brigade's deployed to the left of the turnpike, on this ridge and the next."

The major drew his belt tight. He picked up his whitened hat, and bowed coldly at Dan. "This is my son, Mr. Bale. Lieutenant Billy Glenn, also of the Eighth Illinois, Gamble's brigade."

Billy muttered a word. His eyes were hazel as his father's, but opaque and chilly; they were the eyes of a killer, ruthless with all the hatred of nineteen.

"We've dirtied up your house, I'm afraid," apologized the elder Glenn.

"That's all right."

Clatter, squeak of leather, the father and the son went out to the front door, and Dan followed slowly. A line of carts moved in the road, carts all alike, all small and enormously loaded with anvils and tubs and protruding bars of metal. "The farriers," remarked the major, idly. "I didn't think they'd be up yet." Two horses stood in the yard chewing at the grass, reins trailing; one was the major's; he climbed stiffly upon it. Light as a mounting Sioux, Billy was on the back of the sorrel gelding. He juggled the single rein and squeezed his knees; the sorrel whinnied nervously, swung high on its hind-legs, dropped its fore-feet and headed toward the fence, head low. It flashed over the short pickets, slipped on the dusty grass of the ditch-side, but rose before its belly had rubbed the ground. One creature, horse and boy, they galloped up the hill past the row of rumbling carts.

"Billy's dug up your yard, Mr. Bale."

"It doesn't matter," Dan told him. He wondered through how many eternities he would be saying those words. The broad wheels, the shambling hoofs, dinned and ached in his ears. There was some commotion next door . . . Mrs. Knouse's voice shrieked up—she was laughing, a delirious old-lady screech. She stood on her porch, a huge basket on her arm, and around her crowded a mob of soldiers to whom she was giving something. "I'd just like to give every boy of you a nice piece of bread-and-butter," she cried. They laughed without humor. "Lady, if you did you'd spread more butter than ever woman did before—"

The major did not look toward them; he was settling his boots in the hooded stirrups, loosening the belt about his waist, and trying to make himself comfortable in the saddle. He flashed one glance at Dan—a shaft of baffled disapproval.

"You're fortunate to have your son with you in the same regiment," Bale said.

Glenn swung his hand against his hat rim. "I did have three," he said. He cantered down the graveled path, past the dead horse, and rode away up the slope without looking back.

7.

By six o'clock, Bale estimated that at least three thousand men had passed along the Chambersburg Pike and through adjacent fields—more men than he had ever seen at one time before. They were squatting on the seminary campus, in the upper end of Fanning's pasture, and all along the Fairfield road. Dust had risen, a solid blanket to lie from valley wall to valley wall, and every tree baked in its powdered coating; beyond Oak Ridge the stirring of the soldiers and their horses could be heard—a constant, muddled resonance as of untold tribes gossiping and herding together.

Dan bathed and put on clean clothes, but he had no great appetite for food. Nor had he eaten well since he returned from the west; when he looked at his naked trunk there were bones which he had not seen for years.

In the yard, his pump kept up its patient gouging. A hundred buckets had been filled, men gathered in the fresh and grassy mud to thrust their heads beneath the wooden spout, and still they came. A noticeable path had been trodden deeply through the new-cut weeds, marking across the rear lot to the rail fence, and another path marred the front yard. Men came booted, in neat jackets, in stocking feet; men in putrid undershirts, hard-faced youths who chewed tobacco. The windlass at the Fannings' creaked endlessly, but Mrs. Knouse made it plain that bread and butter were the extent of her offering to the National army. She scampered back and forth from her larkspur bed to the front gate, warning gangs of water-seekers away. At first she tried to make apologetic explanations, but in the last hour her voice had grown raw, angrily peremptory. "Now—now," she was hooting as fast as the soldiers appeared: "now—now, you men stay out of my lilies. It ain't no need for you to be here; you get a drink some place else."

Dan had not seen Irene Fanning since Sunday afternoon. He spent the better part of an hour standing inside his kitchen window and staring across the open field: she is caged over there, I am caged here, by the hateful circumstance which has come to us both . . . He knew that he would need an authentic excuse, to cross to the other house, but every impulse demanded that he go to his woman at once, and share the menacing passage of time with her. Cybo had been jailed somewhere, out of sight; Demon went limping on foot to the village, and returned almost immediately . . . The sun moved into the top fringe of Oak Ridge trees. Excuse or not, with no palpable necessity—Dan could wait no longer.

He shut and locked front and rear doors; the side door had not been used for years, it was painted shut and probably nailed as well. Holding himself to a lounging stroll, he crossed the field. A gray mule with a U.S. brand and a ghastly sore on its flank, was poking about, strayed or wilfully abandoned. It stood squarely in the path, glaring at Dan with rheumy eyes. He threw a clod, and the mule stumbled aside, braying horridly. On the high expanse of grass near the seminary, wagons were arranged in park—a wall of soiled canvas covers before which the men shuttled like actors on an arranged stage: actors who were not certain what their lines might be, or what business they would be called upon to perform.

Demon huddled on the kitchen step, sullenly watching the soldiers who ringed about the well. He stood up, blinking at Dan as if he too were suddenly become a stranger. "Mist Fanning he sick, Mist Dan," he mumbled.

"Sick?"

"A bad misery in the head, and now he got pain heh." The old negro patted his stomach.

"Did you get hold of a doctor?"

"Miss Duffey she say Doc gone out to Culp's, wheh somebody sick. And maybe he stop see 'bout Miss Wade baby."

Dan echoed, "Wade—"

"She got boy baby, Mist Dan. Huh man, he soldier."

He meant the elder of the Wade girls; Dan remembered; she had married a man named McClellan. There was a baby, born the day the Confederates marched through . . . out by the well, an old Irishman with a pleasing baritone was singing *Lula, Lula, Lula is gone*.

Irene called from the kitchen, "Come inside, Mr. Bale." The windlass crunched, wrapping its links tight on the wooden drum of the well. Dan entered the house; Gretel was rattling dishes in the pantry . . . *Irene, I cannot even take your hand*, he wanted to say. The noise of the encampment stuttered through all bounds of hearing. It seemed that this was a bizarre picnic, a male nation loosed amid the austere woods, and frightening all the birds away.

"How are you people standing all this?" Dan asked.

The woman's eyes were holding pain and weariness. "Very well, except for Mr. Fanning. He is ill."

"Demon told me. Do you want me to go and find the doctor?"

"It's inflammation of the—abdomen. He's had attacks before, and the strain of this week has brought it on again. Mrs. Fanning is with him upstairs . . . No," she said, "he seems better within the last hour, and perhaps he won't need any medicine. I think he'd be better without too many drugs to upset him." Her eyes fell away from his; mechanically, she motioned him on into the sitting room.

He said, "You and Mrs. Fanning must not be alone with—"

"There's Demon, and Gretel. We're—"

Tyler's mother called down through the hallway: "Daughter. Who's there?" Her voice was droning, lifeless. "I am greatly abused by all," she was saying.

"It's Mr. Bale, mother."

"Oh." She ordered, with sudden energy, "Have him make those soldiers go away from the well. They bother father—" (A wraith of Mr. Fanning began to expostulate weakly in the distance beyond her: "No, no, mother—they need the water, they must—")

In the yard, Dan approached the circle of perspiring men. He said, "If you can make as little noise as possible, it will be appreciated. A man is sick, in this house." Their tanned faces turned on him. The bucket plunged down again. "Is that a fact?" a young man sneered. "We wear out our butts all day to try and keep the rebs outa his precious farm, and now he—"

"Shut up, Anson," somebody said.

Dan told them, "He's not young. His son is in the army." There was silence, then a grumble which might be assent. "Just as you say, brother. But you better station that darkey here to warn the rest of the boys. They won't know about it, less you tell 'em." Their voices dulled down; they worked the crank slowly, and its squeal was more evident than before.

Dan went back into the house. "I will stay here," he said defiantly to Mrs. Fanning.

The girl sat stiffly in a straight-backed chair, the western windows behind her, the sun skewering through wistaria vines that darkened this room. The level light made brass of her hair, and painted the outline of her soft neck; she wore a gown of Spanish linen, and it did not become her as well as most of her dresses.

"Very well," she said. "Very well."

No one in the room . . . he bent over her, lifting her icy hands. "You don't want me to stay—"

"You know that. Not—here."

"I have to be with you. There is something ominous about this military business. I have a strange horror—"

Her gaze searched his face, firmly, steadily. "Yes. That thought . . . I've had it ever since they first rode past." Her shoulders moved under their tight linen sheathing. "Do you think there'll be a—fight?"

"There's no one here for them to fight; doubtless they will move on, by tomorrow. But there are three thousand men at least, scattered over this mile or two. As long as Mr. Fanning is ill, I want to be close at hand." He paused for a moment, but she said nothing. "Under any circumstances—even if I scarcely knew you, it would be the thing to do. No one would wish to bother Mrs. Knouse!"

This was a house of ugly enchantment. Its walls stood ready to mute any common thought or speech between the woman and Dan. (Tyler lived here: he was a baby, crawling over these floors. He toyed with his blocks and baa-lamb in this hallway; here he was punished and fondled, long before any sin ever existed between us, before we ever came together.) I tell you, Dan wanted to cry, events are surely sapping the life and pungency from us. The world will not leave us alone. Oh, I should have taken you away last Friday night, no matter what roads were cut by the Confederates—

Mrs. Fanning came groaning downstairs. Father was a poor, sick man. She could not understand why the cavalry had felt it necessary to stop in Gettysburg; they should have gone on west or north or wherever they intended to go. "Let them be chasing rebels, that was what the State demanded. If honey boy were here he would send them packing out of the yard. And Daniel, you go out and see that they aren't stealing our wood."

The moon made itself felt, even while the western sky was pink and hollow above the vanished sun. Red spot, chasing scarlet varnish, orange spotted and speckled in the thin woods, score after score of colored blotches: fires were shining. The bugles and the horses neighed together; three thousand men were eating, boiling coffee along the entire ridge, and forever the light horse-artillery rattled in the side roads. This division of cavalry went about secret plottings in which the country people could have no part; even the tired horses knew plans which civilians could never be allowed to know.

Mr. Fanning slept quite comfortably, and much of his pain had gone away. Downstairs, his wife read the Philadelphia paper aloud to Dan Bale and to her daughter-in-law. Poil de Chevres, all-wool Delaines, Challies, Mozambiques—Pacific Lawns at eighteen-and-three-quarter-cents the yard—and all to be had at H. Steel & Son's in North Tenth street. She remembered with approval the fine organdy lawns she'd bought the year before, from Eyre and Landell's.

Some women, she declared pointedly, didn't feel that Philadelphia shops were good enough for them; for her part, she thought it downright unpatriotic for ladies to send abroad for things they might as well buy in their own country . . . Irene made no remark; she had a palm-leaf fan in her hand but it did not move, it might have been glued there.

Oh, my dear . . .

When Mrs. Fanning was gone upstairs, Dan wound the girl in his arms. She did not resist; they stood knotted together for a long moment, perplexed by a thousand forebodings. "I wish you'd written that letter," she murmured weakly, ". . . yes, I know, I asked you to write nothing yet; it is my fault; but if you had written, or gone to find him, I'd feel that something had been done about it."

Mrs. Fanning called over the stair rail: she wished that Daniel would sleep on the couch in the sitting room, where he could hear anybody if they tried to break in.

He went first to look at his own house. No one had disturbed the place, but there were mounted sentries padding in the road, and another battery of small cannon toiling past. A sepulchral silence had fallen over the hills—a silence in which wagons and guns still grated far away, seemingly muffled in sound by the very moonlight which revealed them to the eyes. Miles to the south rose the dull reflection of other fires: more soldiers off there behind those creamy ridges. Dan wondered if they were rebels . . . The dead horse lay beside his gate, and the moonlight made richness out of its swelling carcass.

He sat on the Fannings' porch, all alone in dusty midnight. Cybo whined from the cellar. Insects hissed ferociously, and upstairs Dan knew that Irene was lying on her bed, staring at the ceiling with open eyes. It did not seem that either of them could draw warm, undisciplined breath again until this weight of muddling armies was lifted from their hearts. Back and forth, from bedroom to silver-white porch, their disordered thoughts poured one to the other, and the sprawling brigades lay too thickly and too close to them, bearing them down with cruel impassiveness.

Book Four

JULY FIRST

1.

Toward morning Bale slept at last with the peculiar, hopeless discomfort of the sleeper who knows that some unsolved problem is looming close at hand—whose dreams are shaped but vaguely, and yet carry in them a devilish succession of accusing faces. He was awakened at five o'clock by the deliberate pound of hoofs and crunch of saddles, and Mr. Fanning's voice saying, "If you will come inside, gentlemen, you shall have a cup of it."

Fully clothed, Dan got up from the sofa and opened the door which led from sitting room to rear hall. Beyond, in the outer doorway of the kitchen, Mr. Fanning stood wrapped in his wife's gray shawl, and still wearing his night-cap. He looked like a masquerader, half parson and half witch; his eyes were gelatin in his haggard face. A tall coffee-pot bubbled furiously on the stove; its nutty odor scented the room, and even at this hour the stove fire had made the kitchen stuffy. With midday the place would be a baking hell.

Fanning returned to the stove, nodding nervously at Dan. "I felt the need of coffee," he said in explanation. "Mother allowed me none yesterday, but now I crave it. Sadly."

Dan asked, "How do you feel?"

"I am greatly improved. All pain is gone—" In the

yard sounded a mutter of voices, a clatter of dismount-
ing men. "A party of officers just crossed the lawn,"
whispered Fanning, "and they commented upon the
odor of coffee. I made bold to offer them some. You
will join us, of course?"

"Thank you," Bale said. "I'd like to rest up a trifle."
He went to the farther end of the rear hall and entered
the dark wash-room. Beyond the heavy, closed doors
he could hear soldiers tramping into the kitchen; men
seemed to move with a thunderous tread, once they
were girded for war. Dan filled the lead-colored bowl
and buried his face in the cool, dark water. In the
dim mirror he looked at himself as he combed his
hair. He thought that he appeared very grim, discon-
solate to the point of soullessness, perhaps because he
needed to shave.

He would have preferred to leave by the east door
and go home across the field, now that Mr. Fanning
was once more astir and accountable . . . He went
back through the passageway: at least he would be
compelled to stop for a moment. There would be no
seeing Irene at this hour, and he was glad that he could
not see her until he had established a waking equilib-
rium. The dreams, many of them, were about her and
Tyler. They were wretched illusions of weeping and of
death.

The kitchen seemed stuffed with uniforms, although
only four men had come in to accept Mr. Fanning's
invitation. A short-necked officer with a wide brush
of sandy mustache, sat beside the kitchen table; he
wore the stars of a brigadier-general, and his inferior
officers stood across the room, helping themselves to
cream and sugar . . . The general nodded at Dan; his
square hand stirred briskly the steaming cup before

him. "General Buford," said Fanning, "this is my neighbor, Mr. Bale." He turned to the staff officers. "Are you gentlemen getting sufficient—?"

Their boots scraped on the white floor. "We're coming first rate."

Buford poured out a saucerful of coffee and lifted it to his lips. His parched eyelids closed momentarily over eyes strained by wakefulness, the eyes of one who was very tired. "Good coffee," he murmured.

"I have been ill, and was making some for myself when you passed through the yard. I—"

"We shouldn't levy off you," the soldier said.

Mr. Fanning choked in his cup. "My pleasure, General. My only son is with the army. Captain Tyler Fanning, the Seventy-second Pennsylvania Volunteers. Perhaps you have met him?" he asked.

A young officer snickered, and Buford shot a hard glance at him. He put down his saucer and poured more coffee from the cup. "I don't believe I recollect the name, Mr. Fanning."

Outside, a horse plunged skittishly. "Hold on, Pretty," droned a voice. A man in blue stood beside a gray mare, grasping a net of bridle reins in one hand, and in his other the pole of a brief flag which flashed crimson in the climbing sunlight. The folds twisted in and out, winding, unwinding against staff. A numeral: *I*.

Mr. Fanning nodded toward the door. "Your man outside—the standard-bearer or orderly or whatever he may be—will he—?"

"No, sir," said a young captain. "He doesn't drink coffee."

"Morris?" asked a major in a checkered shirt. "Why, he has religious principles against it."

No one spoke for a moment. You could hear them all sipping noisily at the hot liquid, tapping their spoons against the china cups as if they liked the sound. The captain belched.

General Buford turned, gazing at Dan Bale and again at his host. He had a soiled hat balanced on his knee, and his breeches were soaked to the crotch with the moisture of bushes through which he had been riding. "Did either of you see the rebels hereabouts, yesterday?" he asked.

"Rebels?" repeated Mr. Fanning.

The general shrugged. "They were here, according to farmers out along the turnpike, west."

Dan said, "I was at work in my yard most of the forenoon. I saw none."

Mr. Fanning asked once more, "Rebels?" His hand shook brown splashes from his cup.

Buford drained the last of his coffee. "At least a scouting party of infantry. They were seen near the school up here, but they cut for it when our folks came to town . . . No, thank you. No second cup." He stood up, twisting his tired shoulders, rubbing his buttocks. "Well, gentlemen," he said to his staff. He turned toward Mr. Fanning. "That hit the spot, after a night in the saddle. Is your family here?"

The older man raised his eyebrows. He still wore the white night-cap. "Certainly. My wife and my—"

"Get them into the cellar as soon as you hear any firing."

The room was still. Far away sounded the rumble of wide wheels—wagons or artillery, Dan could not tell which.

"Firing." Fanning's jaw clicked. "Do you expect—?"

Buford slapped his hat against his thigh. He swung on his heel, facing the door; he spoke with flat detachment, relating a very tiresome fact. "It'll be fought at this point. I'm only afraid it'll be commenced before the infantry can get up. We're thankful for the coffee, Mr. Fanning." He walked out to the stoop, his damp boots squeaking in leather agony at every step. His officers followed, saluting, saying their thank-yous, jingle and crunch across the floor . . . a rapid thud grew into hearing—a horse, and galloping. "Here's Colonel Devin, sir," the young captain announced.

Buford's dry voice rapped out, shrill and curt. "Hello, Tom! Are your videttes all in place, as ordered?"

A man on an ugly, short-barreled horse came trotting through the open gate from the north pasture. Dan could see him leaning forward, saluting, pivoting in a quick circle. Buford had moved out of sight.

"General, I've got them out, but there's not such necessity as you think."

Through the chatter and trampling, the commander's words found their way. "You'll see, Tom," he said.

The officer laughed. "I'll take care of all that will attack my front in the next twenty-four hours."

Buford came into view again. He was forcing his boot-toes through his stirrups, reaching forward and adjusting the curb-bit as his big chestnut wrenched her head about . . . There seemed to be a fatal weight of experience riding his body, making him appear years older than he was. Through the doorway, Bale stared at the blue-clad man with his ragged leather gloves and his shapeless mustache. The war will kill him, Bale knew suddenly. He will die of it. I am looking at a man who is close to death, and seems to know how close.

"No, you won't take care of them, Colonel," the general declared. "They'll attack you this morning and they'll come a-booming when they come—skirmishers three deep. You watch! You'll have to fight like the devil to hold out until supports get here. I only hope Reynolds is routing his infantry out of bed afore this."

The colonel laughed, with little humor but no hint of mockery. "You seem pretty certain, sir."

Buford nudged his mare a few steps forward and jerked his forefinger in Colonel Devin's face. "I haven't been riding all over these hills for nothing, all night long. This place is damn important, and the enemy knows it if he's got half an eye. They'll sweat their guts out to take this ridge. We'll be lucky to hold it, I reckon." He said, "All right, boys, come along." The whole posse rode up across the farmyard.

Dan stood watching, his coffee untasted in the cup he held. He heard himself saying, "I hope his fears aren't realized. There is no—"

"Listen!" exclaimed Mr. Fanning. He lifted his palm, fingers stiff, his arm quivering under the fold of gray fringe. "Listen." His mouth drooped open.

Bale turned. In the cellarway, Cybo sniffed and scraped against the door with his toe-nails. The chickens were clucking, a comfortable barnyard monotone outside, but faintly above all the domestic clamor pattered the sound of shots—a medley of them, so distant that they seemed half imagined. Then the blue morning fell away into nerveless silence again, and only the waking camp stirred with its innocent pandemonium.

2.

The dead horse lay in the ditch still. Its belly was swelling rapidly, and the two left legs no longer stretched on the ground but were lifted horizontally by the steady bloating of the carcass. From the front porch of the Bale house could be heard an increasing hum of shiny green and purple flies which crept on the taut skin or twisted in the air above.

Mrs. Knouse was fastening a sign at her gate—a ragged wafer of cardboard hung from a stretched cord. She had printed the legend with red keel: *No Tresspass.* She pushed back her sunbonnet and stared belligerently at Dan Bale as he came through his yard. It was well after six o'clock; the sun burned above the church spires and the distant tower of the college, and already its warmth could be felt on the face.

"There's too many of 'em," Mrs. Knouse said. "I wouldn't have a flower left if I let 'em traipse in here after water."

"Who?"

She nodded toward the long rows of wagons near the seminary. "Them." Bugles had talked and ordered; hearty streams of cavalry had ridden over the ridge and vanished among the meadows beyond; still the groves twitched with moving men. It seemed wholly senseless for people to engage in any such activity on a morning like this. Farmers would be cradling their grain.

Bale asked the old woman, "Did you hear the shooting?"

She was molded there, a stubborn and unbelieving image with jaw agape.

"Half an hour or so ago," he told her. "I've just inquired of a soldier. He said it was a skirmish out in the picket line: they seem to think there may be fighting close by. You'd better go down cellar if there's any trouble."

She echoed, "Trouble, Daniel? A war? Fighting—" He went into his house, leaving her among the shafts of larkspur, bewildered by this incredible idea.

The house had the hollow dampness of a brick house tightly closed for many hours. The Seth Thomas clock and a smaller gilt clock in the library were counting the minutes, stirring their hidden cogs. Dan went out to the kitchen, opened the stove, and arranged a handful of kindlings in the fire-box. Yellow flame hunted deliberately along the resinous splinters, curled and mantled up through the pile. As soon as the fire was burning well, he filled the tea kettle and set it over the open stove-hole. If he intended to shave, he'd best be about it before the day grew warmer.

Something, he thought, must be done with the dead horse. If the troops weren't going to dispose of it, he would have to secure assistance and haul the thing into a field where it could be burned or buried. A few gallons of coal oil and some dry logs might do the trick. There would be an ungodly odor. Perhaps it wouldn't take too long to dig a hole. Out west, a dead animal was dragged far on the prairie; the crows and the elements had their skillful, wilderness way in such matters. He thought, "A dead horse lying beside the Chambersburg Pike! No, that would hardly do. The town council will be up in arms if they learn of it."

He set a mirror in the kitchen window and went about the business of shaving. This was the window outside which Elmer Quagger had stood, so many ages before. Time was more certainly relative than ever Bale had realized; these weeks in Gettysburg had taught him the fallacy of ordinary reckoning. Echoing years, since first he took his neighbor's wife ... Through the window, past the corner of the mirror frame, the Fanning house lifted amid its sheds and vines, an engraved landscape which he would see for years to come, and always with poignancy. He decided: *she's up and about by now. I'm glad I left, and did not wait for her to come downstairs. There is so little we can say over there; the walls come close and muffle our words, the furniture haunts us. Mr. Fanning is recovered from his attack of illness, thank fortune. I did not need to stay.*

He cooked a skillet full of bacon, and brought out a jar of preserves. He sat at the kitchen table with the food before him, and a novel he had bought in Chicago as he came east. Now he opened it for the first time. An author named Melville ... the story was of remote islands, and two young seamen who fled their ship. *Typee.* It sounded like a word in the Pottawattomie language. The woman kept coming between him and this narrow print. She was saturated in the agony which she had suffered in his dreams ... *Most evil circumstance, most disheartening subterfuge, and we have enmeshed ourselves accordingly. I wonder,* she cried to him, *if ever we'll be free of ourselves.*

There were soldiers at the well pumping intermittently, trudging with their splashing buckets, but no hordes such as had come the evening before. Their conversation heckled through the open door. *The old man sold her after that. Pshaw, she wa'n't no good for work in the field. No, I guess she wouldn't be. And liable to run away if the women-folks drove her ... one of the trimmest shapes you ever say. Nice, round*

little boobies, and no feller had ever touched her be-
fore . . . couple of brass guns whacking away, but we
come in under them. They started to limber up and
retreat when they saw we meant business. Yah, I re-
member. Goodrich was there. Was he? Yah, just after
he joined the calvary . . . in a valley beyond, in a secret place far from the harbor, men could hide forever in the flowery shade. But the valley of Typee was
a place of danger. They must find another valley . . .

Eight o'clock, rang the Seth Thomas. It offered its
cozy announcement, a loose spring clicked, and the
little hammer lay back to await another hour. Bale
looked up from the book. A scrap of bacon lay in cool,
white grease on his plate—yes, he had eaten breakfast,
he had been reading. Soldiers came for water, soldiers
talked and annoyed him, and all the time that black
aching in forbidden corners of his brain—

Chinese crackers. The boys—they've bought crackers at Pock's store. The Fourth is only a few days
away, and how Elijah and I used to trade torpedoes.

Again the distant spatter of explosions like a far-
away string of little red tubes, popping round-echoed
under the hot sky. Dan stood up suddenly, and the
chair teetered and went over with a crash . . . He was
out in the yard, in the candid frying of sunlight. Bang:
one lone cracker off beyond Oak Ridge. Patter, snap,
bam-bam, the others retorted. Muskets and carbines;
now he knew. Close beside the seminary a bugle began
to peal, startled from some sluggish dream. It was a
round yellow throat, braying with spirited hoarseness.
Ta-ta-tata-tatala, ta-ta-tata-tatata. Near the first trees a
man roared: "No, No! Lieutenant Pennybacker said
for you to stay till you was relieved!" Then all the futile
squibs, the gilt-wrapped Chinese foolishness, seemed
to mass in a single powder charge, hollow and effort-

less and sullen. The hot grass felt the ground surge underneath and then lie still again.

Off to the southwest rose a growing medley, yells and horse sounds, where a drift of mounted men scurried among the trees. He could see them plainly as they poured across the yellow glades of sunshine which tilted toward the crest. They were swinging from their horses: rapidly the landscape resolved itself into struggling knots of animals, little cores and festers of brown horses, flipping manes and tails, and each four horses held by a lead soldier in painted blue. A lone volcano blasted its earthy cap, out on the Pike; again the yard wriggled underfoot.

Even as Bale turned to look at the long row of parked wagons, one of the vehicles wrenched out of line and went jolting across the uneven ground toward the Fairfield road. Then the third, then another much farther along the wooden rank. The butchered air seemed to crack with the sound of their wheels, the sudden snarls of drivers, and all the slapping of dead leather on living hide. They looked like dirty gray chickens, chickens with cumbersome wheels instead of legs, staggering away from a shelter once friendly but now approached by the menace of a hawk. Underneath their pressure dry branches snapped on the ground, and uniformed men and men in black aprons went scuttling out of their path. In the country west of the ridge, far down near Willoughby Run, the spatter of carbines grew more distinct. *Take care,* a cursing quartette burst out, *where the devil ye're* ... a wagon swayed to one side, turned left and went over with a resounding smash against a farrier's cart. One of the horses was down. Through the dust and the spasm of kicking legs, men came tumbling to cut the tangled harness.

Northwest, where the new railroad grade cleaved the ridge, more bugles were signalling a repeated message. The steady fall of horses' hoofs, trained creatures, a mechanized fragment of this remarkable horde: they were thundering up the Pike, a gun which had been left behind in the village and only now was rocking out to join the trumpets which yelled for it. Twenty-four bony legs tearing into the dust, teams swam high above the road, and riders on three of the horses were strapping savagely. The tawny metal tube bounded from side to side behind them. "Why," Dan said aloud and to the strange silence which clothed the empty yard—"that general was a prophet, all the time he drank his coffee. He said this would happen. *Come a-booming when they come—*"

Maybe this frantic little cannon was part of the supports which he had mentioned . . . A single horse skimmed up out of the railroad cut and across the field toward the Pike. Its rider threw himself to the ground as the animal halted, sliding broadside by the high north fence. He flung against the rails; one went down, another, another—Dan could hear them thumping and rolling. The horses and the brass gun roared past, lathered in grit, red-striped clowns clinging desperately to the cubed gun carriage. The man at the fence mouthed: "Calif's straight ahead on this road!" His scream cut itself short; the churning dust wiped across in front of him; the gun went bounding up the slope, horses and limber and all, and when the haze had drifted low Dan could see that the man was once more mounted—he was past the breach he had made in the fence, and pounding toward Stevens Run in a new storm of his own making.

Here was war of some sort, tormenting the roads; war which staggered with flapping, canvas-weighted wagons. Dan had the notion that he was expected to do something about this—he did not know what to do. Tyler should be at hand: he was a soldier, such things were his responsibility, and let the bastard be there to accept it.

Mrs. Knouse wailed through a crack of her kitchen door: "Daniel, is there going to be a battle by the seminary?" He yelled, "Stay in your house. Go down cellar—mind, now! There's apt to be bullets flying round." And dimly, he thought he heard them high above his head, tired insects whispering, long m-sounds against the pale oven of the sky.

Irene Fanning was not inside the house, where she belonged. She was out in the vegetable garden, slim bust and spreading width of green gown; she was exposed to this unearthly riot. He vaulted over the fence and ran across the pasture as fast as he could run. The lone army mule was trotting in a three-legged circle, round and round and round, with a knot of insects buzzing over the great ulcer on its flank. It lunged away from the path as Bale raced past. Demon scooted out of the barn, waving halters in his fist; the two old nags, the long-retired carriage team, cantered off with their heads held high.

The fence bars were contrived for delay, for the purpose of tripping and bruising ankle bones as one sprang over them. Dan crossed the garden. The girl watched him come. She wore a bonnet with a wide, starchy brim and there were long gardening-gloves drawn over her hands and wrists. She held a tin dishpan, half full of lettuce.

"You'd better go into the house at once," he cried. "This is a battle—a real one. They may be all over this land in another ten minutes."

She looked at him very soberly, then made a thin

smile. "At first, when I heard those big explosions, I thought workmen were blasting on the new railway line. It sounded like that, when they were blasting out rocks in the hill."

"No, it's trouble. More than anyone wants, I'm afraid." He clenched his hands, wondering at the calmness with which she faced him. "Look here," he said, again, "you'd better go inside." The m's were skating through the air, high above: invisible birds, they seemed. From a great distance came a hollow reverberation, and as if in delayed answer a ball of noisy smoke frayed up, north of the Schmucker house on the ridge. The woman did not move, though she clutched her pan of lettuce more tightly . . . *Loo,* men yelled, *looroo aaray,* incoherent howlings, and out of their jargon launched one shriek which shafted higher, higher, a sliver from all the agony ever born in the world. Dan's hand clutched Irene Fanning's elbow; he drew her along with him. "That scream," she whispered, "oh, heaven, what—?" "Horse," he said.

He helped her up on the stoop; Mr. Fanning opened the door for them. His face was drawn, pearl-colored. "I believe," he said, "that we had better take refuge in the cellar. Gretel is already there." He cried, "Mother! Mother, come down from upstairs—" and hurried lamely into the front hall. Irene put her pan on the kitchen table, and drew off her gardening-gloves. "Are you coming to the cellar with us?" she asked.

Dan shook his head. "You'd best take drinking water, and perhaps some food. If the shooting comes near, this kitchen will not be safe."

"You speak as if you knew."

"I do know," he said. "There were hundreds killed in Minnesota during the uprising last year. I may not be in the army, but I know how bullets can go through plank doors."

She made a grimace. "Will you reach me some candles? They're up in the high cupboard." The front stairway was shivering as Mrs. Fanning grunted her way down; window glass kept up a constant vibration under the impact of artillery. "They haven't got many cannon," Dan said. "Maybe it's just as well for those of us who live here."

"The rebels—perhaps they have more—"

He stood on the wide shelf and handed down the bundle of white candles, and a glutinous block of old-fashioned matches. "No," she said, "not those. The parlor matches are right there in a box. Over farther. There."

He pressed a sheaf of loose matches into her hand . . . fingers I have fondled, fingers which have caressed me . . . "Thank you, Mr. Bale."

Fanning cried from the passageway, "Daughter. Where is Demon?"

"He's out in the field," Bale answered. "I'll go fetch him."

"Thank you," Irene said, again. "I believe he is trying to drive Pansy and Pincus into the barn."

Dan told them, "Do you go down cellar. The firing's coming nearer, rapidly." He felt the woman staring at his back, felt the dull fear and increasing trouble of her breathing. He went out into the yard; the light outer door banged on his heel, and now he could see a slow fog of saffron staining the green tops of Oak Ridge. The sun puffed higher, intense and mighty, a desert sun.

Demon was out beyond the chicken-run. He had one of the team safely inside the stable, but the old white mare eluded him. She stood on a rocky knoll, lifting her hoofs one after another, as if the soil were too hot to stand upon. "Demon," Dan yelled, "go into the house."

"I got get Pansy," the negro wailed.

Bale said, "I'll get her. Mr. Fanning said for you to hurry!" He took the old servant by his shoulders and turned him around, and gave him a slap in the small of his back. Demon scampered toward the back door, his loose clothes bagging around him, his silver poll glistening. "Pincus tied in the bahn!" he howled. "He tied, Mist Dan—"

Bale propped the stable door with a slanted board. He caught up some small stones and sprinted out into the pasture. Pansy tossed her head and whinnied peevishly. He threw a stone: it caught her in the ribs. She turned toward the barn, and the man raced abreast of her, still throwing stones. Stiff-legged, she tried to swing toward the garden, but he cut her path. Then she lumbered into the stable. He shut the door and sank the wooden bar into its notch.

The last of the big wagons, a final straggle of black-smiths' carts, rumbled hastily toward the village along the Fairfield road. Above the constant crackle of rifle fire, and punctuated by the empty slamming of larger guns, Dan could hear a far-away sound . . . strange sound which he had never heard before. It was high, windy—it seemed to possess all creation which lay west of those racketing woods.

He went back to the house. Mr. Fanning was pattering from room to room, closing windows, his slippers whispering over the carpets. "You must come into the cellar with us, Daniel."

"No, I must go home." He said, "I wish you were all over there instead of here, though the cellar itself is tiny. A brick house would be safer and less apt to be fired."

Fanning's unhealthy face at the door. "Merciful Heavens, sir! Do you think there's a possibility—?"

"Well," Dan said, "it's war." He drew the sofa out of its corner, hauled it through the door and into the passage; the cellar doorway was wide enough to admit it. " 'Way below," he called, and moved backward down the damp stairs, dragging the monstrous piece after him. He could feel long-unused muscles trying to rip themselves loose within his shoulders. " 'Way," he gasped . . . The sofa began to slide; he leaned forward, breaking its descent until he could rest the bottom legs on cellar stones. Then he swung the higher end around.

Bedford Fanning came down slowly, holding at the sides of the stairway for support. "Mother," he said.

She sobbed, "I feel so kind of sickish—"

Irene had lighted two candles. The gloom was thick—it smelled of potatoes, of long-stored vegetables and wines, and of the cool seepage where lizards crawled. Gretel was squatting on an upended box beside the wall, a round-bellied little woman with padded cheeks which now were crimsoned by excitement and fear. "Ach," she kept whispering, "good God, Missis Fanning, and rebels come with pistols by them."

"You can be a little more comfortable with the sofa," Dan said. He looked quickly around the place. "Only two windows, and they're small and facing the south and east."

Mrs. Fanning sighed, "Now, father, you lie down and rest." Dan knew that she was making a most laudable effort to expunge her own dishonest misery, in the face of her husband's greater need. She took the man's hands and drew him toward the couch. Her hair was disarranged; long tails of it hung raggedly around her shoulders, and the wire ringlets across her forehead were limp and feeble things. In this mossy gloom, she appeared as an elephantine sorceress. She moaned again, "Yes, Bedford. You lie down—what if you should get another spell—"

Somewhere in the house above sounded a tinkle of breaking glass. A window-pane. Dan went up the stairs to bring cushions and the folded afghan which he had dumped from the sofa when he dragged it out of the sitting room . . . He turned, his arms loaded, and found Irene standing behind him. "Oh, go down," he commanded roughly.

Her dry whisper came: "I wish you would stay."

"With them? I'd go mad. If you were with me, alone—"

She cried his name, softly. "Oh, what is wrong? I have the utmost horror of this thing—a hideous—"

"Yes," he said, and understanding the truth only as he spoke it for the first time. "These armies have come between us." The room was breathless with caged summer, now that all the doors and windows had been closed.

She said, "Kiss me goodbye."

He bent down. There was a scuffling sound in the kitchen; they broke apart. Demon scraped past the door. He had a thick book he had brought from the little shed which was his. They heard him go creeping fearfully down the cellar stairs, murmuring some few words to himself, over and over.

Irene stifled a sob. "Demon has his Bible. He cannot read, but he owns a Bible; now it is a refuge for him."

"He is more fortunate than we," Dan said. The

windows jiggled; it seemed that boards in the floor were spreading and quivering with each fresh explosion.

The woman pressed her lips against his mouth, against his chin, and dragging down into the hollow of his throat. "I have brought this upon us," she whispered with full belief. "Dan, I have. By my—selfishness. It is some kind of judgment—"

He growled, "Oh, stop saying that!" Her eyes held his for a moment; they were set and dry and devoid of any expression; then she picked up a book, a newspaper and a mending basket from the table, and went out into the rear hallway. She descended the steep stairs in front of Bale, and she did not look at him again. Mr. Fanning was seated on the couch beside his wife; her bulk sagged deep in the creaking sofa springs. The man gazed up as Dan placed the pillows beside him. Candlelight gave a false color to his face.

"Did you see the dog, Daniel?"

"Nowhere. Isn't he—?"

"He scampered out, some time ago."

"I'll shut him up if I see him," Bale said. "Goodbye." The mutter of uneven firing rose into a stormy pulsation, without the barest second of silence in which no report was echoing. Dan saw Irene's hair, froth of old gold; it appeared finer and silkier than ever he had seen it before . . . Goodbye, the voices ached. Take care, take care.

He felt the doors all fastened on the inside. He crawled out of a window, and dropped to the ground a few feet below. The nervousness of musketry ran behind Oak Ridge, north across the railroad cut and seemingly as far as Oak Hill. Cybo was nowhere in sight. A few chickens still scratched industriously

beneath the gaunt plum trees, but most of the flock
had been driven to shelter by the sound of battle. A
shell came hissing from the west; you could hear the
whirring gush of its propulsion, and half see the quick
cleavage of the air. Then it burst in a fan of spraying
white feathers, near the Johnson house at the ridge's
crest.

Inside the seminary cupola, men were moving about.
Dan saw their heads waggling at the apertures, and
sunlight dazzled for a moment on some brass about
them. Across the barrier beyond the upper end of
Fanning's pasture, a group of soldiers gathered around
something which lay on the ground. One by one,
slowly, through the smoky shade and across the
open green of the seminary lawn, dingy figures came
hobbling.

Wounded men: they began to dot the whole expanse, dragging themselves close to the trees, and still
in the west you could hear that windy, wailing sound.
Bale thought, it must be the wounded; those who are
hurt—they are making that vast crying. Christ, that
there should be so many of them.

A soldier scrambled over the broken fence and ran
down the slope. His face grew rapidly ... now he
was near, he was in his undershirt, and one of his
arms seemed painted to the elbow. He whooped, "Let
me have some water!" He trotted past the corner of
the granary, his thin ribs puffing out against his
soaked flannels. "For God's sake—" he wailed.

There was a bucket beside the well. Dan wound
the windlass furiously. The boy stood swinging his
hands; his face was marked with fresh tears. "Ma
said to look out for each other," he kept repeating,
"Ma said to look out. Jesus, hurry up with that water!" He snatched the full pail and darted off again.

There would be more of them, Dan knew. He found a wooden bucket inside the open door of the carriage house. He emptied an accumulation of chaff and straw, drew the pail full of water, and went up the field toward the frosty, sliding smoke.

The wild-faced boy had stopped beyond a heap of stones at the fence corner. He was on his knees beside a flat mound—a man who wore a tight, yellow-trimmed jacket drenched with winy stains. His legs kept bending and straightening again as if they worked an invisible treadmill. "Ike!" gasped the boy. He slopped a handful of water across the soldier's face. *Ike.* The man had been shot in the jaw; a few strands of damp beard hung down, dotted with fragments of white teeth; his mouth was a spongy red well from which curdling streams trickled along each cheek. "Oh, my God," said the boy beside him. "Do something, mister! This here's my brother." The wounded soldier said *ull,* and his knees began to relax. "Our Father which art in heaven hallow'd be Thy name—" the boy shouted. He raised his dirty face and stared at Dan with wild blue eyes. "Oh, look at him. Oh, my God. Oh . . ." A huge bubble formed at the opening of the shattered mouth: it broke, spattering the face above with a sticky spray. The long, yellow-striped legs stretched across the grass, the outflung hands cupped lazily. The man lay very still, his eyes looking at the smoke which spread reluctantly toward the zenith. "Oh, he's dead. God, oh, my God," cried his brother. He began to whine, beating his fists against his knees . . . Farther up the campus, a hoarse query: "How about some of that water over here, friend?"

Dan heard a voice, deep and calm, say, "Right away." It was his own voice, he knew now, but it seemed as if he were standing back in the dooryard, gazing at this hill, this looming academy where so many theological doctrines had been learned. He thought: Elijah should have waited. He'd have had fighting enough, right here . . . He wondered where Elijah had gone, and how it was with him; then he found himself the center of muddling men, who sobbed and gulped as they strove to suck the water from groping palms. He left the bucket with them, and went on toward the higher ground. Increasing, peppery with burnt powder, the smoke sagged in murky strands. Someone called, "Non-combatants to the rear!" but when Bale turned he could see no one beckoning at him.

Beside the seminary stood a knot of horses, patient, heads bowed, their empty saddles shining like chocolate mirrors. That same man who held the little banner with its embroidered figure *I* was Morris, the man with principles against coffee-drinking. General Buford must be inside the building . . . The acrid haze spread apart for a moment, and Dan had a clear view of McPherson's woods and the glittering fields which spread away to the north. On that ridge dwelt a fuzz of toy men who wriggled from stumps to walls, who lay behind the ragged shrubbery and fired rapidly toward the west. There were no enemies to be seen, no sign of their existence save for a rose-colored cone which bobbed out of sight in the valley ahead. "I've seen a battle flag," Dan said: so that is what men follow to their death . . . Then haze went up from the wheat and down from the sky, closed together and shut those warring pygmies in a ruinous world of their own. Closer to the ears, the constant cry kept trilling beyond the rifle reports, as if five thousand ghosts were howling together.

A man crept out from the first line of trees; he came on his hands and one knee, crawling methodically and apparently without pain. One leg dragged loosely behind him; his boot was torn half off. Bale went toward him. Something said *wasss* close above his head, and a few leaves flickered past. The crawling man constructed a terrible grin of his whitish face. "No." He shook a stubborn head. "I can make it, easy. This isn't the first time for me." He padded rapidly past, and then turned and called, "If you're dead set on it, there's plenty worse wounded that need help. But I'd advise you to retire. No place for citizens."

Dan asked, "What is that sound?"

"Sound?" Wearily, the man lifted his hand and wiped the jewels of perspiration from his forehead. "Yelling noise?"

"I thought it must be the wounded. But—"

The soldier smirked fiendishly. "Rebels. They always do that." He crept on toward the seminary . . . "Hey," someone cried. "Hey. Civilian!" A thin, bald-headed officer had risen from behind a log, and was beckoning with the field-glasses in his hand. He jerked his head toward the rear. "Want to get killed," he was shouting—"get back out of this." The guns exploded, exploded . . . Dan came back; still he could detect the greasy hum of bullets close around. The officer shook his sunburnt head at him. "It passes understanding. If I were out of this, I'd not tempt Providence."

"Will they come this far?"

The officer spat a cud upon the trampled sod. "You'll be safer in—say, Philadelphia. Take yourself in that direction before a minié bites you." He crouched once more, and lifted the glass.

Herr's farm, Minnigh's farm, the Germels house, were swallowed by a popping, resounding fog. Out near the turnpike a battery of guns fired without a pause for breath, but all this roar could not drown the falsetto howl of human throats . . . the rebels, the *whoooo* of desolation that walked with them as they drilled their way closer.

Bale reached the crawling soldier and lifted him upright, thrusting an arm under his shoulders. The trooper grimaced painfully. "Well. Thought you was headed towards the war." He leaned heavily against Dan, using him for a crutch; he exuded the rancid odor of one who was long unwashed. They moved across a flower bed where the pink geraniums were trodden to rags by a hundred boot-heels. "Here," the soldier ordered, "set me down against a good brick wall. I don't want a case shot in my hind end." Dan lowered him to the ground in a corner near the seminary door; the sun scorched around them.

"Don't you want to be in the shade?"

"Nope. Good, clean sunshine is the stuff for crawlers. Gray ramblers . . . prob'ly you never had any. I'll wait right here until a beautiful lady comes with a dish of brandy-peaches, or something. Take care!" He saluted weakly, then took out a jack-knife and began to slit his shattered boot.

Through the door of the building, a slim youth came springing like a monkey out of a box. He sailed into the saddle of a little bay horse and went pounding up across the lawn, heedless of the wounded men who tumbled out of his way. "That's a mighty hurry," a cracked voice declared. "Old John must be getting his dander up . . ." The surf of firing slid higher, the reports were sharper, shorter, more metallic. "There go the Colts'," remarked the same voice. "Ammunition's going." The owner of the voice racked past Dan Bale; he stared curiously at him, then lunged on, a wizened, long-armed man with two carbines for canes. High overhead, Dan heard a sudden cry: "That's it, sir! First Corps guidon, or else—" He looked up at the cupola. An officer was leaning out, a telescope clamped against his eye and pointed toward the south. From inside the building sounded a trample of hurrying feet: General Buford came out on the steps, drawing on his ragged gloves, though the sun was cooking every grass-blade. The major with the checkered shirt limped behind him; he had a red-stained cloth wrapped around his groin and upper thighs, like an enormous diaper. "Here he comes," said Buford.

A bearded man in a slouch hat was trotting up the slope, threading his horse among the apple trees, bending low to avoid the gnarly boughs which reached down. "It's Reynolds himself!" the major exclaimed. Bale had a clear view of the newcomer as he came past: his horse was soaped from neck to flanks, and little clots of sputum blew from its muzzle. Sad soldier . . . this man who hurried under the fruit trees was drawn taut by enormous unhappinesses, blistered by cruel loads. His scrawny beard was sugared with dust, and in spite of the temperature he had his blouse neatly buttoned, the tight seams overlapping; his shoulder-straps were crusty with stars.

He wheeled in front of the seminary, and waved his hand. "What's the matter, John?" he demanded. The guns sounded in a crackling welcome.

Bulford ran down the steps, his spurs tinkling. "There's hell to pay. They jumped me first thing this morning, General. Is that your folks down the road, coming from Emmetsburg?"

The general nodded. "The First Corps. They're on

the road." He looked back across the valley behind him. "I can get Wadsworth up here in short order, behind this ridge we're on. Do you think you can hold out until his infantry is in line?"

"Reckon I can," the cavalryman said. Dan walked on toward the fence. General Reynolds rode toward the crest of the ridge, with Buford and an aid scrambling upon their horses and turning after him. The Confederate lines must be toiling closer; their endless soprano drone was more distinct—it seemed that the hills would never be free of its wailing.

Bale circled the wrecked wagon and the motionless horse which lay snared in clipped ends of harness; he stopped at the pasture fence. The dead soldier lay in the same place—the soldier named Ike. Noisy flies were gathering above his face, and his brother was nowhere to be seen.

"Gone to git him some rebels," said a weak voice.

Dan turned. A soldier sat propped against the trunk of an apple tree, twenty feet away. He had torn his shirt off, and was stuffing the rags against his bloody side. He breathed rapidly, nodding at Dan. "Hain't you the fellow who was here with water, spell ago? You might cover his face, fellow, so's the flies won't eat him all to once't. Here, take this thing."

Feebly, he tried to throw his discarded jacket across the intervening space. Dan picked it up, and went to the corpse. "Martin's gone to pick him some Butternuts. It's a mercy—he'll shoot the gravy out of any that gets in his way . . ." He coughed some blood and saliva into his beard. "I know them boys well; they come from Indiana, same as me. That's kind of you, fellow, to cover up a poor fellow that way who can't help himself. How'd you like to be et by flies? No more would I."

Oh, Dan wanted to say, shut your gossiping mouth. Guns still built their prodigious mountain of smoke above the ridge, driving a spiteful punctuation into that approaching scream. A muted thudding passed close at hand; one of Buford's officers fled through the orchard, and out over the pasture. He cut across the Fairfield road and went rocking on past the extension of Middle street. *Oh, Marthy,* said the Indiana trooper, and groaned seriously. A fat man in a silk hat came clambering over the fence behind the Bale house. He looked sullen and dogged in his isolation, and a brown satchel dangled from his hand. Dan ran toward him, motioning him back. "Doc!" he yelled.

Duffey waved, but did not pause in his lumbering scramble up the briary incline. Whole sections of the seminary fence lay flat; he floundered across the loose rails, and his face was reddish purple. He began, "Now, never be minding any discussion. I wasn't stopping any of those men on the road—they're able enough, if they can get away so neat. I thought I'd be up and visit the invalids."

"You'd better get out of here," Bale said. "They've ordered me away."

The doctor licked his lips. "This won't be as dangerous as the cholera. You should have seen it in Philadelphia—folks dying like flies, and you never knew when it would be biting you." His webbed eyelids rolled up, and he cocked his head toward the man who sat propped against the tree. "There's one bad hit, I judge. Come along."

They stopped beside the man from Indiana. "What have you been letting them do to you, friend?" Duffey went down on his knees, sighing.

The soldier clutched the old man's sleeve with a

greedy grasp. "Do something fer me," he gasped. "I got a ball in my body—"

"Then you're half a man at least," rumbled the doctor. Gently, he lifted away the poultice of crimson rags which the man had bunched against his side. There was a purple hole the size of a dime, from which the color oozed. "Open my grip," Duffey ordered, and Dan clicked the fasteners. "There's lint on top." He lifted the fuzzy mass in his coarse fingers. He winked at the anxious face which gaped up at him. "Don't prepare for glory yet, my friend—you might be disappointing yourself. Unn . . . it's through the diaphragm, if I mistake not, at about the eighth intercostal. Doubtless it's to the left of the ensiform cartilage extremity." He rattled the words.

The ground quavered beneath them, like a crust over a deep jelly pie. The trooper wailed, "Reckon I'll never see Marthy again. That sounds like an awful wound." He whined and shuddered under Duffey's inquisition. The doctor said, without raising his head: "Dan. Get me some water." And he told his patient: "Sure, you're sound as a cherry stone. Only pray to whatever church god you want, and bear in mind that folks have come all the way from Harrisburg to let me fool with their innards."

When Bale came back with the water, he found the man lying in the shade with a bundle of grass under his head and Duffey's coat around him; the wound was newly bandaged. Duffey wiped his hands on a cloth. "Give our friend a drink," he directed, "and come along." He led the way toward the seminary with Dan bringing the water pail and the satchel.

Someone screamed, "Wait! Wait where you are—" A man with the face of an enraged child trotted across the rutted grass, his long blouse dangling open, his buttons glittering. "I'm Captain Amos Larrabee," he cried. His voice was wiry and girlish. "Who are you, and what are you doing here? Who told you to attend that man?"

"President Lincoln sent me a telegram." Duffey's eyes protruded, hard and pink. "He said, 'They're having a war out past your town. Go out and try to be the Christian you've never been before.'"

The officer shook a white finger at him. "You're absurd, sir. We can't have country doctors fiddling with our wounded! I am a medical officer, in charge, and I order you to leave the field."

"Come, Dan Bale." The doctor lowered his head like a bull. "I see a poor man lying beside the school, and nobody caring for him." The captain stepped aside, his smooth jaw quivering. He shrieked, "I'll summon the provost and have you hustled out of this in two shakes!"

Duffey grunted, "One shake will do." They went on to the seminary. The man whom Dan had helped into the corner, was still there. He had removed his boot and swaddled his foot in a jacket. He looked up, nodding, and made a weak gesture with his hand.

"What have you got?" said the doctor. "It may be the gout." The roar came around them like water. Duffey opened the sticky wrappings: he found the foot to be a grotesque tangle of loose skin, blood and pink-sheathed bones gleaming through. He mourned, "Oh, the metatarsus is wrecked. You'll be a-losing this."

The man whispered. "Thought so. Well, I don't tend bar with my feet—least I can set on a chair to do it. Maybe you don't know it, but I invented the first Apricot Bouquet that was ever drunk in Chicago . . . Do you want to cut it off, now?"

"Not here," the doctor gulped. He was adept at strengthening human spirit when it was faint, but he had no words to greet his calm acceptance. He bound the damp mass in a clean bandage. "Find the sulphate of morphia," he told Dan, "for I've got some in there. I'll give you one-quarter grain now, boy, and have you got a watch? You'll be needing more every second hour."

He prepared the dose; his fingers were as steady as wooden levers; the little bottle became a part of him, and the wounded man could not take his eyes from it. "Will it stop the pain, sir?" Duffey nodded; yes, it would help. "For God's *sake*—" the man bubbled . . .

"Easy. Easy. Here we are, lad."

Then the soldier drank from the pail which Dan held for him. He settled back among the crushed poppies of the flower bed. He droned, "Come in to Patrick O'Carna's Family Resort, if ever you're in Chicago. You can have plenty of refreshment and never spend a copper."

"Don't invite me too reckless," said the doctor. "I'm an old man now, but my name is still Duffey. I'll see to you later, if that he-sow of a medical officer doesn't get himself underfoot. Likely it's his sort we read about in the papers, that feed the soldiers on calomel." He stood up, fanning himself with the wretched silk hat. Sweat dripped from his thick eyebrows; he smelled of other sweat.

Bale said, "There's a new noise coming out of the south. Hear it, Doc? If Elijah were here he'd say we were being flanked." They started across the lawn; the doctor waddled behind; he had found his pink-and-white handkerchief, and he was using it on his face.

Up in the cupola a man whistled shrilly. For a moment he leaned far out—they could see his brown hatchet-face hanging above them, etched against the wood structure and the sulphurous sky. He waved a hand indefinitely at everyone in the yard. He howled, "Now you'll see the Johnnies get their ass kicked. The First Corps's coming up!"

When they moved beyond the nearest clump of trees, they could see a long parade of soldiers crawling like a snake past the orchard by the Bliss farm, a blue-black worm spiked at intervals with striped flags. They were roaring as they came—a deep and serious chant, the blending of a thousand single humors and profanities.

"Flanked by more Nationals," said Duffey, "and maybe they'll be keeping this war out of your garden, Dan." The sun threw its resisting waves of heat across the long ridge, it contorted the fence-rows and trees, but still you could see more caravans in the Emmetsburg road—horses and guns, a speeding migration which sent the dust mounting.

They struck the rack-backed line of mortised fence: the rails flew. Now they were separate figures who had built themselves into a wholesome tide. They came with a kind of horrid desperation; the officers trotted beside them, all horses long since led to the rear; the officers carried their medieval swords. They were howling, *Step fast, men! Shoot low when we go in, remember, keep your fire low.* The infantry dipped across the Fairfield road; now they were aiming to the west of the Schmucker house, and all around you heard the murmur of weary cavalrymen, half mocking and half fervent: they said, there's plenty of Secesh down ahead by that crick, and they don't care who they hit. Hello, Wisconsin! . . . The head of the column swerved sharply, and a mob of horsemen

raced by. The seasoned, religious face of General Reynolds again; he had his staff with him. Muddled hoofs
clipped at the hard pathway as they bunched across;
the general swung his horse to the right and reined in,
waving toward the grove behind the seminary. His
crisp voice above the jolt of the thrashing horde . . . *go
in . . . left through this timber, Meredith! Gamble will
retire as you advance through him.* A flat voice sang:
"left-oblique"—and a dozen other voices rattled it
in fainter echoes. "Left-oblique, left-oblique . . . *ha.*"
The flags looked rich and glittering, even in the corro-
sion of their gilt and fringe. Blue standards, national
colors, they dipped and waved as the lines swung toward the west.

"Look," the doctor murmured, "they're all a-
wearing black hats. It must be a new style." The
long, dark row sagged back, evened again. "Clean
'em out, Michigan," a vast voice roared—"here we
go. Twenty-fourth!" The line seemed beaten flat,
much thinner than when it had rushed forward in a
column, as if those fields which it had crossed were
an anvil where it was pounded to a narrow tough-
ness. Reynolds and his staff slapped on along the
summit of the ridge; the bouncing riders kept turning dusty faces, looking back.

A drone went up: *foorwooord.* They yapped it,
back past the Schmucker house, all the way to the
steaming road. *Foorwooord.* The rope of men edged
into the smoky shade; the hill kept wiggling, and
there was a new swarm crawling up out of the southeast valley behind them. Now you could look past
the northern boundary of the grove and see the infantry stringing through the shallow valley, past the
dry run, and up the gentle slope to the next stockade
of trees. Again they vanished. Beyond McPherson's

ridge the wail of the Confederates rose more shrilly; fresh reports spanked out, applauding buffets from end to end of the confusion. The infantry let its first volley go, a racking gash which whipped high above the heads of the stubborn, dismounted troopers who lay crouched in their path.

Duffey drew a long breath. "Here we stand," he said, "when folks are needing me to see after them."

"Are you going to amputate that man's foot?"

"Not in the flower bed, I can tell you. I left my carryall in your yard, and maybe poor Salt will be killed, though I tied him in your old stable. But I was thinking we might take some of these unfortunates down to your back porch: it's a handy place, and nobody is turning a finger for them. And plenty of water close by, at the well." He unrolled his shirt sleeves, nodding briskly at his own decision. "I'll be starting down there, Dan. You might bring that man with the foot. I'm never one to let an honest Irishman catch the gangrene if I can help it."

He lifted his satchel and trudged across the lawn; ahead of him, the rocky field was dotted with the figures of men who huddled, crouched and exhausted under the staring sun, or who toiled on toward the village and whatever succor they might find there. A crunching thunder of wheels was born in the south—the squeal of beaten horses. One after another four guns jounced out of the road-trough and came quaking along the ridge, the six-horse teams all dripping with dirt and foam, and men clinging crazily to the caissons. Behind each wheeled chest a long brass barrel bowed and bounced, its prolonge caught up, its muzzle low. The artillery went on toward the Chambersburg Pike; blank-eyed boys gazed carelessly at Dan as they passed. They were without coats, but each wore his little cap clapped tightly on one side of his head. As if performing some observance of ritual, a blue monkey-shape lifted his hand to his nose and wiggled his fingers at Bale as the last limber whistled past.

Dan had some difficulty in finding the wounded Irishman; the man had crept out of the sun and behind a stiff hedge of burning-bush near the steps. He was drugged by the morphia. Duffey must have given him more than one-quarter of a grain. He opened his eyes as Dan lifted him. "It's O'Carna's Family Resort," he said faintly. "Don't you forget it, friend." He blew a damp breath from his lips, then lay back with his head sagging across Bale's arm. The weight was quite enough; this man was heavier than he appeared to be, however many toes he had lost when the flying iron struck him. Two toes gone, Dan thought—if he's lost two, it must be at least two ounces of his weight gone. Maybe four. He wondered how much a toe weighed, and where it went when it was shot away . . . He circled the upset wagon, stepped over the jack-straw rails and went down across the field.

The eternal firing had shriveled; it could not mean as much as it had meant before. At first it bludgeoned your ears and tried to break their drums, but if your ears were tough, resisting—if you would not be torn by the grind and concussion, then indeed you would triumph. The spasms, the tangling doom, each separate slam of each separate gun, all would be muted as if your brain had wrapped itself in a sound-proof shroud. You could no longer be aware of the keening bullets which strayed across the hill.

Bale thought: here we played war, here I wounded Ty Fanning with a sharp weed. Here, good God, here behind this lichened bowlder I lay flat and plotted that I was Robin Hood. Here I conducted my growing self and lay spread on the ground, and looked at the stars. And at this place I filled my pipe and smoked it, and talked to Hud, and laughed at him for his prophecies.

The wounded man twisted, sighing. He began to vomit; the froth dripped down across Bale's arm and splashed upon his pantaloons. It was odd to see him vomiting, when you knew that his stomach was not pierced. Dan stopped and lifted his knee, supporting the load until he could wriggle his arms into a better position. Then he went on, quartering across the pasture toward his own house. Through all the stormy world, he could make out the sound of his own pump—squeaking, squeaking.

One man was coming forward up this slope where so many others went down. He wore a white hat . . . "I have observed that hat many times," Dan said, "and long ago . . ." He could see the hickory-nut face, the bony jaws and gummed jowls of a very old man. He thought of a jail where night rain dripped tenderly; he thought of a lantern. "Hello," he said.

John Burns moved out of the path. He had a long-barreled musket in his hand, and he was coughing, with all the road dust and smoke which had settled across the field. "Is that fellow bad hurt, Mister Bale?"

"He'll lose a foot," Dan said. He looked at the musket.

The old constable spat, and nodded. He hoisted the gun. His hands were stringy, colored with the lavender stains of age. "Now," he remarked as if in apology, "this ain't what I would of picked. It was a good enough gun in its day; we fit the British with such as this here." His eyes hunted past Dan and the unconscious cavalryman in his arms. "Hah," he whispered. Bale turned. A soldier sat among some bushes—he had a wet handkerchief, and he was swabbing at the blood which sopped in his dark hair; his face and beard were tinted from it. He snarled, "Haven't you people ever seen blood before? Go up there and see how you like it!"

Burns told him, "I aim to go." He went over to the man and picked up the rifle which lay beside him.

The soldier blinked up at the old constable. "Well, damn me to hell. That weepon belongs to Uncle Sam, granddad."

"I'll mind it for him. Give me what ca'tridges you got, sonny."

Blood sluiced down, wavering channels of it, unchecked and unrubbed by the handkerchief. "I'll call you, old man," declared the soldier. He handed up a leather cartridge box. "Here's balls, too. Go out and get your hair parted, and give 'em one for me."

The old man emptied the ammunition into his pockets. He leaned his rusty musket among the bushes. "I'll git that later if it hain't be stole," he said. "Much obliged. I fit the British, must have been before your Pa was born. These rebels laid hands on me when they were here afore this, and hauled me around and tried to get gay," he told Dan and the Irishman in his arms, and the man who sat in the weeds. This was an explanation which he was making to all the world. "I'd like to see 'em scorch for it . . . come fighting round our town, this way. Well." He inserted his arm in the leather sling of the rifle. "Teamed awhile with the army down in Maryland," he called back to them, "but they said I was too old. They made me come home, and I been constable ever since." He walked on, head bent, the strap gleaming across his knobby shoulder.

Bale said to the man beside the path, "Come across the fence to that brick house. There's a doctor there who'll look after you." He could hear the soldier stumbling through the grass after him as he went toward the fence. He put his burden on the ground and removed a whole section of the fence, so that others might come through. Then he lifted the unconscious man once more and went toward the house, with the other man staggering behind.

Already Duffey had entered the kitchen. He had brought out several pans, and a torn sheet which he was spreading like a carpet over the boards of the rear porch. "Here, Daniel. Lay him down, poor soul. And you got me another patient as well. But you're not bad," he diagnosed. "Not bad at all. Set down and await your turn." He said to Bale, "Now you'll see me for the butcher I am." He began to unfasten the wet wad of bandage; his fingers went fast and assuredly about their business. The man sighed, and retched again. "Now, my boy," reproved Duffey.

He squinted at the mass in his hands. It looked like veal. He poured a tin of water, and watched the red glue soaking away. The man chanted stupidly, "My-foot-hurts-it-God-damn-hurts-oh." He began, his eyes tightly closed: *Dominus nostri in*—

"I'll remove the articulating surface of the tibia and calcaneum," the doctor said, "then bring the cut surfaces into apposition. Go fetch my other bag, Dan; I left it on the front stoop, not knowing where I'd go. I've got a bit of ether." He wiped his juicy hands. "And bring some whiskey from inside the house, some of Pentland Bale's whiskey. Praise Peter, and he didn't live to see amputations in his dooryard."

Dan hurried through the house to the front, and unlocked the door. At the road gate sat a tall scarecrow

on a black horse. The rider was hatless, his face rubbed
with charcoal, and one arm hung loose at his side; he
sat very still, with all the ridges rocking behind him
and smoke foaming high. His horse was rusted thickly
over the withers. The man sagged stiffly, as if somewhere in his middle was a pain which cut him, and
yet held his sundered nerves together by its very intensity.

"Major Glenn!" Dan heard himself calling. "Major,
come in and—" The officer's head drooped sideways;
he scanned the yard and the front of the house, and
seemed wondering as he stared. Then his shoulders
straightened themselves. "Billy," he yelled. He nodded toward the man in the doorway, without seeing
him at all. "I did have three of them . . . it's the Eighth
Illinois, Gamble's brigade. He never knew what hit
him, nor did the sorrel." Then his horse started away
of its own accord; he rode slowly down the Pike,
bending in his saddle, and the dust of artillery pouring out from the village to meet him.

3.

As the hours boomed by, the Fannings had prayed,
and Mr. Fanning had read a chapter from Demon's
Bible. Lizards and tiny unnamed creatures—things
which were damp and jeweled and scaly—scurried
on the stone ledges, and you felt their pin-point eyes
watching you . . . The man and his wife talked of
their son; they were thankful that he was not in this
battle; they hoped that no battles would overcome
him, in Virginia or wherever he might be. The young
woman listened to their prayers and to the other

things they said: and now they discuss my husband, the person who never made me ecstatic, and to whom I have done a cruelty.

Gretel came to regard this war as an electric storm. She made Demon set to work with her, after she had discovered that the explosions would not penetrate the cellar and strike her down. She sorted rows of fruit jars and pickles and jelly glasses. These pears were spoiled, they oozed with smelly brine, they must be thrown out. The melon pickles could go on that lower shelf, and the jellies on the ledge beside them, and here was the bottle of blackberry wine which Mr. Fanning thought had been stolen. Under the little woman's directions, Demon worked handily, and he divided the battle into Big Ones and Little Ones. "Big One," he said. "Now come mo' Big Ones. Reckon Mist Ty, he captain, he not mind no Big Ones."

Mr. Fanning found a certain comfort in the proximity of his precious carpet-bag. It was here, tamped beneath clay and brick dust, where he had buried it after retrieving it from the old cistern . . . They heard voices moaning or bawling at one another; they heard the windlass at the well. And they crept up to the cobwebbed windows, but the windows faced the south and east, and all they could see was a fat man in torn breeches who climbed over the fence into Mrs. Knouse's field. Irene sat on an overturned tub, close to the flickering candle, and she read aloud from the newspaper. *Latest advices convey the information that General Hooker is preparing to set his forces in motion at once, or has already done so at this writing. Whether the impending conflict with rebel General Lee will be a second Antietam, seems a moot question.* You could buy superior Light Zephyr cloth cloaks at J. W. Proctor's. Harrisburg despatches declared that General F. W. Smith had assumed command of the volunteers there assembled, on the 27th instant. Black dress Grenadine at Eyre and Landell's, Fourth & Arch . . . She read in a slow, unworried voice—a voice which was not anything of her making, and which she had never employed before. She read many things which her mother-in-law had read aloud, the evening before, and which she did not recognize in repetition.

For nearly an hour there was a foreboding lull, then the noise wrapped closer around them. It seemed splintering through hidden orifices, ready to possess the entire cellar and drive them out like chipmunks from a hole in the ground, smoked and tortured. Demon said that there were a lot of Big Ones, now . . . Through the smudgy south window there was little to be seen except stunted rose bushes, but one small triangle of landscape was visible, and that triangle shivered with swarms of distant ants. And near at hand endured a groaning noise which might have come from ungreased wheels, or from a daytime banshee.

Irene said that nothing would hurt her. It was safe enough to go into the kitchen and dip fresh water from the pail, and bring down anything else which was needed. No, no, she would go alone; perhaps Cybo was at the rear door, whining to come in; perhaps that was the little agony they heard . . . She went up at twelve-thirty, for all their wailing and protests, and she found that no bullets had entered the kitchen. The rooms were stuffy and stale from the torrid glare outside. She crept into the sitting room, then to the library. Through the hot window glass she could see whole colleges of men tramping up the Emmetsburg road—why, she thought, it must be the entire Union

army; there could never be more than that; they are
blue and black and alive with metal. They drift aside
in sturdy little streams, and then bulge together again,
and I was right when I thought of ants.

Tyler would be there. She wanted to call down
through the beamed flooring: "You are wrong. Your
prayers are not worth the saying! He is here—the
whole army is here, and this must be the battle in
which he will be killed." Her hands pained her . . . she
looked down and opened them and saw four sore,
ruddy dents in each palm.

There was order in this approach, she knew, but she
could not identify it. Rapidly the uneven avalanche
rolled toward the village; they came like molasses spilling over a platter. "There might be that many people in
Philadelphia . . . ," she whispered aloud. "Where on
earth did they all come from?" The house twitched
on its foundations; it was ill or intoxicated, it would
never be a healthy house again.

Niedes'—they were in the Niedes' grain. Dust
came decently and smothered the Niede farm and
every little cluster of trees beyond; the dust was of this
valley, waiting for soldiers to come—it loved them, it
lay upon them heavily, but they trotted on beneath its
weight with their baby flags nodding and flickering.

Up through the floor rose Mrs. Fanning's wail:
*Daughter, oh, daughter—what on earth is happening.
That noise—* She laughed wisely, and pounded on the
floor with her knee to let Mrs. Fanning know that she
had heard. Tyler and the entire army, or so it seems—
that's what is happening. It's the Seventy-second
Pennsylvania and thirty other Seventy-second Pennsylvanias; some of them are in the Emmetsburg road
and some in the fields, and some have bulged the very
fences aside. And these are cannon and they come

helter-skelter, and behind our house I can hear other cannon in the Pike. The village is being possessed by all these Seventy-second Pennsylvanias or heaven knows what you call them.

Well, she told herself, I heard a car of war coming over the hills, and I could have told anybody this would happen. Dan said there were three thousand men here last night. If three thousand men came between us as they did, what will ten times that number do to him, and do to me? Oh, at any time I would have fallen ill to see them coming, but they are a menace of the darkest order, they are poison for all their glistening and in spite of their speed and their banners—they are worse than any cancer which ever ate at flesh. Because I craved him, I quiver and lived my limit inside his arms, and he within mine. Heaven, she cried without a word, I wish you'd send one of those bullets through the window . . .

No—grief, not that—not to die. I want to live; I want to go away; I want to get out of this. I want to go away from this war and this town which was a quiet town, a stupid and affable place before the rebels and the rest of them came. Let me get out—crash this glass, cut my way though it, run across the field as I did last Friday, be beside him and hide in the wilderness. He said we should do it. Heavenly Father, why didn't I go? Tyler's coming—somewhere within these swarms he will be snarling and hooting at his men before the bullets pare him down.

She felt a sodden futility, leaden through every vein. She knew the same unwicldy bitterness which had possessed her as a child, when her mother lay dead in the parlor, and she curled in her cold bed upstairs, listening to the hushed tread of servants and the sepulchral whispering of relatives whom she had never seen before. It was a certain, blank tragedy which supplanted all other consciousness.

Oh, give me some sort of a prayer, she thought—Heavenly Father of whom I had been taught but from whom I have shrunk away! Even give me an unread book, to carry around with me as Demon carries his.

At last she got up and found Mr. Fanning beside her, bending down, crying. "My dear little lady, why didn't you answer, you have given mother such a turn—come at once." "Yes," she said, and went with him into the rear hallway. She imagined that the roaring multitudes who chased along the ridge were going to a fire—maybe they had buckets, maybe they would put it out . . . "I hear groaning again," she told Mr. Fanning. "It is close. I think out on the stoop—we heard it, before—" They unlatched the door and looked out. There were two dusty shoes sprawled close beside the door, and legs stretched down over the step. In terror, rushing, saying brief words, they hovered over the man. He had been shot through the throat—somehow he had made his way to this porch, and here he was. He kept rolling his eyes and squeezing his tongue out through fat, steel lips. His hands had torn the clothing around his neck, and had raked furrows in his flesh as well. *Aaahh* he kept murmuring, a secret which he whispered to himself countless times. They dragged him up on the porch; he was about eighteen, Irene thought, and he had a pale skin dotted with tiny orange freckles. His clawing fingers, the nails crammed with shredded skin—they grew from hands which were as slender as a flute player's, and all raw and blistered by harness and guns. The gasping cry which he uttered was changing now, even as they brought him into the kitchen. His green eyes swiveled in raw sockets, and saw nothing of the room or the faces above. Then moisture came up in his throat; he made a trilling sound, and blood coursed across the clean-scrubbed floor, and he wadded the woman's gown in his hand as he died.

4.

General Reynolds fell quickly and easily, without a sound. Lieutenant Steele saw him go; he had had no premonition of the general's death, and it would be long before he grew accustomed to the knowledge that the well-remembered dark face, the silent manner, the alert eyes, existed only in decay and shroudings.

John Buford kept urging Reynolds to be more careful. The major-general was guiding his horse among the torn mounds of shrubbery, springing it lightly over dismantled fences, pausing with his upraised field-glass at the most exposed fence corners. "For God's sake," Buford exclaimed in his tuneless Kentucky drawl, "take a little care, sir." For a long time the superior officer did not pay any attention to this entreaty, and when he did observe it he only laughed. He had a close-clipped, scrubby beard, and a way of appearing neat and on parade even when the hollows of his cheeks were larded with grime and his horse's legs all plastered with mud and manure. When troops waited on a march, and fell out in somebody's pasture to lie beside their stacked arms, Reynolds made it a habit to notify brigade commanders if their men had time enough to boil coffee.

Lieutenant Steele would cheerfully have washed Reynolds' boots with his tongue, and accounted it a privilege.

Then a soldier from Major Van de Graaf's Fifth Alabama battalion—a young man about twenty-one, named Rufus Canty—poked his rifle through a bank of thistles. It was a five-round Spencer, captured from a Yankee only two months before, and Rufus Canty was very proud of his gun. Forever he was trying to see what it would do.

He lay a few feet in advance of his line, where Archer halted in Grandpa Germels' east pasture, and all along the weeds his companions were firing. The reports rang solidly, in varying volume: there were Springfields and Vincennes muskets, and Colts, and Spencers, and even a few Henrys, all clanging away at the blue lumps who waited beyond the creek. This little nest of weeds had a cool, minty odor; it spoke of frogs and creeping green grasshoppers . . . Rufus Canty thought of a church-meeting in the woods back home. He had wandered away with Araminta Bates, and they lay among some such weeds as these, making love until the stars came out. Araminta was afraid of snakes which might be crawling around, but he only laughed at her. "Sho," he said, "I'm not going to stop loving you because of some old snake." Later, Araminta had been right scared; she thought she was in the family way, but it happened that she wasn't. He wondered what old man Bates would have done about it . . . The weeds smelled like church-meeting. A couple of wings of cold fried chicken: now, that wouldn't be bad. Dinners in baskets, roasting ears in the fire, and a big hunk of vinegar pie. The preacher chuckling to Rufe Canty's mother, "And, Sister, I never knowed a chicken had any parts besides a neck, till I was growed" . . . he nudged the barrel of his Spencer, fondly. It was a good gun.

One hundred, two hundred, three hundred yards. That was asking a lot of a gun. Of course you could take any ordinary old shooting-iron and bang away up to half a mile, and trust to luck that the bullet might find lodgment in the ragged yeast of Yankees. But now there was no mass of purple Yanks, wheeling and sparkling; only an elusive row of smoke-stabs behind that stone fence and in the fringe of timber. On his left, Welch Myson called: "Hey, you Rufe."

"Ya."

"Yore so blame still Ah thought you was kilt."

"Ah ain't kilt yet." The line of hidden rifles pecked at him.

He pushed the Spencer out, and rested its barrel in a green crotch of thistle. Through the higher woods he could see a huddle of riders who scouted mysteriously under the shade. Then they came into the smoke; half screened by fences and lone trees, they drifted along the ridge. Like to have me a big telescope, Rufe Canty thought—like that officer on the big horse. Like to have me a telescope big as a locomotive; reckon I could see all the way back home, with a telescope like that. If I aim mighty high, I reckon I could hit that horse.

He pulled the trigger, and the butt mauled his sore shoulder again. Watching through the hot mist, he could see the Yankee officer falling limply from the horse, half a side fall, half a backward fall, and his arms flying wide as he went. The horse leaped nervously and turned, sniffing. Then dull smoke got in the way—blurred all the dark blue shapes, and dulled the gleam of metal about them. Rufe Canty's throat was suddenly dry. By God, he said to himself. What do you know.

He called, "Hi, Welch Myson. Jest got me a big Yank, clean on top that hill."

"You did like so much hell."

"Ah hope to shout, Ah did. He was hoss-back. Reckon he was captin."

Then the yell and the orders pulled him out of his nest. He plunged forward through the thistle brake, bending low, holding the Spencer tight in both hands. He began to scream with the rest of them, burning his throat by the very friction of sound: *whooooo* . . . they made a few rods forward; it began to be muddy under foot; there were willows, bending, nodding, green tufts flying as the Yankees talked back. A solid volley chewed across their front—here was a new cry ahead, and the feeling of an unconscious enemy who suddenly roused up and hit out with both fists . . . They crouched along the willows, and peeked at the ridge ahead. "Thar come them ole black hats," Welch Myson squawked. "That hain't no milish—hit's the Army of the Patomack, shore—"

Reynolds made no sound which Lieutenant Steele could hear. There was the little, spiteful slap of the ball, and the next instant the general was on the grass; he seemed to bounce as he struck the ground. Steele got to him before anyone else. He said, "God—sir!" and put his arms around the firm, muscular shoulders. Reynolds looked rather canny and knowing; the lids sagged slightly over his eyes, and there were straws caught in his beard, and his hat had fallen off. There was a blue hole in the skin where his neck joined the head, squarely behind his right ear, and a larger hole in the left side of his head, higher up. Something wet and hot, a soggy scrap, fell on Jack

Steele's naked wrist. He cried, "God damn dirty sons-a-bitching bastards—"

Dead, and he had never known about it. Steele carried him back to the shelter of a big beech tree, and put him gently on the ground. He stood breathing from the exertion; Reynolds was not a tiny man. The staff kept bending over the general, and mumbling dazedly; nobody else cried, no one except Lieutenant Steele. Not just then . . . The lieutenant heard the thud of hoofs approaching across the shade; he looked up at General Buford and saw the amazed frown which drove between his eyes. "Is he dead?" Buford demanded.

"Yes, sir," a thick voice said. "Shot through the head. Must have been a sharp-shooter."

"I'll give you a line to General Meade." Buford turned his horse, so that he would not be facing the prone figure under the beech tree; he took out his notebook and began to scratch with a lead pencil. "General Doubleday's at the school over yonder," he said, without looking up. "One of you gentlemen will notify him at once. I reckon he's up in the cupola."

Steele cried, "Yes, *sir!*" He beat Captain Fane to his horse, and went scuttling away, the mouldy acorns scattering, the bullets crooning overhead. He was grateful for something to do, though it seemed like basest treachery to desert Reynolds, now that he was so quiet and saying nothing. And he was supposed to be a captain, himself, only it hadn't come through . . . stared blankly into General Doubleday's sirloin, thick-mouthed face, and saying: "Regret to inform the general that General Reynolds has just been killed, sir." Doubleday said, "What-what-why, what is that, sir, hold on, Lieutenant, repeat what you were saying."

The batteries over on the Pike were going full-tilt, and it was hard to deliver or receive a verbal message.

Steele could never recall much of what happened, for some time afterward. He remembered that Doubleday said something about retiring General Reynolds' body to a place of safety; Meredith's brigade and the rebels were fighting like fury down the hill toward that biggest creek, and it looked like the enemy might come through at any time. You could see dun clouds of rebels, far across the northwest fields, whenever the fog thinned enough . . . Steele had four privates with him, and they had placed the body on a stretcher. The canvas was dry with old death, black and scaly. Steele removed his blouse and spread it under the general's head—he was not willing for that face to press against the blood of God-knew-whom. They went past the seminary; Steele halted the men, and entered the building and somewhere he found a clean tablecloth. He didn't ask permission; the masters of this academy could God damn well let John Reynolds have their tablecloth when he needed it. The lieutenant would have shot anyone who tried to stop him, and he would have done it seriously and considerately.

With two men carrying the stretcher, and the other two walking beside it with fixed bayonets, Steele went past the skimpy orchard, down the slope. He walked behind. He dramatized each moment with an intensity of self-torture. He must follow, follow . . . *whither thou goest, I shall go.* Perhaps it was "I will follow" or "there also will I go"—Jack Steele wasn't a close student of the Scriptures, although his father was a Methodist deacon. Men—wounded, most of them—kept coming up and asking in hushed voices,

"Hey. Who's that you got there?" and the privates
would whisper out of the corners of their mouths:
"Reynolds. He's dead," until Steele snapped them into
silence. Halfway down the rocky pasture below the
school, he was approached by a big, smooth-shaven
man in civilian clothes who came through a gap in the
rail fence and hurried toward the stretcher. The man
had sober, gray eyes and powerful hands; his shirt
and trousers were stained with blood in varying degrees, though he didn't seem to be hurt at all.

He said, explosively, and not as one accustomed to
addressing officers: "Bring him over here to my
house. There's a doctor, with instruments and medicine— He can—"

The lieutenant told him: "He can do nothing for
this man. He is dead."

"I didn't know you bothered carrying off the dead
ones," the civilian cried. There was a defiant challenge in his gaze, a bitter accusation; Steele recognized it dully, but he was too broken to take issue. He
felt his nostrils swelling. "Sir, this is the body of General John Reynolds! All right, men—" and on they
went. He thought about the big, blood-stained civilian hours afterward, and wondered who he was.

Turn and turn about, they carried the body into a
house on the road which quartered southwest from
Gettysburg; that seemed safe enough for the moment, and well past any position which the Confederates were apt to attain for another hour or two. It
was the house of George George—an utterly impossible name: you wouldn't have believed it unless you
were there. Later came the ambulance, and more soldiers, and orders. The guns still argued sternly out
past those low hills; the sun hissed.

Steele went with the body, and they jolted along a

country road into the south. He thought of the fifes, and that labored two-four they often played for a guard-mount: *when we go down to Washington, when we go down to Washington, I was shot five times in the ankle-bone and once at Manassas Junction.* Here he was, going down to Washington. Horses flashed past them—untold dust, now rushing north, now south. They saw flags ahead, an approaching horde of troops. The columns deployed to let the ambulance rattle through. Steele rode in a daze, and he looked down at perspiring faces, and he heard a name passed from man to man. Reynolds. Reynolds. You kept saying those two syllables over and over, and soon they meant nothing at all. Flies got into the ambulance—occasionally Steele would climb in at the rear and drive them out with his hat.

The sun worked hard at melting the green and gold world which glared up at it. You imagined at times that the fences were melting, that the groves had become soft and were pouring green candle-grease into the shadows of the hard little valleys . . . A face was looking at him: severe eyes, pointed mustache, wide goatee. "How did he meet his death?" inquired the rigid voice. "He was at the lines, sir. A sharp-shooter picked him off; he was struck in the temple, instantly killed, sir." Hancock said, "Can I see him?" "Yes, sir. He's—" Hancock came away from the ambulance; he turned and clicked his boot-heels. Then he went on toward Gettysburg. It was the hottest day which had yet come in that year of heat.

5.

Until nearly one o'clock Adam Duffey worked like a slave. Dan counted twenty-nine men whose bodies he had stitched or cut or swabbed; two of them died quietly, lying on blankets in the shade of the cherry tree. Then ambulances pitched in at the gate, and there was a coatless medical officer who roared orders in mixed German and English as the soldiers carried off the dead and the wounded. He did not criticize Duffey for his ministrations, save to object to a double-flap method of hip amputation which Duffey had employed in one case. The house seemed very quiet, after these murmuring cargoes were led away; between lulls in the firing you could hear flies gossiping above loose-turned dirt in the garden and knowing well what lay underneath.

Duffey said, "I'm a tired man, Daniel. And getting old."

He came slowly into the kitchen and sat down on a bench against the wall, wiping at his arms with a tea-towel. The floor swam in dirty water, and the stove reeked furiously with its burden of steaming pans. Diluted blood made strange raspberry whorls in the puddles near the door.

"We should have something to eat," Dan said.

Duffey blew his nose. "A bite of whiskey wouldn't hurt me. And I've just thought about old Salt—"

"I gave him some water awhile ago. He had a bait of oats I brought from Fanning's barn."

The doctor lifted a quart bottle from the table; it was empty; he let it roll across the floor. The rumble of guns drowned his whisper: "Some of our patients were hogs—"

"There's more in the keg." Bale raised the trapdoor and crept down into the pit beneath. While he drained whiskey from the Monongahela keg, he could hear Adam Duffey talking in the room above. Talking to himself: it was the first time Dan had ever known the doctor to do it. Artillery made a flat, metallic orchestration of his words; he talked as if he were explaining to another, sterner surgeon who would hold him responsible for all he had failed to do. Sure . . . would have been glad for a better opportunity. Something like . . . a young man, and devil a bit of good it did him. The damn ball comminuted the surgical neck of the left humerus, and the coracoid process of the scapula. But there was more awaiting me . . . just below the clavicle. A better chance . . . Dan came up with the whiskey and Duffey poured out a full teacup. He drank it, grunted, and coughed heartily when he was done. Some of the whiskey trickled out of his nostrils, and he wiped his face with fingers still stained. He left a smudge on his lip.

He said, "That right eye. You'll be remembering. He was a howler, and will you blame him?"

"Do you think I am insensate, merely because I say nothing?" Bale barked at him.

Duffey stared with moist, blank gaze. "It must have been a fragment of a bombshell. Evacuated the humors of the eye, as near as I could make out—and the nasal bones were a pretty mess. And the right superior maxilla."

Dan said, "Look here. You go in the other room and lie down. You're wholly exhausted."

"No, for I might be shot in my sleep."

"It's safe enough. I looked at the other side of the house: some bullets have struck there, but they are mostly spent and they flatten out on the bricks. I'll move the big secretary to the head of your sofa, and nothing could strike you."

The doctor stood up. "There are folks in town that I must see to. Take Katie Huffmaster. The child will be frantic in all this heat." It seemed a long moment before he found his balance and stood with weight adjusted on his quivering legs.

You could do nothing with him. He was knowing a shock far stranger than the common crudity of physical exhaustion; he babbled of nasal bones and masseters all the while Dan was bringing old Salt out of the weedy stable and harnessing him to the carryall. Duffey had courted this agony, and willingly would have embraced it for more hours than he could stand, but once the stimulus of torn bodies was taken from him, he said that he would go and he let nothing dissuade him. It was fantastic to think that he expected to find his ordinary routine awaiting him, a life without disruption, hours unshaken by Parrott guns. Ten pounds had evaporated mysteriously from under his skin since morning; his eyes lay in papery pockets, baggy envelopes falling against his cheeks. "There's cannons and horsemen making hell on the Pike," he kept saying, "but they must let me pass because I'm a physician. I can keep one wheel across the ditch until I come to the bridge, and I'll be out of their way if they go trying to run me down." He drove out of the yard; the smoke and the noise claimed him once he was in the highway.

A man bent from his plunging horse and howled in Dan's face, "Where's that old fool bound for? Doesn't he know this is a fight? If he was *my* father—" and

then rode swearing away. The turnpike length was tur-
bulent with messengers and tumbling wagons of ammunition. Old Salt danced and sawed between the
shafts, but Duffey kept him bravely in his course along
the ditch; the oilcloth curtain at the rear of the carryall
was bound up in a tight roll and through the aperture
you could see the doctor's head rolling on his shoulders, his hat jammed tight, his arms straining against
the reins. He did not look back. Dan had the notion
that he would be killed by a stray shell before he got
out of sight. With relief, he watched the vehicle sag at
last around the curve and vanish into town through
mauling dust.

The ring of war had spread northeast across the valley beyond the railroad ditch; now the battle was a
milling crescent from the Fairfield road to the alms-
house. At noon the village had been possessed by new
Federal troops who roared up the Emmetsburg road.
They brought with them a fresh and enormous dust
cloud to settle over the village, making it unreal and
misty. Within ten minutes you could watch them edg-
ing out from the northern limits of the town, wary little tides of dark figures overspreading the fields. They
stopped, thinning, dammed by an unseen obstacle
which shunted their bulk toward the west. Miniature
horses dragged the many-wheeled batteries into position and let them begin to pound.

Dan stood for a moment on the front porch. He
had a pipe in his hand . . . what was he going to do
with it . . . he looked at the fields across the Mummasburg road, and tried to think of water-fowl on a
prairie slough. Smoke drifted in soapy puffs from the
woods in front of the McClean farm, and beyond the
college buildings endless torrents of men disintegrated
among the gleaming planes of wheat. Field by field,

the ripe crops went out of existence. An hour, two hours before they had been happy lakes of tan; then they were trodden flat, and lost their color forever. Out of the farms to the north came moaning billows of dust, turreted with more of the rosy flags. A fuzz of smoke cooked between the two armies, and the wheat broke down and was forgotten.

Well, he thought, I must keep alive. No matter what they do to this country and to each other, I have my right to continue. Feed, stuff my body, put into it the breads and the meat and the lumps of butter, the pitchers of milk . . . no, there is no milk, The Germelses' elves did not come last night; steel hoofs walked their farm.

Only when he opened the buttery door and smelled an air of cheese, only then did he feel the nausea of a man unused to wading through such puddles on his floor. He closed the door and went out into the yard. The high sun roared at him; the whole round horizon bulged up and down, pimpled with noise. *Didn't know you bothered carrying off the dead ones,* said a voice. Then he was inside the water-closet: Mrs. Knouse must not see him, sick. In all the horrid sweat which drenched him, he knew that he was incapable still of retching in his own dooryard—the war had not beaten him yet.

He strangled for a long time, leaning forward with the top of his head against the rear wall, but no relief came. He went out to the pump and splashed his face with water and lay down, clutching the grass in his fists, holding tight to the terrible earth.

Perhaps he slept. It was a kind of unconsciousness which had never visited him before. Once he jerked and sat up, aware of peril, staring dizzily at a horse without a rider which came screaming out of the thin oaks—a horse with saddle crooked and stirrups swinging, and knots of pink and gray hanging from its rear. Head low, it plunged through the old rails at full gallop and drove into the side of the barn. The rotten building trembled for a moment; the horse lay shuddering, and screaming no longer; it had made the cry which resounds for hours after the parent impulse has vanished. Bale lay back and looked at the sky. Again he tightened his convulsive grasp on the sod.

And again he saw the Fannings in their cellar . . . She is safer there, he told himself, the horse-scream still inside him. She would be more alarmed if she should see me now; if I made my way over there and rapped at the cellar window and tried to talk to her, it would reawaken something which must sleep until this noise has stopped and the armies have gone away. Here I am, strong as an ox, lying in the yard like a schoolboy who has smoked his first cigar. If only I hadn't gone into the buttery, if only I hadn't thought to eat.

Now he vomited as surely and completely as ever Tyler had done, and he rolled over in the grass away from it. The ground kept going up and down. People whooped and yodeled; the inveterate guns made their lingo; people dashed by with troops of horses, but no more of them came into his yard to die.

After a long while he arose, all alone in the middle of the lawn, giddiness still whirling behind his eyes. Somewhere in this unwinding landscape the Knouse home came to rest; he imagined that he had stayed the crazy dance of the entire countryside, merely by putting his hand on the stone rim of the nasturtium bed. He wanted to call to Mrs. Knouse, deep in her cellar refuge, clutching her spoons and her dead husband's watch and her best green teapot—cry out to her and say: "You wouldn't believe me at first, you hag! Now you'd better hide under the beef barrel. They're yelling in this direction, much closer than they were before; the guns are louder and more numerous, and you watch what happens to the village now."

He looked toward Fanning's, and when he had put the house in its proper place he could see that the rear door was open. Demon dragged something out to the stoop.

A little howl came up in Bale's throat. He began to run, a clumsy fashion of running, but the garden fled rapidly behind him. "God," he cried, "and don't tell me that one of them is dead!" He fell across a knobbed post which once had been the leg of a living horse; he got up and ran on. Now Demon had the limp thing completely past the door . . . it was blue, and none of the Fannings wore blue, thanks be.

He halted beside the first big bowlder of the field, and bellowed: "Demon! What is it?" but there were too many armies having their say. The old negro ducked back into the kitchen and clapped the door shut; again he would be latching it. The air exclaimed *pshaw* in a split second, and a dark spot snapped into being among the lichens of the big rock. Dan thought, I'd better look out . . . The blue image, however it got there, had best lie abandoned on the rear steps of Mr. Fanning's house; there were too many other concerns of treacherous importance.

This had become agony—the vengeful artillery with their false little lulls, their commitments of fresh sound, and now the doubled, baser noise which would vanquish armies by sheer cruelty to the ears . . . The man went back into the shelter of his stable and looked out past the tree-fringe. The sun was a red pancake in high haze of the west, and chemical smoke made it spin and wink with purple blushes. When unexpectedly the seminary wrenched out of its acrid wrappings, he could see a horde of workmen digging alongside it, laboring as no hired diggers had ever done. Shovels and picks vibrated crazily out of the suffering troop, and droves of other men were running along the ridge with fence rails, flinging the rails down and darting back to the fields for more.

I suppose, he considered, those are what they call breastworks. The Lord knows why—they'll never be breast high in an hour, at that rate.

The northern end of Adams county exploded. Dan went out to see the pit which must have been made. Now he felt the quaint, whimsical strength of the rejuvenated invalid—he could afford to watch the wheat fields suffering, with a casual eye, since he had suffered as they. But when he reached the front yard, there was nothing to see but a dark smother of old smoke in the north. He opened his mouth, relaxed, listening. At first it sounded like a storm, and then like a dream of Halloween; it was the same wail which had been resounding all day in the west, and now came in from the north and northeast as well, bound to come all the way this time. If the rebels advanced from the north, these Nationals would be driven off Oak Ridge, crushed between two tides of their enemies. They'd better retreat while they could, and start back to Emmetsburg or wherever they hailed from.

The smoke blew high, like a cover lifted from a hot dinner dish, and it exposed a sauce of brownish armies spreading in toward the Pennsylvania College grounds, seasoned with pimento flags. The other lonely, white-striped flags scuttled ahead into the village, nodding and hiding behind the barns. "Looky there," a harsh duet ripped out, and Dan turned. Wagons had been rocking past, still hurrying up the slope on demoniac errands, but this wagon would go no farther. It had stopped in front of the Knouse gate . . . Mrs. Knouse's little sign hung there swaying on its cord, saying *No Tresspass* to them and all their brothers . . . the drivers were standing up on the seat, hands grasping the front bows of the wagon-top, heads turned toward the northeast; then, saying no more, one of the men leaped down and seized the halters of the lead team. He wore a round, straw hat; he did not look at all like a soldier. The wagon swayed as the front axle turned to its limit—the teams brayed and struggled—they were brought about. The big ark went rumbling back down the turnpike, with the straw-hatted man clambering up over the tailboard, and a long whip crackling around the mules' ears.

Now it was a very odd noise which the whole length of Oak Ridge was making: the guns contributed little, and the afternoon ached with their cessation. It was mainly the sound of men, uncounted tribes of them, each exclaiming or muttering and beginning to leave the crest of the hill. They clung together in blocks or bunches, each regiment with a flag or two for its nucleus, but they moved more rapidly every minute and soon they would be running. The foremost swarms jogged out of the woods and gathered momentum. Men—a multitude of them, and dressed mostly in dark blue clothes—had been attending some sort of a political rally on that hill; suddenly a fire had burst out, or a hurricane came close, and everybody was going home.

6.

A new kind of thudding possessed the yard, and Mrs. Fanning knew that people were not being careful about the garden. No matter what lashed these soldiers in their madcap exploits, it was indecent of them to ruin the cabbages and the parsley borders, and that was what they were doing. She wailed, "Bedford, I've a great notion to go up and complain to the officers. Honey boy wouldn't let his soldiers go wrecking other folks's gardens! He—" There came a faint, musical crash as someone plowed through the cucumber frames. Irene heard herself soothing falsely: "Mother. Please. I will go up. No, I'm not in the least afraid. The guns have stopped. Maybe the fighting is all over, and the rebels gone." A savage blast shook the towering house above them, and made the cellar stairs complain; Mrs. Fanning squealed; the girl went up, all the same.

She was not afraid of those smudges on the kitchen floor . . . He had been such a baffled, innocent person—no one to fear, but certainly a youth to be mourned time out of mind. Mr. Fanning was stricken by the utter conclusiveness of it; he suffered no further inflammation of the bowels, but a deeper and more serious burn, and it showed in his eyes. He had groped away to the cellar, and slid to the sofa with his hand over his eyes. "Mother," he asked, after a time, "read a chapter." It was a Psalm; the Hebraic passion had a rich sensuousness, even with Mrs. Fanning mouthing it fearfully. Irene thought about David. She wondered if the freckled boy had been named David, and she rather thought that he had.

Much later, her father-in-law came to the actualities with a sudden start. "Demon," he ordered, "go to the kitchen and take that poor lad outside. The room is closed—this heat and— Return immediately, before you are hurt." His wife kept crying; she was no longer fit to read a Psalm or anything else. She drank some wine and it made her head ache as always; the hours had wallowed before her eyes, wounded and bleary, and at last she was tortured by the thought which sat as a certainty in Irene's mind: this was more than an ordinary battle—more brigades would be trotting out of Maryland, and Tyler with them.

Giants dragged their sofas up and down distant cellar stairs. They dragged them with the utmost carelessness, letting them fall three or four steps at a time, dropping the massive legs on vast boards which rang like kettle-drums. You felt the wistaria roots, the wide skein of tree roots which netted around the yard, all clinging desperately beneath the soil, shivering with a strangle-hold amid the loam which had never treated them this way before.

And then came the medley of running feet, the stoppage of artillery mouths, and confusion which told Mrs. Fanning that her garden was wrecked. Faintly above the other sounds, Irene heard a dog barking. It was Cybo. Anyone would recognize his bark, and heaven knew where he had been all day. Later they learned that the Schmuckers had shut him in their woodshed, and he escaped through a window after the retreating lines had excited him to a frenzy.

Irene went into the kitchen, and a window-pane flew apart as she opened the door. Yellow plaster spat crudely from the wall beside her and powdered her shoulder. She turned and looked at the wall: here was a gray boil which had burst within the clean paint, and it was a wonder they had never guessed it was there. They had thought this house to be solid, incorruptible, and only now were riflemen teaching them the sad truth. The boil held a bright little core of metal sticking in it; the girl touched the lead morsel; it burned her fingers. She said, "Well," and her thin voice echoed in the oven of the room.

She went to the window beside the stove and turned back one panel of the inside shutter. There were a lot of men scooting past the farm buildings, dodging between the sheds, hurdling the fences. Two of them flung open the stable door and ran inside; she heard the old team whicker in surprise, heard them plainly through all the shouting and the pattering shots. Then the men were out of the door again and sprinting east across the garden, huge knapsacks bobbing on their backs; they had decided against remaining in the barn.

She thought, I have no business here by this window, the glass is apt to shatter at any moment, and there would be a hole in my body instead of in the plaster. But still she leaned there, dully conscious of the dry stains on the floor behind her, and wondering why these men were running so fast.

Past the sheds she could see a crowd of soldiers pouring down the pasture. Now the Mercuries, the fleet ones who ran ahead, were flinging themselves over the southeast fence and into Mrs. Knouse's weedy acres, unchecked and not looking back. The first solid row of troops reached the fence; up they went, and over, gabbling, lifting a National flag and a blue flag high, and then milling on again; they left some of the rails tumbled from the post-slots. A second fringe reached the fence; there was a lean man in a black hat who straddled on the peak, waving a tinny sword, yipping; the men behind him swung around doggedly and dropped to their knees. Their rifles lifted out of the grass, pointing high above the heads of the troops who followed them: ragged jabs of flame tore loose with a munching crash. Then the uneven rank swarmed over the barrier and trotted on, southeast.

Cybo barking . . . Irene could not see him. He was somewhere behind the trees up toward the seminary. She opened the rear door of the kitchen, and a storm of noise poured through. The turnpike beyond Dan Bale's house was a crowded torrent of dust, seething with wheels and rearing teams; the guns bounced furiously along, stiff on their axles. Retreating batteries, with inky gunners and beaten horses, implanted the whole understanding which the woman had not grasped before.

Running away, she cried to herself. They've quit— they're going to the town, and what will happen now? In all the turmoil of pastures and roads, there lived a piercing cry long-caged behind Oak Ridge and now rising, whelped and eager, from close beside the brick school.

The family had come up from the cellar; their feet skulked in the passageway. *Miss Irene,* came the old negro's frantic whisper, *Miss Irene! . . .* and the spasm of Fanning whispers, *Daughter, Daughter,* and Gretel's squeals. "It's a retreat!" the girl called to them, but she could not turn; she must stare at these plunging herds. Already the fastest runners were swallowed in village dust and village trees, and on the other side of the house you could hear the Fairfield road squirming under more runaways . . . Something fan-shaped grew enormously out of the garden; she fell back against the side of the doorway and flung up her arms instinctively. The house staggered under the concussion, and things of some sort had been flying high when the shell burst.

Irene sobbed to her father-in-law: "The dog—he was out there—" Another geyser, another thunder, one, two, three, brown bouquet after brown bouquet springing from the field. She thought: where is Dan—they missed his house that time, but the next explosion may— A man leaned soberly behind a bowlder, one human island in the noisy river, working his ramrod into the barrel of his musket; then a bursting pin-wheel blotted him from her gaze. Oh, that scream—Dan said it was a horse, it is the same scream which began this morning, and all this time it has been spearing high above the heat, on, on, higher than the larks ever flew, higher than the buzzards above Codori's farm.

The rebels were close, she could see them: an endless row of gray paupers who glided toward the apple trees at the seminary. They were howling like winter wind, firing at will; the guns pecked with constant, anxious reports. The last scurrying blue lines were only half a field ahead. They began to fall, one by one, sprawling and thinning as the rifles rang. This was something which had taken place in a legend, whispered by firesides to awed generations; yes, the woman knew, I heard about this before—someone told me, and now I see it happening. The populous fields were dotted with horses which kicked or reared, or stood stock-still, or lay clubbing the weeds with frantic legs.

And here appeared Cybo, officious as ever, yelping and snapping in and out among the fugitives. He could not understand what possessed them, or how they dared come into his domain and do these crazy things, and then run away before he could bark at them. He hurtled from man to man; now he was lost in a changing muddle of uniforms, now he came closer, speeding on the swarming flanks, pealing shrilly as he herded them. He loped behind one hopeless, laboring figure, a bearded man with a glistening bald spot atop his bare head, a man who could not keep up and was losing ground to the howling brown rank which breathed behind. The girl found her voice: *Cybo, Cybo*—she screamed endlessly, and he did not hear her. He worried beside the man's heels, a white avenger, four-legged and wholly mad. The soldier kicked out at every other stride; the dog circled him, flew wide, and came snapping in again. The man flung up his hand; he had a revolver, he took steady aim, and fired, and then went staggering on again.

The dog began: *I-yee-yee, I-yee-yee!* . . . He shrieked it as if he had held the sound ready for this emergency; he had been shot; he knew what to do. He dove for the pasture fence and wriggled under. *I-yee-yee, I-yee-yee* . . . came up across the butchered carrot rows; his hind quarters were beginning to drag, he left a thick trail of blood behind him. He was crawling, now; the tongue lolled out, the eyes were rolling. He snaked toward the back porch, his cries still rusty and piercing, but weaker at every breath. Irene stepped over the body of the freckled soldier; she went down to the dog, and meant to lift him in her arms, hideous as he was. His eyes were back in his head and the froth matted his mouth. He stopped his scream on a high, chopped note, a bird-like sound, and lay with his hind legs stretched foolishly behind him and the thin urine tickling out from under his belly.

7.

Eva Duffey thought, That man. I'd like to wring
his neck . . . Each day she made such an exclamation within her mind, but she had waited thirty-two
years without carrying out her threatened desire.
This morning she knew well enough where the doctor was going when he drove away; she could not
have called after him, Stay with me because I need
you, and you are apt to be killed. There may be a
great deal of pain out there by the Sem, but there is
always a great deal of pain in the world. Stay, Adam—
stay—

Her enduring love was of the sort which exhibits
itself in small disparagements, in caustic bantering—
the refined and dangerous emotion of a woman who
has but a small store of active affection, and only one
opening through which to shed it, and only one person ever to shed it upon.

Her barrenness, or his, had been the bitterest thing
she found in life. Duffey met her at the table where
he boarded for a time, in Camden; the small-pox
came long before he did, but still Eva was earnestly
hopeful of marriage. It was years before she realized
that no one else would ever have asked her. When
nature did not assert itself in the ordinary conception which came all too easily for most women, Eva
worked to strengthen their planting. Covertly she re-
sorted to old wives' remedies, queer recipes written
on scraps of yellow paper, superstitions and shibbo-
leths whose inadequacy she knew well enough. The
doctor laughed at her for awhile; after they had been
five years married he never mentioned the subject of

their having a child. His wife escaped the shrewdom
or the maudlin mother-soulfulness which would have
claimed many another. Her maternal instinct seemed
dried into a staunch pith all through the heart of her;
her words were sharp, her thought even keener; she
believed Adam Duffey a great man, and possibly she
was the most deeply contented woman in a civiliza-
tion where ordinary contentment was a matter of
Gospels, jet earrings, rich cooking and immense cow-
barns.

So she suffered through the hours when her father
and mother danced in their wide gilt frames on the
parlor wall, when torn dust lapped across lots from
the west. Beyond the Joe Leens' garden she could see
whole streets-full of blue men with bayoneted muskets, jogging out into the fields north of town. Once
she took her sunbonnet and went as far as the Deffenbaughs': young Mrs. Gubbe shrieked from the
door of a cellar, *For pity sakes, Mis' Duffey* . . . She
waved at the Gubbes, and walked on until she was
ordered to return. A wheel had rolled from a gun-
carriage; red-striped boys clustered around the gun,
lifting and straining, the sun seeming to pick them
out with especial ferocity. She felt very sorry for them
and she wanted to call, "If you wouldn't get in each
other's way you might get that thing fixed," but for
once she felt that she would say nothing. There was
no sign of old Salt coming across the Diamond; nothing but more yellow mist, and more teams plunging
through it, perverted in their anxiety to meet the
thunder which grumbled in the north and west. Then
a lone brown-faced youth with high, creased boots
(he looked like someone she had known once, but
she couldn't place him; he had a precious fuzz of
mutton-chop whiskers, and heaven knew he had sat

up nights to raise that much) came scampering toward her on an ugly pony, and he yelled, "Thee had better go home before thee gets run down!" and he whirled the white-eyed pony in front of her, to compel her to turn back. She cried angrily, "My conscience!" and stepped among Mrs. Deffenbaugh's honeysuckle bushes, but she did obey him, and turned back. Hours later she could have sworn that the youth was one of the Copes she had known in West Chester; he had the same nose and upper lip which Edge and Samuel and Edgar Cope all had. The Copes were Friends. It was absurd to think of Quakers scurrying through the dirt-clouds with big revolvers bumping against their saddles.

She went into the doctor's office and touched things with nervous hands; no patients tapping at the door; it seemed odd. She picked up a copy of *The Scalpel* and found herself reading what Doctor Edward H. Dixon had to say about subcutaneous fractures. And all the time enormous paws were pushing against the house. The hot sky crackled and crackled . . . *but not mentioned by Sir William Fergusson in his "System of Practical Surgery" published, if memory serves correctly, in 1846.* She could feel perspiration soaking out between her thin ribs, gluing her shirt to her body, and she wished that she might take off her corsets and lie down upon the bed with a cool cloth over her eyes. When she heard the carryall creaking to a halt outside, the room vanished in prickling grayness: she found her balance and her voice after Duffey came in and patted her hand . . .

"No," she squawled, "not out again!" His eyes looked blank and startled. "The girl," he said. "I hate to be thinking of that fracture box, and maybe I can get her eased a trifle. If the horse was going to run away with her, he should have done it in December. After I'm through with Katie, I'll drive out to Culp's."

His breath reeked of whiskey which was not agreeing with him, but his hands were steady as he repacked his satchels. "Yes," he said, "I looked after some soldiers, but they took them away from me." And now she realized that indeed he was going into the streets again, and nothing she could say would keep him at home. She went to get a glass of milk for him, and a piece of sponge cake; he thanked her with dignity; after he was gone she saw the milk on his desk with only a finger of it missing, and the cake not touched at all.

She got her Bible out of the parlor. It was a dog-eared pile of thin leaves with the backbone gone, for she read it every day and at length. Her family had frowned upon her marriage to an Irishman, even one whose Catholicism was only a boyhood recollection, and had tacitly murmured that God might never forgive. She had not been inside a church for more than thirty years, except to attend funerals and church programs, but she could have told Reverend Solt a thing or two about the prophets. Gettysburg regarded her as a queer piece, but felt the primness of her faith as opposed to the doctor's flagrant agnosticism.

It was Jeremiah, and she had read a chapter and more before she saw the terrible error of her selection.

Behold, I will send and take all the families of the north, saith the Lord and Nebuchadrezzar the king of Babylon, my servant, and will bring them against this land, and against the inhabitants thereof, and against all these nations round about, and will

*utterly destroy them, and make them an astonish-
ment, and an hissing, and perpetual desolations.*

*Moreover I will take from them the voice of
mirth, and the voice of gladness, the voice of the
bridegroom, and the voice of the bride, the sound
of the millstones, and the light of the candle.*

*And this whole land shall be a desolation, and an
astonishment.*

She wanted to laugh at the book, and cry to Jeremiah that this was another of the cryptic inaccuracies
with which his text was sown. *Behold,* he might have
said, *I will send and take all the families of the
south . . . and bring them against this land.* Then it
would have made sense. Likely enough the rebel Lee
was meant to be Nebuchadrezzar . . . *whole land
shall be a desolation.* She went out upon the porch
again, her mouth and lips as dry as fire-brick, and she
strained her eyes into the low storm which drifted
across people's gardens. The sun came through the
haze with a queer half light—it was like an eclipse,
and you ought to have smoked glass to look through.
Not a spear of grass moved, along the whole street;
only a few birds kept fluttering nervously in and out
among the drooping elms, moving with the uneasy
flurry of fright—much extra waving of wings, and
whistling noises which they had never made before.
Behind them lived the bulging wall of sound.

There existed still the New Testament, in spite of
all the discomfort which Jeremiah had given her, so
she went inside, and found after a long time that she
had been sitting on the carpeted stairs of the hall,
reading Luke until Jesus had eaten the pieces of
broiled fish and the honeycomb. The doctor did not
come back; it was time enough; he should be through

with the Culps by now, or with Emmy Funk and her tumor, or whomever he had gone to see. She wanted to stand there in the dim, hot closeness of the little hall and scream, and scream.

The lines north of town went to pieces about four o'clock. You could hear the crowds of Confederates brawling closer as retreating Federal artillery roared south across the Diamond. Eva Duffey watched the distant flakes of red and white which were the national flags, being hurried away through the town, obliterated suddenly by opposite barns and houses, lancing out again into the dust, carried by lumbering groups of blue men who stumbled and fell and sometimes didn't get up again. She had never thought that war could be like this, with such a desperate casualness about it. War was fought in fields: there was the field of Shiloh, the field of Antietam, the field of Fredericksburg. She knew; she had read the papers. The papers mentioned nothing of people running across back yards and knocking down the clothes-props as they went.

Suddenly she looked out, north through the window of the front parlor, and it gave her a thick feeling in her lungs to find that the entire end of the street was blocked by a mob of ragged men, white with dust, and lugging soiled cerise flags along with them. They came at a dog-trot, spread across the road and up over the cinder paths at each side, their feet resounding whenever they pounded across a section of board sidewalk. A horse flashed through them from the rear; its rider looked gaunt but graceful, he had a white silk shirt which had been badly torn and flapped in ribbons from his shoulders. He turned, and waved his hand at the trotting men . . . had long hair blowing in tangled gold as the sun found it. He called in a shrill voice, "Fo'm on the left of the Fifty-seventh at the next squeh!" and then dashed past the house, leaning low over his horse's neck. A moment later Eva Duffey heard the rapid explosion of shots from the direction of York street. The ragged men began to scream. They sprinted ahead, no longer trotting, and two or three of them seemed to trip and fall forward on their hands and knees.

Mrs. Duffey found the front door. She thought, If they've shot Adam they might as well shoot me, too. She pushed open the door and stepped out on the porch. Through the curtain of morning-glory vines she could see a little knot of dark blue figures at the intersection, behind the picket fence of Deffenbaugh's wide lawn. A horse was trotting in at Grandma Leen's gate and up across her flowers; its saddle was empty. The swarm of brown men roared over the picket fence and the purple huddle behind it. More shots rang, isolated in all the confusion from every side, and she could see hands lifted high, waving out of the crowd . . . Several soldiers came running back up the road and bent over something which lay there. It was the man with the torn white shirt. They didn't pick him up; they bent down one by one, and then arose and moved back a foot or two, and stood looking at him.

The rebels possessed the entire village. When Adam Duffey had not come back at sunset, his wife started out to hunt for him. The battle seemed to be over, mainly, though firing jangled intermittently out near the cemetery. Columns of Confederates were swinging in from the north and east and west, and the Diamond was a turmoil of wagons and guns. A few citizens crept out of their houses. Mr. Pock was in his store, even so soon, and selling things.

People whispered that the Union troops had taken refuge on the hill at the cemetery, and they had such a mass of cannon up there among the rocks that the rebels dared not attack them. Probably the Nationals would be in full retreat by morning, and the enemy after them . . . An endless double-file of men in blue uniforms tramped north across the railroad track, marching without their weapons, and herded along by a sprinkling of armed rebels. Mrs. Duffey went down Baltimore street almost to the tannery, until a sentry told her that she could come no farther. Every once in awhile a rifle sounded, somewhere inside the tannery building, and it would be answered by shots from up on the hill.

"I'm looking for my husband, Doctor Adam Duffey."

The sentry nodded toward the shady slope beyond. "If he's up there, he might as well be in Africa as far as you're concerned, ma'am. Can't pass here."

"Maybe he's hurt . . . did you see a carryall and—?"

He shook his head. Then, possessed of a sudden and understanding pity, he bent down and pointed at the tannery. "Look. There's some of our people over there. Sharp-shooters, with telescopes on their guns. They're having a shooting match with some Yanks up by that brick house."

She asked, "The double house? MacLeans live there—and the Wade girl, Mrs. McClellan. She's got a new baby. Do you rebels mean to tell me that you make war on babies?"

"No, ma'am." He had curly black hair, long untrimmed, and his face was very dirty. "But those friends of yours ought to tell the Yanks to get out of their yard. They keep shooting at us down here, and we have to shoot back. Now, ma'am, please go back home."

Fearful, shuttered houses so silent and unpeopled on each side . . . a gun at the tannery said *gam*. Eva Duffey turned and took a few slow steps; the soldier came behind her.

"Now, lady, I mean—"

"You don't talk like one of these rebels," she told him.

"Maybe that's because I was raised in Pittsburgh," he said, and waved her on.

She felt eyes glaring at her, all the way. Men roosted among the guns in the Diamond; most of them were munching doughnuts. Somebody had been selling them doughnuts—a small boy in a gingham shirt, with an empty basket on his arm. She caught his shoulder and whirled him around. "Frankie," she cried, "have you seen the doctor anywheres?"

His father had been killed at Fair Oaks; his mother had four children; yes, he had been selling doughnuts at five cents a piece. "He drove down Baltimore street a long time ago, before they started to fight in town. I ain't see him since, Missis—"

"Then he was out at Culp's or the Funk place," she cried, and trying in all anguish to believe it. "He was out there, and the armies got between him and home. He couldn't get back. There's shoot-sharpers at the tannery and they— He can't get back." From every street came the mottled rumble of moving teams; sidewalks and roadways were littered with caps and knapsacks and muskets and much manure, but the rebels had men going about and collecting everything which could be used. There was a row of dead bodies stretched on the porch of the Emblem Hotel.

She went on home. There was nothing to do but wait until the next day. The Federals would be gone by morning, most likely, and the rebels would start after them. Then Doctor Duffey could return to the village. He would despise this war more than ever; there would be no tempering his views, and who knew but what Stanton's spies would hustle him away to Washington and the Old Capitol prison, as a suspicious person or a traitor . . . *Wring his neck,* she sobbed, and hurried on. A man bawled out and tried to snatch her arm; she felt his beard brush her shoulder; he was drunk. "Arrest that man!" somebody snapped, and there was the sound of running feet, and a struggle. Now she had best remain at home.

A woman with no hat or bonnet, a little woman, was walking slowly up and down in front of the house. Eva cried, "Syrena! Adam's drove out to the Culp place, and he got caught by all those soldiers being in the way! He'll be cursing something terrible, and I'm frightened to death. They're still shooting, out by the cemetery."

Mrs. Huddlestone had a darning-ball in her hands, she kept twisting it around and of course did not know that she had it. She nodded at Eva, with a plaintive smile half seen through the dusk. "I kept thinking maybe Lijy would be with our soldiers," she explained, "so I come out to look, but I couldn't see him at all. The Enemies come down the street; they liked to knocked me over. Soon as the shooting stopped I come out again. But I couldn't see him anywhere. I'll be glad when I know just where he's at, and make sure he hain't been taken to a prison pen by The Enemies."

They went into the house, and Eva Duffey made tea; they both wept as they drank it, and in the gloom the carriage house looked horrid and empty without the back of the carryall sticking out . . . Ragged men skulked up to the door and asked for a little sugar or a little this-and-that. Many of them were heathenish and menacing. At last the doctor's wife barred all her doors and dragged chairs against them, and wedged the chairs underneath the doorknobs. Mrs. Huddlestone stayed all night; neither of them slept well; there were shots and noises all the time, and men singing. God knew why they should wish to sing.

8.

The Second Corps had reached Sangster's Station before Tyler Fanning caught up with his regiment. Afterward, he remembered Sangster's Station chiefly because it was the place where a pretty girl with a soiled green apron was picking flowers in her yard; she had a willow basket half full of late roses, and she refused to look at the marching troops. The men called, "Hello, sissy—how about a posy?" "Pshaw, Dobbs, she won't give you none; she's picking those for the Secesh . . . Centreville." Eternally he was ill, and he rode for two hours in a burden wagon, by order of the colonel . . . head ached, and loose boards in the wagon kept chirping as they rubbed together, and the driver was talking to a sutler about the land his brother had bought in Iowa. The land was inside the bend of a river, and no cyclone could strike it there.

Iowa brought the thought of Dan Bale. The letter from Elmer Quagger came, and it seemed that every man in the company knew what that letter told about the captain's wife. He saw that a third corporal was bucked and gagged that day, for stealing, and he knew that the man would not have been bucked and gagged on any other day. Mrs. Captain Fanning has betrayed . . . and night came upon Thoroughfare Gap with rainy haze, like a rubber blanket laid over the short clover.

They were there until the 25th, and Fanning could follow his letter all the way north: see Chaplain Kraal posting it in Baltimore, see it laying in a mail pouch, see the pouch lifted about and transferred at the Junction, and handled by many people as it traveled . . . The corps packed up and began to move. Owen's brigade existed no longer, as such. The new commander's name was Webb: a New Yorker. He was said to be a smart enough soldier . . . Scrawny mobs of the enemy hung worrying on the heels of the advance, and there were a few casualties and a few wagons were lost. The Potomac looked browner than Ty had ever seen it, weak coffee talking among its rocks, and people called the place Edwards Ferry. The despot's heel is on thy shore, Maryland, my Maryland. Cherries were ripe, and wheat in the shock.

Poolesville, Barnesville, Monocacy Junction. The first time he ever called upon her, she played the piano for him. He stood and looked at the dull polish on his shoes, but he did remember to turn the music each time she hesitated and a sheet needed turning. She wanted to know whether he had ever heard Jenny Lind; no, he said, he didn't know much about songs or singers. "You should know," she declared. "You should." "It looks extremely difficult, Miss Lorrence." "Oh, not at all, Mr. Fanning." Her dress was cut quite low; he thought of the things his friends talked about, at college. He had never done *it,* not in all his life. He had had dreams . . . Her tea-rose silk, heavy and gathered, puffed out above its tight belt. Not at all difficult. "Well," he said, "I would be a willing pupil." They laughed. Her aunt came to serve the tea. Japanese cups—her father had bought them in Paris. Yes, she had been to Paris, too. Then her aunt said something about President Buchanan, and Tyler talked, somewhat violently, about the President. The women sat and listened to him. That was in September of 1860, and he was twenty years old.

Despots' heels or not, whatever kind of heels, they trudged doggedly all day on the 28th. It was sultry; the dun sky let its drizzle leak at them, but the roads weren't bad. Then the sun again. A persistent rumor scouted up and down: old Joe Hooker had quit, old Joe Hooker had been busted square in two—Hooker was sick, or drunk, or both, and had gone to Washington. Tyler talked with the captain of Company D, and Lieutenants Eldridge and Oliver, when they halted early in the afternoon. Eldridge got out his little collapsible chessboard, and Oliver carefully re-arranged the chessmen as they had been aligned that morning. The halt had overtaken the Philadelphia brigade at a decent spot, for once; they sprawled in chestnut shade, dozing the precious seconds away; the speckled grass was soft and cushiony as the soldiers lay in it. Ty came back to Company D, and found the captain sitting with his shoulders against a rock, eyeing his men reflectively and pasting a wrapper around a mashed cigar. He said, "Fanning, how's the inner man? . . ." "All right," Ty told him. "What news?" "None, that I know of. Baxter's got a notion that it'll be somebody new . . ." "Probably McClellan again," Tyler suggested. "Well," said the captain of Company D, "I'd just as soon. I mean that, seriously. Do you believe the tale about Hooker's being dazed when a shot struck the porch-post he was leaning against, at Chancellorsville? Drunk as anyone could ever be! I talked with a man who was at headquarters that day. No doubt whatever . . ." Then Oliver and Eldridge began to chime in—

None of them was two hours older before he heard the truth. It was George Meade. The men caught the story from the air, as always, and chewed it back and forth. They were marching at ease, arms at will, and they felt like talking. No one knew much about General Meade except that he was wall-eyed, and some man insisted that he was a Spaniard. Meade. Now, isn't that a hell of a Spanish name? "It's Dutch," somebody said. "No, English." "Well," the soldier insisted, "he's a Spaniard and come over here from Spain." "Aw, shut up—he lived in Philadelphia before you was born." Tyler cried, "All *right,* men!" They went into a hushed mumbling.

Liberty, Johnsville, and Uniontown in the evening of the 29th. It had been trying to rain, most of the day, and the provost guards kept gathering stragglers out of the fence corners. Lieutenant Eldridge was acquainted in this neighborhood; he invited everyone to a doings at the house of a Mr. Royster, who was said to be a good Union man. At first Fanning thought he wouldn't go—he needed sleep, as did everyone else. But he went at last. He sat out on the piazza with a Miss Walthall from Dover, a visiting niece or something, and listened to her chatter about Longfellow. She wanted to know whether he had read "The Courtship of Miles Standish," but he hadn't; he didn't care much for poetry. Then she wanted to go to the spring across the road, and get a drink.

It was dark as Egypt, though the drizzle had stopped. Her aunt would be crazy if she knew how Belle was slipping out like that—all alone, with a man . . . she did want a drink from the spring. It was clear water: *aqua pura,* cool and mossy on such a stifling night. They went. Miss Walthall tripped in the dark and fell, she fell against Tyler, he had her by the hand. She cried softly. "Oh, *Captain,*" and he kissed her, but it tasted as all kisses tasted to him. They had their drink and went back to the house and Hugh Ridgeway said, "Fanning, you sly dog, where have you been hiding Miss Walthall?" And Fanning said, "We've been to Dover and back, and I find Dover charming." She went to waltz with Hugh. Tyler sat out in the yard, on the edge of a flower-bed made from half an old hogshead, and he smelled the flowers which he squashed as he sat upon them. Whenever he tried to think about home, a lot of carriage wheels began to spin inside his brain. They went slowly at first; he could count the spokes. They had only ten or twelve spokes and he knew that they were not cannon wheels. Artillery wheels had fourteen spokes, mostly; he had counted them often enough.

He had always heard that in such moments a man should envisage the woman—construct her amid the nightmares which hung about him, watch her features take shape and slowly fade again. He tried hard enough to invoke his wife. But now he could see no wraith of tea-rose silk, no hands on piano keys— nothing except the smudge of his cigar, and camp fires spread russet all over the nearby farms. The house lights shone on ornamental leaves overhead, leaves cut and clipped by invalids who had nothing better to do, and masking whatever stars there might be. It was useless to attempt envisaging Irene or any other woman.

Tuesday night the whole corps lay at Uniontown

still, though the Fifth Corps and the Pennsylvania Reserves passed on to the northeast. Farmers gathered around the picket lines with dire stories about the rebel cavalry, and how they had raided Westminster, a few miles to the right. Roads were noisy with staff officers hammering up and down, and lanterns glowed in the headquarters tents; the vast, mysterious honesty of moonlight made the red fires ashamed of themselves. Tyler Fanning felt the familiar, groping bulge in his stomach. Organs would ripple in loose-drawn knots . . . it wasn't more painful than the law allowed, but it was damned annoying. He sat on his rubber blanket, opening his clothing and massaging as Doctor Duffey had instructed him. If he went to the surgeon, the surgeon would only give him calomel. Well, there were a lot of snakes or little slimy beasts of some kind, wound up in his innards. The scarred hide was pulled together in a pink squeeze, like the neck of a paper sack, and the animals curled and uncurled inside, and refused to let him rest. Lose it, he thought, and feel better. He walked away from his snoring flock and stood among some weeds and put his finger down his throat. Afterward he felt weaker than a cat, and the tips of his fingers were buzzing. His feet, also, and a watery whirlpool inside each ear. God damn it, why couldn't he be sleeping on a mattress?

They made thirty-five miles the next day. Thirty-five miles with gas booming inside him, even though he did have a horse to ride. There had been no rain in these northern counties; the dust was hot talcum. Men leaned over the fences all afternoon and yelled about a big battle up in Pennsylvania. Taneytown . . . this was a joke. Going home, home, home said the horse's dragging feet, a muffled k-sound at the end of every beat. Home to find what's what. *To my certain*

*knowledge, the informant has never told an untruth,
at least not in the years I have known Said Informant, which is a long time.* Elmer Quagger had testi-
fied in church, often enough—Ty had heard him,
little boy sitting between his father and his mother . . .
If this is true, I have done right in telling her, and I
suppose that I must confront Bale. He will be a surly
customer. Somehow he has been so queer and philo-
sophical since boyhood—his education was a deep
dye, and so I didn't think that women interested him.
He has learned new tricks, out west. Cannot try them
on me, a captain . . . Ty drew his revolver out of its
holster; it was extremely heavy; he let it drop back
into the leather case again, and his tingling fingers
had difficulty in anchoring the flap.

I was twenty, and I had not been wounded . . .

Going home, home, home. How remarkable if we
pass through Gettysburg. Have Colonel Baxter and
the adjutant to supper, and see that Gretel cooks
some chickens in the German way.

And now the colonel put a hand on his bridle, and
looked very severe. "Fanning—you are jaundiced—
you look green as a pea-pod. Get into a wagon!"

"I'm all right, sir," he heard his own voice squawking, and angrily, because the men were looking up at
him with red-rimmed eyes. Each of them had a
good sixty pounds of blankets and crackers and tin
cups and under-drawers and playing cards and Bi-
bles and India rubber, strapped to his shoulders.
Forty rounds in their cartouches, sixty rounds in their
pockets. They were thinking: lie in a wagon.

"Go back to the train, Captain." Baxter jerked his
thumb. "We may need you badly tomorrow."

Once more he lay in a wagon, rations bubbling in
his gullet as if he had never chewed them. The dust

found him. He could feel it drifting into his nose. Well, he prided himself, the old man recognizes that I'm of value. Nobody else could handle the company as well as I. Lieutenant Wicks becomes hysterical under fire; the men would suffer if I were killed, or if I died of my snakes and stomach-dwellers. The wagon wheels said: going-home-to-Gettysburg-and-see-your-pretty-wife-going-home-to-Gettysburg-and-spare-your-precious-life. "No," he had told the girl from Delaware, "I don't care much about poetry." And here he was, building miles of red-hot poems out of the wheels . . . He became amazingly hungry, and the only food which he imagined and which he most craved, was sliced radishes and lettuce leaves. With vinegar and sugar. It would be so good; he could eat a barrel of it, if he had some.

In late afternoon he felt much better. The train made a brief halt; Fanning went up to the door of a yellow farmhouse and got some milk. The woman made him pay twenty-five cents in currency for a small pannikin of it, and he wanted to tell her what a wrinkled beast she was. The milk stayed down, and it might placate all impulses in the secret pit of him.

He untied Jinks from the rear of the wagon, watered him at the farmer's trough, and rode through solid dust to find the Seventy-second. They were just coughing Foorwoord—*cha!* again. An ambulance came from the north, and a dread story came with it. "General Reynolds. Yes, he's killed. They've been fighting along the mountains." "No, he was only wounded." "You're crazier than a hoot-owl; the driver told me. He *was* dead. There the ambulance goes, back there." The men kept turning and looking back.

Pennsylvania had slid down beneath their sore feet. "And folks call the rebels foot-cavalry!" a cracked voice jeered, but few soldiers were wasting their breath in talk. After dark they went into line across the road, a half-mile past the Truckenmiller farm. Every once in a while they heard a far-off sound which might have been a shot, though there wouldn't be much shooting now that dark had come . . . Tyler formed a notion that he was coming home with college mates, or with some foreign aggregation of which he was very proud, and with which he would astonish the villagers. If fighting had actually taken place close to town, he'd have every opportunity to snatch a few minutes at home.

I wonder, he thought with sudden horror—maybe my letter made her so angry that she went home to Philadelphia. And that would be a ghastly scandal; the town would never get over it.

Breastworks, came the order, and the sleepy men had to be kicked out of the grass where they lay. Too tired to swear, they fumbled weakly in the gloom, dragging fence rails and turning up a shallow ditch across the cornfield. "Well enough," grunted the sergeant. "All right," said Ty "—let them sleep." And they all lay down and died, some with the tools still in their hands. There were but eighteen stragglers in the whole brigade.

The moon seemed surprised to find itself confronted by guns. It slid up out of the eastern ridges, a brass bangle, and waited motionless above the hot, black trees. Old Baxter had been wiser than he knew. Now, if another battle occurred, Tyler would be available for duty. He could make these youths hold their first volley until they counted the wooden buttons on the rebels' shirts . . . Thirty-five miles. Ty lay back and slept with the lemon moonlight on him. His stomach awakened him about eleven o'clock, and the awful carriage wheels began to turn inside his brain.

Book Five

STARS CEASE TO SHINE ON THE BRAVE

1.

In that half world which lay somewhere between nightmare and fact, an existence claimed by sleep but never subservient to it, Irene heard the sounds of the house and yard. She was conscious of sheets wrapping her naked legs, of the damp nightgown coating her.

The terror of past hours would not let her rest. One face swelled like a sun: high forehead, green-grape eyes, the lips gone back from flat teeth . . . He breathed through locked jaws, pain leaving him at every breath and filling him once more as he sucked again. He lay on the floor of the sitting room, his soaked bandages gluing the carpet. The surgeon stepped carefully from place to place, over one body, past other whinnying men; he had removed his shoes, and his feet were immense in their ragged white socks.

The girl could not reason or understand, in the snare of this obsession, but the face with green-grape eyes stayed before her. It was a background, an awful platter whereon other faces were arranged like poached eggs, the ethereal paleness of them overlapping, melting together. Sometimes she pushed herself up through the cast of sore muscles: again she was in her bed, again there was summer night and wistaria and the dense moonlight outside. Sounds crowded close outside her door and window, a herd of them, and singly they slipped inside and made themselves known.

Dog barked. Not Cybo; Cybo was dead because he had barked. Surgeon in big knit socks, and the floor squeaked under him. Throat, throat, throat, the endless cough and swallow. Far away, the dog; far away the skirmishing wheels. That's a shot—little round bubble from a hidden drum, tom-tom on the long ridges. Throat, throat, and there is a mystery of movement in the Fannings' room; they suffer and grow old together.

How long, she thought, did I sleep? Went down into a mine shaft where ghoul-sounds existed amid my descent, the insects buzzing behind them. Oh God, it's . . . the word was lost in other strangulations. Forever the wagons and teams encompassed the country; forever the laborers clicked their axes. Flat voice said contritely: "Christ Almighty, let me die and get rid of this oooh."

They were downstairs. Dining room, sitting room, library and hall were paved with long-legged bundles. Water and lint and silver probes, and all night the flickering candles would feel sorry for them.

She helped the doctor until long after dark. These were rebels, but incapable of stealing horses. Sometimes, as a young girl, Irene had imagined herself in a war like tapestry design, and in that tapestry war she held cups to thankful lips, she put her hands on clean, dying brows, and felt the skin of knights turn to clay as she touched them. Now she had Gretel bring a sack of bran from the storeroom, and together they worked in the kitchen, tearing clean white rags into sixteen-inch lengths, folding once, stitching the sides, pouring a stuffing of loose bran, doubling the seam at the end and basting hastily across. They must have made four dozen pads, and the surgeon said that he could use more in the morning.

Horror in the barn, wild horror in the carriage house. The gig, the carriage and the old sleigh had been dragged out to make room for straw and the long rows which lay in it. A lantern hung upon a nail and watched the men turning heads, twitching, or becoming fatefully quiet. There were a few horses in the yard, and always someone at the well, but for the most part the invaders stayed away from the house; only a few soldiers came and went, always in pairs, and always carrying burdens between them when they came.

A man with a kinky red beard had ridden into the yard soon after the Nationals retreated through the town; got off, bowed and excused himself, walked through the house and came out on the front porch, tugged at his beard, called to a big soldier whom he designated as Doctor Pell.

"Sir," Mr. Fanning cried hopelessly, "this is my home—we have been ill and—"

The general nodded. "If you forbid us—" He turned his rusty hat in his hands, and when he looked up at Bedford Fanning there was an accusing gleam in his eyes. "You have relatives with the Northern army? Ah. A son. I beg you to consider . . . if this were Virginia, and your son lay wounded—" He said, "Thank you. We're grateful. There are hundreds of wounded hereabouts, and we are compelled to use certain houses for headquarters and others for hospital purposes."

But, he said, the family might remain if they chose. Already Mrs. Fanning had crept to her room; she lay across the bed, her eyes simmering in tears, her padded

hands grasping the quilt. Irene came. "Just—let—
me—alone—daughter. The turpentine spirits," she
begged in a voice out of the grave. "Can't I bring
you some wine, mother?" "No. No. Let me be."

When Mr. Fanning came up, Irene returned to the
first floor. She made no explanation of her going, and
he did not protest at her mingling with these enemies
who began to troop through the rooms and fetch their
dreadful luggage inside. Each member of the household
had become a separate organism, going a solitary way,
eyes veiled, ears deadened to the tiny screech of nerves.
Demon stood at the well, drawing pail after pail of
water, and explaining to the Confederates about his
Freedom Paper. They kept teasing him; many of them
were very young.

The woman told the surgeon that she would help,
and he nodded as if he had expected nothing else. She
wondered in how many other houses he had moved
about as he was moving here, whistling soundlessly
between his tight lips. "Spread a sheet over that table,
Keedy, that'll do well enough . . ." He told her about
the bran; hot water, of course; and if there was any
milk for milk punch, or any soup— He said little
enough, and not once did he thank her or annoy her
with fulsome apologies. She was a woman, she was
in this place, this was what she should be doing.

Only once when he looked at a steel engraving of
Boston Common, which hung in the library, he seemed
wistfully human.

"You are from Boston, Madam?"

She said, "Philadelphia."

"My home is in Roanoke—wife and two children—
but I pursued my studies at Cambridge. Harvard,
'fifty-five."

An invisible broth, the smell of perspiration and

unwashed bodies and fresh blood, saturated the rooms. The surgeon and his assistants kept the library door closed—that was where they did awful things, that was where they had the tubs and dishpans, and where the yells came from.

... Northern soldiers as well, and strangely they smelled as did the rebels; they made the same sounds; their blood was the same color. Sometimes enemies would be side by side, and sometimes both of them would be conscious. Irene would come in and find them looking at each other, and they'd be talking. Delirious or not, agonized beyond all hope, the feverish sneers would be bubbling in their mouths. "Hallo, Reb." "Howdy. Yawl shore high-tailed it." "Aw, just goin' down the line to get a few friends and come back and whale the muss out of you." "Where you got hit, Yank?" "Guess my spine—feels dead and froze, it don't hurt, but I can't move my legs, what—you—got? Down here . . . oh, that's hard lines . . . could I have a drink, Miss? We hate to bother."

A voice railed from the corner. "You God damn white-livered rats!" it burst, all in one breath. "That's all she's good for, Yankee slut! She—" A man kicked out with his foot, and there was the sound of leather driven deep against a yielding body, the arrowy scream after a whole second of silence, the thrashing about, the gabble of the rest. Doctor Pell was at the door, several Doctor Pells with berry-juice hands and berry-juice all over their shirt bosoms. "Madam," all the bearded doctors spoke together, "I suggest that you stay in the kitchen: it'll be better."

She sat in the steaming kitchen with her naked elbows on the table; once she slumped forward and the candle flame licked greedily toward her hair, and the sizzle of it burnt keenly through all other odors. "The poor young Missis," Gretel wailed. "Ach, and it is bad they make you to work so hard." A frail voice questioned slowly, "Hard? They make me—work hard? No. Not at all. Go—on—with your—soup."

Muffled by library doors and other closed doors, a tortured animal continued his insufferable yelling. It sounded as if he were crying, "Ahoy!" over and over, very rapidly. Gretel began to hiccough; her soup ladle clattered on the floor and she went down to join it, shuddering with her blue apron up over her face, the petticoats bulging around her fat brown-cotton legs as she slid lower and lower on her haunches. "Missis," she gasped, "and I feel it so sick inside!"

Irene had the wooden spoon in her hand and she was wiping it clean; she stood before the hell of the stove and felt it searing her face with its hundred white-hot cracks. "You've done your share," she told Gretel, "and more. Do you get to your room and try to rest. I will finish this."

Pale flesh bubbling, soaked from slim little bones, the chicken swam in its pot. She could not discern the fragrance of it; only one odor could come to her. She rolled the sleeve higher on her scorched arm: stir, and stir, and round again, and round. The wall-lamp flared in its bracket. She would keep this up, she would go on stirring chicken broth forever, and after a while the swollen skin would pop from her arm, and her own meat would season this potion. The man in the remote library began to shout once more, muffled hootings which someone was trying to stifle with a hand pressed across the mouth. Horses and wheels roared through the barnyard, then another batch; they were moving guns from one place to another.

Men drifted near the window. "No, I was mighty

suspicious when he saw him laying there. He had three hits—guess he'd lost a sight of blood. Sergeant said, 'How come you got this gun, and you a civilian?' He said 'twan't his gun—"

"Wawl see him thar, and he said he was constable down in that-thar town. Reckon he was seventy-five if he was a day. He tolt us he was wounded a-crossin' the field; reckon he tolt a lie. I wouldn't make trust with no Yank if he—"

She repeated the words to herself, the queer little camp-following gossip. Why, she recognized, if he was an old constable he must have been that old shoemaker, Burns. He has been wounded . . . Steam came up in her face, cooking her eyes; still she could not close them.

The door opened behind her, and a young orderly slid into the room. The woman thought, I like the way that little lock of black hair droops over your forehead. You should not be here, lad. Somewhere there is a farm; your mother bakes peach pies, she—

"Lady, Captin says as how if that soup—"

"Yes." Remote S-sound of the word—who said that—some dark shape whispering in a corner? "It's been finished for some time." She said, "Now I must go." The ladle lay upon the table, smoking. She went into the rear passage; that door, a narrow back stairway like a turret stairs in a castle, it was too narrow for Mrs. Bedford Fanning to use. Up she went in stuffy blackness. Tiny blossoms of color burst before her eyes; she said, "My mind is gathering forget-me-nots, one at a time. Cannot hold the whole bouquet."

Then she was in her own room, and had turned the wooden button on the door. Through the open window came army sounds: the axles and the braying, a lunatic scream, the crackle of flames and the sound of a banjo being tuned. A jovial soul was saying to Demon, "Then I'll ask Gen'ral Lee to take you back fo' to be his own nigger—he's got jest scads of 'em— fool free niggers he's cotched up Nawth," and Demon was sullen. No, suh, young Mist Rebel.

"Irene Lorrence," she exclaimed in crazy wonder, "how does it happen that you are here?" Still in the darkness and without lighting a candle or closing the shutters, she unfastened her clothing. Her girlhood came closer and more distinctly to her at every moment, rushing in a charge out of the caverns of the past. Years when she was a child, the baby years screaming behind. She saw the covers of forgotten but now familiar books; she tasted raspberry ice, she remembered the taste of muffins; she was rolling a hoop, she was practicing at the piano, now Aunt Cynthia was whispering in a voice brittle as straw: *When you are older I shall tell you more. All girls are the same.* There was a cat named Pumpkin, and it had a fit. She toiled for weeks in pink and blue cross-stitch, with an endless chain-stitch border: Pride is an evil which all do deplore. I pray for humility and for no more. Irene Victoria Lorrence 1849 . . . And in this babble of her life, she perceived the faces of playmates and little-known cousins, which speedily clustered and shaped themselves in one hideous amalgamation of features.

Jaws set tight, and ivory tusks framed in scrolled lips; a high, narrow forehead and eyes like green— All she's good for, Yankee slut! Now she had slipped the night-dress over her head; the room and the outdoor and indoor sounds made a nasty whirl around her, she fell upon her bed.

Again she started up before any nature of sleep had come. "Heavenly Father," she cried, "Tyler—*Tyler.* I did that to him. Because I wanted to. I went seeking it. I found out what it was like, I craved it and went again and again. All that time he was believing me to be his wife, or else he was drugged with the disaster I brought upon him. The only peace he had was for a week after he left, and that was a false peace soon to be broken. The rebels declare that the whole Army of the Potomac is here, or on the way, and at this moment Tyler may be lying on a library table in some other house."

Something. There was something . . . She groped amid the tumult. Said: "It happened before the Confederate general came here—while the flood of soldiers was pouring down from the seminary. It had to do with Cybo . . . had his head in my lap, the awfulness of him stained my clothing. Indeed—" she said— "now, now I have it! It was Daniel Bale. (When she recalled his name, immediately she could feel him loving her in the dark; it was rape, and nothing else.) He ran between the trotting columns, officers howled at him to get out of the way, but still he raced on, and grew larger and more formidable every second. He was past the ruined fence, running through the wreck of cabbages. He called, "Are you all safe?" "Yes," Mr. Fanning answered, wholly beaten— "yes, Daniel, we are safe except for the dog. See, he is dead."

Bale looked at her; he must have been tending some of the wounded during that day, for he had stains all over him. Blood upon them both. Her gown, his pantaloons and shirt—her hands, and his. The car of war came trundling across from South Mountain, spoiling all the crops. She stared at him . . . tried to say, Lover, I am here.

"This must be the end," her father-in-law was lamenting. "Nothing but the dissolution of our country can result from these endless defeats. The Nationals broke and ran like . . ." His throat went dry, and there was nothing more for him to say. Now the rebels were in the barnyard.

"I'll be at hand," Bale said, "if you need me."

"Daniel, I see troops in your yard— Yes," he said again, "I will go back." Most of the soldiers are past, now . . . more artillery. He stood looking for a long moment at the body of the dead Federal soldier, the one who must have been named David. It had fallen off the step and lay on its face; the elbows were bent and stiff, the neck seemed swollen above the collar.

She tried once more to meet Bale's gaze and give him whatever it was he wanted, but she could still hear Cybo going *I-yee-yee* and see him wallowing toward her.

"Call me if you have need," the man told them again, and went back across the pasture.

That was it, that was what happened late in the day, it was the Something. A-whirl on her giddy bed, the woman paraded this all before her. It was a circumstance which might have meant a great deal if she had not been a wicked woman. But she had been one. "Tyler," she whispered aloud, and it made a terrible sound in her mouth. "Husband," she said, and the word was just as shocking. Forever, my sin and my tremendous responsibility. In this same hour he may be on a rack, and my own arms cranking his sockets apart, my ears receiving his outcry. Whomsoever God hath joined together, let them not rack one another asunder . . . Then, for the first time, she screamed. It was not a loud scream, and no one heard her.

2.

More than anything else, the thick scent of decaying flesh made Dan awake. It was the chestnut gelding beside his front fence, now forty hours dead, a vast balloon frosted with a thousand flies. He wondered how the rebels could endure it; there were plenty of them in the yard tending their own horses, or merely sitting on their heels and eating crackers. A wagon had stopped in front of Mrs. Knouse's gate. It was loaded with loose shoes, and a swarm of beggarish soldiers clustered around the tailboard, passing the shoes from hand to hand, throwing their old foot-gear aside, trying on the new.

There was no water in his pitcher and he must go down to the pump before he could wash. He tried to count the mornings . . . two days ago he had been scything weeds. Yesterday he awoke at Fanning's; yesterday cannon took the sky apart. Now the morning air was heavy with a foreboding warmth. Clouds which could not be identified by size or shape or color, but which existed nevertheless, lay like cloth across the sun and its shadows were dull and hazy.

Downstairs he found the rooms blue with bacon smoke. The double doors of the library and front parlor were drawn tight; the general must be asleep still, for he had been riding about until very late; dimly, Dan had awakened to look out and see the horses trooping home, all silver in the dust and shine of the moon. Men muttered about The Old Man and Lee and Up On The Hill. The Confederate Commander's headquarters must be there, at Johnson's or the seminary.

In the kitchen, a nervous man with blood-shot eyes got up from the table and offered his hand. "Haowdeedo. We've taken possession, as you see." He spoke with the swift, run-together slur of the martial Britisher.

"I expected that you would. Excuse me—I want to go out to the pump."

The officer shrugged. He wore a soiled, stiff-bosomed shirt and gray breeches. "No use, I'm most sorry to say. *Dis aliter visum.* It is dry, my deh felleh. The niggah had to fetch water from some place, God knows wheh. But he has managed to contrive some most excellent coffee, and I shall be most happy—" A smile slipped across his thin, sharp face. "This is most awkwahd—your own kitchen, eh? Do join me at breakfast!"

A black man came from beside the stove, and put another chair in place. Bale sat down. He thought, Doc won't believe me if I tell him this has happened. Civilized warfare . . . he said, "I'm sorry. There are a number of officers here, and you came together—"

The Englishman's coffee cup shook in his hand. "Captain Aubrey Campbell-Slaughter, A.D.C. to General Rice Duncan, Heth's Division. Late Her Majesty's Coldstream Guards." His pink eyes were steaming above the rim of his cup, and for all the frying meat you could sense a mist of whiskey around him.

More Confederates came into the kitchen. Dan heard himself murmuring banalities, accepting apologies which he did not want or value. "Ruining your carpets with our spurs, sir." The burden of The Invaded. Somebody laughed. There was a face with prodigious waxed mustaches thrust out like knives beneath the broken nose. "I always say, sir, that I've waited a long time to sleep in a Pennsylvania bed." No one laughed, then—only a whisper snapping toward Captain Campbell-Slaughter: "I tell you, English, you'd better stiffen up before the general's abroad . . ."

A sheaf of swords stood in the corner, loose belts trailing. The clock ticked behind its painted glass pane. These men ate heartily, like boys on a spree beyond the authority of parents or schoolmasters. Only one of them was past thirty. In the haze by the hot stove, the silent negro toiled at his cookery. He had not touched any food from the larder; the coffee was better than that sold by Mr. Pock, the bacon not so good, and there was a crock of fresh butter on the table. A major said to Bale, "Yes, we've got expert foragers. Better than the Yanks, if you'll excuse me."

On the rear porch someone was singing softly: *oh, let not, my own love, the summer winds winging their sweet-laden zephyrs o'er land and o'er sea—* When Dan came out the singer was gone, and he never knew who it was . . . the staff officer had been correct; the pump was useless. You'd work the handle endlessly and bring up only a few spasms of turbid water. Men had been drawing water from the well at Mrs. Knouse's, despite her warning sign; there were trampled paths all through her flowers. Bale walked past the stable and looked across the field toward the Fanning house. Dun figures strolled in the yard—one soldier carried a pail into the garden and dumped something from it, then went back to the barn. A squad worked in the pasture, and at first Dan didn't know what they were doing. They had a long row of colored wads on the ground and at the end of the row stood two soldiers with shovels. They'd roll one of the wads away from the rest, cover it with swift waves of loose dirt, and then roll another wad beside it and start digging again . . . wads, wads, he thought, blots of blue and tan on the landscape. My God— they give them short shrift, once they are dead.

The Confederate army had spread along the ridge: past Schmucker's, past the Schultz house, far beyond McMillen's and the Blisses', the farms were alive with a gray-black froth of men and teams. Bale looked toward Granite Ridge, and there existed some sort of germ-life as well, remote and dusty with the constant stirring of the Taneytown road, but still a life which gave off sound.

Irene and the Fannings would be sleeping late, or keeping well to their rooms. Dan wondered if the Union army were retreating—they'd had all night in which to retreat, and he had thought that the rebels would set out on their trail at the first crack of dawn. But in this stifling morning there seemed no hint of running away, or of pursuit. All around the valley rim strange picnics were taking place: the broken grain waited, splintered by the wheels of artillery which hunted along the slopes.

He turned. Mrs. Knouse's little box-house, so still. It frightened him. The rebels had not taken possession of it . . . he didn't know why, he wasn't a soldier. He hated all armies. He climbed over the fence and walked around the Knouse place. The doors were locked, the windows shuttered. He rapped at the kitchen door, and cried the old woman's name. Two officers came out on his porch and looked across curiously.

There was no inside cellar entrance, Bale remembered. He thudded his fist on the folded doors of the outer cellarway. She did not reply though he called and called.

"Who's down there?" they asked, across the fence. Dan said, "My neighbor. She's old . . ." And she'd been down there for twenty-four hours. Dan set his hand around the ridge which covered the crack between the two doors, and pulled; the strip ripped off with a shattering. He slid his fingers through the crack and pushed a wooden bar inside. Then he could lift the twin doors, and the morning sped down ahead of him.

It smelled of fruit and potatoes, of damp spices and the queer, old-lady herbs which would be sacked and put away in such a place. There was no window. Bale stood for a moment in the cavern, blinking at darkness. Shadows of the two officers shafted across the cellarway. He heard himself informing them, "Here she is," and all the time he thought it strange that Mrs. Knouse should have been killed by this catastrophe which had barely crushed down her hollyhocks. She lay on her face between two tubs, a limp rag of checkered gingham from which claw-like hands spread out and patterned the loose dirt. He picked her up and carried her out into the garden.

She was not dead, but her pulse fluttered like an imprisoned moth, captured inside the wrinkled brown wrist. Her face looked very shrunken and accusing. "Water," Dan said, and one of the soldiers ran to the well. The other man, and he was the colonel with the broken nose, took up one of the homely hands and began to rub it gently. He declared, "I always say, sir, that war is worse on the widows and orphants than on us men who fight it."

They bathed her face but her eyes did not open; once she swallowed on nothing; the pulse still capered, however feebly. The colonel brought out a green glass flask and held it speculatively to the light.

"This here's Maryland liquor. I don't know that it's scarcely fit to drink."

Dan forced Mrs. Knouse's lips apart, and let the whiskey seep between her snag-teeth. She gagged, and swallowed again; one hand lifted, fell back.

"I'd say she was coming 'round."

Dan said, "We'll see. If she'd lain down there awhile longer—" All the time a strange, horned Reason stood behind him, shrieking that there was no justice in reviving this decrepit witch, merely because she was a woman; the burial party was covering better wads than she, and dozens of them, and heaven knew how many other burial parties there were.

She whispered, "Rebels," and mourned about it for awhile, gurgling. The sun grew hotter, and all the time these men ministered to her they were ruining more of her garden. They gave her additional whiskey, and her eyes opened warily as if expecting enemies to pounce, and ready to slide behind their pink lids at the first attack.

"Mrs. Knouse," Bale entreated.

She told him "Rebels," again, and then she whispered, "I never durst. No. No." At last she sat up in his arms and he let her head lie against his chest, the sunbonnet all askew; he had been the torment of her life with his childhood cats and his pop-guns and currant thievery, but now she was a frightened baby for him to woo and reassure.

"Yore all right, Ma," the youngest Confederate tried to make her believe.

She said, "No," with suspicion and then she had a chill, even with the larkspurs withering around her. "Who are these critters, Daniel?" she wanted to know. "Just soldiers." She choked, and said that she knew, they were rebel soldiers and they must keep away from her well. She knew. She had heard them at the well all night long. They thought she didn't know, but she did know. "The sign," she cried weakly—there was a sign at her gate, and it was not for them to bother a woman when she had no men-folks by her.

They heard someone hurrying through the grass, and when Dan turned he could see Irene Fanning coming across his yard. Her gown was shielded by a great apron which must have belonged to her mother-in-law; her face looked too firm and set, as if the skull were built of limestone under soft skin. She was holding her skirt with both hands as she ran . . . The old woman moaned in Dan's arms.

Irene stopped at the fence, lifting one hand to grasp the spear of a picket. "I saw, from the house, and came as quickly as I could. What has happened?"

The two officers had removed their hats. Dan rose; Mrs. Knouse let her head nod limply . . . yes, she might have been whispering, yes, I reckoned this would come about.

"Nothing's happened," he said. "Mrs. Knouse was in her cellar since yesterday morning, that's all."

The old woman hissed, "They come in my yard anyway."

Irene said, "Bring her over to our house. We must care for her."

"Why," he heard himself remonstrating for no reason at all, "she—"

"They will take my bulbs."

Mrs. Fanning moistened her lips. You've got middling black eyes, Dan thought, and always I believed they were green . . . The colonel was close beside him, fumbling for a hold on the gingham dummy. "Here," he drawled, "you come and visit me a spell, Ma'am, while yo' neighbor gets over the fence." Bale swung himself across the spikes. "Daniel," Mrs. Knouse kept wailing, "I want you should make them come no more to my well, and they have trod my speckle-lilies."

Once more he took the burden, and he followed Irene across the pasture. She stayed a few yards ahead of him as if she had a peculiar creed against walking at his side. The Fanning house was a cavern of hot smells. "Not in there," the girl ordered, when he turned toward the sitting room; "bring her up the back stairway." He carried Mrs. Knouse up the dark, winding case and then he was in the second story of the big house, and it was the first time he had been there since he was a child.

"Where?"

"This is the spare room. Here, on your left. We offered what beds we had but Doctor Pell said No." The bed was ancient and curtained; the curtains had a motif of little girls leading faded lambs. Irene drew the drapes apart, and Bale put Mrs. Knouse into the dim sanctuary of linen and goose-feathers. She said, "Speckle-lilies, and there is my canary-bird in the cellar still." "I'll get it," Dan said, and he went out to the hall.

He stood looking into the dark pit of the rear stairs, and a few shafts of sunlight slanted past him. He heard Irene murmuring reassurance to the old woman, and promising tea and an egg; he heard her opening the window. She came out and closed the door.

"I'll go for her bird," he repeated. Downstairs, other men said other things: a damp and unhealthy chanting of many voices like sleepy children, and you could not make out their words. The girl stood beside him and her shoulders were drooping. He took her hand. She did not attempt to withdraw it, but her skin was all too cool. "Irene," he said.

Her eyes came up and they showed hollow desperation which he had not seen there before. Some assurance seemed broken within her mind.

"I want to see you."

"What?" he asked. And then, "Irene—oh, darling, I—"

"Oh," she said, "don't talk about it now." She drew her hand away. Her lips were caked. "It's about Tyler," she explained. "That's what it's about. But I have things to do. I—have things— Will you come later?"

He said with a dreadful casualness and dignity: "Certainly," and then went ahead of her down the staircase. There were too many people in the kitchen— Gretel and Demon and shirtless strangers—fresh blood, blood not so fresh. A hollow-chested youth with a stained cloth pinned across his front, was warming something in a pan on the stove. In the closed sitting room, two men competed in a horrid vocal contest. One said "Lucille," over and over, and the other kept talking about "They're only militia, Bobby, only militia—"

Dan crossed the pasture, circling wide to avoid the workers and the few wads as yet unburied. There was something happening along the Pike in front of his house. He came through the yard to find the fence lined with boys and men who took off their hats as a group of riders came by. There were seven of the horsemen pacing down the hill from Johnson's house, and foremost rode a big, gray-bearded soldier on a horse nearly as pale as old Salt. The man wore a pearl-gray hat, and he had some glasses in his hand. He bowed toward the front porch, acknowledging a salute, and he called in a clear voice: "I shall want you in about an hour, General, at General Hill's headquarters," and then rode on toward the town. He did not look as Dan had thought he would look . . . that same expression Bale had seen the day before, in the eyes of the dusty Reynolds who trotted toward the seminary under the apple trees. They were trying to kill men, each trying to kill the other's, and now one was dead and one still alive. It seemed too strange that they should have the identical far-seeing obsession in their eyes.

3.

As the dead cavalry horse in the ditch underwent its chemistry, so Daniel Bale felt that his brain was bloating before an inevitable extinction. Dimly he tried to think, If I had stayed in the west, if I had let Grandfather be buried without my coming . . . Beyond that cowardly chiding he could not continue. Every main-stay of his intelligence was exhausted: Plotinus, Eckhart, Tauler were distant words, not even names, and he had not the courage to reach for any philosophy. He knew certainly that he would never be able to bring it back.

He thought now that he was losing every ambition and dream for the future. Quite as a boyish lover, before this war completed its circumscription, he had toyed with a vision in which he saw himself and Irene gone into the haze of western sky, following a long road across the mounds of blue-stem. Together they could take the mystic refuge of wilderness as it was offered, and not question or analyze it. He had seen them driving through Big Hell Slough, and had watched her wonder at the million blackbirds which broke away from them, fluting, brushing their scarlet humps against the sky. He had wanted to show her the prairies; he had wanted her to sleep in a wagon box with him, and come to the grist mill which once he had owned and now might own again if he chose.

The frontier had been a refuge for others like him and like this woman. People such as they broke with the east; they reared a life as tall and succulent as the upland reeds around their homes, and as unstable. Life in the prairie country had little of the toiling triteness which symbolized these Pennsylvania farms: the very solitude and wonder of the pillowed clouds made a pathway into something fresh and luring . . . you slept soundly at night, you fancied cobalt castles amid the gum-weed, you ate hungrily.

Just as a wise man had said, the soil would breed poverty and ignorance; no paradise could withstand them. But before people put their noses into the furrows there were open years when every windy ridge abounded in exultant madness, and those were the years Dan Bale saw himself spending with this woman.

Such a passion, he had come to believe, must have more than the body behind it. It would be rounded, all-embracing . . . these books we will share, we will laugh over this carded wool, over oatmeal and axes, and each will listen when the geese and pelicans ride the sky to the north, and will say: *Hear them, hear them?* Even our rages and the human squabbles curling between us will have the mutual brand; good and evil, the magnificent and the more frequent trivial, both will be ours.

He did not know how to importune or persuade with forethought. The first joustings, brief as they were, had been only a pretense to hide their instant eagerness, the hearty instinct to blend their bodies and see what it would be like. She had whispered and confessed as he had; both of them knew; nothing was covert, and even in this sodden fear there was no flavor of suspicion.

"Wants to talk to me about Tyler. Well, by God," he said—*by God*—

He made his errand. The terrified bird rioted in its cage all the way, and he hoped it would not die of fright before Demon carried it up to the spare room. When he returned, he entered through the rear door of his house; there were sentries round the front. Double doors into the hall were open and the nasal voice of General Duncan was saying, "No, he's sending Anderson—he's got five brigades. Just as glad. Didn't we get pounded enough yesterday to suit you?" There were officers in the hall. Someone chattered, "Archer wasn't wounded when they took him—I have it from a Yankee prisoner—Archer was completely cut off by those willows . . ." The staff moved aside to let Bale pass, and he went up the stairs. Looked down over the balustrade, and through the library door he saw General Duncan standing beside Pentland Bale's desk, with the miniatures of Pentland Bale's mother and father just beyond . . . a bitter pine-cone of a man with a feel of whips and livery stables about him. He was reading a note written on crumpled blue paper. Dan went into his bedroom and shut the door.

He lay down upon the unmade bed and tried to close his nose to the increasing stench of horse-meat. They could burn it, he reiterated, just as I considered doing—few gallons of coal oil and a lot of dry wood. Or bury it. Never drive out west with her. I know it. I know it as surely as I am lying here. The impact has flung us into a rubbish heap where we lie quivering.

He tried to make an occupation out of the sounds in the yard, voices coming up through floor and windows. It might be possible to identify voices even though you'd met the men only once or twice; if you were exceedingly skillful it could be done. "Well, see the quartermaster, Colonel Cornwall! See the quartermaster. I am not your quartermaster. I am—" He looked like a dried pine-cone. "Oh English," someone called. "I suppose that British officer drank himself out of the Coldstream Guards, and that is why he is here. I have heard that such men are demons in battle . . ." Demon. I wonder if he saw us when he went through the hall with his Bible—saw us beginning our kiss? What matter if he did?

Rolled over, and buried his face in the stuffy bedclothes, and began to curse Demon. Servile, cringing, gabbling humbug—he is tainted as surely as Tyler is tainted. If she stays with them she will be spoiled in the same way; it is the Fanning taint, I know there is such a thing, and how I loathe it.

Horses clattered away from the gate. "I shall want you in about an hour, General, at General Hill's headquarters." Who was General Hill? Tyler must despise all fate because he isn't a general. Let them kill him; power to their powder, ruthless selection to their lead.

The room had grown much hotter . . . very long time. Paralysis like sleep overcame him, and yet his eyes were open every hour . . . He heard a stutter of gunfire, another Fourth of July. Such a sound you heard for a great while before you were aware of it; how long had this been happening? Big boots pounded around the house, men running toward the stable. The firing rose out of the distant south and faint as it was, each single report seemed more fanged and vicious than any firing Dan had heard yet.

At last he went down to the yard and he could see

smoke soaring at the southern tip of the ridge: a battle, near where the Emmetsburg road crawled up out of the flat valley, two or three miles away. General Duncan and his family were gone but a rim of men roosted on the old stable. One sat in lonely state atop the privy, arms wound around his doubled-up knees. Sometimes a stratum of impenetrable air hedged in front of the firing and for long minutes you couldn't hear the sprinkle of shots—only watch the smoke stealing beyond McMillen's. A gun or two talked, over near the cemetery; those were big guns. Dan looked at his watch. It was ten minutes after twelve. Now, surely, it was late enough; he had waited, and he would cross the field to Irene—she could not expect him to remain patient forever.

He declared stubbornly, "I'll eat something first. When I cross that field, it shall be as slowly as ever I crossed it before . . ." In his kitchen, the perspiring slave brought out cold bacon and bread and a bottle of peach brandy. "Yasso, how you like you eggs?" "Don't bother to fix any . . ." He ate, and a staccato whisper still came from the south. He thought, you bastard guns, if you knew what you were doing . . . Some meek privates hung around the kitchen porch and begged for food, saying little, staring with eloquence. Dan gave them whatever was within reach; the big negro drove them away with a torrent of curses and threats, and glared at Bale for his prodigality.

Dan stood up and finished his brandy. He walked out of the door, down the yard and into the scorching pasture; the air was smelling here as well. It seemed as if he were walking through deep water, with the heat waves trailing like tissue as he crossed the field. Irene was waiting for him at the fallen fence beside

Fanning's garden, and for awhile they stood without speaking, listening to the unrest of muskets.

She wore a dress of rich golden-brown, the false tucks falling smoothly over her hoops. She had done her hair since early morning, but had never been tending wounded rebels in that gown. He said, "It's beautiful. I never saw you wear that before."

"Can we walk for a moment?" she asked. "Away from the house. Anywhere."

He looked around. "It's all the same—you dare not go far. They've cleared things up a bit, around close."

"I don't mind. I have camphor on this handkerchief. I want to get away from the house."

He took her arm and said, "Very well." They went past the barns and through the open gate. The girl started toward an upper fence corner but Dan drew her back; he remembered the man from Indiana who was in that fence corner, unless some squad had found him. "Over near the oaks above my place," he suggested. "There was little or no fighting at that point." She said, "Anywhere. I —want to—walk." The sunlight, weakened by thin clouds, made a sulphur pool out of their shadows and washed it ahead of them.

They came up to a slanting bowlder which had not been marred or distressed by the war; blackberry wires lay about it, dotted with red clusters.

"Do you wish to sit down?"

"Thank you. This will do." She leaned beside the bowlder, with the silk handkerchief crumpled beneath her nose, and she looked with curiosity at the weeds as if she hoped to know their botany.

He knew that he had picked a berry or two and said, "Not ripe," but she had answered nothing. "May I see your wrist?" he asked, and lifted the limp arm which she extended. Her scar was turning from pink to blue; it still looked raised and new, but some day all trace would be gone save for a silver hint when the light fell upon it in a certain way.

She said, slowly and believing it well: "He is going to be killed."

"Who?"

"Tyler. I have known it for some time. There is something fearful in the thought."

He didn't know what to say. Her arm slid away from him, and he watched the heat doing things to her shadow. "You really believe—?"

"Before," she said, "I didn't care."

There was a quick snarl in his throat; he couldn't help it. "Now you do, eh?"

"I do not love Tyler. I never have. I was not a good wife."

He asked angrily, "What is a good wife?"

"It was frightening," she said. "Not quite a dream. It has seemed as if I saw him struck down with a sword, and the man who struck him down was sorry he had to do it."

"You don't find many people struck down with swords in modern warfare. We had scores around the place yesterday, and not one of those suffered a saber wound."

She kept looking at the grass. "A sword. It's been in my mind."

My dear—my dear—look at me! and he let his hands agonize hers. She did look at him but it was not the look he wanted; it was neither resentful nor accusing, but there seemed to be a thick pane of glass between them. "I've been thinking about Tyler," she went on, and now he realized that she was calling him Dan no more—she might never speak his name again. "I am forever damned if he dies, believing as he does. Before this I had no conception of what war meant. Now I have the notion. There is war in our house . . . yesterday, too. His name might have been David. I guess it was."

"Do you know how you are talking? As if you were—"

"Oh, yes," she nodded. "Mad. I want Tyler to believe a lie; I want him to comfort himself with it. He has been in the war for two years; for two years he helped keep such a thing away from us. He helped to keep David from dying in our kitchen—kept him dying somewhere else, where we couldn't see or hear him, for two whole years. Maybe it wasn't just— maybe it is not right for anyone to be killed, but that is what Tyler did. He deserved better than I gave him."

"God," Bale told her, "you were in love with him all the time."

"No. I desired you. That was real." She said, "We've had a Confederate general at our house: he commands this army hereabouts. It's called a division . . . a man named Heth, and still unconscious; Doctor Pell said he was struck by a spent ball, and it glanced around the paper he had folded inside his hat. So many officers keep coming to see whether he has his senses back, and I've heard their talk. That's our whole army, over there beyond the cemetery. They all say so."

He asked, "What of it? It just means more fighting, but not in this pasture."

"Tyler's over there. I want you to go to him."

"My God," he said.

"He'd believe you."

"No—I don't think he—"

"Yes. He would. He thinks you are strange—he disapproves of you and your ideas, but he would believe anything you told him." She patted the handkerchief, and folded it again and again, and still she looked at the weeds in front of her.

Dan's throat was stiff and sore. "How do you know he's there?"

"He must be. I heard them talk about the Second Corps. Maybe they took prisoners. Probably that was it: Tyler's in the Second Corps—he had that little clover-thing on his hat. You could find him, and he would listen to you if you said that Elmer Quagger had—That you and I—"

"If he is killed, it doesn't matter what he thought."

She said, "I would always feel it. It's—cruelty. Wanton. This is the first time in my life, and God would not forgive me."

"I doubt that you truly believe in God."

"Then I wouldn't forgive."

He pleaded: "Look at me, oh, darling, why must—" She raised her eyes to his. He stared for awhile. "Oh, all right," he heard himself droning. "I will go. But what about Quagger?"

"You can settle with him, some way. I do not know how. You'll know."

He said again, "All right. What is it: Tyler—"

"The Seventy-second Pennsylvania Volunteers. I think his brigade is commanded by a man named Owen, and Colonel Baxter was a friend of my father's. They call it the Philadelphia brigade. It's in the Second Corps, but I don't know what part."

Dan declared, "You want me to go over there and lie to him, and I will do it," and there was hate in his voice. Not hate for her; she was to be pitied, she could not help herself. "But if he's killed, will you agree to marry me?"

"You should know what I will do. But this way . . . he mustn't die believing me—thinking that I did—"

"Well," he told her, "I'll have difficulty in getting to the cemetery. Of course there is no such thing as a pass. Doubtless I can find a way tonight." .. The distant musket-skirmish had died out; it was replaced by another sound, slight and insecure. It was a human sound behind them among the rocks and bushes, in heavy oak shade.

Bale said, "It's a man," and he found him under some vines. He was a Union soldier. The black blood crusted all over one side of him and he looked as if he were dead, but he wasn't. Dan picked him up, and one swollen arm failed to hang limp even by its own weight. Bale moved the arm—the man screamed from the bottom of hell, and a knot of squirming white bulged from under his armpit.

Good God in heaven, if only she didn't see that! But when Dan looked at her face, he knew that she had seen. "Take him over to the house," he heard her say, and he nodded. How often, he thought, must I carry these victims around? He crossed the pasture with the squawling thing in his arms, and when he turned he could see the girl coming along slowly . . . The Confederate surgeon said, "Ha, when they've got the worms you can't wager much. There's one like that inside, only worse—trochanters and neck of the left femur shattered, ball lodged near the acetabulum, and maggots by the wagon-load . . ." Dan searched for Irene in the kitchen and rear entry; she had gone to her room. There was nothing for him to do but walk to the village and hunt Elmer Quagger.

4.

All this had been recited by the Book of The Revelation. It did not coincide word for word or verse for verse, but still it was the sum of a vision: the Reverend Solt walked in Washington street as far as they would let him go, and he recognized that the same lightnings and thunderings which had overpowered the countryside on Wednesday afternoon were recurring on Thursday, and Saint John the Divine might have suggested that there would be two days of it.

The throne could be the cemetery hill, and the sea of dust, baking in its hundred degrees, could be called a sea of glass like unto crystal. But Saint John had noted only four beasts and here were many thousands of beasts, quick and dead . . . Seals? There would indeed be a hundred and forty-four thousand people sealed, if this kept on. Already he had seen a hundred soldiers sealed with thin red wax, lying like sots in yesterday's storm.

So it had begun again in spite of the heat, in spite of Christ, in spite of the very hills which stood in the way; it began about four o'clock, and there was little to be gained for God if you sat by your kitchen table, making notes for a sermon on Romans, Fourteenth Chapter, Seventeenth Verse: "For the kingdom of God is not meat and drink; but righteousness, and peace, and joy in the Holy Ghost." He had not learned to write until he was thirteen years old, and the notes on which he depended were a slavery done as penance for his long benightedness; he had not entered into the Kingdom until he was grown a man . . . He searched Romans for a better text and thought he had found it in the Eleventh Chapter, Thirty-fourth Verse: "For who hath known the mind of the Lord? or who hath been his counsellor?"

Sister wailed from the potato bin: neither had she known the mind of the Lord, but she hoped that He was guarding her among the potatoes. "Simon," she cried, "Simon—a big ca'tridge went through Vandercook's garret yesterday—please come down cellar, oh, Simon—please! . . ." Reverend Solt opened the stair door and called past the row of milk crocks, "No man is safe from what wrath is in store for him, Annie. You should recollect the Psalms better than you do. 'O God, why hast thou cast us off for ever? why doth thine anger smoke against the sheep of thy pasture?' I am going down to the corner."

He progressed as far as Quackenboss's woodshed, and this was the Revelation come to life: the yellow smoke coughed above Gettysburg . . . Henry Niede's farm. No, it was far past there—somewhere near the Sherfy place. The ground felt its rock foundation sundering underneath, and a bucket of nails fell from a shelf in the woodshed. Then a gun exploded, close beside the minister, and he turned his white face to see the two bare-armed Confederate soldiers who sprawled in Quackenboss's bean patch and poked their guns between pickets of the warped fence. They were aiming toward the cemetery; you saw the cones of fir trees, and felt the sun mirroring on tombstones up there.

"You better get to hell out of here, Uncle. This is hot."

A hot pebble grazed the shed, gouging a long furrow of splinters. "I tolt you the first time," growled the sharp-shooter.

They had long, glistening tubes fastened atop their rifles; these were no guns such as Reverend Solt had ever seen before.

"He's a pusson," said the other man.

They both grinned over the sedge of beans. "I'm sorry, parson. Didn't notice the cloth. I wish you'd get for home, though."

Another gouge at the woodshed—lower, this time—and an echo clicked among chimneys of the nearby house. Reverent Solt creaked down to his knees, and took out a blue cotton handkerchief. He patted his wet neck. He asked: "Are you prepared?"

The guns clanged in unison. Again brown eyes studied him. "I hope you are, parson, if you stay around here."

"Them's mean Yanks, pusson."

"Especially since they're liable to throw a shell down here any minute."

"That is in the Scriptures," the minister said. "All of this is. 'And they ascended up to heaven in a cloud; and their enemies beheld them.'"

They chuckled among the beans. "I don't reckon I want to be beheld, do you, Dart?"

Reverend Solt wiped his face. "I would not jest, my son. Not in the sin you are doing."

"Listen—" drawled the brown-eyed man. His face was smooth-shaven and tanned as honey; a rusty bandage was wrapped around his right shoulder. He looked bitterly at the minister. "Your folks are doing the same sin and doing it just as hard as us. Look at those bullet marks on the shed, if you don't believe—"

"No," he insisted, "not the same sin. 'But these have altogether broken the yoke, and burst the bonds.'"

The soldier swore. With his unwounded arm he

hitched himself forward, and propped the rifle barrel higher. "That's Old Testament, and you're talking about the Right of Secession. Oh, yes, you are—"

"'Wherefore,'" quoted Simon Solt, earnestly, "'a lion out of the forest shall slay them, and a wolf of the evenings shall spoil them, a leopard shall watch over their cities.'"

The other Confederate said, "Aw, poop." His gun slammed. "You high-tail it off with yore fine talk. Wawl don't want no more."

"Shut up, Dart," muttered the younger man. He nodded at the minister. "My pappy was a church follower, too. I had to read the Word till I was black in the face. Seems like this is somewhere thereabouts: 'Go ye up on her walls, and destroy, for the houses of Israel and Judah have dealt mighty mean to me, saith the Lord.'"

Reverend Solt shook his head, and the air was creasing close above him . . . "That is Jeremiah, but you have not spoke it right."

"It's right enough for me. Now let us alone, and scoot out of here before Elijah or somebody comes to fetch you in a pillar of fire by day or—" Something went *put*. He said, hoarsely, "Nuhh," and the burned hands slid down from his gun . . . his head cocked forward. The other soldier rose suddenly on his knees. "Lane!" he cried. "Hi thar, *Lane!*" The limp head tumbled against the bottom runner of the fence, and the rifle clattered loose.

They dragged him into the shelter of the woodshed, his boots making furrows through the green garden. His face had a little velvet hole close beside the left eye, and a drop of red wax slid down from it. "Sealed," Reverend Solt whispered.

The dusty-bearded survivor raised up on his haunches. "I reckon yore glad, you Yankee psalm-shouter! Lane had two little gals to home."

"Glad?" cried Solt. "Man, man—listen to me—" He looked at the long body; it seemed twice as long as it had seemed a moment before; a thin, giant height pressed flat among old ashes and chick-weed. He began to cry. "Oh, Lord," he sobbed, "our Father, our Heavenly Guardian and Redeemer of all, we—we come to Thee in a—midnight of sorrow and loneliness—beseech Thee to shew us that our way is not Thy way—that—" His tears seeped into his beard . . . two little girls, two little girls, and he could see them fairly. The Confederate was staring grimly at him, as if Reverend Solt had brought this about and should be held solely accountable.

5.

Dan saw a little group of men crouching amid bushes on the south side of Breckenridge street in front of the old Angwald place. None of them was fat enough to be the man he wanted, but in hours of searching he had exhausted the few clues available. His temples rattled in the earthquake of artillery . . . At the Frielings' he could arouse no one, though he tried in the faint hope that they would have some knowledge of the tenant whom they had driven away.

He slid behind fences as rapidly as he could, and welcomed each breadth of wall. A thousand phlegmatic Georgians waited along Middle street and they hadn't wished to let him pass. The yard fences were demolished to make a barricade. The rebel skirmishers lay scattered far ahead, and there was a right smart of bullets coming out of the cemetery. "But if you ain't got sense enough to stay to home . . . go 'long," they said, "and mind them Yankee sha'p-shooters."

He minded them as well as he could. Balls droned, clattering among the shuttered houses. A black-and-white cat sat out on the Gerbers' horse-block and washed its face. Dan came from behind a wall opposite the Angwald house, and started across the road toward the men who hid in a nest of honeysuckle.

"Look out!" came a yell.

The dust fluffed beside him . . . he was in the bushes, and looking down at two pale boys of twelve or fourteen, and a moss-bearded man who squatted with a crutch in his hands.

Bart McKosh told him, "They almost got you that time, Bale."

"Have you seen Elmer Quagger?"

"Quagger?" repeated McKosh. He turned the word over, and examined it, and did not like it. "No, I hain't seen him. Nor want to." His sour eyes came up and hung on Dan's. "He's a Copperhead. You ought to know that."

"Yes, I want to see him . . ."

McKosh jerked his elbow toward the two boys beside him. "Showing my nevvies what wars looks like."

"They ought not to be here."

Bart grunted, "Well, they would come." He turned to the youth nearest him, and pointed through the bushes. "Look close, Amos. See them little shiny knobs right in front of the gate? Three-inch rifles— it's a whole battery of them. If you notice over on the Pike you'll see how the rebels have got Parrotts and rifles and twenty-four-pound howitzers all mixed up together. They've got lots of captured Union guns."

He nodded at Bale. "I guess this is more war than folks around here ever had a smell of. They say there's two or three corps tangled up down around the Trostle place."

Somewhere, closer than cannon and musket volleys, a thin wail was hinging up and down the scale. "That noise," Dan said.

"I hear it." McKosh spat into the calla lilies, and poked at the place with his crutch. "We thought it was a cat yowling, but I couldn't see him nowhere around."

"There's Puss Gerber out by the road," said one of the nephews. "Angwalds haven't got a cat—it got froze last winter."

His uncle nodded. "I like to got froze at Fredericksburg." Dan looked down at the thin shoulders and stringy neck, the empty trouser-leg tacked up against his belt . . . The boys said, "Still yowling."

There was a sudden wrenching of wood at the house ahead of them, and something pale fluttered among flowers beside the foundation. They all watched it. It wasn't a cat.

McKosh drew a long breath. "Well," he said, "somebody waving—"

Bale could see a thin hand flapping from the cellar window. He stood up and started out of the bushes. A branch flicked, leaves twinkled loose. "For the love of Jesus!" ejaculated McKosh. He fastened his hands on Bale's pant-leg and hauled him back. "Mr. Bale, those National folks have got their eye on this yard! I heard the guns go off. Don't go over there—they'll take you for a Butternut and you'll get shot on the way." His nephews were squirming backward out of the honeysuckles. "Get behind that big sycamore," he ordered them.

Dan said, "But somebody's waving, over at the house—"

The veteran grunted, "Let 'em wave." He wriggled a few inches forward, and cupped his hands. "Hey," he called.

The hand ceased flapping. *Wurr,* a voice sobbed.

"What?"

"*Water* . . . Who's there?"

"Bart McKosh and—and Daniel Bale. What you want?"

Still the cat was mourning . . . Mrs. Angwald had a shallow voice, wholly beaten and despairing. She quavered, and they could barely hear her: "We've been down here since yesterday and the children just dying fresh drink-a-water."

McKosh scratched his head. "Well," he hallooed, "where'll I get water? Where's a bucket?"

It was a child crying. Dan said, "Well, hell—" He rose and started forward. Bart made a queer noise in his throat; he was pointing. In the low sun's glare stood a fat man, outlined against the yellow fields. He was at the old box well, fifty yards away, winding the windlass. He looked crumpled and straw was sticking all over his clothes.

"Quagger," Bale said. Before he thought, he had taken a step and was clear of the bushes. A short brown furrow smoked in front of him: he stopped. McKosh was dragging at his trousers. "No sense in two of you getting shot! He's got the water, not you."

Dan cried, "Where in damnation did he come from?"

"How'd I know? Out of the barn or woods or somewheres. Up from hell with the rest of his stripe—"

Elmer Quagger walked across the open yard. There were barns and fences at the south end of the property, but they lay well below the sights of the Federal rifles. You could hear the angry *pak, pak* of the marksmen, round little beats against the immense storm in the south. Quagger walked carefully, holding the dripping bucket far out at his side and balancing it with an extended left hand. A window went to pieces, on the other side of the house. The bullets sank through the shrubbery, they kicked up from rocks bordering the path. "They're bound to get him," grunted McKosh. "You kids stay behind that tree."

The sun was spoiled by a landscape of powder smoke hanging in front of it, but somehow its level stare came through and rested vengefully on the man with the pail . . . He stopped for a moment and looked back at the well; some water splashed over the bucket's rim; he went on, groping for the cellar door. Then the corner of the house hid him.

Bart McKosh rolled over and looked up at Dan. "Some folks are born fortunate. If that'd been me I'd a' had a dozen holes in my gizzard." After a time the front door of the house opened, and closed quickly behind Elmer Quagger. He stood on the stoop, gazing toward the men in front. The one-legged veteran cried, "Well, come on if you're coming! Keep the house behind you and you're safe." Quagger walked down the path and through the gate.

Masked by the long barricade of green, Bale crept to meet him. "You're not hit?" he asked.

The fat man shook his round head. He looked at Dan with frightened eyes. His voice seemed as flat and mushy as ever. "No, sir. For a minute I thought they'd shot the pail, though."

That was a fool thing to do. McKosh called with grudging admiration. Quagger didn't look at him. He said, haltingly, "What you got on your mind, Bale?"

"I guess you know," Dan said.

With a flabby hand, the Copperhead brushed some straw from his sleeve. "I've been praying," he said, "but somehow I can't get right with my soul. And I've been upset and sick with my stomach. I—"

He followed Dan across the narrow street and behind the wall. "Sit down," Bale told him. Quagger slumped upon the ground; his hand gathered a sheaf of grass and clung to it, shaking. He raised his voice against the roar behind them. "You—know about—that letter I wrote to young Fanning?"

Bale thought: This is a hypocrisy I never dreamed . . .

"Why did you send it, Quagger?"

"I was mad because you pushed me in the bushes. I got to thinking about the Huddlestone boy—I knew you two was in cahoots—and when he started out there that Sunday night, I followed on. I don't know—I thought maybe it was a militia secret, or something."

"Well," Dan said, "it wasn't."

Quagger took up the bunch of grass and squeezed off the ripe grain of the heads. "I guess not. Well—I was besides the fence in the dark, and I followed Huddlestone away, and then I thought I'd come back. The Devil had me in his grasp." He said, "Honest," and sobbed dryly for awhile. "I kind of figured I'd give you a poke in the face, and cut away, because you had cursed me and slung me in the briars. Then when I looked through the window, the young Missis was with you. Thinks I, that's better than a clout in the nose! I'll just—"

He looked up with a fearful, shamed face, and then down again. "Well, Bale, I done you a lot of harm. And the lady. Didn't I?" His fat chins shook; his voice was fat.

"Did you see anything wrong?"

"Just her being there. It was real late at night."

Dan said, "She was walking, and hurt herself on some thorns. I was doctoring her in the kitchen."

"I recollect, now. You had some cloth and stuff. But the Devil was besides me, I tell you. I went back to town and set down, over to Frieling's, and wrote that letter, and sent it to the Junction with Barney Endsor. If I hadn't been mad clean through I wouldn't of done it."

Dan thought, "Here we sit—the world goes apart— here we sit, tugging grass," and the knowledge of his own vileness sang through his brain . . . Now there is another part to it: I must get within the National lines. I told her I would, and I must go.

"I'll say to him that I never saw a wrong deed, and I'll ask the lady's pardon," Quagger was beginning. He had a shiver of eagerness in his voice. "See—old Bedford sacked me from the factory when I joined the Knights. I haven't had nothing but misfortune ever since. Now I haven't got no money or situation, and I've been sleeping in the old haymow back of Angwald's. If you could get me a situation—"

Oh, God, Bale thought.

He stood up. "I don't know," he said aloud. "Maybe I could. Where have you been eating?"

"I've got three dollars in greenbacks left to my name," Quagger told him, "and what food I bought, I bought at Pock's and Shick's and the bakery. But my digestive system has been terrible. Nothing but trouble and misfortunate things have happened to me for the last two years, Bale. I must be being punished by God's justice. For something." He lifted his head. "Anyway, I've always been honest and out-and-out until now."

Dan said inside, If he knew, if he knew . . . "Can I lend you some money?"

"I guess I oughtn't to accept no favors from you."

"The devil," Dan said. He found seventeen dollars in his pocket; now he believed the legend about evil money burning one's fingers; he put the notes in Quagger's hand. "How did you come to be at the well, just now?"

"I'd heard that baby caterwauling for a long time, where I was lying out there in the old barn. If I hadn't been scared I would of gone before. And then," he added, simply, "I guess God spoke to me and told me to get it. He said like, Elmer Quagger—you go get water . . . They didn't have a drop in the house. I came up through the kitchen floor-door, and there wasn't a drop."

They were in hot shadow, folded by the wall; a titanic outcry rode the sunset farms beyond, and it was made of increasing muskets . . . Get away from his awful honesty, the utter penitence of him, while I'm still able to go. "Good-bye," Dan said, "I must be on my way. Now —" he stammered: his voice went on and declared more lies to Elmer Quagger . . . when he rose, head and shoulders above the wall, the sun had slid down unclouded except for smoke, and the brass sky above South Mountain was as bright as any dawn.

"Bale," Quagger gabbled—"Bale, you never said that you'd let bygones be bygones. I'll go to Fanning and his wife on bended knee."

"Oh, all right," Dan cried. The hill. Now loomed the cemetery hill.

6.

He reached Middle street and found a mass of gray marching east, and could not understand why they were going in that direction, when peremptory gun-blasts kept summoning them to Ziegler's grove. He thought of Elijah...take them in the flank. That was one of the phrases Hud had always loved to roll on his tongue: a flank movement.

Undeniably he was a citizen in brown trousers and saffron shirt, but a hundred rebels were no more in uniform than he. He had a vision of a shrewd Federal watchman following him with the sights of a rifle... not that way, not just as I come toward them. He wanted blue. He found blue in the next yard; it sent him sprawling. A sturdy body swollen by summer, lying on its back beside a cistern, with a black blister for a face. Dan got up and came back; despite all horror he knew what he must do. The dusk sifted around him; he heard the regiments tramping toward the east. *Sorry,* came between his lips.

He unfastened the trouser-band that stretched so tight across the round abdomen. The legs were stiff as boards but the shoes were gone—some rebel had taken them—and it was that much easier to draw the cloth over puffy feet.

Huddled amid the rhubarb he worked savagely, kicking his own legs into the terrible trousers. They would do; they covered the brown pantaloons, and now a Federal sentry could not believe that he was shooting a rebel, even though Dan wore no blouse. I would have spared you this if I could, he wanted to say to the dead man...the wraith hustled beside him as he crossed the intersection diagonally at Baltimore street and sped east through back lots. Wait, it cried, explain, explain—I expected death at one time or another, but why should I have such indignity? I was a virgin, a German, a good wrestler, twenty years old: my name was Emil, my uncle said I was a reliable boy and cried when I went into the army, and now you leave me naked in the sight of a relentless world.

When he came abreast of the silent, quick-moving column the darkness had already claimed them. He heard soft voices muttering: *them Looswanna boys goes fust,* and he bent behind a stable wall for fear they would see him. The wall ended at an earthy ramp which led up to the barn door. A constant, muffled chafe of accoutrements sounded as the long files switched out into a field ahead, and when Bale lifted his face above the wall he could see clay-colored blots assuming formation beyond the fence. The village had fallen behind, a black quarry of rock houses bunched against the darkening west.

No smoking, the order whispered off across the pasture. Bayonets twisted around steel barrels; the same sound was ringing ahead; there were advanced masses of troops. Them Looswanna boys goes fust. Dan thought, if I can get across the road before anyone turns back. The dead man's pants made a tremendous brushing, swaddled over his own clothes as they were. He touched the rim of the wall: stones wedged firmly together, and not a one would slide. He squeezed across and crouched, holding his breath. A group of men loomed tall beside him, holding the sunset on their shoulders.

They did not see him. *"Oui,"* said one. It sounded as if he added: *Le too onsommell.* French, Dan thought. I don't know it; whatever it means. Them Looswanna boys. The men fanned past with an eager crunching. He ran across the road and lay down; there was a post fence directly ahead lining somebody's pasture-lot, and he hitched beneath the bottom rail. The grass lay thick, bent under a blanket of dust. *Forward,* came the mutter.

Another wall, a ruined one: it chased up the slope and continued as bushes. Dan came beside the ghostly line, and pressed ahead with them. They were far to the east and south of Gettysburg, swung half around the hump of the cemetery hill and now climbing toward it from a creek valley at the Culp farm. On the height ahead there was noise: hosts and horses dwelling among the rocks. A soldier began to cough. "Stop that!" and the man gagged in his effort to obey.

Gorilla loomed up, beyond the sultry breadth of bushes; gorilla walking slowly, taking a few steps backward, turning and marching forward again. He hissed at Dan, "Close up! They can't dress on you!" and Bale crowded close beside the hedge. On the opposite side another man was working his way ahead; the Cougher; he still made odd chucklings. You couldn't see buttons or buckles or the detailed shape of a weapon—only a smear, only smears trying to hold their breath and proceed as quietly as possible.

In front, surprisingly near, a man yelled: "Who's there? Lutz, have you got skirmishers out in front?" A solitary musket banged, farther on the right: *soor,* said the air. "Fire!" A thin command. "Fire—at will!" All the way from the side of the valley came the stutter of guns, little scraps of orange splitting out. The rebels started, ahhhhhhhh, and now the line was running.

The hillside marred with rags of flame. Dan ran

against fence rails: he wanted to cry, "Wait, hold on, I'm not one of them." He tumbled between the rails and landed in a trodden lane. The world began to come apart with spiteful luminosity, ahead and at his side . . . if they'll stop that yell until I get past the lines. He plunged across an angular bowlder and a spray of dirt stung his face. Lie down, lie down until it stops. A freakish weight of human flesh fell upon him and smashed the air from his lungs. Bale drew up his legs, he could not sob, his chest was killing him, his arms flailing out on each side. The other man had picked himself up and was rattling on.

"God damn," a monster roared amid the crackling orange. "Keep to that wall. *Lieber Gott,* keep to that—hold it, men, hold—" And even in the anguish of empty lungs, Dan distinguished the individual report which wrapped itself around that voice and wiped it out. The noise picked up another combatant and hurled him among the stones; he suffered momentary pneumonia and died of it. Bale wrenched his head from side to side; now he felt clean air coming into his body, cold-water air, it was drowning him happily.

He wept, "Well, had I known this would happen . . ." The hill went up and down, trying to shake off the mange of rifle flashes and the yipping orders . . . well away from the wall, sir. Sky opened in one doomed, terrific split. Dan's eyes went shut and he felt the sides of his head twitching—felt the little membranes of his ears thrilling and lacerated, collapsing at last beneath the oppression put upon them.

Cannot stay here, cannot stay— She insists that I tell my lie.

He struggled up, on his elbows; a body was lying across his feet. He dragged one foot out and shoved

with the other, and the limp weight rolled over into
a depth beyond. Agonized nations squawked con-
tinually: *Don't lettum get those guns.* Now he had his
ears again; he could hear. *Don't lettum get those guns.*
In all the knife-thrusts of fire, he recognized that the
vitality, the heart of it, breathed in the crags directly
ahead. They made a thick barricade with their screeching, a dam through which other noises tried to cut.
*Don't lettum whooooo don't lettum Rickett whooooo
lettum* . . . they were a circus of panthers let loose, and
the flattened bullets squealed off on every side. The
frantic nations were throwing stones, breathing and
sweating and hurling them as they howled, the stones
cracking as they struck the lower bowlders. A blue
spray went sky-high in front of Dan Bale; he felt the
angry smart of a fist in his face. "Got shot," said a
stolid pronouncement, and he lay flat and listened to it.

7.

Voice groaned, *gimme drink* . . . the sky widened
again. He whispered, amid salty constellations:
"Wish they'd stop that," and the blast went ringing
among the rocks. He lifted a hand; thought it was
somebody else's hand; it felt far away. By God, my
own hand, and I don't recognize. Shot in the face—
saw the sparks go.

He put his fingers into his hair . . . so very little
blood. *Gimme drink.* The pale stars looked at him.

He touched his forehead. There was no hole: all a
big lump. It seemed nonsensical, now that he was gossiping about it in his own mind, to have been struck
by a stone when none of the bullets could find him.

He planed his hand up and down, criss-cross, back around to each ear; it sensed the splitting ache inside his skull, but it could find no hole, no spring where blood and brains welled out. I didn't expect, he thought wisely.

"Ow," men repeated off into the spinning curves of distance. "Ow-*wo*." Bale began to repossess his own body again. It was difficult, when he had been away so long.

This hand. He moved again. He occupied himself with testing his feet, moving each foot on its ankle-joint, wriggling his hips, taking deep breaths of the sultry air. And feeling moonlight tint his face. No coolness in the world. The insects stewed above . . . mosquito hymns, wiry and annoying. Woe, woe, woe said a thousand quaint voices, interlarding their general complaint with names and mingled phrases. Where is this? There was a cemetery before.

Then the whole understanding occurred: where he was, and why he was there, and the long day yonder. He sat up with his palms against his pounding temples. His vision cleared, and he saw the nearest bowlders looking cushiony in the moon-glow, and observed the ice of fallen musket barrels. Dim lumps lay along the wide bosom of the hill. Dan shifted his leg; a stone clattered down the incline. Some wide-spread life above seemed to catch its breath— the voiceless second of silence—then several muskets boomed in a merging report, and bullets spattered the granite beside him.

He burrowed flat, and dared not stand. The Confederates had retreated, he lay between the two opposing armies, and any further movement from him might provoke a fatal shower . . . Daylight, he thought. Then they can see my blue cloth. He slid his fingers down and touched the shoddy material, and tried to close his mind to the memory of how it was obtained.

Water and God and Melanie, the wounded men prayed. Who was Melanie? That person kept asking for her. Then he talked in French, and how could anyone know what he wanted? . . . They hooted like owls, all the way over toward Culp's hill. The National army bustled, and chopped wood up past the cemetery.

Moon went higher, hour by hour; it was plastered by a close halo at times, and at other times washed out by a veiling of clouds; still it sent reflected heat against the white hillside and encouraged the mosquitoes. Far down the valley existed spots of light, and turning wheels and nickering horses, and the same sounds drifted over the brow of the hill: part of a background constructed of many thousand men, breathing and whispering and spying at the lower ground before them.

His headache dried up, and the skin stiffened and swelled around the welt at his hair-line. I will go all the way, he resolved, if they kill me for it. I will spite them . . . He even slept in snatches, huddled stiff on the hard soil, and conscious of the outcries beyond and the changing shadows made by the moon. Then he awoke, cooler than he had been, and found the world gray where it was black before. Every film of vapor evaporated from the sky; Dan stretched his neck and looked toward the east, and saw the wild beauty prepared in silver and blue without a semblance of war.

He slid out from between the caging rocks. In the dawn above him swelled a bulk of elms and evergreens and torn turf, with uniformed corpses spread in impossible positions. There was a low stone wall and a movement of life behind it. Dan got up. It was torture to move; he hobbled as he pushed up the hill. Behind, early rifles began to protest—the spraying lead clicked around him. "Take care," the officer said, "he's blue . . ." and the slim Springfields were pulled back over the wall. "Let him come in, men," and Dan had climbed across the barrier, and soldiers were staring suspiciously at him. Over on the other side of Culp's hill a storehouse of Chinese crackers began to be set off. The dawn was growing yellower and yellower.

8.

The boy with the braided shoulder-straps said, "All right. Come on." They stepped over the legs of snoring men and across a low ditch; robins were singing in the cemetery and smoke came up from a dozen little fires along the road, gypsy saucers of glowing twigs where coffee steamed in tin cans. There was the friendly smell of scorched beef-fat: you thought of a kitchen where there were white curtains and geraniums at the window. The smoke of the Culp's hill muskets had already deadened the bright torrent of dawn. Ditch and roadside were banked with men and knapsacks and rolled blankets, edge to edge, knee to knee, covering the earth with a padded human carpet.

"*Was ist ein gefängner,* Schmidt?" asked a tired voice.

The boy turned his stubbled face toward a group of men around a coffee can. "*Nein. Citizen. Wo ist der Über-Offizer?*"

"At the fence, Lieutenant."

Again Dan's guide said, "Come on." He halted at last before a pair of booted legs stuck out of a weedy tangle alongside the cemetery fence. The air smelled . . . my dead horse, Dan thought. No. It is at home. There must be more of them . . . Lieutenant Schmidt saluted the sprawling legs. "Colonel Yotes. Lieutenant Schmidt reporting, sir."

The legs moved reluctantly and a wan, bearded face pushed up out of the weeds. "Yes, Schmidt."

"This man just entered our lines. Says he's a civilian, sir."

Slowly the colonel turned his head. He blinked at Dan. Bale told him, "My name's Bale, live in Gettysburg, I had to come inside the Union lines and this was the only way I could come."

"Why did you have to come?"

"It was necessary for me to see one of your officers."

"My—officers?" The colonel's jaws creaked.

Lieutenant Schmidt said, uninterestedly: "He says he's looking for the Seventy-second Pennsylvania Volunteers, sir."

"They're not in this corps, my man."

"I don't know. It's the Second Corps."

"What ails your forehead?"

"Someone threw a stone."

Colonel Yotes looked at Dan's legs. The robins yodeled behind him; in the southeast the dawn kept crumbling among sodden powder-charges. "Why are you wearing those pants?" he asked.

"I thought it would make it easier," Dan answered. "Your men came near shooting me as it was. I was on the hillside all night."

The officer lay down suddenly; there was water in

his eyes, and now Dan saw that one sleeve of his blouse was black and sticky. He said through a narcotic weariness, "Perhaps you are a spy. Deliver him to the provost, Schmidt."

"Yes, *sir*," snapped the lieutenant. He saluted and left-faced as crisply as if made of stiff paper. "This way," he ordered Dan. They went through the gate into the graveyard; ahead loomed the barrels of cannon, smooth surprises amid the acacias. Men were polishing out the big tubes with greasy rags. The shod hoofs of tethered horses grated against gravestones. "Here," Lieutenant Schmidt cracked out, suddenly. He flung a glance over his shoulder, and the rounded slope hid his regiment and his commander. He looked Bale squarely in the eyes for the first time since they had left the stone wall.

"His Congressman got this regiment for him three weeks ago. Spy! Provost!" He laughed; his face was twenty years old, his eyes were forty, and when he spoke it was with no discernible accent. "Get to hell out of this, and don't come back. I want some breakfast. *Raus!*" He double-quicked back down the incline, holding his scabbard with one hand and hurdling trimly over a dead mule in his path.

Walked here before, Dan thought. He remembered his grandfather's face, and in his mind it would be calm and resigned forever, no matter what happened under the soil. That resignation bought of sorrow and other battles long before Dan was born ... hereabouts, he thought, hereabouts.

The Bearman lot. A lame horse teetered on three legs, eating grass from a great-uncle's grave, and Adolph's new mound was trampled. You didn't think they'd follow you here, did you? ... Faces went by, going about their jibes and their tasks; faces eating crackers. There were ammunition carts crowded beside the brick gate-house where the sexton had lived, and Dan could smell onions frying, somewhere. The odor slit through him. I must eat—I *must*. Keep alive until I see Fanning . . . Culp's hill crackled like a burning woodpile, but none of these men seemed as concerned as he should have seemed.

"Where's the Second Corps?" Dan demanded of curly red whiskers.

"Ich haben none speak."

" 'Way over to the left and forward," someone called. "Damnation, soldier, you're a long ways from home. This is K Battery, First Ohio." "He ain't a soldier," muttered someone else. Another said, "He must be a sutler. Sutler, you got a wagon back there? What's the chances of—" Their petitions followed him, but most of the artillerymen slept on, lumps as motionless as the graves they lay among.

Telitha F., devoted wife of Pentland Bale. Here his family waited for him. The tombstones got up, breaking their roots, and whirled like dervishes. Dan walked on: the cemetery and the sprawled blue colonies, the guns shining in smoky sunlight, interlocking shadows, hot dawn, all flowed past him. A fluent stealth to their passing . . . where in time is the Seventy-second Pennsylvania?

A row of stacked muskets before him. The tired young dead were arising: Culp's hill was the trumpet sounding behind them, and this became the morning of the day of judgment with a million waking tramps past the graveyard, far beyond the green cornfield and woods, far into the torn wheat. Bayonet poked viciously. "For Christ sake, don't walk on Captain— He'll wake up and kick the stuffing out of you. What you say? . . . This is the Ninety-fourth New York. Well, Christ sake, if you want the Second Corps get down past the road toward those woods. That's Hays's Division."

Want the Seventy-second Pennsylvania. If I walk the whole length of the army.

Through Ziegler's grove a few rifles were pattering, all porcelain sunrises forgotten . . . They must think I'm a straggler rejoining my regiment: keep away from officers, for they will call a provost guard . . . "Naw, this is the Fourteenth Connecticut." (This man, too old to be in war. He is older than John Burns, but from his eyes you know that he has seen a lot of wars.) "This is the Twelfth New Jezzy."

"I own property in New Jersey," Dan said, and left the soldier staring after him, scratching his beard.

Again the odor of onions. Faces were more numerous, now, and more and more of them were waking faces with eyes in them. "This," said a clear voice, "is the First Delaware." He looked down into the satiny eyes. "You're a girl!" he blurted, and the eyes were suddenly wide with an admitted terror. Afterward, he didn't know how he was so certain. Her voice—so like a young boy's voice . . . she ran, scooting over the rocks, lugging her drum with her. The pecking rifles were directly ahead.

Men lay flat here in the lower woods; even the officers crouched behind whatever cover offered. Dan heard the m-sounds, the same as yesterday, they would always be the same. This regiment was not sleeping; it lay behind boards and rails and was about a very serious business. "Halt," came the command, and he knew enough to obey.

"Well, get down!" A big man rose up, resting on

his elbow, and glared bitterly at Dan. Bale dropped to his knees. The m's above. "I know," he said, "sharp-shooters."

"What's your regiment?"

He told his story. The man still had the scowl between his eyes, but he nodded as Dan talked. "That's Webb's brigade you want. Got the California regiment in it. I know them well. Wait here." Dan lay back and closed his eyes; the perpetual shooting moved far up into the freshening sky. He heard the officer go crawling away, pebbles scraping. "I'm sick of this, Gibson!" he ranted, some distance beyond. "Take skirmishers—a company, anyhow—and clean out that barn over there. Take Company D; that ought to be enough. I'll answer for it." Tired reply: "Yes-sir." Orders began to click along the woods' edge.

"That'll stop 'em, perhaps," growled the big man when he returned. Bale sat up. "What?" he asked. The officer wagged his swarthy head. "Rebs in a barn out there beyond that road—they've been raising sin with us." His scornful gaze pried close. "Here," he said, "have you breakfasted?"

"Don't know . . . ate something . . . when—" The major told him: "I'm finished. You're welcome to this." He offered a handful of crackers, a chunk of cold sausage and a whiskey bottle in which muddy coffee splashed like tar. "If you can handle it," he added.

"God," Bale said.

The thick coffee ate into his stomach. His jaws were sore; kept chewing and chewing; he was ravenous, but it hurt to swallow. "I know how it goes," sneered the major. He was beetle-browed, and his sneer had been designed for him when he was a child. "But you'd better join the army. If you're going to be shot at you might as well get greenbacks for it. Now you'll have to excuse me, my friend; I've got a war to fight. You'll find Webb's brigade over to the left—we extend Gibbon at the edge of these trees, and Webb's in Gibbon's Division." He peered past the oak trees ahead and over the board fence bounding them. Dan followed his gaze. A crowd of soldiers raced toward the Emmetsburg road, and a few hundred yards beyond was the Blisses' barn with rapid streaks of smoke springing from haymow and windows. "Goodbye." The officer rose. He added, gruffly, "Leave that coffee bottle there in the rocks; I need it. Don't forget. Webb's brigade of Gibbon's Division."

"It's the Second Corps," Bale said.

The officer's angry face exploded. "*This is* the Second Corps!" He went sliding away between the trees, revolver holster swinging against his leg.

Dan picked his way south. There were no more bullets sighing across from the Bliss barn, but around the barn lifted a rally of howls, the rapid spanking of shots, and everywhere men were standing up to watch the action on their front . . . He asked again. They said the something-or-other New York. Then he came out past the trees. There were no buzzards in the sky but an odor washed up through the dry daisy field, over sweltering hay and fence-vines; something dead, over by Codori's, and God knows it's no calf. The climbing sun made a gold rinse on the western ridge and the ridge was quartz—myriad little sparkles of metal over there. That's what the rebels look like to an enemy; now I am almost an enemy; they are not men who sing *oh let not my own love,* men named English, men eating bacon at a kitchen table. Now I know why the buzzards were here.

Sweat came out all over him. They *knew.* He cried it again in his mind. Even Tyler knew . . . Heads turning;

a lounging rim of rifle-stocks and soiled suspenders and brass buttons within the boundary of the board fence. What is this? Something-or-other New York. Still New York. There was the rock-oak copse; blue men were picnicking around it, the little field frothed with people watching the toy battle at the Blisses' barn. All these soldiers had clover-leaves on their caps, and suddenly the color had changed.

Flint eyes questioned him. He croaked, "No, I'm not a soldier. Citizen—" "What in hell?" the boy said.

"Those clover-leaves on your caps. A minute ago they were all blue—back through the woods. Now they are all white."

The boy grinned, a wistful grin in spite of the stony eyes. "Oh, that was the Third Division. Hays'. This is the Second. The first is different too—red. I don't know what you want here, but have you got any tobacco?"

"Yes," Dan said, and gave him the Winnebago-beaded pouch which he had brought from the West. "Where is Gibbon's Division?" Now the boy knew that he talked like a madman. "This is it—Seventy-first Pennsylvania . . ." They lay at ease along the wall, and again they were munching crackers.

"I want Webb's brigade." "Yah, this is it." "I want the Seventy-second Pennsylvania." And then the soldier had had all he could endure. He went toward a slight man with a dirty white havelock hanging to his shoulders, who stood gazing at the Bliss barn through his glass.

"Captain Ballou, sir—"

The man snapped, "It can wait, Private!" He went on looking through the glass for centuries. At last his hand dropped, and his eyes skewered the youth beside him, and went past him to look at Dan. The officer's goatee helped a chin which was frail and childish, but there was a kind of poison in his eyes.

"Well, Grimes?"

"He wants the Fire Zouaves, sir."

Bale said, "I've been through a lot to find them. It is most imperative that I communicate with Captain Tyler Fanning. I am a civilian and have come through the lines for that purpose."

"Who larruped you on the pate?"

"I was caught in a fight, last night."

"Mm," said the officer. "You know Fanning?"

"Yes."

"How are his children?"

"He has none."

"And his father's legal practice. What of it?"

"It's a shoe factory," Dan said. He felt his teeth baring; what was this? . . . The captain's shallow face relaxed. "I wondered whether you knew him, that's all. I am well acquainted with Captain Fanning. But I am sorry to say that the Seventy-second has been detached from this position at the moment. They may be up presently."

"I'll go. Where—"

"Oh, no. You shan't stir . . ." Captain Ballou laughed tinnily . . . "I marvel that you got this far. They'd gather you up and hustle you to the rear so fast it would make your head swim. Excuse me, but you are a walking corpse—with that bruise, and all. Lie down here behind the stones out of harm's way, and wait your chance. I will aid you insofar as possible, but I ought to report you to brigade headquarters. However, you may not have to wait long. Your message would appear to be most urgent. I trust—his family—"

"They're well," Dan said. It—it is something.

He lay in the grass at the corner of the field. The wall went west some eighty yards, then angled to the south. The whole enclosure was full of troops, and there was gleaming field artillery ranged not far behind. Bale closed his eyes: Captain Ballou, he thought. I am becoming acquainted with many of them . . . Close at hand men were gabbling. "Look at them Butternuts go out of there—looks like a rat hunt—they ought to burn that barn. Jehosaphat, they won't let us burn nothing."

And God knew what might be happening to the Niedes, on the next farm. Dan's forehead throbbed. Seventy-second Pennsylvania, and where are they?

She sat by this wall. She wasn't wearing hoops. That day I spoke of Another Field, and she knew what I meant. Tyler was asleep, and it was not a picnic; they had nothing to eat. But the buzzards sensed the strange picnic which was to come, and here it is today.

Far beyond the Taneytown road, over near Rock Creek, guns were slackening their savagery, and there was an echoing whimper of cheering. Dan could feel the sun at work, thawing stiffness from his muscles. *Lie in the grass and let the sun pound me.* Again he closed his eyes. Who's that feller over there? He was talking to old Ballou.

"He's not old," Dan thought of yelling. "Young, and his chin is weak, but that signifies nothing." Then the scorch of sun claimed him, and he slept forever, and the Seventy-second P.V. did not come, ho, to the wars.

9.

There was a dead hush when he awakened. No more guns rang from the east. The sun had him: he was a cricket in the trough of the countryside, and the sun had impaled him on its broad, brass blade. He opened his eyes and saw flattened weeds and corn-sprouts and the stones of the wall; a boy said, "Well, I got two jacks." Dan turned his wet head. They were playing cards on a jacket spread open a few feet away. Blue uniforms made a plump inner lining for the whole, jutting field. The sun burned out Bale's eyes, seeping in sweat, helpless as he was . . . other insects clucked in the grass near his head. He wondered how the sun had ever climbed to that imposing height.

The youth with the gray flint eyes grinned at him. "You looked to have died, mister." He was chewing something, and so were the other men.

Dan's head swam away and then came back. "Are they here, yet?"

The boy shook his head. "They're still back behind the ridge."

"I'll go," Dan told him. He thought that he was stronger than he had been in days; he was strong enough to freeze his face as he talked with Tyler. But he hated his body nevertheless—hated the worms in his brain and the sore tendons lacing him together. "I gave you that tobacco pouch," he said. "Now you've got to give me some food."

The boy tossed a roll of damp newspaper across the grass. Inside was a wad of crushed cherries and gingerbread. The soldier turned back to his card

game. "Fill up my floosh," somebody else demanded.
The dealer said: "How's a diamond, Stemson?" The
ridge toward the west was still pimpled with its
armies; animals crept among the trees, hauling guns.
The sounds of their journeying came in a faint
discussion—all echoes flat and baked by the high
heat of noon, and the mile of grain baking in between.

The cherries and soaked gingerbread were vile
enough; Dan ate as the starving eat. The man on his
right had an open cartridge-pouch between his legs
and was counting paper cartridges into it, and he kept
declaring to a sergeant while he counted: "No, their
powder tests better than ours. Try it—that's all I got to
say—try it. You know well enough ours is half dirt and
too much charcoal, and them that make it are setting
on their fat asses, getting rich."

Captain Ballou arrived with an officious rattle of
equipment, swinging past the angle of the wall to
where Dan sat. Ballou had taken off his blouse and
now wore his sword-belt over a wet flannel shirt.
"You'll have to come with me to headquarters," he
announced. "I've been talking to Colonel Baker about
it. We can't have a civilian sitting at the line with us; I
have orders to evacuate you to the rear."

Bale stood up. He wiped the soggy crumbs from his
hands. "I must see Fanning," he said.

There were deep pencil-lines between the young
officer's pale eyes. "You should be thankful that I
permitted you to lie down and sleep, sir. Now will
you come along, please." The nearby men had fallen
silent; they were watching.

"Wait," Bale cried. He felt for his watch. The chain
hung loose, its links shorn in two.

The captain shook out the folds of his dirty have-lock. "Some of our burglars attended you, I see," and the card-players bent closer over their game. "Well," Ballou nodded, "General Hancock once said that he wouldn't give a damn for a man who was issued half enough food and couldn't steal the other half. They rob the dead: God help the living." He seemed rather proud of his burglars.

"I won't go to the rear unless it's to reach Fanning's company," Bale said with cold defiance. He unfastened the watch chain and slipped it into his hip pocket. It was the first time he had put his hand inside. The dead man had owned a black handkerchief and an onion and a tin box of salve. Dan threw them over the wall, and in the silence of watching men he could hear the articles pelt softly into the grass.

Ballou put his heels together. "If you are ready, sir, follow along."

Dan folded his arms.

Ballou took a deep breath. "I don't know why I was so lax in the first place. Possibly because we were all weary from our long march." He called over his shoulder: "Grimes. Lennihan. You—other fellow—" They were all leaping to attention, saluting, the cards fluttered away and there was a heap of copper and paper currency on the jacket. "If this civilian will not accompany me of his own will, you are to fetch him." His heel dug into the sod as he swung on it.

A sharp sound rapped across from the tip of Oak Ridge, and everyone turned to look. There was new smoke among the trees and a dull, mechanical whirring screeched toward them. "Whitworth!" exclaimed the captain. North, a few rods away, came a grating crash and a column of dirt and stubble flew high.

Somebody cried, "What the hell's that for?" All the men were standing up and looking. Just imagine— them Whitworths load at the breech.

"Well," began Ballou. The western ridge divided itself into booming segments of eruption. The landscape looked funny . . . there was something. Now Dan understood: the Bliss barn was gone—a smoking rubble lay where it had been. "Burned it," he whispered to himself, "and I slept through it all." Nest of wool flew apart, alongside the little grove of oaks. "Ballou," yelled a commanding spirit, "take charge of your company!" and a horse fled past as men tumbled out of its way. The fold of earth south of the seminary was become a round crest of organic smoke, and the hammers came down all around. "By God," yelped the Counter of Cartridges, "so that's what they were kiting around for." The soldiers of this regiment began to clatter their ramrods; they had loaded their guns, they were all worming close to the wall, and hugging the board fence which leaned away to the right.

Ballou had gone ducking toward the front of the angle, gesticulating at heads which bobbed up on each side of the wall. Another spout of earth, back by the Taneytown road, another, another, and Dan Bale sensed the horse-cry which had started its life on Wednesday morning and would exist on these farms until the end of time. Hammers stung against his skull.

The world beyond the valley farms was ballasted with smoke, shot through with colorless jabs of light, evasive pinks and reds which faded on the instant of their inception. The trees of the little copse began to pull apart, their leaves ripped loose and spattering wide. *Get down,* somebody yelled in Bale's ear, *for the lova* . . . dropped to his knees, and the earth jiggled with that ugliness of underground avalanches.

Why don't we open up? They were all hooting. "Get busy, Mister Hunt!" came a bawdy cheer. Did he say *Hunt?* . . . they laughed, the west was a long bulge of lightning and tropical spume. Must have a hundred guns over there. Two hundred going at once, they estimated. Heavier than Fredericksburg if they keep this up.

Through the mutilation a stampede came from the rear: people scuttled to shelter, gun after gun lurched in from the Taneytown road, lining beside the cannon which had been squatting in that upper field since daylight. The gunners tore the harness apart, bounding like fleas, pushing the thick pieces into position, hauling and leaning against the wheels. They straddled the slanting trails, screwing away at tiny wheels beneath each breech. All Dan could think was: how'll I get back? Seventy-second. I can't run toward those guns if they're shooting. He got to his feet and the air was bumped close beside him. A bushel of stones flew from the wall. One of the card-players stood up and screamed. He beat his chest with open hands, shaking his head and rolling his eyes until the whites puffed out and glistened. Hands pulled him down, but he fought with them. The bent pastures seemed wearing away beneath this incessant crash of bursting iron.

Between two swinging mauls of sound a distant voice called flatly: "Load . . . watch your fuses and . . ." The cannoneers were jerked by wires; you heard the rammer-heads driving in. A short-legged man was standing on the nearest caisson—above him a splinter of white bit into the sky. He bent down and scratched his knee, then straightened again . . . faintly through the devouring noise: Number One, Fire. The concussion leveled the infantrymen by the wall; fingers of flame singed at them. "Number Two, Fire." Dan heard somebody laughing—he was in the grass, and Captain Ballou was crawling across his chest, knees and sword and all . . . *more than . . . bargained for.* Ballou looked down at him with eyes as bright as a squirrel's. He crawled on around the corner with his sword dragging behind. "Number One, Fire." The Milky Way came down and flung itself up again.

Bale's ears made a wet sound within his head. He grew against the old stones of the wall foundation, became a legal part of them. Where's Tyler Fanning, he thought. Fire Zouaves . . . the wars. Number Two, Fire. A man screeched. "Son of a bitch if they're not concentrating on us!" Yah, we're focal. Captain Ballou came along the line again; his mouth was wrinkling above his cornsilk goatee. I should say we'll get it presently. Voice said, a whisper born in the ruction: *Thy Kingdom come, Thy will be done, on earth as it is in*— There goes Perkins, praying again. You let him be, Scut—if he dies 'twon't be with no oaths on his— Ballou screamed back at Dan: "You can't go to the rear now. They're shortening on our guns—stay where you are until this stops!" Torpedoes blew with every stroke of the mallets: you couldn't see the world over by the Blisses' and Pitzers' any more. Horses squirmed, dotted all the way back to the road, heads arching and squealing, high out of the dust they were stirring around themselves. "Number Three, Fire . . ." how long, Dan thought. Twenty minutes. He didn't know. The flint-eyed neighbor spat out a stream of blood and tobacco juice. He had been chewing the linings of his cheeks, and the diluted saliva trickled over his hard little lip. "Wish I was out in front," he said. Skirmishers. They're not getting much of this.

Ready. Between the shivering anvils. *By piece. At will. Fire.* Nearer reports merged together, separated again; there was no longer any Number One or Number Two or number anything. Some round object was squeezed into Bale's hand; he looked; it was his watch. The boy grinned eerily at him. Then he squirmed nearer, to howl, "I thought I'd like to have that! But I think I'm going to glory this time. I had a feeling. Can't take no watch along with me." He choked in the smoke, and hitched away. Bale looked at the watch, then it seemed that the roof of his head had flown apart, and a mist of blood was in his eyes. The men were all gagging, blinded by that sound, that splintering crash which blew a hole fairly through the sky.

He managed to turn his head. Red still wiggled across the salty landscape, but when the smoke thinned he could see that the caisson where the officer had stood was gone—forever vanished, and there existed only a tangled sprawl of cloth and earth and dripping spokes, with one cannon barrel up-ended at the side. Chariot of fire . . . forty-five minutes. An hour. An hour of days, with the fields blowing up like crops of geysers, and the whole insane asylum of horses telling their Creator what he had done to them.

All the way across, Dan thought, all the way across Pennsylvania. A thousand miles, from the Round Top Hills to the cemetery. The dead will get up out of the grave-yard and work the guns when the cannoneers are killed: stiff and ghastly in their grave-clothes, they will push the black rammers and pull them out again. He looked toward the higher ground in the north and east—the Ever Green, the Baby Rest Darling place. There was nothing but one rain-cloud of smoke and crawling flame.

ALL PERSONS FOUND USING FIREARMS IN THESE GROUNDS WILL BE PROSECUTED WITH THE UTMOST VIGOR OF THE LAW.

He screeched with laughter, but he couldn't hear his own laugh. A new sound came from the south, past the mound of saplings: the blue huddlers were lifting their heads, craning their necks; they held their guns ready in efficient hands. A lot of horsemen were coming through the smoke, and a sound trotted alongside them. It's him? What in the devil. Yah, it's him. What's he want?

A large man rode through the mist on a big-boned horse. He was a man with a hard face modeled in an iron grin. The men began to stand up; dimly under the roar you could hear the clank of their rifles as they waved them aloft. A boy's voice shrilled: *Prrresent . . . hahm!* The general had his hat in his hand, flapping it limply; his blouse was buttoned at the throat but hung gaping on each side of his round blue belly; the howl came through the copse and around the walled angle of the little field. *Han-cock,* they were all yelling. Three cheers for *Han-cock* . . . the guns blotted them, they poured in stronger again, a wrenching exultation which mingled with the thunder all around: rrrrah . . . rrrrah . . . rrrrah. "We'll show 'em, Winfield," came a screech. He rode past the corner, his staff fighting their rearing horses, and looking very pale. A pin-wheel crackled above the wall and men staggered back. Hancock kept the metal grin on his jaws, his mustaches sticking out above it. "Hold fast, gentlemen. Give them what Paddy gave the drum.

They'll be coming across," he bellowed, "and make them like it when they get here . . ." *Han-cock! Han-cock! Han-cock!* . . . the vapor whirled behind him.

Nobody knew how long. An hour. Two hours. Maybe a day. There wasn't any time in creation. The smoke was thinning gradually and guns were falling silent all along this highland, and you could hear parched throats squawking: "Shake ass, cut that harness, get that three-incher outa there." Mist weighted the mild slopes, falling thickly into the valley, and the infantry wasn't crouching down behind the barricade any more. They were spreading rows of cartridges on the rocks in front of them and as the firing slackened you could hear the squeak of leather; they dug eagerly into their cartridge boxes.

A lone man was racking the whole county with his scream, back where the battery of rifled guns had stood: a man who lay amid the broken wheels and smoking harness, and he had been there all the time but you couldn't hear him until the guns stopped. One of Henry Niede's straw-stacks was burning, near the barn, its tiny sparks squirting up in a thick purge of flame . . . The scream in the rear continued; it stopped; the last haze fell away, and a man in citizen's clothes was there in the wreckage.

Dan croaked, "Doctor Duffey," but nobody looked at him. This seemed a most grotesque fabrication, it was a more violent lie than any he would tell to Tyler. The fat man grew there, on his knees in the hot mess of the exploded caisson. The final crush of Confederate artillery had lightened, and troubled waters gushed in everyone's ears. It was impossible to realize that such thunder might ever have an end.

Bale made his way slowly up the pasture, stepping over the men who lay there. Duffey was a cartoon of

the Duffey whom Bale had known once. He possessed
fish eyes and a seamed, baggy face; he had been
floundering in blood; the cups of his hands were
brown and sticky. "I was back by the stables, back at
General Meade's house," he roared. "This man has
been shot to bits. I thought I would be doing something for him, but he was shot to bits. It's a marvel he
could yell about it, being shot to bits." Only two rebel
guns still fired—distinct reports—you could tell them.
A sulphur bolster swelled up a mile and a half wide,
God knew how long or how thick. The silver sun tried
to get through it.

Dan cried again, "Doc! . . . Well? . . ." Duffey seemed
to say: I know you, you were once my friend, once I
was a man and had friends, we are both here, what
does it matter? His enormous voice blurbed: "Cut off.
I was cut off, that day, with old Salt and the carryall.
I've been here—since—"

Dan said, *I came* . . . seized Duffey's arm and
hurled himself backward, and together they fell out
from under a scurry of horse-legs. Here were more
guns, different guns, they came down across the field
over the dead and the living, cracking outstretched
legs with their bounding wheels. Order, wiry and high,
a hawk-voice from the heat overhead: "Will you get
your Napoleons in line at once, Lieutenant Cushing?"
Yes, sirrrrr . . . all the rebel cannon had stopped, and
the smoke was spreading wider; the sun burned it
away with fast-recovering strength. The orders talked
like neighborhood gossip along the twice-bent wall.
Across the valley, the flat extension of Oak Ridge
seemed to grow and wiggle. Codori's house and barns
were out in front, still, the Niede place was there and
the Emmetsburg road, but something queer was happening beyond.

Bale said, "Look." Everybody said the same thing. Look at. There's a plentiful number of them . . . a generous wedge of dirt color, dotted with spikes of pale red, crawling steadily out of the trees more than a mile away. Duffey went down on one knee, then rose again: he staggered and put his hand on Dan's shoulder. He mumbled thickly: "What—doing here—Daniel—" Bale cried, "I had to see—" and the activity of the batteries covered his words. The cannoneers were drenched in lamp-black, faces, hands, bare chests, ragged pants. Lieutenant told them, coolly enough: "Load. Cannister. Double."

Duffey's head seemed to come loose on his thick neck. He bowed, shaking it, and pushing his sticky hands up over the mat of gray hair. "I've men back there by the barns," he said, "men to see after. Will you be with me?"

"I can't," Bale told him. "Got to wait here for Seventy-second Pennsylvania, don't know where they are, they must be coming down here soon." Be sure and let the skirmishers under your range before you fire, a lot of aggrieved people were saying. The men began to squat down, all along the stone wall. Doctor Duffey went back toward the crest of the ridge, going rather blindly. He stooped above one man, got up and went on.

The western face of the flat valley was shifting, a brown sand that turned itself over and over, and now the pale red spikes became flags. Plentiful number. Bet a paper dollar they don't get to this wall. Take you, Charlie; sure as hell they will. Dan looked into the face of Captain Ballou. "Oh, great God in heaven," the captain howled, "now I know you're crazy! Get to the rear, man, while you've a chance!"

Mounted officers poked up out of the advancing

mass, lone and remote. There was a faint scattering
of fire down along the Emmetsburg road—from
Codori's and Niede's yards. Bale thought, That can't
be Uncle Otto shooting at them; probably the whole
family's run away. They should have . . . little blue
morsels behind every rock and fence corner, and toy
puffs of smoke marking them. The dirt color fell wider,
wider, spreading, spreading, you could see lines: three
immense billows of dust and steel-shine, filling the
dish of the valley from Sherfy's all the way up past
the Bliss place.

They'll get it on the left. Naw, it's coming this way.
The devil you say—it's coming all along. Must be
their whole army. Suddenly a man wheeled away
from the wall and started toward the rear, his gun
hung loosely from his hand. He kept looking over his
shoulder. "Come on back," several voices yelled.
Captain Ballou sprinted after the man. He cried,
"What do you mean?" The soldier began to sob . . .
"Only a youngster," someone grunted . . . He crouched,
whirled, and raced back to the wall once more. Over
by the copse they were crying, "Get some rails on top
of that wall. Pile it up, Appleton, pile it up" . . . brown
swarm had legs; it was all men as it flowed toward
the road, but you would never have known it before.

Blue morsels oozed in retreat, firing back as they
came up the field from the highway. The last dirty wave
was well out of the groves across the valley. Anxious
cannon started in to the right and left: *Gom—g-g-gom,*
and bursts of white and gold appeared in the middle
of the swarm. They came on, seriously and steadily. A
tiny, mounted figure fell from its horse, the horse
stood motionless, the sea came past, vermillion flags
and all. They began to make a sound. "That Noise,"
Bale said. His finger-nails bent against the stones

where he stood, watching. It was a wind, a gusty sighing that gained volume and shrillness as it trampled ahead. The colored flags, blue and rosy alike, bowed and nodded. The dust of exploding shells was thicker across them. *Whoooooooo*.

The rifled guns by the cemetery were clanging, and all the way along the upper ridge, when you turned you could see the stubby fingers of metal bounding between their wheels, and sizzling vapor got in the way. "Well," Bale said, "I'm damned if I stay here and be killed. Seventy-second. I don't hate these brown men, they ate in my kitchen, they slept in my house—I don't give a good God damn what Elijah said about them . . ." He swung around and started toward the Taneytown road, his head bent beneath the explosions and the howl running up the fields behind him. He reached the first fence. A voice he'd never heard before cried, "You cowardly bastard!" and something struck him across the shoulders.

He whirled, doubling his fists. A boy with a set, greenish face confronted him. "I'm not a soldier!" Dan cried. The youth shook his head; he couldn't hear, now that the guns were going without a pause; he dropped his sword and ripped out his revolver in one quick motion. He motioned Dan toward the wall at the front of the field beside the copse.

Well, Bale thought, be killed one way or another. The boy officer found a gun in the weeds, and picked it up and put it in Dan's hands. It was set at full cock—a Vincennes musket—Lucas Mite had one, during the Indian uprising . . . The boy came behind, revolver shaking in his hand. The brown mass was at the Emmetsburg road, split by the Codori buildings, and fence rails rolled or waved high as they came over. Dan reached the wall. "There's twice that many on the right," a man said. "Lookit." Behind them echoed a livid blat: *Ready. By Piece. At Will. Fire.* The family of brass guns flamed.

The Confederates began to lie down on the ground. They lay down rapidly, sideways, forward, blotted flat in tumbled crops . . . *whoooooo* . . . wrench of sparks along the whole front of them, and splinters flew from rails atop the stone wall, and the man who had said "Lookit" stood up and lay down across the rails with his hands dangling. "Lettergo at will, boys." The wall uttered a sundering cough.

God, they're dressing. Lookit that—dressing—crazy as— Anyway, that's prettiest movement ever saw executed under fire. The ramrods clattered. Gray nations straightened out and swung to the right, arching in toward the slope. The nest of guns gave out their bile, spurt by spurt. Bale said aloud, "Something dead, over by Codori's—must be a calf." Persons found using firearms will be prosecuted utmost vigor. The yell went tussling along the dusty tribes; rapidly they began to have faces. Most of them were lugging their rifles at their sides and working the rods with their right hands as they came. Crust of smoke sped out to meet them.

They kept roaring, every throat wide open with sound. The Nationals were standing up, man by man, standing up and falling down and standing up and falling down. Pink flag dodged forward; the smoke shredded and let it through, and a struggling clay torrent screeched behind. The front runners kept flinging out their hands and sprawling forward, and others tumbled over them to do the same thing. The flag bobbed closer, supported by a tight-locked mass of bare arms. Squarely in front of the rolling haze, a row of men came out and knelt; their muskets flamed, but you couldn't hear the sound any more. There lived a single ocean of pulsation and wail, a bursting rattle which knit all solitary explosions together. A man in a green jacket ran forward and put both hands on the wall beside Dan—he didn't have a gun or anything. A rifle-butt swung, and the green jacket was spattered.

Gray bodies; they smelled of sweat and chemicals; the red flags wavered, bunched together, there were a dozen of them in front of the trees. "That ain't milishy, looky them clovahs," came a discordant howl. Dan felt people pressing him back, staggering over rocks and outflung arms and legs, and always that rim of wolf-faces pushing him. A black-nailed hand tore the sleeve from his shirt. He still had the gun—he didn't know what to do except go back with the others. Through the mist before the wall, a block of blue soldiers tumbled out at the left of the copse, striking toward the side of the shrieking swarm. Ahead of them ran a young man with a contorted face; he swung a hatchet over his head. The guns in the rear had ceased firing. The nearer world was too unsupported, though ghosts of detonations still made the ground heave, it would be jelly forever. Bale felt a metal-tired wheel strike his back, and he slid around it. Back this far, he thought. Face poked up beside him and said, "Get outa the way." *Nuther shot.* Claw hauling at a string. A stem of flame crushed the wolf-heads, crushed everyone's eyes and ears as the cannon went off. Dan slipped, his feet were tangled in something slimy. Felt like ropes: good God, they weren't ropes.

Here's Fire Zouaves. New yell rose up in the rear. They yelled, *Raaaaa* as they came swarming past. Dan saw a man with wooden face and narrow eyes; he was coughing as he ran. Dan yelled, "Ty—for— *Ty.*"

The reserves smashed past the single, silent gun; Tyler swung around, he was announcing something, his face looked like no face he had ever worn before. "Be killed," Bale said in his brain. He couldn't hear anything Ty was saying, and Ty couldn't hear him. Thinks she's damned if he dies before I talk to him. More important than that—

He swung up the muzzle of the gun in his hand and knocked two snarling wrestlers aside. *Ty,* he screamed. There was a bald man in a gray jacket—he was middle-aged, he held a sword high above his head and he was crying aloud. Again Fanning turned to halloo at the blue froth beside him—he had lost his hat, and his hair was all tousled and childish. Sword glitter . . . bald head, you cannot do that . . . Dan pulled the trigger. The middle-aged man stumbled. His hand grabbed at the big barrel of the brass cannon, it was steaming, he coughed and said something about cold steel, and went down under a stampede. Dan dropped the musket.

Once he saw the tops of little oak trees trembling as the bodies pushed against them. There was a remarkable and increasing patter of shots on the right and the left; pink flag came down, and its staff glanced off the cannon barrel. Lonely outcry, *Ah Surrendah* . . . the stubborn clay washed back and disappeared, the musket rattle lessened, increased, and lessened again. "Go to the rear," people were calling. Oh-my-God-oh-my-God-oh-God-kill-me oh-God-quit-it-oh-God-stop-it-oh . . . *go to the rear.* Lay down them guns, Johnny. The crush thinned and distorted itself; men were sliding down on their hands and knees. A red and black image fell against Dan Bale, the arms convulsed around him and then turned to dough and collapsed.

You could see a soapy gray remnant sliding back toward Codori's, guns still popping, but most of the mass had lain down or gone staggering to the rear. "Ty," Bale said. "Where in damnation. He can't be dead." He started to look around. Guns near at hand had all stopped their crackling. He yelled, "Fanning! Fanning!" and there came some kind of a responsive drooling. He climbed across the retching, gargling pile. Tyler leaned back, his face chalky, his shoulders against the cannon wheel. "Here," he whined. He saw Dan and blinked at him. "The devil," he said at last, and then lifted his wet hands and made a foolish gesture—he had been caressing his thigh and it was all soaked and purple.

Dan got down beside him. Was going to tell him something, he thought: what? I had to see you . . . the distant, stubborn volleys fought to take his words away from him. Tyler rolled his eyes this way and that . . . "What-you-doing-in-the-army-ahhh," he said.

"I came through the lines to see you. I was here—"

The pale eyes went around again. "Had to tell you," Dan railed at him—"it's not true. You see, it's not true. That letter . . ." Tyler said, *Bluhhh,* and his lips went away from his teeth . . . "That letter, Ty, it's not true, not a word of it, it was all a fabrication, I was here and killed somebody—he was middle-aged—I shot a man, just to tell you—I tell you, I shot him— you God damn dirty son of a bitch, do you hear, do you hear, do you hear?"

Fanning slid lower and began to vomit; his lips were fish-gills. He mourned, Tell me what's not true . . . *Bluhhh.*

"Your wife." Fanning opened his eyes, and closed them, and opened, and closed. "Aw," he sighed with the yellow dripping from his chin. "Aw, that."

"Do you believe me? I killed a man just to—"

"What? Yes. Of course, I— Leg . . . aw . . . aw, my Christ."

There were some officers bending over a man just ahead. National officers—one of them was spitting blood but he seemed strong enough; the other man was naked to the waist, but you could tell he was an officer. They lifted a limp, bald-headed figure in shabby gray, and their eyes met as they raised him up. "Yes," one declared, "we must take him back to the stretcher-bearers. Did you hear?" "Yes," said the other, "I heard. *He has called for help as the son of a widow.*

The hospitals were back in the valley of Rock Creek. Darkness came on, stinking and thick. Dan found a surgeon kneeling in the middle of a moaning waste of straw and wet rags.

"Who?" the surgeon asked. "He was mainly bald, and had stars on his jacket collar? Ah, yes." He nodded sadly. "You refer to General Armistead of Virginia. He was mortally wounded."

10.

In still another hospital Doctor Duffey worked among the awful population, and Dan worked with him all evening. Tyler Fanning had been carried here with most of the other wounded from the rock-oak copse; the chief surgeon and his assistants rigged a barn door on the rocks to serve as an operating table; between probings the surgeon petitioned shrilly for food—hard-tack, biscuits, anything to help hold the life inside the men. It was surprising how many of them had eaten nothing since they could remember. The evening groped on, and no crackers came.

Can't do anything for our colonel, a young lieutenant continued his insistent delirium. *I tell you, gentlemen, you can't do anything. He's killed, I tell you: killed. Send all the doctors you wish, but you can't do anything for him. My name . . . tell you what my name is. My name. Walker. William H. Acting as adjutant. Twentieth Massachusetts.*

More fiends drowned him out—then he'd come through them again with his stern announcements. *I'm shot through the hips. Can't help the colonel. He's killed. He's Colonel Paul J. Revere, colonel, Twentieth Massachusetts.* Another boy kept chuckling from his den in the humid blackness. "Read it in the *Atlantic Monthly*—hah, you don't know what *Atlantic Monthly* is—I read everything he's ever written— *it was one by the village clock when he galloped into Lexington. He saw the gilded weathercock swim in the moonlight as he passed.* Know Paul Revere," repeated the Chuckler—"learned him out of magazine at the academy."

It was well after midnight when they heard feet sliding down the hillside and a voice sang out of the gloom, "Here's your damn crackers." The surgeon cried: "Whom do you think you're addressing, sir? Give me your name!" Dull shapes flew away as he came closer with his lantern. "Give me your name," he roared again, and then began to entreat: "Officer of the day, oh, officer of the day— !" A voice jibed, "There's only officers of the night around here," and the ancient joke went trembling off amid the groans: "officer of the day, if you're officer of the day, what the devil are ye doing out at night?"

The surgeon fell against the box, and swore, and set his lantern down. It was smudged with blood; the light shone pink. He said, "Only one box," and began to tug at the lid. Bale went toward him; he felt something sharp under his foot. A bayonet. He came into the pale circle of light and offered the bayonet. The officer's face was wan and ugly under its ragged beard. "You get it open," he ordered, and stood breathing noisily while Dan broke the lid and ripped it off in pieces. Then the surgeon bent close, swinging his lantern over the open box.

"Smells like mice, and God only knows when those were packed. For the war with Mexico, probably. Do you mind giving out one apiece as far as they go?"

The men heard him, and they relayed the word through the underbrush. "One piece. Mexican war—wouldn't that physic you? Oh, mother, I'm cold as . . . say that Lincoln and his cabinet are living off the fat of the land while we . . . *dy*ing, I'm *dy*ing, and I don't want to *die*." A man screeched, "You won't die as long as you can yell like that!"

Up the hill beyond them mumbling wagons began to carry a deeper resonance, as if they transported drums eternally beaten in a muffled roll. "I can't distribute these in the dark," Dan told the surgeon. The officer swore again, pressed the wire handle into Bale's hand, and went scrambling off toward the lights beside the barn door . . . Face. It was white and severe and somehow princely, and the eyes were closed. Dan said, "Here's a bite to eat." The face didn't twitch or open its eyes. "I'll take his," sobbed another man, and reached up a perspiring hand . . . Face. It grinned softly; it was an ugly Scotch face, and you thought it was listening to bagpipes of enchantment, droning wickedly in a rainy world beyond. Scotch face couldn't hold the hard-tack, it fell against his corrugated neck, but he grinned with inarticulate delight . . . Face. Sober and firm as steel; one eye stared without blinking, the other socket was a coagulating pool. "Thank you, friend," the soldier whispered. "I think I hear artillery again."

"Wagons," Dan said.

The man smiled, his single eye clicked shut. "My error, sir. God's cannon . . ."

Dan kept listening as he worked his way among the trees. Now he identified the deep murmur up above; it did not live with the wagons but far beyond them, enormous palpitations in the overcast sky. He could feel the sweat seeping in his armpits and through his crotch; the moisture was turning cold, even as he worked; the poison of heat was cooling away. Why, he thought, there'll be nothing to cover them if it should rain.

A strip of lightning dashed overhead, and all around came the resigned trickle of leaves wavering in a sudden wind and falling quiet again. Bale found Tyler. Ty had his back propped against a tree trunk, and was swaddled in an old jacket. He grimaced into the lantern glow. Dan asked, "Do you feel like having a cracker?" and knelt beside him.

"Feel like," Tyler said, "feel like——"

Bale put his hand on the wrapping of cloth around Fanning's leg. The hemorrhage seemed stopped. There was some dampness, but the bandages were not soaked. "I can't find any more brandy," he said, "but here's a cracker if you want one."

Tyler's eyes were puffing and angry. "No. Not now."

Another light toiled up the ravine toward them. Silhouetted against it was a bulb of black which went up and down mechanically—a head thudding against the ground. "Here," Adam Duffey's voice cried out, "why can't you—" A man interrupted in a fearful exclamation, "You can't stop him, sir! He's been banging himself that way for the last hour."

Bale wrapped the blouse tighter around Ty's shoulders and went down toward the doctor's lantern. The bulb kept thudding, thudding, though Duffey tried to hold it still. Their combined light showed a soldier who lay on his stomach, rigid from the waist down but with a bruised and unrecognizable face—the mouth a wide welt of dirt and blood. "I remember him well," whispered Duffey. "I remember them striped pants. The only thing would have been to lay bare the calvaria and apply the trephine, and it couldn't be done at the time." The head struck against the ground again, again. This man made no sound, though his face was sticky with leaf-mould. His glassy eyes protruded; he did not know that he lived.

The trees bent under the sudden smash of rain; it came with no more warning than that, and in a solid layer.

Maggie, Maggie . . . they began to whimper, all the way along the ravine and all around the universe outside, a weak volley of complaint as the water roared over them. Bale held the lantern close against his legs, humping himself above it. Voice said, through the driven sheets, "You ought to know what's good for him: one thing, Doctor." Thunder struggled across the sky; for a moment the rain thinned, and there was a hopeful hush among the prone men—then the sea mashed the trees again, and now they might as well die.

The clear echo went round and round inside Dan Bale's brain. As the son of a widow . . . son of a widow. I will always hear that talking to me, he thought.

Crackers in his hand began to soften as the water found them; in a few moments they were a glutinous dough which slid between his fingers. Cover the box, if it isn't too late. He climbed back toward the thicket where the box of hard-tack lay. A lavender flash made a starchy design of all the faces among the trees, and found the silver in every eye . . . far down by the creek sounded a piercing yell.

Once Dan looked back at Duffey's lantern, still stubborn with its flame through the torrent, and it seemed that the doctor was busy attending the man with the bloated head. I wonder, Bale thought with ghastly reckoning, I wonder what. He felt every pore of his skin lifting in nervous goose-flesh; he went on, sliding among the pasty leaves.

Little rivers whispered down the hillside, growing wider and taking loose twigs and rubbish with them as they curled among the drift of roots, a steady music in the darkness. A log rolled against Dan's feet and said Uhh. "Look out there," he heard himself crying, and then he had found the cracker box. Some shrubbery had helped to protect it but the top layer was wet. He said aloud, "If I only had something," and an arm reached out and tugged at his pantaloons. *Here,* the growl rasped, and the man was offering his coat. Bale spread the garment over the box; the lantern told him that this jacket was gray . . . He went hunting Tyler Fanning. Ty's face was spectral and collapsed, but he was conscious. He complained, "I'm fairly soaked," and after a moment— "Go on, if there's anything you can do for anyone else. This is— pretty mess—must say."

The little colonies of lanterns, guarded with a new and frightening jealousy, were wandering toward the creek; they danced, they were hurrying. *He's drowning,* a howl came floating up, *for God's sake hurry up . . . just slid off in the river . . .* Rock Creek had a sullen, mounting roar not to be disdained. Dan tried to run; a tree-trunk scraped the side of his face. He blundered on toward the lower ground. Lights were bobbing like glow-worms, and with no leadership or ordered purpose. He felt a curl of water around his shoes, now he was splashing, the stream whistled eagerly between his ankles. It was spreading, and this seemed a cloudburst which nature had sent to punish them all . . . His lantern found a muddy face, and he groped through brown foam for the man's hand, and then the flood killed his lantern forever.

At least he held his hand, and he would not let go. He yelled, "I've got you," and the tired mumble told him, "For Christ sake hang onto me," and then an ungodly spasm—*you done got my hurt arm, for Christ sake leggo!* He wrenched his arm under the man's shoulders and dragged him back, fighting through the water as it tried to steal his breath from him. They came up on some sort of a mound where the creek no longer sang around his legs. Bale said, "Wait till I get my bearings."

His black burden announced, "Guess you're a Yank. This is a deeloodge, like the Bible tells about."

Dan fancied he could see the trees; he dragged the man farther, and the safe slope began to tilt under them. "All right, now," the rebel said. "You can let me drap anywhere. Thought I'd not get home to Nawth Kalina again."

Two out of three, Dan thought, it's the same story

this time. He yelled, "There seem to be a lot of North Carolina folks around here."

Voice gurgled, "Reckon it's because they always put us in the hottest place. I'm most thankful to you for pulling me out of the deeloodge."

He could do nothing in this cascade without the lantern. He left the wounded man burrowing against a rotten stump, and went splashing downhill, trying to light the lantern again as it swung on his arm. It was no use: the matches in his pocket were all too wet. A few lights still wavered along the rapid stream ahead, faint wailings still came out of the water. The rain threshed with a steady roar.

"Cloudburst," Dan said aloud. He leaned heavily against a tree. Slowly a hand went around his ankle. A voice came up, full of certain knowledge. "This is a judgment which follows. Always."

Dan cried, "Who are you?" and he bent down to touch the twisting mound of cloth and leather and cold fingers. "Are you alive?" he demanded crazily. "Are you—?"

The man loosed a shrill laugh. In any light his face would have shone prophetic and ghastly, but now he was only a nightmare voice dwelling underfoot. "Alive," he repeated proudly. "Mister, I've seen it happen before. Was you in many battles before this? We tear the world with our cannons, and Providence brings this upon us. There's—" he wailed on, his words imprinted by the constant thunder—"always a cloudburst, afterward. Always, after a battle—"

Dan tore the clutch from his ankle; he went on, stumbling from tree to tree, trying to reach the lights which still survived. But they went out, one at a time, before he got to them. Now there was no beam left in the world; the bubbling entreaties became weaker, forgotten in the murmur which trilled along the higher ground; in the darkness no one could rescue any more men. Rock Creek swam above its banks and carried them away.

The rain weakened with dawn, and Dan found Adam Duffey in the grove farther upstream. The doctor brooded like a patron witch among a tangle of bodies. He was adjusting a scrap of oilcloth over one man, wiping water from the face of another. He nodded at Dan through the gloom, and when he had recognized him he stood up and rubbed his hands together, "Do you remember the one with the swollen head on him, Daniel?" he asked. And when Bale said that he did, the old doctor bent close and lifted his blurring face. "I cured him," he whispered, "I cured him, as sure as I'm a foot high." He put his mouth close to his friend's ear and said again, *Cured him painlessly. I bled him.*

11.

Dan went into Gettysburg at noon, walking near the edge of the Baltimore Pike. The road was a narrow mire where wagons and guns argued for the right of way, with officers flapping heedlessly past them. Word had spread across the hills as soon as the first troops left the cemetery and crept warily down toward outlying houses: the rebs moved out, they're laying on that higher ground over past the town, and maybe old Bob Lee's had enough.

A squad of pickets waited beside the cemetery, and another squad near the intersection of the Emmetsburg road, but it was easy to avoid them by crawling across tumbled walls and striking north along the grassy slopes. Endless, shoddy rolls clouded the sky, a purple menace near the northwest horizon; there would be more rain. Out over the eastern valley you could see a long column of cavalry moving toward the village, with outriders on either flank holding far ahead of the advance.

The guns still bickered inside Dan's ears . . . when he looked back across a lane he could see that the tracks he left were sliding and uneven. Duffey had been sound asleep when Bale left the hospital, and could not be roused out of the damp blanket in which he had wrapped himself. Tyler Fanning was delirious, and demanding shrilly that the entire army be bucked and gagged.

Bale came up into a garden behind a brick house on the hillside. A few soldiers and a sobbing woman were gathered around a long shape shrouded in a pink comforter. Two men with shovels scooped out a grave among the muddy onion-tops. The soldiers looked at Dan with lusterless eyes, and the woman had her face buried in a shawl . . .

He asked, "Who is it?" and a fat sergeant turned and rubbed his nose with a black finger. "A lady," he told Dan. "She got hit by a bullet through the door of that house. They said she was killed instanter."

Dan looked at the house—a double one, of brick, and he did not know who lived there. He walked on through the adjoining garden. Two pale women peered from their cellarway, watching the burial party.

"Who is it?" he inquired again.

They said, "The Wade girl. She was making biscuit dough. It was yesterday morning," and he could see that they were wondering who he might be.

"Wade girl." He walked on a few steps, and then

turned. "Which one?" They said, drearily enough: "Ginny. The other'n's Mrs. McClellan." Dan kept thinking: buried in a pink comforter. The rebels killed her, and probably did not know it, and they did not know that those girls were named Virginia and Georgia . . . heard a child coming up on Grandfather's porch and saying, "Ma sent your new shirts. She says tell her if the cuffs aren't right."

The Diamond was all mud and horses and soggy files of blue men. Dan went lurching along Chambersburg street; from every house he saw pinched faces peering out, and there was the incessant crying of children—crying monotonously, as if they had made that their business for many days. Limber chests and upset wagons and dead horses lay along the street, and now in the dull distance he could see a line of faded blue, spread out past the curve in the turnpike. Far ahead sounded two or three shots, lonely and trivial under the thunder which growled overhead.

A sentinel set a bayonet in front of him. "No thoroughfare," he ordered.

Dan caught at the yard-fence beside him. "Aren't they—gone?" he asked.

"They're on the hill ahead. We got skirmishers feeling along the edge of town."

"I would like to reach my house. It's—"

The soldier shifted his tobacco cud. "No, sir. See those batteries up the road? No telling when they'll open up and fire. But I think the Butternuts got enough—Lord knows we got a bellyful ourselves."

In a dreamy void, he started back toward the square. The houses swam on each side with the utmost stupidity; he heard a young girl call, inside a doorway, "Ma—ain't that Mister Bale going past?" "Pshaw, Nellie," and it is some other man comes … behind him the solitary musket-shots kept ringing across the north-west fields near his home, but they were isolated shots. He said, aloud, "Quite unenthusiastic," and then a fence flew up and stuck him sharply on the cheek … lay there with crickets in his ears. "Hey, Al Kendall, looky there." Horses stopped in the road, and two soldiers came to pick him up.

They said: "You'd better go in here somewhere and let people tend you." "If you're not drunk," they added.

They set him on his feet. "Can go it alone," he said, and started on. He did manage to cross the Diamond, sliding on the cobbled crossing, and he found the Duffey house squatting in the same place where it had always been … Eva Duffey had her arms around him, and she was crowing: "Do you know where Adam is? Do you know where—?"

Lay on a couch; it started to glide through the wall into immeasurable wildernesses beyond. "He's all right, I tell you," a chorus of voices told Mrs. Duffey. With him all night and with the wounded. He was not wounded or killed or wounded killed wounded killed as soon as wakes up will get back to town.

It rained again, undammed torrents to wash away brigades of wounded men, and Dan turned over on the couch and looked out of the window. The water walked as erect hail above the dusky lawn, spouting from the eaves-trough in a solid trunk against the rain-water barrel.

"Now," she said, "here's some hot potato soup I fixed special," and he roused up greedily, leering at the bowl with its white steam and freckles of pepper. "My," the woman declared, "you look a sight better, even with that bad bruise. I washed the mud off your face while you slept, and you never budged."

"What time is it?" The soup scorched into the aching core around which his body was built.

Eva Duffey looked at the bustling clock. Her eyes glittered, keener and icier than ever, and the little house cap she wore seemed as always: a trap wherein her face was caught. "It's half after four, Daniel. Tell me about Adam." She stood caressing her hardened fingers, waiting for him to begin.

"Yes," he said. "Then I will go back to them."

12.

They used to keep Irene's piano in the sitting room but that room became sacred to Tyler's convalescence when he was on furlough after his Antietam wound, and Demon and Mr. Fanning had hauled the piano into the library. There it stood, yet, a green baize drape over it and stacks of music gathering dust underneath. The girl had not played . . . she did not know how long since she had played. So many months. She recalled sitting there and picking meticulously at something of Liszt's, in a German musical magazine, when the bare fields were brown, ages before.

It was odd now that she should desire the touch of ebony and ivory—wish her slippers to feel the felt-wrapped pedals, and experience the ache of the novice as she spread fingers over the octaves. She went into the library alone, in the dusk of Sunday night, and lifted off the cloth (it stuck; something sticky had been laid upon it days before, and now she must get a new green baize covering).

Am not a widow . . . she thumbed the music sheets: some were fresh and unexamined, some were dog-eared folios which came from her home in Philadelphia when the piano came. Chopin, Op. 35, No. 2. Well, she thought, I'm not afraid of it. Dusk was damp as autumn. She could barely see the keys. Mrs. Fanning would not mind her playing, if indeed she could hear through the walls and floors and depths of slumber where she buried her breathing. Am still a wife, with a husband who was alive yesterday and must be alive still.

She faltered a little after the third measure and then secured new confidence and went on, holding her face close to the sheet and wondering why she didn't stop to light a candle. When she reached into the higher blacks, something rattled and fell upon the floor. It sounded like a coin. Irene went to get matches and candles, and looked for the object when she returned to the room. A reek was all around her, cologne would never take it away, nothing could serve for a remedy but the years ahead.

And she found the metal thing that had fallen: it was a round, gold-rimmed wafer of ambrotype which had been set in someone's watch case, and God knew why it had been removed. Identification . . . it was a girl with dark hair drawn close around her face, neck and shoulders bare; she might have been beautiful— there was no telling, with only candlelight and glossy tricks of photography to inform. On the back was scratched in square, firm lettering: *Triggie Richmond Aug 1861*. Triggie, Irene thought, he is dead and you do not know it. He must have died on the library table, and Doctor Pell took this out of his watch to give to somebody, or to keep, so that they might tell you and give you back to yourself. And they forgot you, Triggie Richmond Aug 1861, when they went away with the wagons.

Again she heard the last crooning of the weak rows as they were hustled outside and laid hurriedly in the straw of the wagons. Rain would have drowned them yesterday, she prayed, before their wounds had time to become raw from the rubbing.

She put the rimmed picture on top of the cabinet. Her hand fell against the bass and made a mighty discord. Then she stiffened, and peered once more at the music . . . there came a rest, somewhere. Here.

Mrs. Duffey appeared in memory, as she had appeared in the flesh on Saturday night, but now part and parcel with Chopin. Mrs. Duffey in a baggy waterproof of the doctor's, and with a boy soldier behind her. "I just made him bring me, dear—I gave him two dollars—he said it was against orders to let folks pass, but I persuaded him. Now please give him some food to take back with him . . . Well," she gasped, dropping into the nearest chair and letting the muddy water drip unheeded from every part of her, "I got good news for you folks and for Tyler's mother. He's all right. Tyler is. So's Adam. Dan Bale brought me word, but they wouldn't let him come any farther out this way than the Tiber Creek. I'd most given Adam up for lost . . . yes, he has got a wound—your husband has—but Dan says it isn't in his vitals. Great heavens to Betsy, girl, but this house smells to fury . . . Confederates, poor souls, poor awful souls. You should be glad they didn't leave them to die here, but carried them off with their army.

"Dan's gone back to where Adam is, out where they got the wounded. He says it's along Rock Creek, and he'll bring Tyler home as soon as ever he can. Well, I don't know, but he thinks they can do it. They've got so many thousands of wounded, and he guesses nobody will make inquiry if they kind of carry him off quietly. He says old Salt ran away and smashed the carryall to smithereens when all those cannon were shooting on Friday, but he didn't break a leg and now they've got him safe over at the George Spangler place. I 'spect they'll be coming home most any time, and you folks mustn't worry but only trust in Divine Goodness."

Let her call it Divine Goodness. Call it whatever she pleases . . . Irene was placing Chopin on the heap of music when the door of the room squeaked open.

It was her father-in-law; he wore his night-cap and dressing-gown, and his face showed the pale, relieved looseness which it had shown ever since Mrs. Duffey's visit. He whispered, "I heard music."

"Oh," she said. "I was just playing."

"Aren't you too worn out, daughter?"

"I only thought I'd—"

He went over to the window and peered through the clammy dusk. "Mother is resting well, but I could not sleep. I heard wheels go past some time ago."

"It was only an army wagon."

"They're finding Confederate wounded," he said. "More of them. Demon says the soldiers are finding them everywhere, in barns and fence corners. They were compelled to leave many behind. The Nationals have gone in pursuit."

Again she said, "Yes," and went on turning the music with her china hands.

"You used to play a few hymns, my girl. Mother enjoyed those . . . I wish Tyler were more concerned with spiritual matters. Perhaps he will grow that way." The house remained quiet and pained, as they

talked: it would be haunted, there would be an eva-
nescent suffering about it, to the days of its demoli-
tion.

Irene said, "If you wish me to play a hymn—" She
began, soberly, *From Greenland's icy mountains* . . .
She was amazed at her consent to play it. She thought,
Maybe I shall become worthy of playing his, in future
years. The noise of her own unalterable damnation
whistled in her mind; far beyond, she heard the
moderate little hammers falling against their tuned
wire.

Bedford Fanning interrupted, "There is something
coming up our lane. It looks—" Then they both went
to the front door and out upon the porch. Straw was
scattered all over the dooryard, and the house lights
touched wet canteens and abandoned muskets in
the grass. The black carcass of a dead mule was in-
flated and grotesque, half buried among the un-
blossomed phlox.

This was a two-wheeled farm cart, and it stopped
beside the wreck of lilac bushes. An unrecognizable
voice was yapping, "No Poinsett tactics for the infantry I said no Poinsett tactics introduced in company
drill . . ." Laughed. Mr. Fanning went to the head of
the steps. Two tramps came out of the gloom, and
they had the shine of an oil-cloth shape between
them. "It's—" said Mr. Fanning, sharply, "it's—" and
then they had reached the porch.

Duffey told him, "We have your son, man," and
began to back laboriously up the steps. The girl could
make out the figure of Dan Bale at the lower end of
the improvised litter; something clicked behind her
eyes. Tyler said, "Wicks, take the company. Let them
go into double file, Wicks . . ." Now his head had come
into the light as the doctor backed through the door,

and it was a head like the head of a wounded Confederate, exactly; dry wads of his hair stuck every which way, and the skin seemed transparent under its dirty blonde beard. There was odor, here, putting the reminiscent odor of the vanished wounded to shame.

Doctor Duffey growled, "Where do you want him put?" and when they bent over Tyler, unable to speak, he cried with anger: "Well, say where!" "Upstairs." Irene found herself going ahead of them and calling, "Gretel, Gretel, please come at once."

She lit a lamp in the upper hall and pushed open the door of her room. He was here before, she told herself, and it must be the best place for him now. "In here, please. I'll turn back the covers." They laid the lengthy weight of wet cloth on the unstained sheet and Duffey said, "Now," and "Easy," and worked a wide board out from underneath. Tyler screamed.

His father had a handkerchief, and was wiping froth from the plump-eyed face. He quavered, "You are at home, my son. Home. Good God," he sobbed, "is he out of his mind?"

"Mainly," Duffey grunted, and stood back, wiping the sweat from his own face. "I'll look to his wound, and then I must go. Eva'll be that crazy. There's other wounded—twenty-five thousand."

Irene heard Dan Bale going down the stairway, and she had not looked at him since he came inside. "Wait!" she cried, earnestly. And then, "No, no! I mean— Go on. I will get water." There were other sounds in the house; Gretel downstairs, and Mrs. Fanning awakening and blundering about in her dark room, calling for Bedford, crying, "Have they brought him? Is honey boy here?"

The leg was hairy and swollen, the part you could

see; from knee to crotch it was wound with brown-soaked rags, dirty rags, pieces of torn underwear, part of a muslin curtain, part of a shirt. The odor choked the whole room. "Get water," Irene said, and then she was on the stairs and looking down at Dan. He stood with his back to her, gazing out through the front door, and when he turned it gave her a shock—she did not know his face, it had not been shaved for four days. There was a bulge of mottled colors on his forehead.

"Well, he's here," he said.

She attempted to face the knives in his eyes. He was mud, old mud and new, from head to foot. "You went there," she told him.

"Wasn't that what you wanted me to do?" His voice boomed.

"Please. Not—so—loud."

"Oh," he said, "it's the cannon. Everybody talks that way, afterward. One becomes deaf. Can hardly hear you."

Tyler was making a shrill whine upstairs; he mingled names and incoherencies beyond all reason. "Sutton Jones's killed God damn it," he cried, "Andy McBride killed to hell I said's dead's said's lieutenant's name's Griffith's dead let go me let go me let go."

Dan called through it all, "You insisted that I go, didn't you? I killed a man." Blindly, she turned and went into the dining room; he followed her. She cried, "That's right, Gretel—that's right—build up the fire, we shall need hot water at once."

A bugle was ringing somewhere not far away.

Bale told her, still speaking far louder than she wanted him to speak, "Did what you demanded that I do."

She turned. "I am going mad," she said, rapidly, "going mad with this! With—I cannot talk to you, now. You should know that. He's suffering so hideously. Oh," she shrieked, *"why won't you understand?"* She flung her hands against her face and felt her head beginning to fly apart.

For a long moment he said nothing. Gretel was making a great fuss in the kitchen, clattering pans and spilling water, and upstairs Tyler hallooed and hallooed . . . Bale said, more soberly, "Well. Must make certain allowances."

"Indeed," she struggled to say.

"Have—you—others here?"

She saw nothing except a gray blur with eyes in it. "Not now. Mrs. Knouse went home this morning, wholly recovered. The rebels carried away their wounded yesterday, and our five wounded Unionists were— They are making a hospital of the seminary."

"We shall talk, later?" He asked it hopelessly. "This is—not a part of—"

"Strange," she said.

"Do you please tell Doc I've gone to my house. If it's still there. He can drive back to town alone with no trouble."

Irene said, "I will tell him," and then she heard Dan going across the porch and down the steps and away into the wet grass. She felt her feet leaving her; Gretel screamed from the doorway. Irene thought, All the shadows varnished and fleeing fast, and everything gone smooth to the touch . . . Doctor Duffey said with something of his old kindliness, "There, child. Be taking it easy," and she looked up into his face, and Gretel's, and felt water soaking uncomfortably around the drenched collar of her dress. "Said you can drive back alone," she said, thickly.

13.

Mrs. Knouse was still awake, and the light from her kitchen showed Dan that his back door was standing wide. He went inside and struck a match. Drawers had been pulled from the built-in cupboard, and knives and forks and napkins were scattered all over the floor. Everywhere were the marks of muddy feet. In the living room it was the same, and in the front parlor and library. Pentland Bale's desk stood gaping and ravished; letters and books and receipts were inches deep over the carpet. "Camp followers," Dan said. Sons of bitches.

Evidently the marauders had been frightened away before they completed their tour of the entire house. The upper rooms were in some disorder, but only the disorder of an army staff compelled to leave in haste, and nothing was disturbed in Dan's own bedroom. His money was safe enough, all the time, in the belt fastened around his body . . . Keepsakes. Probably they took silver, and whatever else they wanted.

He stood for awhile with a lighted candle in his hand, gazing at his bed and desk, at the sedate curtains of the corner closet. Monongahela, he thought . . . maybe some still left in the cellar keg. As he went back down the stairway he could hear footsteps in the path outside. He walked out on the stoop, still holding his candle.

An agonized, tallow face lifted close to the light. "Oh, you are safe," came Julius Orcutt's voice, and Dan could see that the lawyer was bareheaded. He carried a huge umbrella. "I feared that you were killed. No one had seen you for days."

"I'm all right," Dan said. "Come inside, sir."

Orcutt crowed, "No, no. I am walking, walking."

"Where to?"

"It came with all the mail they brought in by wagon today," Orcutt said, much more rapidly than he was accustomed to speak. "You will understand—I am walking because I cannot endure the house. Mrs. Orcutt has her sister with her . . . I came in at the gate to see—"

Bale cried, "For God's sake, what is it?"

"It came in the mail from Hanover Junction. Benjy—" he wallowed over the name somehow. "Vicksburg. They wrote from the hospital where he—"

Dan said, "I guess you mean he is dead, don't you?"

The tallow face came close again, and Orcutt chewed his lip for a time. He announced, at length, "Yes. Dead. There is no doubt. The doctor wrote. He signed himself D. F. Albright, Surgeon. It was a bullet through the head. He did not suffer long."

"I'm sorry," Dan said. He was trying to tame his voice; the batteries still rumbled in his ears. "I—" He reached through the darkness and found Julius Orcutt's skeleton hand, and wondered how it could be hot instead of cold.

Finally, the lawyer withdrew his hand from Bale's grasp. "Walking," he said. "Do you believe it was true, Dan? The letter? I cannot endure the thought of his suffering."

"Oh, it must be true."

He banged around with his umbrella, and went away down the path. "I have walked miles," he said, and then something else which could not be understood. Dan stood for awhile, listening to those feet swishing in the mud. He went upstairs and lay down on the soiled bed-clothing. The world screwed away, high and dry, and left him in a mine.

Once he got up, remembering the decanter on his desk, remembering what was in it, and he staggered through sunlight into Mrs. Knouse's yard and took a drink from her well. There was a constant rattle of vehicles in the Pike; he heard them dimly, after he was in his room again. When he awakened the second time the sun was shining still. Or shining again. He thought it might be Tuesday forenoon, and later learned that this was correct.

Weak and ravenous as he was, he brought water and managed to bathe and shave. There were still clean shirts left in his bureau, and one suit of clean underwear. Now he lived in a feverish and blasted world, and suffered the knowledge that he had helped to make it feverish and blasted. A terrific accumulation of unsolved problems were mountainous before him, more problems than he would ever be able to deal with. When he shaved the ragged whiskers away, he found that his cheek-bones did not fit his face, and how could anyone know him now?

No, she did not come near. She did not reason how it might be with me . . . strange pack of anxiety stowed within this head. I should have something— some philosophy—

When he had dressed it was past noon, and starvation thrilled his toes and fingertips. A farmer in an old Germantown gave him a ride to the Diamond, and Dan went into the Emblem Hotel and found a vacant chair in the dining room.

The town shuddered with a formidable invasion. These were civilians and their women, these were not soldiers, and on every side you realized why they had come to Gettysburg, and you knew that the town would groan for months beneath their anguish and their crusading. They crowded in doorways, they buzzed on the hotel porch, and every hour brought recruits in wagons and buggies, dark parades pouring from the north and east and south, now even beginning to drift in from the west.

Muskets were corded like firewood on the sidewalk of York street, and Chambersburg street still lay tense with its broken caissons and rotting horses.

Eva Duffey found Dan as he came out of the hotel dining room. "Oh," she cried, "what you must have been through!" "We've all been through it," he heard himself assuring her. "What now? I've got a shadow of myself back."

"Make the rounds," she told him, twisting her hands. "Look for Elijah, Dan! I tremble to think what will happen to his mother if we don't get track of him soon. She sits and rocks, all the time. She— I've looked and looked, but there are so many thousand wounded." She whispered, "*Adam*. Daniel, Adam's in *liquor*. He won't sleep, but he drinks and drinks. He's off tending the wounded now. I fear he may poison some of 'em. He frightens me." Then she burst into tears, and went away down York street to the Huddlestone house.

"Where's the bulk of the wounded?" Dan asked of a soldier on the corner.

The soldier jerked his head. "South," he said. "Still out in the woods at corps hospitals. Town's full, too. All these here colleges and a lot of houses. Full—clean full. You might start down there at that church, if you're looking for anybody special. The Christian Commission are right good help."

There was white powder all over the wet roadway like a fall of snow, in thin windrows as the scattering

shovels had tossed it. From some distance away
Bale could see a limp red banner dangling in front
of the church; that narrow flag was the insignia of a
hospital, and flags such as that hung on many of the
houses. Boys gathered around a horse-block at the
edge of the street; every now and then a sharp explosion would sound from the center of the group, and
the boys would all be laughing delightedly. They had
whole boxes of percussion caps and they were touch-
ing them off with a hammer . . . A group of women
came down the church steps and trailed drearily toward a New Rochelle wagon which waited in the
road, with its driver holding the halters of the nervous team. He called, "You kids better quit that mon-
keying!" . . . The women moved slowly, for two of
them were supporting a slight, white-faced girl between
them. "It's God's mercy, Genevievey," one of them
was saying in a tuneless voice. "The Lord giveth and
the Lord taketh away. And the folks said he would
have been a cripple, always, if he had lived. We must
praise the Lord that he ain't lying in an unmarked
grave." The girl said, shrilly: "Never got to see him."
They pulled her along.

Dan climbed the steps; the smell came out and
struck him like a board. A woman cried, rather peevishly, "Yes, yes, sir? Please don't stand in the door."
"I beg your pardon." "Oh, Mr. Jarvis," she called past
him to somebody in the street, "don't forget the tincture of sesquichloride of iron. Then she said," "Yes, yes,
again," and looked up into Dan's face, patting her
hands together.

She had a face like an unripe peach, fuzzy with gray,
wind-bitten and yellowish. Her eyes were good eyes—
clear and vigorous with a militant pity.

"I'm looking for a man named Huddlestone."

"Dearie me," she said, "we haven't their names on the reel, sir. We don't know half. But you can come in and see. Are you certain he's in this hospital? This is the Harrisburg Christian Commission. You can come in and look. Look a-plenty."

They were in the pews and on the floor as well. The pews had been turned face-to-face and pushed together to form wide troughs. The men made a murmur like a colony of water-birds, gabbling and cooing in concert. Dan walked slowly between the rows, looking down at hairy faces. "No more lemons," one hoarse person kept insisting, at the far side of the high-ceiled room. "No—more—lemons." The eyes rolled listlessly, following Dan as far as they could, and then staring at the space he had last filled.

A fat man in a broadcloth coat got up painfully; he had been on his knees beside a patient on the floor. He cleared his throat and addressed the gaunt woman who bent beside him. "It's a sloughing ulcer," he told her. "I'd use free applications of bromine, and hope for the best. There is a mighty discharge of sero-purulent matter from the wound." His marbles of eyes turned toward Dan: the only life in his drooping, unshaven face. There was the smell of liquor discernible, even in this stench. "Daniel," he said, abstractedly.

Bale told the doctor, "I'm looking for Hud."

"Hud," Duffey repeated. And after a long pause, "I would have found him if he was here. Indeed."

"Doc. How—are you—?"

Duffey put his spongy hand on Bale's arm. "Now that is a strange one. Over there with the tartan shawl. He got hit on his bottom with a cannon-ball." The woman turned and hurried away with a pan in her hands. "It was an exploding shell, I mean to say. Took off the integuments of the gluteal and lumbar regions, and a large portion of the gluteal muscles on the right side. You should see it, Daniel. Come over here and I'll—"

"God," Bale exclaimed. He seized the old doctor's coat and halted him. "Elijah's mother is going crazy with anxiety. We've got to find him. I feel that he may have been with the army, all along."

Duffey chuckled; the laugh hung deep in his chest; his eyes were very dry—it seemed to Dan that they had been peeled, as fruit, peeled with a sharp knife and all the color gone out of them. Just the pulp underneath. "Elijah? Sure, he's a cadaver long before this. You're wasting your time." He went away down the aisle, lurching, and bent over the man under the tartan shawl.

Clearly, a phantom church audience began to lift up its hymn books and sing: *When I read my title clear, to mansions in the skies.* Dan could hear them; he did not believe in ghosts, he did not know what to think of this song, but still he heard it droning through the invisible forest of gurglings and spoken words. He started along the opposite aisle . . . the peach-fuzz woman met him and said, "So your man ain't anywhere about," and went whisking on before he could answer her. He watched the faces—brown, bearded, baby-face, yellow (that is the shadow of death, and there seems no end to them). The choir began, *By Life's fair stream, fast by the throne of God*— He stopped, and then went back to look at a man who lay turned on his side, drooling a puddle from his half-open mouth. He had a bandage wrapped tightly around the upper part of his head, covering the eyes and forehead. There was something about the mouth and chin.

He touched the man's shoulder. The blank, bound head turned slowly. "Har," it said.

"Don't I know you?" Dan asked.

The caked lips shook for a moment. "Voice sounds . . . who are you?"

"My name's Bale. I live here in Gettysburg."

The voice said, weakly, "Oh." And after a long wait: "Hid in your pantry. We did."

"Pantry," Dan repeated. "Jesus Christ." He got down on his knees. "Your name's Fisher."

Fisher told him, "Never see again. Hard lines, isn't it? They haven't told me, but I guess I know. It just looked like a lot of milk spilled over everything, milk that was boiling. It put 'em out for sure."

"Where is Huddlestone?"

The boy groped around, patting his bandage with uncertain hands. "We left the horse. Those folks' horse. It's a farmer named Crawley—hell of a name, like crawl—right near Uniontown, Maryland. You see if we didn't."

Rooo, came from the next pew.

"Can't you remember about Huddlestone? Elijah Huddlestone. He was with you."

Fisher whispered, "That truss." Reluctantly, his hands slid down from the bandage. "Well, it was the Army of the Potomac all right. We went along. The rest of the Penn college boys will wonder about that, I guess. It was the One Hundred Forty-eighth Pennyslvania—"

"One Hundred Forty-eighth Pennsylvania—"

The boy repeated it again. "Yes. That was it. So many folks from college in Company C. They welcomed us. They did."

"Can you remember about Huddlestone?"

"He had a rupture. We thought we'd let our beards grow. He had a start, by that time. Never shaved."

"Where did you fight?"

"It was wheat."

"Was Huddlestone with you?"

Fisher didn't answer. Dan took his hand and shook it in a frenzy. "Now, listen," he said. "Fisher. Listen to me. It's his mother. She wants to know what became of him. Is he still with the army? Did they enlist you both, or just let you come along with them because you were part of that temporary regiment?"

The young man swallowed and swallowed. "It's quite dark," he said, clearly. "Looked like milk at first—I saw it. Milk in my eyes."

There was a smell more fiendish than any of the others. A man and two women carried something past Dan's back and down the aisle and out of the door . . . wrapped up with a patchwork quilt. "That's gangrene." Fisher spoke with assurance. "They can't fool me by now. I heard them talking." His hands came up and hunted around. "Where'd you go?" he cried.

"Huddlestone," Dan said. "Hud, you called him."

"We—had a picnic there—one time and—and tamarinds. I remember the place, too; it was by that rocky hill, and we climbed up there with the girls. I looked back and I could see the hill, just the same. Rocks."

"Little Round Top. Was that it?"

Swaddled head nodding. "Little—little— And we walked in the wheat. They were all along the fence. Those men of Hundred Forty-eighth Pennsylvania thought we wouldn't be able to shoot much. But showed 'em we could too. They said Home Guards. I was too young."

There was no need to say goodbye; it would mean nothing. Little Round Top. There was a lane running down past the Trostle farm and a wide wheat field on the other side of it, to the south. "He can't be dead," Dan said aloud, and then he was on the steps. He stood there, looking up and down in the hot sunshine. In the next square he saw an old single buggy with a sorrel mare hitched to it, and a man in a linen duster climbing down over the wheel.

He ran along the sidewalk and waved his hand. Finis Sketchley turned, stopped, started up toward the house steps, and stopped again. "Oh," he said, when Bale came up, "I didn't know who that was, sonny. Ought to see the ruination up at Ever Green. They've marked it up terrible. I ain't been hardly able to eat or sleep with—"

Bale said, "Where are you going now?"

The old undertaker jerked his thumb toward the house with its hospital flag. A soldier came out on the porch, limping, leaning on a mop-handle. "Two just died in here, Dan. I never been so busy in my life: I've laid out a fair hundred."

"Lend me your mare and buggy for a couple of hours."

"Can't do it. You better go to the livery stable."

"The devil," Bale said. "There aren't any horses left around here. I couldn't get a rig for love or money—there's too many strangers. I'll pay you—" He said, "Anything." He fumbled in his pocket and found a ten dollar gold piece. "Here," he said.

Sketchley's crazy eye kept winking at him. Then, reluctantly, he reached up his bony hand. "All right, you take her. Be sure to gentle her. I can walk back to see about my ice. Think of it," he said, "a good ten thousand corpses. Yes, I guess ten. There's doctors

and doctor students coming here from Philadelphia
and York and all over; plenty corpses won't ever get
buried."

Dan climbed into the buggy and slapped the reins.
Sketchley cried in alarm, *Gentle her!* and the mare
went puffing away . . . Bale drove out Baltimore street
past a train of toiling wagons, and swung right at the
Emmetsburg road intersection, then left again at the
sluice which led up over the hill. He could make better time across the fields, littered as they were, with all
the fences down; the Emmetsburg road would be
blocked by splintered cannon and fallen horses.

When he came out on the open ridge it looked as
if all the universe had been swabbed with molasses,
to catch flies . . . it had caught a million bugs. They
lay in a sticky padding, steaming out into the yellow
distance of the afternoon; the smell rode in a solid
wave. The bugs were blue and black and gray and
brown, so many shades of each color that they
blended in a confused, dun crust laid on the green
and gold of the fields. The bugs were horses and artillery caissons and mules, and people named . . .
people named . . . "think of it," said Finis Sketchley,
"a good ten thousand corpses." Little farms sat squat
and horrid in this vast, decaying lake: Niede's house
and barns, the Codori place . . . tiny, moving images
walked here and there; soldiers and civilians who
went searching, searching, holding cologne-soaked
cloths over their noses.

The buggy wheel racked up over a log; at the peak
of the rise, the log collapsed with a sound. Dan
looked back. He thought he was going to fall out of
the buggy; the spasm struck him suddenly; he reined
in the mare, and she stood quivering all the time he
was sick. As soon as his vision cleared he drove on.

The horizon would incline, slowly, palpitating—the same jelly which the guns had made of it. There was a vile mist clinging in every hollow, despite the sun. He looked back at a shattered house—General Meade's house, Duffey had called it. He began to count: one horse, two, three, four five six seven eight nine ten eleven . . . you complained about that one by your gate, he thought. Said that the town council would not allow it.

He headed the sorrel into the field on his right and went quartering along the west face of the ridge. Not all of the Nationals had followed after the retreating rebels; there were still living soldiers in this country. They hitched along in couples or in straggling files— far and wide amid the wilderness of swollen bugs— some of them had spades, some had stretchers, some still carried guns, they looked like French peasants. It was a picture; he had seen it; French or Irish or Dutch peasants cutting peat out of a sedgy moorland. They were stolid clods come to life, and moving slowly.

Haven't got a handkerchief, Dan thought. Left it somewhere. He began to drive with one hand, holding his sleeve across his mouth and nose. His gaze fell toward the front buggy wheel; he let the mare pick her own path; somehow she was more accustomed to this rank spoilage, than he. Well, he thought, she's hauled Finis Sketchley around for years and— Wheel went over a roll of blankets. Playing cards. Underdrawers. Cup. Revolver. An open book . . . it was insane of him: he pulled on the reins, got out and went back, stepping over muskets, and picked up the book. It was Irving's *Sketch-Book,* and the greasy wheel had mutilated across the page where Master Simon explained the feudal antiquity of peacocks. On the fly-leaf was written in faded ink: *Artie's Christmas book. From Coz. December the 25, 1842.* There were rusty spatters all over the cover. Dan threw the book as far as he could.

Well, he thought, I didn't think we were here so soon—not at this place. I had never intended to come here again. Some birds flew up past the rock-oak grove; there were plump gray and purplish pillows, long-shaped, covering the whole daisy field and heaped thickly across the low wall. A young soldier stepped from behind a shredded stump and a tangle of wheel-spokes . . . caisson blew up, it made a hole in the sky, Dan remembered that noise, he would remember it forever. *Called for help as the son of—*

The boy sentinel had a handkerchief tied across his mouth and nose. He dragged his musket, trailing the butt across the ground. His eyes looked bilious. He croaked, "Lezzee yur pass." Dan said, "Whoa." He sat there looking stonily at the soldier. The boy said, "Ain't lettenem go over field thouta pass," and retched between the words. "Lezzee it . . ." "Oh, hell," Bale said. He drove on without looking back . . . He could feel that the atmosphere was disordered, high against the blue china sky, and when he had lifted his gaze from the revolving metal tire he found the whole zenith being ridden by wide-winged birds that wheeled and wheeled, spun slowly, flapped their wings with mighty effort when they did move them. Haven't seen any for years. Maybe these came over from the Blue Ridge. Tyler stood back there and shot at them; they flew.

A lot of teams over along the Emmetsburg road; canvas-topped wagons, most of them. The buggy went over another log, and the sorrel shied nervously, her ears sticking up like trowels. A pot-bellied negro was sitting squarely in the path, his back against a rock, his arms flung wide. "Get up," Dan said, and sawed on the left rein. It wasn't a negro, no, no ... the mare trotted for a time, whickering uncomfortable; the buggy jounced over things.

Twice Dan had to get down and push impediments aside; fence rails, and other things. There were a lot of playing cards on the ground, and crackers all soaked by the rain, drying into the trampled grass once more ... flaky. Perhaps they were manna. He had always thought that manna would look like crackers. He passed opposite the Weikert house. The farmer was out in his dooryard, wandering aimlessly amid the scattered blue and gray bundles. Dan kept on, south, in a narrow glade between the creek and the steeper ridge. He passed a few more living soldiers, but they did not offer to stop him. Probably I don't look like a robber of the dead, he thought. And I did not keep the *Sketch-Book*. I threw it away, away.

Little Round Top rose up, to the left. It was carpeted with dummies of blue and butternut, but mostly butternut. God had had a whole barrelful of dummies, and he had dumped them out on top of the rocky hill; they went tumbling and rolling down the steep, smooth sides, lodging here and there among the rocks; adhesive dummies, they lay fat and contented on some of the sheerest slopes. Now Dan headed the horse west in the lane which cut across, all the way to the Sherfy farm. I walked this, he thought, that day so long ago. Met Elijah with the Niede girl, in a cut-under buggy. That was the day Irene said, "Dan. Desire you, desire you—'"

That wounded Fisher said wheat. He was sure it was wheat, near the bone-built hill.

The wheels splashed through thickening puddles.

They went over Plum Run; it had been very high, and
was gone down into its banks again, murmuring feebly. On each side swept a fly-ridden mass of rusting
guns and old clothing and weeds and loose shoes, and
more playing cards and crackers. The fringe of bright
wheat glimmered ahead—its fences were thrown far
and wide, and it had been harvested by a million
hoofs, beaten and pounded and mauled this way and
that. In some places there were clumps of it still standing, proud, catching the sharp sunshine. Steam and
birds went up from the bloating horses.

Dan tied the sorrel to a gashed plum tree. He began to walk through the wheat, peering cautiously,
watching where he stepped. No use, he thought—I
can't make a thing out of all these colored people,
blistered as they are. Why do they stick out their
tongues at me? But when I talked to Fisher, I felt that
I dared not wait to come.

Some people were moving, over beyond the west
fence, coming out of the thin woods. When they had
passed the trees, Dan could see that they were not soldiers but citizens. Three men. They had a two-wheeled
cart and a horse; one of the men led the horse and the
two others strolled behind. There was something familiar abut the leader; he had a sullen, methodical
gait; his arm swung curved at his side.

"Mr. Niede," Dan called. They all stopped and the
leader turned, staring. Bale climbed across the broken rails and pushed through the fringe of bushes; he
fell over something; it, too, made a sound. He got up
and went on.

Henry Niede said, "Well, Dan Bale." The two men
behind the cart moved closer together. They were
both bearded; they wore straw hats; one of them was

playing with a gilt watch-fob that dangled from his waistcoat.

"I was down here, looking—" said Dan, and then he stopped. He walked over to the cart; something said, Go and see.

"Take care," barked the youngest man. His beard was silky. He looked frightened. The cart had something in it covered with canvas ... Henry Niede clutched the horse's bridle with both hands. "Now, look once," he began hastily. "They spoiled my wheat already. I guess I got to live. Anyway, these things should be got out of the way."

Both of the others said, "Take care," and sharply. Bale pulled back the dirty piece of canvas. He couldn't tell much about it; there was a black mustache. He felt something fiery turn over in his stomach. He reached forward and touched the cargo. There was a numeral in brass; it said 26. Voice announced, We're the Twenty-sixth, now. The Gettysburg boys make up Company A.

He rearranged the canvas and walked around to the front of the cart. Niede stepped back and let go of the bridle. One of the doctors cried, "Just a moment, my good man!" Bale didn't look at them. Niede yelled, "And maybe I should starve to death if they make a mess by my farm? I never got my wheat; and now there is a hole in my house roof costs fifty dollars. *Ja*, it costs maybe sixty. Three dollars apiece is all I get for these here."

Dan said, "That's Elijah Huddlestone." Niede's gaze groped for a moment; he looked genuinely startled. "*Donnerwetter*," he whispered. Bale struck him on the chin as hard as he could and sent him rolling. He turned around; one of the men had picked up a stone.

"Put that down, or I'll kill you," Dan told him. Niede was making a terrible noise, but not loud. The men fell back a few steps; the one with the stone breathed rapidly, and looked at Dan.

He called again, "Put it down," and the man dropped the stone. "I broke his jaw," Bale said. "Felt it go." He was amazed at having that much strength left. He took the bridle of the old horse and led her across the field, the cart wheels crunching through stubble. They bumped up over the rail pile, and out into the road. Dan tied the bridle to the rear of Sketchley's buggy and started off, slowly. It took him almost an hour to reach the cemetery.

There were soldiers working around, hauling unseated cannon out of the splintered tombstones. The Huddlestone lot was not far from Pentland Bale's grave, past a big cedar tree; only one of the stones had been ruined, in that section. Baby. Rest, Darling was crushed into five pieces, and there were deep wheel-tracks across Pentland Bale's mound.

He asked two soldiers to help him, and they came quietly, chewing tobacco. They buried Elijah deeper than most of the bodies were being buried, though not as far down as his father lay. Before the sun was very low they had the mound well-shaped. "We mark it with the name, usual, if we can git hold of it," said one of the men. "Stick a musket at the head, or put the name in a bottle or on a shingle." Dan thanked them. "I'll take care of it," he said. "He's a friend of mine."

The soldier had brought out a dirty notebook. "We're s'posed to keep note of any we bury."

Huddlestone, Sergeant E. 26th Pennsylvania—"I don't know," Dan said. "It was temporary infantry or unusual infantry or something like that." The man wrote down 26th Pennsylvania, and went back to his work.

Bale left Henry Niede's cart and horse in the Diamond, tied in front of Pock's. Niede would find it, or send someone, even if his face was ruined. Finis Sketchley came out of the hotel; he had been waiting anxiously for Dan to return with the mare, because he had two coffin-makers coming from Harrisburg, and they might have to walk all the way from where the railroad was torn up if he didn't go after them.

Through the white lime, Dan walked over to the Huddlestone house, and he was seventy-five years old. Elijah's mother sat in her rocker on the porch, and Eva Duffey and Amelia Niede and Mrs. Joe Leen were all there, talking to her. Amelia was knitting something with red wool. They all began to flutter and call anxiously as Dan turned in at the gate: What news? He thought, Get it over while they're here together. "I've got bad news," he said, and surely they could have told that much. "Elijah was killed in the battle . . . Yes. I said— He was killed. He's dead." He said, coldly: "He and young Fisher joined the Union advance, and fought out by the Trostle farm. Fisher was wounded but Elijah was killed. We've just buried him, up at Ever Green."

Amelia went down in a pile across the steps. She began, savagely: "Oh-ho-ho, ho-ho-ho-ho." Mrs. Huddlestone stopped rocking; Eva Duffey stumbled toward her, and Dan turned away and left them.

He walked along Chambersburg street and didn't notice anybody. At the fork he turned out on the Fairfield road, and went with the ruts mashing under his shoes. There were a lot of rigs on the road, more of them coming into town than going out. People looked at him as they jolted past; they had bundles and boxes on their laps, and so many of them were women. Christian Commission, Sanitary Commission: make milk punch for wounded folks and say, "Don't forget the tincture of sesquichloride of iron." He went in at the lane leading up to the Fannings'. Mules and horses lay here, but they had been dragged out of the track; the smell was thinner than south of town.

There was an officer's horse tied to the front hitch-post, and a new-looking carryall around in back—he didn't know whose it was. He went up to the front door, and Gretel met him there. "Tell Mrs. Fanning—Mrs. Tyler Fanning—that I'd like to see her a minute," he said.

She asked him to come inside. Straw was scattered through the hall and library; Demon worked in the sitting room with a hammer, taking up the carpet; there would be a new carpet, now.

Dan heard someone on the stairs. Irene wore a blue gown with white dots in it, and she was wiping her hands in a tiny towel with a lace border. "Oh," she said.

There was no one else around. "I came to see you," he said.

"Tyler is to lose his left limb."

Bale looked at the floor. The girl wore shining, ebony slippers; he could see the tips of them under the hem of her dress. "Yes," she said, "I believe they will amputate it tomorrow. The surgeon says he will recover. You did—tell him . . ." She said, "Didn't you?"

"Yes," he cried. "Surely. He believed every word I said. Didn't he act—as if he believed it?"

Demon started pounding in the next room, pounding God knew what or why. He was supposed to be pulling up tacks, not driving them in. "Yes . . . He has been delirious most of the time. Though I feel that he—believed you."

"Well," Bale said.

"He's my husband," the woman whispered. "He'll have only one limb. Don't look at me like that."

He told her, thickly: "If you only possessed sufficient courage—"

"Oh," she sobbed, "you—to talk about our courage! Tyler has been twice wounded."

"I suppose you feel that you committed— It was something wicked, you believe, for which God can never forgive you and which no one else—"

She said, "Of course I was wicked. I pray that he won't die. I could never stand it if he did."

"All right." Desire you forever, whether my mind wishes it or not . . . astral voicelessness which is your spirit. He turned and found the door.

She said rapidly: "Don't act—that way. Think—if you were up there in bed instead of— How would it be?"

"I don't know," he replied. He went out on the porch. "By the by," he said, "Mr. Fanning's colt— Dazzle—was left in Maryland. I shall write to the man, and send money, and have the colt brought to you. Elijah Huddlestone is dead," he said, over his shoulder, and knew that he could never tell the rest to anyone. He walked down the steps and around the corner and toward his own house: its upstairs windows were pure gold. He looked back, once, and thought that he saw Irene watching him from the rear window of the upper hall, but he could never be sure whether it was she. There were a lot of other people in the house.

He said to himself, "What was that Chinaman's name? Lucas Mite had a book—" Kept thinking how

Elijah looked, on the two-wheeled cart. He went into the buttery and opened up the kitchen cupboard as well; he gathered all the food which would spoil, or which might attract vermin, and carried it out to the rear porch. Most of it was spoiled already. Some one would find it and carry it away. Mrs. Wurke had good, substantial relatives . . . must think of everything. He fastened all downstairs windows and shutters, and barred the back door.

In his room, he changed his shirt and put the few remaining clean clothes into the extension case. He didn't take any books except *Typee*. He counted: he had six hundred and twenty-nine dollars in gold and greenbacks, in the money belt. He put fifty dollars in his pocket and left the rest in the belt.

It was near twilight. He carried the bag with him down the stairway, got his hat, and locked the door on the wreckage inside this house. The dead horse beside his gate was fairly seething. Dan walked back to town along the noisy Pike.

As he passed the Emblem Hotel, he met Julius Orcutt. "Going away?" the tallow-face asked. "Yes," Dan told him. "I will write . . . how is Mrs. Orcutt bearing up?"

The lawyer said, "Bravely." He asked, "Daniel—you are not going West?"

"No." They stepped aside; a lot of Commission folks came past. Dan said to Orcutt, "Please assume the care of—everything. I shall have to write you the details, and arrange about a will; I wish to make the Duffeys and Mrs. Huddlestone the beneficiaries. Do the trains to Baltimore go through, yet?"

Orcutt nodded. "They do. Every four hours, or so I am told. Daniel, do you mean to go into the army?"

"I guess so." There was a long, dry silence between

them. "You're a Mason, sir," Dan began. "Is it something Masonic if you do this: call for help as the son of a widow?"

"Why on earth do you—ask that?" Orcutt demanded.

"I heard somebody say that," Dan told him. "I was pondering it. I assumed it was some kind of a lodge business."

They shook hands; Dan wondered whether Benjy Orcutt had lain long unburied, after he died, and if he had looked like Elijah. Probably there would have been no telling them apart, after just so long . . . "Not going—now—Daniel?" "Yes," he said. "You are the only one I have seen. Here is the key to the house, and I will write from Washington or somewhere."

He started east along York street. It was four miles out to where the railroad began to function, since the track had been destroyed by the first invading rebels, and Bale would have to walk the distance unless someone offered a ride. Orcutt stood there in the middle of the sidewalk, watching him go. The dusk was thick with chloride of lime. Orcutt began to cough.

Bibliography

While the background of this story is supplementary to the development of the characters, it is earnestly believed that the battle fought in these pages is the actual battle which was fought, and not a fictive hullabaloo which never existed at Gettysburg or any other place.

Obviously it is impossible to offer a complete list of sources when many of those sources were living men whose remembrances were available only after the cultivation of their friendship. Likewise one cannot catalog definitely many years of reading on this and allied subjects. However, the author feels that he must express his debt to the files of the New York *Tribune* and the Philadelphia *Press;* to the publications of historical societies in various states—particularly Pennsylvania, Massachusetts, Rhode Island, South Carolina and Virginia; to original records of the United States and Confederate States War Departments, and of the U. S. Surgeon-General's office; and to the books and pamphlets listed below. In each case there is reason for gratitude.

An Address Delivered at Gettysburg, August 27, 1883. Alexander S. Webb. Philadelphia. Porter and Coates. 1883.

An Aide-de-Camp of Lee. Sir Frederick Maurice. Boston. Little, Brown and Company. 1927.

The American War of Secession, 1863. Philip Hugh Dalbiac. London. S. Sonnenschein and Company, Ltd. 1911.

Anecdotes of the Civil War. E. D. Townsend. New York. D. Appleton and Company. 1884.

Annals of the War: The Gettysburg Campaign. St. Clair A. Mulholland. Philadelphia. McLaughlin Brothers. 1880.

The Attack and Defense of Little Round Top. Oliver Wilcox Norton. New York. Neale Publishing Company. 1913.

Battle of Gettysburg and the Christian Commission. Andrew B. Cross. n.p. 1865.

The Battle of Gettysburg. Samuel P. Bates. Philadelphia. T. H. Davis and Company. 1875.

The Battle of Gettysburg. Samuel Adams Drake. Boston. Lee and Shepard. 1893.

The Battle of Gettysburg. L. P. D'Orleans, Comte de Paris. Philadelphia. Porter and Coates. 1886.

The Battle of Gettysburg. Franklin Aretas Haskell. Madison, Wis. Democrat Printing Company. 1908.

The Battle of Gettysburg. Francis M. Pierce. New York. Neale Publishing Company. 1914.

The Battle of Gettysburg, 1863. C. Stevens. Shakopee, Minn. n.p. 1890.

The Battle of Gettysburg. Jesse Bowman Young. New York. Harper and Brothers. 1913.

Battles and Leaders of the Civil War. (In four volumes.) Edited by Robert Underwood Johnson and Clarence Clough Buel. New York. The Century Company. 1884.

The Battles of Chancellorsville and Gettysburg. A. H. Nelson. Minneapolis. Published by the author. 1899.

Before, at and After Gettysburg. J. Watts DePeyster. New York. C. H. Ludwig. 1887.

The Campaigns of General Robert E. Lee. Jubal A. Early. Baltimore. J. Murphy and Company. 1872.

"The Cannoneer." Augustus C. Buell. Washington, D. C. The National Tribune. 1890.

Chancellorsville and Gettysburg. Abner Doubleday. New York. Chas. Scribner's Sons. 1882.

The Charge at Gettysburg. Samuel A. Ashe. Raleigh, N. C. Capital Printing Company. 1902.

The Civil War in Song and Story. Edited by Frank Moore. New York. P. F. Collier. 1889.

A Colonel at Gettysburg and Spottsylvania. Varina D. Brown. Columbia, S. C. The State Company. 1931.

The Crisis of the Confederacy. Cecil Battine. London. Longmans, Green and Company. 1905.

The Fifth Army Corps. William H. Powell. New York. G. P. Putnam's Sons. 1896.

The Fighting Quakers. A. J. H. Duganne. New York. J. P. Robens. 1866.

Following the Greek Cross. Thomas W. Hyde. Boston. Houghton, Mifflin Company. 1894.

Four Years Under Marse Robert. Robert Stiles. New York. Neale Publishing Company. 1903.

From Manassas to Appomattox. James Longstreet. Philadelphia. J. B. Lippincott Company. 1896.

Gettysburg. A Complete Historical Narrative. John J. Garnett. New York. J. M. Hill. 1888.

Gettysburg: As the Battle Was Fought. James T. Long. Harrisburg, Pa. E. K. Meyers. 1891.

Gettysburg, Then and Now. John M. Vanderslice. New York. G. W. Dillingham Company. 1899.

Gettysburg. The Pivotal Battle of the Civil War. R. K. Beecham. Chicago. A. C. McClurg and Company. 1911.

Gettysburg. What They Did Here. L. W. Minnigh. Gettysburg, Pa. Tipton and Blocher. 1924.

Gettysburg and Lincoln. Henry S. Barrage. New York. G. P. Putnam's Sons. 1906.

Gettysburg in War and Peace. Published by the Western Maryland Railroad. Baltimore. 1890.

Gettysburg Made Plain. Abner Doubleday. New York. The Century Company. 1888.

The Great Invasion of 1863. Jacob Hoke. Dayton, Ohio. W.J. Shuey. 1887.

History of the 148th Pennsylvania Volunteers. Edited by J. W. Muffly. Des Moines, Ia. The Kenyon Company. 1904.

History of the Philadelphia Brigade. Charles H. Banes. Philadelphia. J. B. Lippincott Company. 1876.

History of the Second Army Corps. Francis A. Walker. New York. Chas. Scribner's Sons. 1886.

History of the United States Sanitary Commission. Charles J. Still. Philadelphia. J. B Lippincott Company. 1866.

Human Interest Stories of the Three Day Battles at Gettysburg. Herbert L. Grimm and P. L. Roy. Gettysburg, Pa. Times and News Publishing Company. 1927.

Leaves from the Battlefield of Gettysburg. Emily Bliss Souder. Philadelphia. C. Sherman, Son and Company. 1864.

The Life and Letters of George Gordon Meade. Edited by G. G. Meade. New York. Chas. Scribner's Sons. 1913.

Life of Winfield Scott Hancock. Frederick E. Goodrich. Boston. B. B. Russell. 1886.

Lincoln and Episodes of the Civil War. William E. Doster. New York. G. P. Putnam's Sons. 1915.

A Little Fifer's War Diary. C. W. Bardeen. Syracuse, N. Y. Published by the author. 1910.

Martial Deeds of Pennsylvania. Samuel P. Bates. Philadelphia. T. H. Davis and Company. 1875.

Military Memoirs of a Confederate. E. P. Alexander. New York. Chas. Scribner's Sons. 1918.

Minutiae of Soldier Life in the Army of Northern Virginia.

Carlton McCarthy. Richmond. Carlton McCarthy and Company. 1882.

Mr. Dunn Browne's Experiences in the Army. Dunne Browne. Boston. Nichols and Noyes. 1866.

My Story of the War. Mary A. Livermore. Hartford, Conn. A. D. Worthington and Company. 1889.

New Jersey Troops in the Gettysburg Campaign. Samuel Toombs. Orange, N.J. The Evening Mail Publishing House. 1888.

New York at Gettysburg. William F. Fox. Albany. J. B. Lyon Company. 1900.

The North and the South at Antietam and Gettysburg. William E. Spear. Boston. Published by the author. 1908.

North Carolina at Gettysburg. Walter Clark. Raleigh, N. C. n.p. 1921.

Notes on the Rebel Invasion of Maryland and Pennsylvania. Michael Jacobs. Philadelphia. J. B. Lippincott Company. 1864.

Numbers and Losses in the Civil War in America. Thomas L. Livermore. Boston. Houghton, Mifflin Company. 1901.

Original Photographs Taken on the Battlefields by Mathew B. Brady and Alexander Gardner. From the collection of Edward Bailey Eaton. Hartford, Conn. E. B. Eaton. 1907.

Our Boys. A. F. Hill. Philadelphia. J. E. Potter. 1864.

Our Campaign Around Gettysburg. John Lockwood. Brooklyn. A. H. Rome and Brothers. 1864.

The Photographic History of the Civil War. (In ten volumes.) Edited by Francis Trevelyan Miller. New York. The Review of Reviews Company. 1912.

Pickett and His Men. La Salle Corbell Pickett. Atlanta. Foote and Davis Company. 1899.

Pickett or Pettigrew? W. R. Bond. Scotland Neck, N. C. W. L. L. Hall. 1901.

The Pictorial History of the Civil War. (In three volumes.) Benson J. Lossing. Hartford, Conn. Thos. Belknap. 1877.

Recollections of the Civil War. Mason Whiting Tyler. New York. G. P. Putnam's Sons. 1912.

Reminiscences of the Civil War. John B. Gordon. New York. Chas. Scribner's Sons. 1904.

Reply of the Philadelphia Brigade Association to the Foolish and Absurd Narrative of Lieutenant Frank A. Haskell. Philadelphia. Published by the Philadelphia Brigade Association. 1910.

Reports of the Battles of Gettysburg. Abner Doubleday. Montpelier, Vt. Walton's Steam Press. 1865.

A Short Story of the First Day's Fight at Gettysburg. H. S. Huidekoper. Philadelphia. Bicking Printing Company. 1906.

Sketch of the Battles of Gettysburg. T. Ditterline. New York. C. A. Alvord. 1863.

Three Weeks at Gettysburg. Georgeanna M. (Woolsey) Bacon. New York. A. D. F. Randolph. 1863.

Three Years in the Sixth Corps. George T. Stevens. New York. D. Van Nostrand. 1870.

The True Story of "Jennie" Wade. J. W. Johnston. Rochester, N. Y. Published by the author. 1917.

The Twentieth Regiment of Massachusetts Volunteer Infantry. George A. Bruce. Boston. Houghton, Mifflin Company. 1906.

Twenty-sixth Emergency Infantry. Samuel W. Pennypacker. Philadelphia. n.p. 1892.

Two Days of War. Henry Edwin Tremain. New York. Bonnell, Silver and Bowers. 1905.

Vermont at Gettysburg. George C. Benedict. Burlington, Vt. Free Press Association. 1870.

War Memories of an Army Chaplain. H. Clay Turnbull. New York. Chas. Scribner's Sons. 1898.

With Gregg in the Gettysburg Campaign. William Brooke Rawle. Philadelphia. McLaughlin Brothers. 1884.

With Pen and Camera on the Field of Gettysburg in War

and Peace. Holman D. Waldron. Portland, Me. Chisholm Brothers. 1902.

With the Sixth Corps at Gettysburg. H. Hall. Lawrence, Kas. Journal Printing Company. 1896.

Woman's Work in the Civil War. L. P. Brockett and Mary C. Vaughan. Philadelphia. Zeigler, McCurdy and Company. 1867.